Rock

by

Laura Kitchell

"A band of rock gods mock the idea of true love until, one by one, each is swept away by that unique woman who knows his heart in this romance anthology, Rock Band." Katherine Alexander

Ellen,
Rock on! Enjoy!
Laura Kitchell

Rock Band

by Laura Kitchell

Print Version
13 – ISBN: 978-1497564862
10 – ISBN: 1497564867

Dedication

A very special and loving thanks to Susan, a talented author, dear friend, and inspiration for this project. To Lara, who had the patience of a saint and the creativity of a genius to see me through to this amazing cover. To my husband and daughter, whose support made this anthology possible. And to the extraordinary authors of the Quality Novelists Coalition, whose mad skills and talents ensure that you get a quality product when you buy this book.

JUSTIN TIME

Chapter One

Raking stiff fingers through his hair, Justin stood on shaky legs and retrieved his carry-on from the first class overhead bin. He hated flying.

Worse yet, he hated how the words had stopped. Ever since he'd received his ex-girlfriend's wedding invitation, he hadn't written a single song. His band, Smashing Glass, would go on tour in two months, and he didn't have anything new to bring to their show.

He rubbed a hand over his tired face as he waited in the crowded aisle to exit. He shouldn't have come, but three months lacking inspiration had left him desperate. If he had somehow missed an emotional attachment to the bride he hadn't realized existed, he only hoped going to the wedding would sever it.

"I'm losin' it," he muttered.

"Excuse me?" asked a woman with a slight accent he couldn't place.

He glanced over his shoulder. A gorgeous set of green eyes, framed by long, black lashes, gazed in question at him from a porcelain face that struck him as vaguely familiar. Her full, wide lips curved slightly, and she gave her auburn hair a flip past a slender shoulder. His breath caught in his throat.

"Nothing," he said, the last part of the word floating on a sigh, and returned his attention to the unmoving passengers ahead.

"You're Justin Time, aren't you? Justin Keither?" she asked quietly, her face so close he felt her breath caress his ear.

It sent a shiver through him. To cover his reaction, he switched his small suitcase to his other hand. Irritation rankled along his spine. He hadn't expected to find a fan in the first class section of an airplane. Certainly not one who'd flirt so physically nor one who'd draw his attention so unwaveringly. One glance had been enough. He didn't dare glance at her for fear he would stare.

"Yes," he replied curtly, not sparing her a look.

"It's a pleasure to meet you."

French. Her accent, though faint, was decidedly French. He sighed. Her rich, warm voice caressed his nerves, washing away his post-flight shakes. Dangerous. When would they open the hatch and let him off?

"I'm Desiree Renault." She pressed against his back.

Okay, Smashing Glass needed to buy a plane. He could practically feel her firm, warm breasts through the thin cotton of his white button down. He began to harden. Releasing a frustrated huff, he despised this woman's ability to undermine his control. In less than a minute, she had weakened the composure he'd spent years to build. Who was she? No fan had ever undone him like this.

"Would you mind moving forward a little?" she whispered. "The man behind me—" She squealed.

Justin stepped into the opening in front of his seat. She stumbled forward a step, and the portly, forty-something man behind her lost his grip on her pert rear end. She stabbed her elbow into the man's chest, and he bent slightly on a chuckle.

Anger heated Justin's neck as he fisted his free hand. He wanted to pound the asshole square between the eyes.

He couldn't risk an arrest that might keep him from the wedding, though. Instead, he met and held the man's gaze and firmly stepped between him and Desiree. As he rubbed the spot where she had struck him, the scumbag visibly shrank and his licentious grin melted. Justin hooked a finger into his collar to reveal more of the fire tattoo that climbed his throat from his chest. A hint of unsure fear glinted in the man's stare. Good. Justin warily gave the asshole his back.

"Are you alright?" he asked her. He cut a glance over his shoulder and found the man checking messages on a blackberry.

"I will be." She trembled a bit.

He laid a supportive hand on her shoulder. She was tall, but he liked it. At six foot three, he towered over most women.

He glanced to her feet. She wore three inch black and white zebra print pumps. He followed slender ankles to shapely calves and knees. A black leather pencil skirt hugged thighs and a firm ass. It cinched at her tiny waist where a sleeveless, sheer blouse did nothing to hide a black bra on its way to sexy auburn waves. How had he flown all the way from Chicago to Norfolk without noticing this beauty?

Her long, pale fingers gave his hand a pat. "I'm fine, thank you."

Guilt twisted in his gut. He'd ignored her while that jackass had groped her. Now that he'd played white knight, he couldn't escape a sense of responsibility for her. It wouldn't hurt to treat her nicely for a few minutes. The moment they stepped off the plane, they'd be strangers again. Relaxing, he offered her a brief, reassuring smile.

He released her shoulder and took her hard-sided carry-on. The weight of it wrenched his shoulder a bit, and he readjusted his hold on its handle. "Do you have rocks in here?"

She glanced at him, her large green eyes sparkling in a smile that revealed straight, white teeth. "My equipment. I'm on my way to Kill Devil Hills to photograph a wedding."

That made no sense. Wedding photographers didn't make enough to wear designer clothes and fly first class. He glanced at her left hand. No wedding ring.

"I'm going there for a wedding, too," he admitted, cringing inwardly. Why had he told her where he went? Now she'd want to see him there.

"I thought you might be." She faced forward as the hatch opened with a thud.

"Why do you say that?" He tried to gauge her expression, but only the curve of her cheek showed past the flowing mass of her hair.

People moved toward the exit and two smiling flight attendants. Part of him clamored to get to that hatch and escape her and the protectiveness she inspired in him, yet part of him dreaded it. As though his body openly defied his brain, Justin hung closer to Desiree than he needed. She smelled so good. Like a garden.

"You don't remember me." She chuckled. "Of course you don't. I'm being silly."

Now she had him intrigued, but their climb onto the causeway leading into the airport made conversation difficult. Had he met her? No way. He'd remember. A woman like her wouldn't escape his notice, even if she stood amidst a pack of sex-crazed models.

At the gate inside, he marched to a line of empty chairs. He set her case on a seat but his fingers curled around the handle. "You're saying I know you?"

"Sort of." She sent a thick, lazy curl past her shoulder.

Granted, the measure of her features tugged at his memory. He needed to hand her the lead-weighted suitcase and bid her goodbye. Instead, he studied her, trying to place her face.

"When my family moved to America from France, my parents bought a house in a neighborhood where a girl named Mandy lived. I went to a private school, but she became my friend. She went to high school with Jet. Anyway, he invited her to your first performance, and she asked me to go with her."

He smiled, remembering how excited they'd been to get that job. "What a dive. I still can't believe that bar manager let us play there."

She nodded. "The Hole. Wasn't that the name of the place?"

Justin laughed. "That's right. I'd almost forgotten."

Desiree's eyes glittered. "Nobody carded us. We walked right in. Mandy was scared by the bikers and rough-looking dockworkers, but I thought it was great. Everyone loved your music. You showed your greatness, even back then. I knew your band would be famous someday."

He released a slow breath. "It's good to know somebody believed in us. I think you're exaggerating about that first gig, though. We've never been so nervous. Jet sang off-key for half the first song, and C.J. kept dropping his drumsticks because he couldn't keep his palms from sweating. He bought his first fingerless gloves the next day."

She laughed, a delightful, subtle sound that lifted his spirits. Damn, he needed to walk away. Now.

"So why did you say you thought I might be traveling for a wedding? How did you know?" He mentally thumped his palm on his forehead. What was wrong with him?

"You dated Cassidy Baines in high school. Mandy told me. It's why I didn't flirt with you at the Hole. You're on your way to her wedding, right?"

"You know she's getting married because...?"

"It's her wedding I'm going to photograph."

Her fingers itching to touch him, Desiree clutched them behind her back. Justin Keither stood in front of her. Justin Time Keither! She'd crushed on him so hard in high school that she had cried herself to sleep too many nights after meeting him at The Hole. It embarrassed her to remember.

Now he was famous and rich and still didn't know her. He had changed, too. Become a man. His white shirt didn't hide a muscular but lean physique. Neither did it hide the tips of orange and red flames licking up his neck. He wore his dark brown hair long and pulled back in a black ponytail holder. His jaw hinted at stubble, and masculine angles had replaced youthful lines from eleven years ago.

She eyed his hand resting casually on her camera equipment. He'd rescued her from that lout on the plane then carried her case. His gentlemanly behavior renewed old affections even as she fought them.

She wasn't a lonely French schoolgirl in America anymore. Now she traveled the world and enjoyed her success. She'd earned her American citizenship, too.

Besides, he'd come to his ex-girlfriend's wedding. Who did that? He had no beautiful wife to flaunt in the bride's face, so he hadn't come to gloat. No, he could only have come because he'd never gotten over Cassidy.

"I wasn't expecting that," he said with an uneasy chuckle. His smile withered and died. "Where are you staying?"

"At the Radisson. The wedding and reception are being held on the beach behind it, so I figured a room there would be convenient."

"Sure." He tapped neat, short fingernails on her case. His brown eyes considered her. Then, as though some invisible force dragged the words from him, he said in a slightly strangled voice, "I'm in a cottage down the street. I've hired a helicopter. It can get us there in twenty minutes. If you drive, it's more than an hour. Why don't you come with me?"

Did he just flinch? Her immediate impulse urged her to accept, but her good sense gave her pause. She took in his dark blue jeans and brown boots. He could've been a businessman on a weekend golfing excursion. She knew better.

She always paid attention when his name appeared in magazines or made mentioned on television. Anyone who followed Smashing Glass knew Justin Keither rocked hard. He had earned a reputation as one of the best rock-screamers in the industry. He rivaled the best axe men in the business, and he'd won eight awards for songs he'd written.

He toured. He lived the life. Maybe he didn't sport dark circles under his eyes or telltale signs of drug and alcohol abuse, but she had to assume he partied like the best of them.

"You're hesitating." Amusement quirked his lips and put a light in his eyes. Or was it relief? "You don't have to—"

"Yes, thank you. It's very generous of you." She exhaled on a breathy laugh. Of course. Her excess caution had no grounds.

His lips parted on a grin that bordered on victorious, yet a flash of something hesitant darkened his gaze. Her heart skipped a beat. She'd thought him cute those long years ago, but now he was blatantly handsome.

"Come on," he said and headed for the front of the airport.

Adjusting the strap of her purse on her shoulder, Desiree followed. What could a helicopter ride hurt? They weren't strangers. Not really. True, she hadn't seen him in eleven years and he'd spent that time as a rock star, but people didn't change in character. Did they?

No. He'd proven that on the plane.

Smiling, she took a few running steps then strode by his side. "Is your date meeting you there?"

"I'm alone." He stared straight ahead.

She swallowed a groan. She'd used the question to fish, and she suspected he recognized it.

"You wanna be my date?" He spared her a glance that bordered on panic before he stepped onto a down escalator.

Did he play some kind of game – pursuing her while giving her looks like he didn't really want to? She grasped the escalator's handrail so tightly her knuckles went white. She wanted to be his date in the worst way. "I can't. I'm working the event."

"Right." At the bottom, he waited for her to step off then crossed to the airport's baggage claim. "Then how about dinner tonight?"

She opened her mouth to accept, but he'd disappeared from her side. Frowning, she glanced around but couldn't see past a crowd accumulating near the carousel. For a second, her stomach plummeted. He had her equipment. She released a steadying breath and turned her attention to the conveyor. No point panicking. They were going to share a ride. Maybe he'd gone to secure a taxi to take them to the helicopter pad.

Her suitcase came fifth in line, a pearly blue piece she'd purchased her last trip to Italy. Its tag scraped along the conveyor's metal guard, her first name scrolled in large letters on a diagonal in bold black marker. She bent to retrieve the case as it meandered around the conveyor's curve, but a hand got to it first and plucked it off its track. Justin had returned with a luggage cart.

He sent her a broad smile and added her large case to their two smaller ones. He collected a big black suitcase from the claim and said, "Let's go."

"I'm perfectly capable of managing my bags," she said, though her mood didn't even approach irritation. "I appreciate your thoughtfulness, but the luggage has wheels."

A double glass door opened automatically, and he pulled the cart outside and to a waiting cab. "Why manage them if you don't have to?"

The driver came around and loaded their cases into the car's trunk while Justin opened a door and gestured her inside. She couldn't help smiling. The man really had grown into a gentleman.

When he climbed in beside her, she said, "I'm glad your rock-star life hasn't ruined your good manners. And yes to dinner tonight. I have no other plans."

"Great," he said, his tone duller than she expected.

She fingered the collar of his button-down. "I've only ever seen you in T-shirts."

Smiling, he ran a hand down his front. "I always dress when I fly first class. I know I paid for the ticket, and I should wear whatever I want, but some ticket agent or flight attendant always has something to say. I don't need the hassle."

"I see." She reluctantly let go of his collar.

His phone pinged, and he checked its display. "Just a second. This is important."

While he typed a text, she told the driver to take them to the heliport then gazed out the window. In less than a minute, the taxi cruised along a main airport road lined by trees shedding the last of their flowers for small, bright green leaves. At the other end of the airport, amidst maintenance hangers and a lot with parked two- and four-seat personal aircraft, stood a tiny gray box building. A sign read Heliport Terminal.

The moment the taxi arrived, a man in sunglasses and a gray uniform rushed to the curb. "Mr. Keither?"

Justin glanced at him, nodded, and hit send on his phone.

"Right this way, sir. Your bird is primed and ready."

"There are two of us."

"That's fine. You're reservation accommodates up to three passengers. Please proceed to the tarmac. I'll bring your bags."

Justin paid the taxi driver a ten-dollar bill then took Desiree's hand and half jogged toward the asphalt behind the terminal. His hand felt warm and firm around hers, and gave her an unexpected sense of security.

"Ever been on a helicopter before?" he yelled as they approached a large black one, its rotors spinning and its motor's whine filling the mid-morning air.

"Too many times to count."

He shot her a look, his eyes searching and one side of his mouth pulled tight as if he hadn't expected her response.

The uniformed man arrived with their luggage. He shouted, "Go ahead and get in."

Justin bent at the waist and headed for the gaping doorway. He still had her hand, which made her smile as she ducked and followed. She climbed in, secured her restraint, and donned a headset.

"You really have done this before," he shouted.

She more read his lips than heard him.

The pilot gave them a small wave in greeting from his seat. "Kill Devil Hills, right?" came his voice through her headset.

"Yes," said Justin, now belted and wearing a set of earphones.

The uniformed man checked their restraints, gave the pilot a thumb up, and closed the door.

The engine roared, and they lifted then tipped into a forward flight. Desiree giggled. That was her favorite part. The pilot confirmed their clearance with the tower then climbed. Highway, trees, rental car lots, and buildings passed underneath.

Justin offered her a genuine grin. Adjusting the mouthpiece of his headset closer to his lips, he said, "Flying in a plane unnerves me every time, but I love riding in a helicopter. I don't know why."

She nodded and thought about striking a conversation with him, but experience had taught her not to clog the headsets with idle chatter. Besides, his thumbs now flew across a virtual keyboard on his phone. Did he write a new song? He was famous for his lyrics. She spent the flight checking and answering emails on her cell.

In Kill Devil Hills, a taxi waited. The pilot personally transferred their luggage from the helicopter to the car, and Justin made a call. She gave the driver her destination, and they headed down a seemingly endless roadway lined by scraggly grasses, sand, and houses on stilts. Gas stations dotted the way, and they passed a good-sized strip mall promising quality souvenirs and salt-water taffy.

"Sorry about that," said Justin as the driver slowed and turned down a road with cinderblock houses on either side. "That was my agent. C.J., our drummer, got arrested last night for lewd behavior and disturbing the peace."

Her heart sank, and she put her hand on his wrist. "Do you need to leave?"

"Nah." He chuckled. "That's C.J.'s life. Jet or Chaz will bail him out."

"Isn't he your friend? Doesn't he need you?" She stared at him, amazed by his casual attitude.

"Look, he does this all the time. Believe me, if he was in real trouble, I'd go in a heartbeat. This is just C.J. being C.J." He gave her hand on his wrist a squeeze then continued to trap it under his long fingers. Guitar-player's fingers.

Desiree swallowed as a thrill blossomed in her abdomen. She wanted to act calm and worldly-wise, but Justin Keither had her by the hand. Sure, she'd barely met him once in high school, but he'd stuck. Throughout college, and now her career, she'd kept up with his band. She'd attended a couple of their concerts, and even had a Smashing Glass poster framed and hanging in her living room.

"I'm a fan, actually," she reluctantly confessed.

"Of C.J.?" One of his eyebrows shot toward his hairline.

The idea yanked a laugh from her. "No, of yours. Of the band in general. I enjoy your music. Your songs are wonderful."

"Thanks." A sadness pulled the outer corners of his eyes downward, and his mouth hardened.

"Did I say something wrong?"

"We're almost there," said the driver over his shoulder.

Justin took his wallet from a back pocket of his jeans. "You're fine, Desiree. I'm just dealing with something right now."

She wanted to press him, but they'd only started this friendship thirty minutes ago. She didn't want to end it before it had a chance. Past the window, tall hotels and squat restaurants and shops created an interesting beach road landscape. From time to time, they passed enormous houses. In between buildings, she caught glances of ocean and pale sand.

The driver pulled in front of the Radisson and stopped at the entrance. Desiree got out and pointed to her luggage so he could give them to an approaching bellhop. She inhaled sweet, clean ocean air.

"Desiree." Justin poked his head out the lowered window. "Is six thirty okay for dinner?"

Her stomach did a happy flip. "That sounds good."

"What's your number?" He added it to his phone contacts as she recited it.

"I'll be ready."

He offered her a too-mild smile. "I'll pick you up here."

Chapter Two

"You did what?" Justin yelled into his phone.

"It's no big deal, man," said Jet. "C.J.'s home now. It's cool."

He resisted the urge to throw his phone across the cottage. "There's nothing cool about leaving a friend in jail all night when you could do something about it. Goddamn it, Jet, he's practically your brother."

"Brenda needed me. She's the love of my life. I'm going to ask her to marry me."

Justin rolled his eyes. "How long have you known this one?"

"Two weeks, but that's not important. Time doesn't determine love."

"Maybe, but it does a hell of a job revealing the flaws we can't live with."

"You sound like my mother."

"That's a compliment, asshole."

Jet's sigh hissed across the phone line. "Fine. I screwed up with C.J. It won't happen again."

"It better not." Justin shook his head then slumped into a beige overstuffed armchair. "Heaven help me if my fate gets left in the hands of my buddies."

"Hey! No fair. You know we'd do anything for you. I know you're having a hard time right now, but it'll pass. I swear. When the words come again, they'll come so fast you'll struggle to get them written before they disappear."

He chuckled, dreaming of the day. "Now you sound like your mother."

A pause allowed a faint high-pitched electric whine to pierce the connection. Then Jet said, "Okay, I confess. I told her your problem, and that's what she said."

"Damn it. Now she's going to worry. I hate that." Justin thumped his fist on the chair's arm. "She better not tell my mom."

"Sorry. She said she wouldn't."

He sighed. "What's Chaz doing?"

"Checking the obituaries like he always does. I swear sometimes I think he's looking for his own to appear or something."

Justin closed his eyes and rested his head on the chair. "Keep an eye on C.J., would ya? I'm going to stay down here for a while. I'm hoping to start writing again after the wedding tomorrow, so I reserved this place for two weeks."

"No problem. I'll get Mom to invite us to dinner. He's always good for a week after spending an evening with my parents."

"That's a great idea."

"So you're planning to hole up in that shack for two weeks? Not see anyone? Not do anything but write songs?"

"That's the plan."

Jet laughed softly. "Spare me. When it comes to socializing, you're as busy as C.J. The difference is, he's looking to get wasted all the time."

"Thanks, Jet," Justin said dryly.

"I'm just asking you to be realistic. Three days after the wedding, you'll be so stir crazy..."

"What? I'll be so stir crazy I'll what?"

"I don't know. And what if the words don't come?"

The heat of dread and frustration built in Justin's neck at the idea. "Don't go there, man. Besides, I may not be entirely alone. I met a woman on the flight down. We're having dinner tonight."

"Dinner?" His friend's voice didn't hide any of his

disbelief. "Do you mean you're ordering pizza to have in bed between rounds?"

"It's not like that."

"Bullshit. That's the only way it is with you. You're the postman. Lick 'em, stick 'em, and send 'em on their way."

Justin sighed. "This one's different. She's a lady, not some nineteen-year-old rock idol worshiper. I'm not even planning to bed her. I just like spending time with her. She's nice."

"Nice!"

He jerked the phone from his ringing ear. "That's my ear you shouted in."

"Don't do this, man. Nice girls are your kryptonite. They cling and whine and get jealous. You said so a hundred times."

Justin chuckled. "More than a hundred, probably. But seriously, I'm not going to get involved with her. She's smart. Someone I can hold a decent conversation with. Someone my age to hang with for a change. Why would I ruin that with sex?"

"Yeah. Good luck with that."

"Whatever. Keep C.J. out of trouble. I'll see you when I get back." Justin hit the end button and glanced at the time. He had two hours before he needed to head to the Radisson.

The thought of Desiree made him smile. She'd said she was a fan, but he'd never met a fan like her. He could listen to her talk with that accent all day and not grow tired of it. She was stunning, and it didn't hurt that he wanted to kiss those full lips every time he looked at her.

No. No kissing. No touching. No sex. He had to somehow pull a song out of his dried up soul, and wasting efforts on chasing ass would only distract him.

Though he liked how she could hold a decent conversation, and her articulation spoke of higher education. More than anything, the way she gazed at him woke something in him. Without a word, she communicated trust, curiosity, and admiration in her eyes. It made him want to take care of her. The way she'd jabbed her elbow in the man's chest told him she could take care of herself. He smiled.

Other than his band, he'd never had responsibility for another person. She stirred a protectiveness in him that he needed right now. His inability to write left him vulnerable, but she gave him solidity to cling to, something tangible. The moment he'd defended her on that plane, and every minute spent with her afterward, he'd shaken free from that vulnerability. Yeah, he'd made the right choice in asking her to dinner.

He went to the bedroom, unzipped his large suitcase, and removed Cassidy's wedding gift. Under it sat his green song notebook. It had only three songs in it – ones he'd written three months ago. The rest contained empty pages. He could almost hear those pages moaning like lost spirits, begging for his words and the tidbits of musical composition he always jotted when they occurred to him.

He closed his eyes. Nothing. No music. No lyrics. Silence haunted his consciousness.

"Damn it!" He took the notebook and pitched it at the far wall.

It slapped painted drywall then landed on the carpet with a quiet flutter, its cover opened like a collapsing tent and its pages awry. He stared at it, waiting for it to leap and attack.

"I'm seriously losin' it."

He went to the kitchen and opened the fridge. It offered everything from chilled longneck beers to a tray of sushi. His agent's assistant was nothing short of amazing. She'd found this cottage for him, booked his flights, and apparently stocked the kitchen with his favorites.

He took a beer, twisted off the cap, and guzzled a healthy swig. He found a bag on a small dinette table. It contained his favorite candy, the brand of toothpaste he preferred and a spare toothbrush, shampoo and soap, a military action novel, and Jamaican rum.

Beside the bag, restaurant menus formed a neat

stack atop a sheet with numbers including a local taxi service and the front desk of the Radisson.

"I guess I'm the only wedding guest not staying at that hotel."

One thing was certain. When he returned to Chicago, he'd send Spence's assistant a huge bouquet.

Butterflies in her stomach threatened to destroy her appetite, and Desiree smoothed a nervous hand down the brown and white silk skirt hugging her hip. She checked the crisp, gold-threaded neckline of her cream-colored blouse and worried she'd dressed wrong for dinner with a lead guitarist. Spandex and cleavage seemed more fitting.

A refreshing breeze caused tendrils from her French twist to dance against her cheek and ear. She patted her updo to make sure the pins held.

Oh, no. She'd overdressed. She sidestepped a uniformed hotel worker then turned for the door. Ten minutes. She only needed ten minutes to undo this.

"Desiree." Justin stood next to the open rear passenger door of a black sedan. He wore a tan blazer over a white polo shirt and brown slacks.

She exhaled in relief, delighted he hadn't worn a black T-shirt, jeans, and biker boots. Joining him at the door, she said, "You look handsome."

He grinned. "And you're particularly beautiful this evening."

She noted that his smile didn't quite reach his eyes. In the car, she settled her gold wedge purse on her lap and fastened her seatbelt. A driver wearing a black hat and coat offered her a nod in the rearview mirror.

"Do you like seafood?" Justin asked, getting in and closing the door.

"I love it." Her stomach rumbled a bit. "Especially when it's fresh. Did you have a good afternoon?"

"Not really."

He didn't say more, so she waited. She didn't

want to ask outright, but hoped he'd expound to fill the silence she created.

"Sometimes being the leader of a rock band is like being a supervisor. I think if I had known what it would really be like, I would've given it a second thought."

"I don't believe that. They're your friends. Besides, what would you have done instead? I promise you, it's the same in nearly any field."

He met her gaze. "Is it like that for you?"

She opened her mouth then clamped it shut.

"What?" he asked.

"Not really. I'm freelance. I set my own hours and go where I like. I have an assistant, but he doesn't give me any trouble."

Justin barked a laugh. "There you sit, talking like you know all about co-workers—"

"I haven't been self-employed my entire career. I worked in college, and I did an internship for three years after graduation. I was there. I know what it's like."

"Yeah, okay. I guess you're a better judge than me. I've only ever done what I'm doing right now." Weariness sounded in his voice, dropping his tone low and sluggish.

"Are you...?" She closed her lips and looked out her window. Who was she to him? What right did she have to ask probing questions?

"Am I what?" His dark eyes narrowed a fraction.

"Hungry. Are you hungry?" She offered him a tentative smile.

He visibly relaxed. "Actually, yes. I—"

"We're here," said the driver.

Justin's eyebrows arched. "Maybe we should've walked."

Desiree lifted a foot. "Not in these."

"I don't know how women walk in those."

She grinned in earnest. "It's a balancing act."

The car came to a halt, and the driver opened her door. She slid out and waited as Justin came around.

"I'll wait. Enjoy your meal," said the driver.

Justin's hand brushed the small of her back, and a shiver of delight shimmied her shoulders.

"Cold?" he asked.

The opposite, in fact. "I'm fine."

Inside, a young hostess didn't look up as she asked, "Dinner for two?"

"Yes," they said in unison. Desiree laughed, glad to lighten the tension.

"Oh, my gosh. OMG!" The girl's eyes widened.

Justin put a finger to his lips. "I'd prefer to stay and eat, but if there's a scene, I'll have to go somewhere else."

"Of course, Justin Time. I mean, Mr. Keither." She squealed, and moisture pooled in her eyes. "Please follow me."

Desiree cleared her throat. "Maybe you'd like to bring a couple menus?"

"Oh, right." The girl backtracked, selected two large menu books, and sent Justin a watery smile.

Desiree hid a smirk behind her hand, positive the young woman would swoon into a faint any moment. As the hostess led the way, she made sharp gestures and mouthed OMG to at least four other workers.

Thankfully, she presented them a table in a far corner where windows overlooked the ocean. Surrounding tables had no customers, so the area had both quiet and privacy.

Justin held out Desiree's chair, and after she had settled, he took the seat opposite. He opened his mouth to speak, but a waiter appeared. The man set a basket of cornbread with individually wrapped pats of butter at the center of the table then took their drink orders with as moony an expression as she'd ever seen on a man.

When the server left, she opened her menu.

"So I was wondering," said Justin, his menu open before him. "How does a wedding photographer fly first class?"

Amusement tugged at the corners of her mouth. "I'm not a wedding photographer. I'm working this wedding as a favor for the groom's father, who reports for the New York Times. He's given me a lot of leads that paid big, so this is the least I can do for him."

"Leads, huh? So you're a photo journalist?" He leaned forward slightly.

"Sometimes. I do my own thing, really. If it interests me, I photograph it."

"Sounds risky."

The waiter returned with their drinks, begged for Justin's autograph, and took their meal orders. He collected their menus and headed for the other side of the restaurant.

Desiree glanced at the white-capped ocean then at Justin. She'd met men from around the globe. Rich men. Powerful men. Influential men. Many of them handsome and interested in pursuing her. But she'd never forgotten Justin. Never stopped wanting him.

"I'm so pathetic," she whispered.

"I'm sorry? I didn't catch that."

She cleared her throat. "I simply asked what's life without risk. It's paid off for both of us." She gripped the edge of the table. She needed to relax.

"I guess so, but it's easier to take a risk at seventeen. I had my whole life ahead of me, so I had room to make mistakes and fail." He took a swallow of beer then traced the bottle's label while keeping his gaze on her.

"We're still young. Most twenty-eight-year-olds are only now beginning to gain respect in their fields. I think you and I are exceptions. Older people don't tend to take twenty-somethings seriously."

"Yeah, but some of us don't deserve to be taken seriously. I love C.J. He's a genius at percussion, and he's a good friend, but his life's a mess. I keep waiting for him to grow up."

"What if he doesn't? There are rockers out there twice our age who are just like C.J."

He shook his head. "We'll deal with it, I guess. Every time he does something stupid, it makes the entertainment news. It's free publicity for the band. Keeps our name in front of people, you know? I don't like watching him suffer, though. He's fighting demons, and sometimes I think he's losing."

Her heart went out to him. He truly cared about his friends. "We're all fighting demons, aren't we?"

His eyebrows lowered. "What demons are you fighting?"

She shrugged. "Less a demon and more a stigma, really. I was a high-fashion model for a few years. Mostly European publications and runway shows. It's how I paid for college and paid for the first year of my photography career."

"Doesn't surprise me. You're gorgeous. And tall."

She chuckled. "Thank you. When I travel, people still recognize me. Sometimes I have a hard time getting them to treat me as a dedicated professional photographer. I can't complain, though. It's gotten me into a few places I needed to go with less hassle than others received. Journalists aren't happy when I simply walk into a hospital or political function where they're barred. So when someone like Bill not only appreciates my work but sends more my way, I have to show my thanks."

"Bill, the groom's father?"

"Yes. Now it's your turn. What are your demons, Justin?"

Chapter Three

Would Desiree think less of him if he admitted he'd lost his inspiration? Justin bought time by taking a leisurely drink of his beer. When the waiter arrived with their food, he used the reprieve to think.

"This looks delicious," she said.

The waiter topped her water. He left for a few seconds then returned and placed a stack of paper napkins and extra butter on the table. "Can I get you anything else?"

"We're good," said Justin, unwrapping his silverware.

Desiree placed her cloth napkin on her lap and sent him an expectant look. She wasn't going to let it go. Fine.

"I have demons. My dad left my mom when I was still in diapers. She raised me on her own. She dated some when I was young, but she never remarried. It was hard for her. I didn't miss much, I guess. She always made sure I had what I needed, and a few things I wanted like my electric guitar and amps and a concert ticket every now and then. She went without. A lot."

Desiree forked a sautéed scallop but didn't move it to her mouth. "How do you mean?"

"She wore her clothes until she couldn't mend the holes anymore, and she wore her shoes until the soles came off. She never went anywhere fun or did anything for herself. She only worked and came home. I helped. I kept our apartment clean and made dinner sometimes. I started working when I was sixteen. I bought us our first home computer, and we got cable for the television since I could pay for it."

Desiree's eyes went soft, and Justin averted his gaze, embarrassed. On guard for a reason he didn't want to explore. Angry and on edge because he didn't want her pitying him.

Adding butter to his baked potato, he released a slow breath then said, "When Smashing Glass made it big, I bought her a house and a new car. She deserved it, you know? She got to retire early and have all her bills paid through my accountant. Now she does volunteer work and has friends. She has a life and gets to do what she wants."

"You're a good son. Do you see her much?"

He shook his head. "I wish I could do more. I wish I could turn back time and make my father stay."

"Where is he now? Did he remarry?"

"We never heard from him. I didn't try to find him."

"Why not?"

"Honestly, I'm not interested." He tried for a smile. He didn't need to meet some stranger to gain fulfillment. He had his mom, and in many ways, his band was as close as family. Still, that pang of regret and guilt never seemed to disappear. Would his father have stayed if he hadn't been born?

A shadow darkened his thoughts. What if he couldn't write songs anymore? He would let the band down. Jet wrote wonderful lyrics, but Justin's compositions defined their unique sound. What if he never heard new music again?

"Justin?" Desiree's fine eyebrows pitched at a worried angle.

He forced a laugh. "You know what? Let's talk about something less heavy. Tell me how Bill approached you about working his son's wedding."

They spent the evening sharing funny experiences and laughing. He signed two more autographs then walked her to their car.

On the road, he asked, "Do you want to come see my cottage?"

The moment the words left his lips, he regretted them. Too soon. Too crass for this sophisticated woman. What had happened to his resolve not to get her into bed? It would ruin everything they'd spent the day building. Sex always created a light, meaningless interaction. That's why he used it to keep women at a distance. When he fucked a woman their first night together, he could consider her nothing more than a temporary good time. Why should he respect a girl who didn't respect herself?

But not this one. Not Desiree.

She studied the purse on her lap. "I'd love to, but I have to be up early. Setup begins at sunrise, and I want to document it for the wedding album."

"Sure. So I'll see you tomorrow." He fisted his hands in his lap, digging fingernails into his palms to keep from touching her.

She was so gorgeous, though. He'd known many beautiful women, but Desiree's eyes mesmerized him, and her smile melted his insides. She had a calm confidence he had lost in his crisis, and he wanted to bury himself in her. To bask in her peace and seek comfort in her shapely arms.

No. She wasn't for him in that way. Friends. They would form a friendship, and he would walk away when the time came. She deserved a man who could love her. A man who would give her a life of peace and fulfillment. Justin couldn't give her any of that.

The driver pulled in front of the hotel, but she didn't get out. She pivoted on the seat and squarely faced him. Her lovely eyes met his. "Justin, I can tell you're going through something. You can talk to me. I won't judge you. I just wanted you to know that."

The driver opened the door, and she stepped out while Justin's insides knotted. Part of him hated that he hadn't hid his suffering better, but part of him liked how she could read him. How she reached out to him. It meant so much. Other women had sought to trap him or use him for his fame and fortune. He'd never met a woman like Desiree. A woman with a thought to help him rather than herself.

Before closing the car door, she bent and offered a sweet smile. "Thank you for dinner. I'll see you tomorrow."

He couldn't let her go. God help him, he couldn't stop himself from climbing out and meeting her as she came around. "Listen, I think you're an incredible woman." He took her hand. "You deserve so much better than me."

She trailed fingers along his cheek. "Why? What do I 'deserve' that you can't give?"

A knife twisted in his gut. He closed his eyes a moment, soaking in her silken touch. "I don't know. All of me, I guess."

"Are you talking about self-sacrifice or commitment? Because I'm not asking for either. I'm only asking for some of your time." This gentle woman seemed to truly understand, and it blew his mind. Here stood a woman who didn't create drama. She had a maturity that matched his, and for once, he recognized someone he could turn to. Could rely on.

He leaned in, and she met him halfway. Their lips touched, and sparks flashed across his vision. This was magic.

Closing his eyes, he let the world fall away. He brought her against him and sighed when she put her arms around his neck. He touched his tongue to the crease of her lips, and she opened. When their tongues met, his body came to life.

Her taste hinted of sweet butter and cornbread. She felt like heaven in his arms. Her tongue, smooth and warm, caressed his. Once. Twice. Then she let go and stepped away. Disappointment burned like lava in his gut. Shit. What was he doing?

"Goodnight, Justin."

"Goodnight, Desiree." He let his gaze follow her sexy saunter to the hotel entrance while he caught his breath.

She was all woman, and nothing like the weak-willed groupies who flocked to the stage door after concerts. Her strong character made her special. He couldn't deny he wanted her, which meant he would need to work harder to maintain his determination. He'd have to give Jet an easier time. Now he realized how a man could fall for a woman in such a short time. Too bad he didn't deserve her.

With a woman like Desiree, there could be no halfway. He couldn't give her one hundred percent, especially since he continued to fail his band. His friends. Himself.

Desiree maintained her composure until she stepped into an empty elevator and the doors swished shut. Grinning madly, she did a happy dance the entire ride to the tenth floor. Justin had kissed her, and he'd been better than any of her girlhood fantasies.

As she headed along the hall to her room, she sobered. He had something weighing heavily upon him. It wasn't a breakup. The tabloids would've notified the world if he'd been seen with a woman more than once, like they did every time Jet got his heart broken and every time C.J. got served in a paternity suit.

Did he pine over Cassidy? His kiss said otherwise, but how could she tell for certain? She didn't know him well enough. She keyed open her door, went into her room, and flopped backward onto the bed.

Tomorrow would prove his test. His behavior would, she hoped, clue her in to his attachment to the bride.

She touched fingertips to her lips and smiled. His kiss had weakened her insides. It had taken extraordinary effort to step away from him when she only wanted to bring him to her room and fulfill every fantasy she'd ever had of him.

Sighing, she heaved off the bed. She had to get

her gear ready for the big day.

The next morning, wearing comfortable flats, stretch slacks, and a white sleeveless blouse, Desiree flitted among caterers, florists, decorators, and a swarm of deliverymen. An enormous white tent shivered in an ocean breeze, which blew through from one open end to the other. It filtered early morning sun and gave her a cool workplace as she snapped photos of Radisson staff carrying in tables and chairs, florists carting in a garden's worth of arranged flowers, and decorators covering tables and chairs in enough fabric to clothe a village. She captured amazing shots of fake saplings strung with tiny white lights, stacked champagne flutes against an ocean background, and a sea of workers arranging chairs under an awning for the coming ceremony.

She worked for hours. Whenever thoughts of Justin Time filtered in, threatening to distract her, she stubbornly shoved them aside. Shortly after noon, the hotel's wedding coordinator led her to one of the kitchens for a hot lunch. While she ate, she snapped pictures of a baking team placing final touches on the gaudiest cake she'd ever beheld.

An army of chefs and cooks labored at preliminary work to ready the afternoon's reception feast. The bride's family had surely paid a fortune for this event.

When she headed outside, some of the guests had begun to arrive. Desiree went into the reception tent and sat in a corner where she'd stored her equipment so she could load a new memory chip into her camera and check the batteries' charge.

"Hey there."

A thrill ran through her. Justin Time stood at the tent opening. He looked particularly handsome in a pale linen suit with white sneakers and a black T-shirt sporting a stenciled skull with musical notes spewing from a crack in the cranium. Very rock-appropriate, if not for a wedding.

She smiled in approval of his irreverent apparel choices. He'd dressed nicely for their dinner last night, but not for his ex's wedding. A good sign, for sure.

"Hey back," she said.

"Been thinking about me?" His grin lacked conviction.

Yes. "No, I've been working all morning. Have you been thinking of me?"

His grin faltered then took on a forced quality. "No. I've been writing songs all morning."

"That's a good thing." She stood and waved him to a stand that held her laptop. "Take a look."

He moved beside her. His cologne, clean and masculine without the bite of musk, surrounded her. It made her slightly giddy. It made her want him to kiss her like he had last night.

She blinked free from her trance and began uploading the morning's images. Pictures appeared one at a time, each lingering on the display for a three-second count. "These are from the setup."

"Incredible." He leaned closer. "They're so vivid and colorful, like stills from a movie or something."

"Thanks. It has to do with the lighting through this tent fabric and the shutter speed I set. This is my favorite camera setting for outside festivals and nature shots."

When the photo of the pyramid of empty flutes appeared, he gasped. "Wow. That one should be in a gallery or something. I can picture it huge, framed, and hanging on somebody's dining room wall."

She beamed. She could see that, too. "You have a good eye. This is one I knew I'd love before I took the picture. Funny you should mention a gallery. I have a showing coming up."

"I'm impressed." His hand brushed hers as he moved away.

Awareness prickled within her. Reluctantly, she strung her camera around her neck. "I have to get back to work. I want some shots of guests arriving."

His gaze centered on her lips, and she warmed from her neck to her brow. She fought an urge to latch onto him and demand what she wanted. His hands on her. His mouth on hers. His body against her.

She cleared her throat. "Okay then. I'll see you at the reception."

A knowing smirk graced his sensual lips, and amusement gleamed in his dark gaze. He offered a barely-there bow then went outside and followed a cluster of new arrivals toward the beach.

She shook, actually shook, with the effort not to run after him. "That man is going to make me crazy."

As guests arrived, she captured scenes of laughter, loving couples, and proud older relatives. She worked the ceremony in silence, trying to remain inconspicuous while attempting to get fabulous pictures.

Against her will, her gaze repeatedly returned to Justin. Each time, she found him watching her. It allayed her fear that he yearned for Cassidy. He hardly sent the bride a glance throughout the ceremony. At one point, she caught him texting. Hardly the behavior of a lovesick man.

Guests who recognized him spent the ceremony dividing their attention between witnessing the vows and sending Justin furtive, curious glances. He didn't appear to notice.

When the ceremony ended, guests strolled to the reception tent. She stayed on the beach and took candid shots of the wedding party. For the final fifteen minutes of the photo shoot, she used a tripod for portrait-style group photos that involved the families. Then she scrambled to collect her equipment and get to the tent ahead of the new couple.

Justin answered his fifth question regarding the stereotypes of a rock star's life posed by a too-curious middle-aged woman and her star-struck teenaged daughter. He glanced around the table, but nobody appeared interested in talking about anything but him.

"I like a wedding on the beach," he attempted.

"Cassidy makes a beautiful bride."

"So in the typical week, how many days do you get high?" asked the woman.

Justin narrowed his eyes, wishing he had a strip of duct tape to tack across the woman's red-stained lips.

Desiree hurried in under a daunting array of photo equipment, and he breathed a sigh of relief.

"Excuse me," he said, shoving back his chair and standing. "It looks like the photographer could use help."

He didn't make it three steps when the bride stopped him. She hooked her arm through his and said, "Not so fast, Justin. I can't believe you actually came to my wedding. I sent that invitation as a lark."

Ha-ha. "I wouldn't miss it. You were my first love. Half my first song notebook is full of songs about us."

"Really?" She blushed a pretty shade of pink.

"Really. You're a beautiful bride, Cassidy. Your husband's a lucky man." He glanced at Desiree, who had come to a stop as she appeared to attempt a controlled crash of slipping equipment.

"Husband. That sounds so strange. He's waving to me, so I need to go. I'm so glad you came, Justin." She grinned, radiant in her happiness. "I want a picture with you later."

"No problem." He moved toward Desiree, who now crouched to gather the items she had dropped.

The woman from his table stepped in his path. "Will you perform for us?"

"I'm a guest," he said dryly. "Not the hired help. Excuse me." He sidestepped her and squatted next to Desiree. He gathered her tripod and a large umbrella.

"Thanks," she said on a weary smile and a winded breath.

"Actually, I need to thank you for rescuing me from the ignorant questions of a weak mind."

Desiree shot him an amused smile. "Sounds like lyrics of a song."

The ignorant questions of a weak mind. Man, she was right. Unfortunately, he left his notebook at the cottage. He followed her to the corner and ignored applause as the wedding party began making toasts.

"I think I'm going to take off." He wanted to get those words written before they fled. "Can I see you later?"

Her large green eyes glinted with disappointment. "I'd love to, but I have no idea how late this reception will go. Are you returning to Chicago in the morning?"

"No, I'm staying. A sort of vacation, I guess." If wrestling with his failure could be called a vacation. He set her tripod on a chair and propped the umbrella against the tent wall. "How about you?"

"I'm staying, too. I have business here for a few days."

Justin fought a smile. This wasn't goodbye.

Chapter Four

As Desiree approached the open door, a surprised laugh escaped her throat at the sight of her photos filling the Kill Devil Hills Art Gallery. It took an effort to keep her mouth from gaping as she slowly stepped inside. She'd expected a wall or two, not the entire place.

"Ms. Renault." A tall, thin man emerged from the back. He had thick white hair in a well-groomed style and wore pastels more suited to a golf course. He clapped his hands once and beamed. "What an absolute honor to meet you in person."

"Mr. Westin." She offered her hand.

"Call me Phil," he said, taking her hand in a firm, welcoming shake. "What do you think?"

"I'm overwhelmed, really."

He extended an arm in a broad sweep that sent her gaze to a series of enlarged black and white pictures she'd taken in the Sudan early in her career. They included some of her favorites. Walking backward, Phil led her into the heart of the gallery where artfully arranged images of faces she'd captured in Egypt, Kuwait, and Lebanon greeted her like old friends.

At the rear, color photos of tropical waters and exotic gardens shocked her senses while stirring memories of each experience. Finally, he accompanied her through a long hall lined with photos of breathtaking architecture and statuary she'd encountered throughout Europe and Russia.

"Did we do you justice? You didn't give instruction on image placement, so I had Geraldine arrange them in a flow that made the most sense and impact." He gripped his hands at the buckle of his straw-colored belt.

"I'm beyond pleased. You've done so much better than I could have."

"I doubt that," he said, his shoulders relaxing. He unclenched his hands. "I wish we could obtain some of your published photos."

She shrugged and followed him to an office. "Once I sell to a periodical, those images no longer belong to me."

"Don't get me wrong." He moved behind a desk and handed her a pen. "I'm thrilled to have these photos from your private collection. My heart skips a beat every time I look at that picture of the Egyptian boys playing in the Nile. It takes my breath away."

"I'm glad." Praise from this man and his trained eye meant a lot. She accepted a file folder and opened it to the show's contract. "Are you expecting a decent turnout for tonight's opening?"

Phil chuckled. "When news got out that internationally renowned photographer Desiree Renault was showing here, we received more RSVPs than our gallery can hold. People will be lining Gallery Row, waiting to get in here and meet you. I expect we'll sell every piece here and have requests for more."

Her heart beat faster. "That's exciting."

"Did you have a chance to read the contract I emailed you?"

"I did, thanks. It's perfectly acceptable, and this looks identical." She ticked the pen tip along each paragraph.

"It is, Ms. Renault. I printed it off the same attachment file. You didn't have any questions?"

"No. The contract is standard. I use a similar one at my studio." She signed on the last page then initialed the bottom of the other two contract pages. "What time do you need me here this evening?"

He took her signed contract and the pen. "Come at half past seven. And bring a date. For some reason, we always sell more when the artist is accompanied."

She smiled. How could she say no when it meant another opportunity to spend time with Justin?

"Grrr!"

Justin tossed his pen onto the coffee table next to his notebook's empty page and strode across the room. He glared at the offending book, wishing for a second he had superpowers to cause it to burst into flames with a single look.

Not only had he lost the words Desiree had said sounded like lyrics, he still couldn't write a song after sitting through Cassidy's wedding. What was wrong with him?

He raked his nails across his scalp. He needed to get out of this cottage. Taking his phone off its charger, he cast the notebook another hateful stare. Then he chose Desiree from his contact list and put the phone to his ear.

"Desiree Renault," she answered.

"Hey, it's Justin. Did I catch you in the middle of anything?"

"Not at all. In fact, I hoped you would call. Would you be willing to go somewhere with me this evening?"

He turned his back on the coffee table. "More than willing. What do you have in mind?"

"A gallery opening."

He cringed. "Paintings and statues and stuff?"

"Actually, it's my opening. A local gallery has contracted to sell my photos."

Now he remembered her mentioning it. He stood straighter. Collecting three candies from a bowl on the kitchen table, he couldn't help being intrigued. He'd really liked the pictures she'd taken yesterday.

She cleared her throat. "What do you say? Would

you please go with me?"

"Dinner first?" he asked, rolling the three candies across his palm while his stomach grumbled.

"It's catered. We'll eat there."

"That's fine with me." He'd hoped to spend more time in her company. He wasn't about to turn down this chance.

"I'm so glad. I'll bring a car and pick you up in an hour."

He gave her the cottage address, popped a couple pieces of candy in his mouth then got in a hot shower. Steaming water pelted stiff muscles in his neck and shoulders but did little to alleviate his tension. He'd thought for sure he'd write an entire album's worth of songs after Cassidy's wedding. Now, true fear began to set in.

Music was his life. Not only his work, but also part of his identity. His relationships with his band mates expanded his purpose. Recordings, concerts, and interviews gave his life meaning. Without the driving force of his music, he'd lose everything that meant anything.

"Damn it!" He punched the shower wall and regretted it when his knuckles smarted.

He quickly lathered and rinsed. He finished grooming at a well-lit vanity then slicked his hair into a smooth ponytail. He donned black jeans, a black T-shirt, and a black blazer. Before he had a chance to put on his shoes, Desiree knocked at his cottage door.

He opened to her, smiling at her promptness. He hadn't looked forward to ignoring the taunt of his notebook, had she made him wait.

"Sorry I'm early," she said, an unsure crook pulling at the curve of her lips.

A white top made entirely of lace showed glimpses of something pink underneath and let him see her shape silhouetted against a landscape awash in sunset colors. Dark blue jeans hugged her firm hips and thighs, and white high-heeled sandals allowed him to see she'd painted her toenails a pretty coral color.

"Come in," he said, stepping aside so she could enter. "I just need to put something on my feet."

She closed the door behind her. She wore her auburn hair loose and curling lazily down her back. "I can't believe how close you are from my hotel. I could walk here."

He moved to the bedroom and put his bare feet into black Italian loafers. "Is the gallery far?"

"About a ten-minute ride. It's on Galley Row off Croatan Highway."

He joined her in the living room and shoved his wallet into a back pocket. "I'm ready if you are."

She led the way out, and he locked the door. A blue Crown Victoria sat in the cottage's driveway, its motor running. The hotel logo graced the front door, and a uniformed driver climbed out and touched the brim of his hat in greeting, then held open the back passenger door.

En route, Desiree asked, "Did you get a lot of writing done today?"

He cast her a curious glance. "I'm on vacation, remember? Maybe I'm taking a break from writing."

"You? Take a break from writing?" She laughed. "Maybe you've changed more than I thought."

His stomach clenched. She hardly knew him, yet she understood how much writing songs meant to him. Not that it was a secret. It came up in every interview he'd ever given, and diligent paparazzi often snapped photos of him scribbling in his notebook.

"Besides," she said. "You told me at the wedding that you'd been writing all morning."

He'd forgotten about that lie. Damn. Too late to take it back. "Do you know I keep them? My notebooks, I mean."

"The ones where you write your songs?"

"Yes."

"How many are there? You've been doing this for eleven years, haven't you?"

"Longer, really. I started writing songs my first year in high school. None of them are any good, but I kept those, too. My last count was sixty-two."

Her gorgeous eyes widened slightly. "That's a lot of notebooks."

Justin chuckled. "That's a lot of songs. Most of them are crap, but the guys help me pick the best, and those are the ones we set to music."

"Why do you handwrite them? I use my phone for everything. Why don't you type songs into your phone?"

"There's something about the drag of a pen tip on paper that seems to add to my creativity. I've typed notes into my phone, but I always transfer them into my notebook. I don't know. The phone is impersonal, I guess. I don't even like using my laptop when I'm assembling compositions, but it's a necessary evil." He smiled and shrugged.

"How many songs do you have in your current notebook?" She folded long fingers together and settled them on her knees.

"Three." He tried not to grit his teeth.

"So it's new."

Hardly. Normally, he would have a notebook nearly full in the three months he'd carried this one. He didn't answer for fear his anger and frustration would come through in his tone.

He released a slow breath and glanced out the window as the driver turned onto Croatan Highway. "This gallery opening... Did you plan it for a long time?"

"Actually, no. Three weeks ago, I added this wedding to the upcoming events section of my website, and the gallery manager saw it. He emailed me and asked if I'd be interested in showing and selling here. I rarely turn down an opportunity to get my work out there and noticed."

"Publicity is everything, isn't it?" He managed a genuine grin.

She returned it, her eyes sparkling. "Here we are."

He held back. Desiree could detect it in the

tightness of his mouth. A darkness shadowed his gaze. Justin had something weighing on him, and she knew only one thing for certain. It wasn't Cassidy.

Desiree studied him as he strolled through the gallery before the opening. Caterers bustled and the manager kept asking her questions, but she couldn't take her eyes from Justin's expression, which changed with each picture he viewed.

His smiles delighted her. His serious consideration added to her sense of pride. He liked her work, and for a reason she didn't dare explore, his good opinion meant a lot to her.

"Wow." He stopped at the end of the architectural pieces and looked her in the eye. "Wow."

She beamed. Happiness and confidence bloomed in her chest like a sun-warmed flower. He didn't need to say more. His one word, repeated in quiet awe, said more than enough.

As they enjoyed tidbits from the caterer's array of delectable offerings, guests began to arrive. The manager had been right. The opening soon spilled onto the sidewalk. And there were so many actual buyers.

Justin refused to sign autographs. She liked how he kept this event about her. He even took an occasional person to look at his favorites, which touched her heart.

Shortly after nine o'clock, a reporter arrived with a photographer. Word had gotten out, and she suspected 'Justin Time' Keither's celebrity presence was to thank. She wouldn't complain though. Like he'd said. Publicity was everything.

The photographer took pictures of her works on display, her talking with buyers, and her in conversation with Justin. The interview was blessedly brief, focusing mainly on her more famous journalistic photographs, what she worked on now, and how she knew Justin Time.

When the last photo sold, it was still early. She shook Phil's hand, promised to get him more pictures the next day, and snuck out the back with Justin.

"I think we can deem that a huge success," he said, heading for her car.

She laughed and took his arm in both her hands as they walked. "You were wonderful. Nobody expected a rock legend to be selling photos at a gallery opening. Least of all me."

"Yeah, I got some interesting looks. It was all good, though. I think."

"Better than good, thanks to you."

He chuckled. "Don't blame this on me. Blame it on your talent."

"Ready to go home?"

He stopped and faced her. "Maybe. But first..." He cupped her face in his hands. "You're so beautiful."

She held her breath as her heart began to pound. He slowly moved in, and she closed her eyes. Anticipation created a delicious tension, and she clutched the lapels of his blazer. When his lips touched hers, she melted against him.

His fingers lightly combed into her hair. He tilted, deepening the kiss. As the world tipped sideways, she inhaled. His cologne filled her nostrils. His strength held her up.

He wrapped an arm across the small of her back and urged her to open. She did, and he gently touched the tip of his tongue to hers before sliding it along hers in a sensual caress. A tight need pulled deep inside. She inhaled sharply.

He drew her close, and his exhales sent warm puffs of air across the fine hairs of her cheek. Excitement vibrated through his trembling fingers and the urgency in his exploring tongue. She entered into a dance, her tongue twining with his then retreating only to return and caress his again. His low moan resonated into their kiss.

Her knees went weak, which told her she had to stop. If she didn't, she'd have him in her room within minutes of arriving at the hotel. Forget early. Forget logic. No, that wasn't how she wanted their first time.

The driver cleared his throat.

On a groan of effort and disappointment, she released his lapels and broke the kiss. He looked sexy, with his kiss-moistened lips and hooded lids. Sexy enough to kiss one more time. But she fought it. She wouldn't have the determination to stop, driver or not.

"Thank you for this evening," she said.

He raked fingers through his hair and readjusted his ponytail holder. Smiling, he said, "Let's go."

They climbed in the backseat, and when the driver pulled onto Gallery Row, Justin gathered her to snuggle against him in the corner.

She sighed. "Tell me about how you met the rest of the band."

"It wasn't anything special or surprising," he said quietly, his tone adding to the intimacy. "Jet and C.J. went to my high school. They were friends, but C.J. was a foster kid. Jet's parents wound up taking him in so the system wouldn't move him away. I met them in the cafeteria. C.J. was drumming a rhythm on a table while Jet fingered a cool tune on his shoulder keyboard. The band geeks were shooting them dirty looks, so I figured they had to be alright."

Desiree chuckled.

"We started practicing together. Mostly top-forty songs from the radio. We realized we were good, but we needed a bass player. Chaz was playing in some nothing band that was going nowhere, but they played gigs on the weekends. Jet and I went to a pizza place where they happened to be playing. Chaz had a solid groove and some good slap."

"And he agreed to join your band right then and there?" she asked.

"He was smarter than that. He'd been through some hard knocks. It took a lot for him to trust us."

"You must've done something right. He's part of your band."

"He came to some of our rehearsals then agreed to practice with us a couple times. It wasn't until we bailed him out of jail that he started considering us friends."

She swallowed, unsure how Justin would take her

next question. "What did he do, if you don't mind my asking?"

"I don't know. None of us do. He doesn't talk about it, and we never asked. Anyway, we became a band that day. It was Chaz's idea that we start playing our own music and become real. He'd found my songs in my backpack when he'd been looking for a pen, and he really believed we could make it."

"And here you are." She smiled.

"Here we are." His voice lacked conviction.

She left his embrace to search his face. "Every time we get together, I can see something's bothering you. Are you fighting with your friends?"

His eyelids narrowed a fraction.

"I could tell you were dealing with something before. Anything I can help with?"

His features relaxed. "You're really nice to offer, but nobody can help me with this."

Chapter Five

Justin let Desiree drop him at the cottage, and ended their date there. He'd desperately wanted to invite her in, and a flicker in her gaze told him she'd wanted the same. But she saw inside him, and that scared him. More frightening yet was how the world seem to become so much bigger than his band and his music when he touched her.

He wouldn't try to write tonight. His earlier frustration had been enough for one day. What he really needed was a good night's sleep.

He drank two shots of rum then got in the shower and let hot water run down his back until he had trouble keeping his eyes open. He barely dried with a hand towel before he fell into bed and blessed unconsciousness.

When he woke, morning sun had his bedroom glowing. He kept his eyes closed and waited for words.

Nothing.

He opened his eyes and swung his legs over the bed's edge. He listened, searching for music in the silence.

Nothing.

Attending Cassidy's wedding hadn't worked. Spending time with an incredible woman wasn't inspiring him, either. Even a vacation from his band didn't help.

"I give the hell up." He flung the bedding aside

and strode to his suitcase. He tossed a pair of flip-flops onto the carpet then quickly donned a pair of running shorts and a tank top.

Outside, the morning held a warmth that promised sweltering temperatures later. This was a good time to run out his anxiety, before the day grew hot.

He made his way around the cottage and to a stretch of beach where wind and pounding surf attempted to fill the hated silence crowding his mind. He stepped out of his flip-flops and tossed them beside a clump of tall dune grass then began a slow jog atop packed sand along the water's edge.

The thud of his feet created a tempo that stirred a single, throbbing note. His heart leapt at the hope of a song.

He increased his pace, and his pulse kept time. A run of fast notes repeated a simple phrase. Guitar? No, keyboard.

His footsteps became C.J. on drums. A gull cried in the distance, hitting the first note he would strike on his screaming guitar.

Yes!

Then he'd match the scream with his voice, prolonging the tension. The rumble of surf made its way in and melted into a three-phrase fill on Chaz's bass.

Justin slid to a halt, digging heel marks into the sand, and turned. He sprinted for the cottage as the melody started. He had to get to his notebook and get this down before he lost it.

Leaving his flip-flops on the beach, he raced into the cottage and found his notebook where he'd left it yesterday on the living room table. He plopped onto the couch, breathing hard from his run, and grabbed his pen. His hand shaking from both exertion and excitement, he drew a clumsy bar upon a blank page and slashed notes into place. He ignored a drop of sweat that fell from his forehead onto the page's margin.

Five bars down, the music stopped. He went still and closed his eyes.

Nothing.

He replayed the last ten notes in his head, but no music followed.

"Damn it!"

He had to get back on that beach. He plucked the notebook from the table and hurried to the sand. Pen and book in hand, he jogged along the water's edge.

His pounding feet brought only the sound of flesh on damp sand. Wind tugged at his hair and shirt. The waves offered a discordant roar. Gulls held their tongues as they swooped and circled overhead.

He ran harder. Faster. His legs burned. His lungs dragged salty air down his throat. Sweat stung his eyes.

When he couldn't take it another second, he came to a halt. He braced his hand on a knee and pressed the notebook to a stitch in his side. Near to tears, he blinked. He fought an urge to pitch the notebook into the ocean.

He stumbled a few steps backward and sagged into soft, dry sand. Sighing heavily, he bent his knees and rested his forehead against them. Why was this so hard? Maybe he needed an MRI.

"Maybe I need to quit."

He heaved to his feet on a defeated groan. For the first time in his life, he was closer to quitting than he ever thought he could get.

Justin took his time returning to the cottage. Instead of seeking a tune or lyrics, he simply listened to the world. Unlike Chicago, this place was quiet. Peaceful. No shouts. No honking horns. No constant buzz of city noise. Only nature spoke this morning.

He wished he could enjoy it, but the turmoil inside him kept him tense. He collected his flip-flops and strolled to the cottage.

Desiree stood at his door in a pale green sundress that hugged her curves, her hand poised at mid-knock. She offered him a tentative smile. "There you are."

"Here I am." Despite the sourness in his stomach over the morning's failure, the sight of her brightened his day a bit.

Her toned, white shoulders begged him to caress

their smooth skin. She folded her hands behind her back, drawing his eyes to her generous cleavage. Her dress wasn't anything spectacular on its own, but clinging to her as it did, it knocked him upside the head with sexy.

"I was hoping to catch you here," she said.

He took a step closer and detected the faint fragrance of her hair on the breeze. He wanted to touch her auburn curls to learn if they felt as soft as they appeared.

She ran the tip of her sandal in an invisible half circle upon the stone step of his door landing. "Here's the thing. I'm scheduled to check out of the hotel this morning, but it seems to me you could use a friend right now. If you want..."

"If I want what?" He moved a step more. A breeze sent one of her wayward curls into a dance against her cheek, and he wanted to wrap it around his finger. He wanted to caress her cheek and test the silkiness of her skin.

"If you want, I could stay. A little longer." Her large eyes met his gaze, and her fine, arched eyebrows lifted a fraction. "If you want."

He caught a whiff of her perfume, a soft, feminine scent with a hint of vanilla. His heart lightened. How did she take him from the brink of despair to a near chuckle?

"Can I be completely honest with you?" he asked.

"Please do."

"A few seconds ago, I was in a really dark place. And now I'm not. Yeah. I could really use a friend this week. I'd love if you stayed, as long as I'm not keeping you from anything important."

Her smile went from tentative to bright. His gloom dissipated as he basked in the warmth of her sunshine.

"I need to take a shower." Plus, he didn't dare get closer since he hadn't brushed his teeth, either. "Will you wait?"

"Actually, I need to return to the hotel, in case I have to move to another room. How about I come back in an hour? Maybe we could go have brunch somewhere."

"I look forward to it."

He'd said yes. Desiree's stomach did a somersault. She refused to examine why she wanted to stay, or why Justin had always meant something to her. Now, as a woman and a professional, she hardly considered a future with a rock musician ideal.

If she didn't see a life with him, why was she trying so hard? She shook her head, unable to answer. He seemed to need her at the moment, and she wanted to be here for him. Besides, a sweet, needy quality he seemed determined to hide appealed to her. She liked him so much better than she thought possible.

The hotel let her keep her room for an extended stay of three more days. Three days wasn't long. Certainly not long enough to form any kind of permanent attachment.

She hesitated. Was she hoping for a fling? A girlhood fantasy of Justin Time fulfilled so she could move on and find her husband? It didn't sound right, but in all honesty, she'd never dated men longer than a few months because they never measured up to him.

Yet she hadn't been fair. She didn't really know him. She held men against who she thought he was. An ideal born of one evening when they were kids. An evening that had meant nothing to him in terms of her.

So maybe she needed this. If she lived the fantasy for a few days and learned he was only a man with flaws, no better than the rest, she could leave this weekend and Justin Time behind for good.

When she returned to his cottage, he met her outside. He had shaved, and his hair hung damp and loose from a fresh washing. The sight of him brought an unbidden smile. She didn't know whether to love it or hate it. Mostly, she feared missing him when they parted. Because if she did, it would defeat her purpose.

He wore moss green, knee-length shorts, flip-flops, and a black classic band T-shirt with cracked lettering from too many washes. He offered an easy smile and climbed into the passenger seat of her hotel car.

"I thought we might go to a place the hotel's concierge recommends. They specialize in seafood omelets."

"Interesting. Let's do it." His smile slipped a fraction as he fastened his seatbelt.

"We don't have to if you have something else in mind."

He shook his head. "Believe me. I have nothing else in mind."

She followed the beach road to a side street then got on the four-lane road that passed for a highway. "Since I'm staying, maybe you could tell me what's been bothering you."

"You get right to the point."

"Sorry." She cringed inwardly. "It comes with the job, I guess. I can't take time for niceties when there's a picture to take. Lighting and expressions can change in an instant, and I can't play. Especially when it's a potential news photo."

"I'm not a picture."

She didn't miss the tightness of his tone. "You're right. You're not my work. I apologize."

Justin didn't look at her, but his hand found hers on the storage compartment between their seats. His palm warmed the back of her hand, and he rubbed his thumb across her fingers.

They didn't speak again until they took their seats at the restaurant. "You really want to know?" he asked.

"I wouldn't have inquired if I didn't."

His dark gaze slid to the window and remained. "You talked about my songwriting and keep asking if I got a lot written while I'm here."

"Of course," she said. "I want to know about you and your music."

"Well, that's my problem." His eyes found hers

and held her gaze with an intensity that made her heart beat faster. "I'm not writing. At all. I haven't written a single word or a complete melody in months"

She frowned. "But you told me at the wedding that you had written songs all morning."

"I lied."

Her stomach dropped. He hadn't written in months? This was huge for him.

He stared at the table. "I'm at a loss. This morning was the first time music has played in my mind, but I couldn't hold onto it. The music evaporated before I could get it onto paper."

Desiree took his hand and pulled it to the table's center. Giving it a squeeze, she said, "Doesn't that give you hope? If you heard music this morning, maybe it's returning."

He raked his free hand through his damp hair. "I'm afraid to hope."

"It's not gone. It came back today." She wet her dry lips with a sip of water.

His voice grated rough and low when he said, "What good does it do me if I can't hold onto it? I need a new song, Desiree. Hell, I need twenty new songs."

Her name from his sensual mouth sent a thrill through her. She brushed the sensation aside. He needed her support, not her desire. "Don't give up."

Pulling his hand from hers, he said, "I want to. I really want to give up."

Her stomach sank deeper. "But *you're* Smashing Glass. What are you going to do? What will your band do if you give up?"

"I don't know." He rubbed his face. When he lowered his hands to his lap and gazed at her, his eyes were red rimmed and had bags underneath. "I'm so tired."

She studied him a moment, taking in tension around his mouth and a sadness pulling at the corners of his eyes. She glanced over her shoulder. The wait staff bustled to meet the demands of their diners, and nobody appeared prepared to head her way. Likely they hadn't realized who sat with her.

"Justin, what do you say to us leaving?"

His eyebrows lifted slightly. "And go where?"

"I don't know. How about we buy a couple burgers and go to the beach?"

A weary smile graced his shapely lips. "That sounds really good."

She stood and accepted his hand. He led her out on a fast stride. To her amazement, nobody tried to stop them. In the parking lot, he took her keys then drove toward the ocean. He made one stop, buying crab cake sandwiches and soft drinks at a drive-through.

He didn't try to make conversation, and Desiree let him have his peace. He'd confessed something personal and important. She could only imagine how his thoughts raced at the moment.

He parked at his cottage, and she followed him to the beach behind it. Kicking off her sandals, she sighed as her toes came free from the leather straps. Hot, yielding sand surrounded them, and she took digging steps to a thick clump of tall, fragrant grass where Justin had stopped to sit.

She settled beside him and accepted a paper-wrapped sandwich. The ocean spoke in varying degree of lapping water at harmony with the whisper of shifting sand and dancing grasses. Desiree closed her eyes.

"I like how you don't have to talk all the time," Justin said amidst the crinkle of paper as he unwrapped his lunch.

Her eyes still shut, she asked, "Does anyone have to talk all the time?"

"Yes. Most of the women I've dated."

She peeked at him from one eye then closed it and tilted her face to the sun. "Maybe you made them nervous."

"Maybe. I don't know."

When he didn't continue, she glanced at him and found him chewing. Her stomach felt hollow, so she followed his example. The crab cake had a rich, wholesome flavor.

"So I don't make you nervous?" He cut her a sideways look.

She couldn't answer around her mouthful of food, and she gladly chewed in silence. She didn't want to admit she'd never met a man who made her more nervous or self-conscious. A man whose opinion she valued so much. A man she'd wanted to kiss every moment.

"I'm glad I don't make you nervous," he said. He eyed his sandwich as if searching for answers. "I'm..."

She swallowed and studied his profile. "What is it?"

He released a heavy breath. "You're solid and confident, and you're not awe-struck by my celebrity. Everything in my life really sucks right now. Everything but you."

A lump formed in her throat. She settled a hand on his forearm.

"You're so connected." He heaved a heavy sigh. "To your work. To people. Even to me. I haven't been connected to anything since high school."

"Connected?"

He closed his eyes. "I haven't felt anything in a long time. I provide for a lot of people, my mom included, but I don't really care about much other than my music. But I want to. You make me want to."

She sensed a deep sadness in him. "Is this about your father?"

He shrugged. "I don't know. Maybe he had it right. Maybe I'm not worth knowing."

"I think a lot of people love you, Justin." She gave his forearm a squeeze. "I think you're capable of great affection."

Staring out over the waves, he quietly said, "Sometimes I don't believe that. Sometimes I think the people I love only stay in my life because I provide for them."

"You are so much to so many. Much more than a paycheck or a roof over their head." She jiggled his arm, urging him to look at her. "I see who you are, but I wonder if you do."

He met her gaze. "I need you. You're a bright light in my darkness, Desiree. I need you."

Chapter Six

Justin's hands shook. He shoved one into the bend of his knee and dropped his half-eaten sandwich into its wrapper. Now that he'd confessed not only his battle with writer's block but also this unexplainable need he had of Desiree, would she deem him weak? Defective? God help him, needy? She said she could see who he was. What did that mean? *What* did she see?

Maybe he was the nervous one. He had a right. He'd never bared his soul this way to anyone. And Desiree appeared to see more than he thought he'd shown. Affection? He hadn't thought himself capable. Not that he even attempted it. It took everything he had to be tough and competent. It's what everyone needed from him. It's what he needed from himself.

Yet here sat this spectacular woman of substance who showed a genuine interest in him as a person. As a man. He wouldn't blame her if she walked away and didn't look back. She'd said he had the capacity for great affection, but she was wrong.

He averted his face, staring numbly along grassy dunes. She deserved a man who could love her all the way. Not just in bed. Not just when he had time away from concert tours and recording. He squeezed his eyelids closed against an ache in his chest at the idea of sending her away.

Her fingers tightened on his arm then slowly traveled to his shoulder. Something kind and compelling made him meet her gaze. The adoration and understanding shining from her green depths had his loins tightening.

He dropped his eyes to her full lips. Her pink tongue made an appearance, ran along her lower lip then retreated inside. It was more than he could resist.

He leaned near. She didn't hedge, so he closed the distance and touched his mouth to hers. When she pressed firmly into the kiss, nervousness fled in the face of a fierce driving force to claim her as his own. He may not deserve her, but he wanted to. He wanted to be worthy of her. It didn't help that he couldn't stop kissing her.

In a controlled fall, he went to his back while drawing her atop him. Their lips didn't lose contact. Her curves fit him to perfection, and her slight weight relaxed into him. Groaning his arousal, he put one hand to the small of her back and the other into her soft hair as he cupped her slender neck.

Her hand snaked to his nape. He urged her to open, and their tongues met. The scent of her perfume surrounded him. Her warmth and sweet taste infused him. Energized him.

Her silken tongue danced and teased until he hardened where her pelvis gently ground against his. Her quickening breaths brushed his cheek and fired his blood. In the warm sand, her nude legs rubbed against his. He wanted all of her, naked and against him, but not here on the beach.

She languidly withdrew from the kiss and opened sleepy eyes. A lazy smile gently lifted the corners of her kiss-puffed lips while her gaze lingered a moment on his mouth then moved to his eyes.

"Let's go inside," she said quietly.

He didn't need her to ask twice. He helped her up. Holding her hand, he returned to the cottage.

She drew circles on his back through his T-shirt while he unlocked the door. When he held it open, he turned where he stood and drew her into a long, sensual kiss. She pressed her body against him. Hugging her closer, he stepped backward inside then kicked the door closed.

Continuing their kiss, he maneuvered to the bedroom and took her onto the bed with him. She moaned softly. Her smooth hands inched under his shirt and caressed his abdomen.

It wasn't enough. He wanted more of her. No. He wanted all of her.

He slid the strap of her sundress over the sweet round of her shoulder. At the same time, she pushed his shirt to his chest. He broke from their kiss to tug it off over his head. When he reached for her, his fingers met air and then comforter.

Desiree stood three steps from the bed and slowly opened a zipper at the side of her dress. Her eyes held his, and her mouth curved slightly on a sensual smile.

Justin's heart thumped insistently as she lowered the top in a torturous, sexy reveal. She wore no bra, and as the firm tops of her breasts appeared, he realized she didn't need one. They needed no help to maintain their pert position.

Her nipples, coral-colored and hard, peeked at the green cotton's edge. His heart thumped harder. As her dress slipped lower, her smile grew. Her glorious breasts, pale and round, had his palms itching to test and measure her.

The dress dipped lower, baring her delicate ribs and narrow waist. Definition along her stomach confirmed a level of fitness he'd suspected. Her shapely arms straightened as she eased the fabric over the womanly flare of her hips.

He caught a glimpse of pink lace panties, but she snagged them with her thumb and shed them with her dress. Curls, dark auburn and shiny, attested to the natural color of her hair.

He grew harder.

She bent, presenting her breasts in heavy relief against her tiny frame, and sent her dress further. Firm thighs swelled slightly to form a triangle gap just below her beautifully trimmed thatch of curls. Justin's excitement graduated to a full hard-on.

Aching and throbbing, he unfastened his shorts. Her dress landed on the floor, leaving her before him in nothing but her gorgeous skin.

He lifted his hips and removed his shorts and boxer briefs in a single shove. His rod bucked in its freedom.

She came to him and traced the tattooed guitar that dominated his chest. She followed realistic-looking flames to the right and an impressive splash of water to the left. "I've seen this on your music videos and at a distance when you were on stage, but up close, it's breathtaking."

He brushed hair from her forehead. "You saw me on stage?"

"I'm a fan, remember? I've been to a few of your concerts through the years. You're more amazing than I expected." She tripped her fingertips lower across the muscles of his abdomen.

He put a hand to her warm hip and rode the curve of her taut waist to her ribs. "You are, too."

Her gaze met his. When she bent to press her full lips to his mouth, her breast shifted into his hand. It was perfect in its fullness and flawless smooth texture. He ran his thumb across her erect nipple and delighted at her quick intake of breath.

He urged her to the bed. A moan vibrated from her throat into their kiss. He opened, and their tongues entered into a lazy, sensual dance.

Her long, sleek leg climbed his until she draped it over his hip. He traced her spine to her hip then ran his hand around the silken firmness of her ass to her slender thigh. Teasing soft hairs at her apex, Justin adored how she set a leisurely pace.

No rush. No awkward fumbling. This sexy exploration heightened his passion and let him truly appreciate this beautiful woman in his arms.

Then she wrapped long fingers around his excitement, and all thought fled.

♪ ♪ ♪ ♪

Desiree couldn't lie to herself any longer. Justin would never be only a fling. Even when she was nothing to him, he'd been everything to her. An infatuation for the idea of him had now grown into genuine love for the real man. A relationship with a rock star had endless impractical implications, but she didn't care anymore.

Sexual energy surged from him and slammed straight through her. It shook her. Sent her heart racing. Clenched her womb until moisture seeped into her throbbing folds. Like this, sexy and charged and bigger than life, Justin typified the image of a rock star.

Affection in his gaze softened the raw edge of his desire. He lacked urgency. Even in his kiss, his control reigned. It showed that despite how much he wanted her body, he truly cared about her. In this moment, he exhibited all the wonderful traits he claimed not to have.

She drank in the feel of him. His fingertips grazing fiery paths along her skin. His cologne surrounding her in a cloud of heavenly scent. The steely length of him as she rolled a condom onto him. The man dominated her, body and heart.

She ached for him. Yearned for him. Each caress of his hands increased her heat until her blood sang in her ears.

His fingers skimmed her belly then traveled low into her moist flesh. She groaned, pressing against his strokes and silently begging for more. Her body opened, ready for his entry.

He shifted her fully to her back and moved atop her. His knees parted her thighs, and a thrill sent a shiver through her. She gasped at an overpowering need to have him inside her.

Their labored breaths mingled and seemed to echo off the bedroom walls, but when he placed his tip to her eager opening, the room went silent. Desiree held her breath and clutched his muscled shoulders. She'd never wanted anything as much as she wanted him. Here. Now.

He eased inside, and she inhaled in satisfaction as he stretched her needy passage. He filled her. His pelvis kissed hers as he went to his hilt. A spike of pleasure made her jerk when he pressed deep.

"Are you okay?" Justin whispered, concern tugging at his eyebrows. "Am I hurting you?"

She swallowed a laugh at the idea that any pain could intrude on the amazing sensations coursing through her. "I'm better than okay."

While hiking her legs around his hips, she pulled him down for a kiss. When his lips touched hers, her body tightened around him. They both sucked in a quick breath.

He withdrew then thrust.

Every nerve in her body tingled, even in her fingertips. She opened her mouth, and his tongue swept inside. His hips pumped on a steady rhythm that matched the caresses of his tongue.

Soon, Desiree ascended toward release. Each thrust of his hips drove her closer. She rounded her spine, taking him deeper still.

His pace increased. His breathing grew ragged. An urgency crept into his movements.

Nearly at the pinnacle of her goal, she broke from his kiss and pulled air into her straining lungs. He braced on straight arms, and she held onto them as she strove.

So close.

Almost there.

Tiny cries of pleasure escaped her with each thrust multiplying her mounting ecstasy. She arched. Her entire body flexed.

Then it took her. She opened her mouth, but orgasm yanked her into a pleasure so immense it silenced her scream. When it released its hold, it dropped her into blissful oblivion.

She came to awareness where Justin lay on his back and held her close to his side. He wore boxer briefs, and her cheek rested on his shoulder. How long had she been out? A puff of cool air from a vent high on the opposite wall chilled a sheen of perspiration on her brow, and she smiled.

"Wow," she whispered. "To quote you from my gallery opening."

He combed his fingers through the hair above her ear, dragging a few wayward strands out of the dampness coating her neck. He kissed her hairline. "Yeah. Wow. You're amazing."

She chuckled. "You, too. Your tattoo looks completely different from this angle."

He held an unwrapped condom between two fingers. "Want to do it again?"

She laughed. She slid atop him and helped him out of his boxers then claimed his lips in a passionate kiss. Her questing fingers found him hard and ready, so she rolled the protection onto him by feel and slid her primed and begging opening around his tip. He groaned against her mouth.

With a lift of his hips, he filled her on a single thrust. She gasped, arching and losing the kiss. His hands closed over her breasts as they found their rhythm.

Her pleasure rushed in faster than she wanted. She couldn't stave it, so she sent a hand behind and cupped his testicles.

His eyes closed. The angles of his face grew sharp. Inside her, he lengthened and swelled.

Her body responded by constricting around him. Pleasure expanded rapidly. Then the fist of orgasm gripped her. Her entire body tensed. Her lungs seized as she shook with the force of coming.

Under her, Justin grimaced amidst his own release. He pressed into her, and his length jerked against her deepest place. She gasped, trying not to pass out from bliss.

They relaxed at the same time, and she kept him within as she descended until her cheek rested at the center of his tattoo. His heartbeat drummed in her ear, slowing in pace with each breath he exhaled.

She fought an unexpected sadness. How long did

they have? Two days? Three? Would this end when she left?

God help her, she was in love with this man. She couldn't dare to hope she meant more to him than a momentary diversion. An anchor to cling to while he struggled with his writing demon. But she wanted his heart. Was she a fool to want the love of a rock god? To want the love of Justin Time?

Forcing a smile, she rolled off of him and sat on the edge of his bed. "I should go."

"Don't." He sat and braced a straight arm behind him.

"I need a shower."

He moved her hair from her shoulder and placed a kiss on the side of her neck. She closed her eyes, savoring the intimacy.

"Use my shower," he said low. "Stay. Stay with me all day. I need you."

His words fortified yet scared her. Where he was concerned, she could easily lose touch with reality. She could find a way to believe he implied a future for them within his declaration of need. She had to guard her heart.

She didn't want to leave, though, so she accepted his offered shower. Hot water soothed her scalp as she eased her head backward into the flow. She didn't want to agonize over Justin. She'd done enough of that during her school days. She couldn't escape it, however. What she wanted stood in direct opposition to what she could have. To what she *should* have. Loving him wasn't practical and put her in line for serious heartbreak.

If only she had the ability to live in the moment. Expectation had no place in whatever it was they had shared on that plane. Every time she closed her eyes, though, she imagined him with her in Chicago. She imagined standing backstage at his concerts. She pictured him on location with her in Venice, Belgium, and St. Petersburg.

"What am I doing?" she whispered. She faced the water and scrubbed her face then grasped a shampoo bottle. "Just enjoy this for what it is."

Now she had to figure out what it was.

Chapter Seven

In shorts and bare feet, Justin went to the beach to gather the remains of their brunch. Seagulls had ravaged the meal, and a couple still played tug-of-war with a sandwich wrapper a few paces along the sand. He waved away the birds and collected the mess.

Inside, he dumped the scraps into the kitchen trash.

"Justin?" Desiree called from the bedroom.

He smiled and strode to the doorway.

She stood wearing only a towel at the foot of the bed. "I heard the door close."

"I had to get our garbage off the beach." He fought the urge to divest her of her cover and have his way with her. The woman was incredibly sexy and remarkably responsive.

A hint of color tinged her pale cheeks. "I had completely forgotten about that."

He grinned. "We were preoccupied."

"We really were."

Something about the downward slope at one corner of her mouth made him take a step toward her. "Are you okay?"

She smiled, but it didn't reach her eyes. "I'm fine, Justin."

"No you're not." He clasped her hand and urged her to sit with him on the bed. "What's on your mind?"

"Isn't that a dangerous question?"

Now she worried him. "Not if I really want to know. I think the world of you, Desiree. If something's bothering you, I want to know."

"Even if what's bothering me is you?"

"I'm bothering you?" What the hell? He'd thought their lovemaking had been astounding. Had he failed her?

This time when she smiled, it reached her big, green eyes. "I'll admit you make me hot and bothered."

He relaxed and chuckled. "You quoted me. Now I get to quote you. I can tell you've got something heavy weighing on you."

She patted his hand. "It's not important. The only thing that's important is getting you writing again."

Her statement put a molten stone into the pit of his stomach. Squaring his shoulders and setting his features into the face he used with his band when they needed to get serious, he got to his feet and headed for the bathroom. "I don't want to think about that right now."

She stood, and he didn't miss a poignant sadness in her gaze. Part of him wanted to learn its cause and give her comfort, but a more dominant part of him dreaded the chance that she might want to talk more about his lack of inspiration. He couldn't deal with it.

He glanced at her from the doorway and said, "I'm going to take a shower. You've got to be hungry. You hardly ate anything. If you can't find something you want in the kitchen, go ahead and order delivery."

He said the last toward the bathroom door then closed it. In the quiet privacy, he rested his forehead on the cool, smooth wood. He hated how the subject of his music had destroyed the easy intimacy they'd enjoyed. Or was it his music that really had him upset? Did she want more from him than he could give? He squeezed his eyes closed. What was wrong with him?

Rushing through his shower, he looked forward to kissing her and reestablishing their closeness. He wanted to know more about her. Since she lived in Chicago, he didn't have to say goodbye. He could continue to see her at home. He simply needed time to...what? Who did he try to fool? He would do whatever it took to win her, but how much of himself could he offer in return? Still, the idea of her with someone else nearly strangled the life out of him. He'd never been so confused.

Her sudden seriousness had him tense, too. Did she regret making love with him? Did she have as much of a problem committing as he did?

He froze in mid-scrub, his fingertips buried in suds atop his head. Could it be she was already involved with someone else?

Rinsing quickly, he stomped an impatient foot. He closed the water lever then grabbed a towel on his way out of the bathroom. Her towel lay draped over a corner of the mussed bed.

Draping his hips, he went to the cottage's main room. When he didn't see her, he called, "Desiree? Where are you?"

She didn't answer.

He strode to the front door and pulled it open. Her car was gone.

"This is such bullshit!"

He hadn't taken her for a coward. He ran for the bedroom, grimacing when he stepped in a couple of wet footsteps he'd made in the carpet. He dragged clean clothes on over his damp skin, sent his bare feet into his sneakers, and raked fingers through his dripping hair. Outside, he ran the three blocks to her hotel.

He'd finally found a woman he respected. A woman with a sharp mind and opinions of her own. A woman who worked as hard as he did, with dreams and a career. A woman who took his breath away both in bed and out.

A woman worth fighting to keep.

He entered the hotel at a fast stride and went to the front desk. "Desiree Renault's room, please."

A thin man in a navy blue suit asked, "May I have your name?"

"Justin. I'm a friend of hers." His stomach

knotted.

"One moment, sir." The man picked up a handset. "Ms. Renault? You have a guest. His name is Justin. Shall I send him up? Yes, ma'am."

Justin drummed fingertips on the marble countertop.

"You may go up," said the receptionist, hanging up his phone. He pointed. "Elevators are on this side around the corner. She's in room three-twelve."

"Thank you." It took an effort not to sprint to the elevators. At least she agreed to see him. He had to hope.

On the third floor, he located her door and knocked. When she opened it, her mouth formed a line and she wore a guarded look. A suitcase sat open on her bed.

"You left while I showered," he accused. "It's not fair. Talk to me, Desiree."

She lowered her eyes and stepped aside. "Come in, Justin."

He passed her and went to the bed. Clothing and personal care bottles littered the bedspread around the half-packed suitcase. "You're leaving?"

"I think it's best."

Anger and confusion warred in his gut. "Best for whom?"

"For me, Justin." She placed a stack of clothes into the bag. "I can't be your light-'o-love."

"Light-'o-love?" He blinked. What was a light-'o-love? "Did I do something wrong?"

"Of course not." She dropped shower bottles into a plastic bag.

"Then how did you go from staying a few more days to suddenly gotta leave? Is this about my problem? Am I a loser because I've lost my music?"

She placed the bag in the suitcase and faced him. "How can you think such a thing? Your music doesn't define you. You may think it does, but it doesn't."

He grazed the backs of his fingers along her soft cheek. He wanted to kiss her so badly. "Why are you leaving?"

She put a hand on his arm, and her gaze lowered to where she touched him. Quietly, she said, "With you, I don't necessarily think straight. I never have, really. My emotions get involved, and then I get hurt. It makes no sense. I know."

Taking her gently by the shoulders, he rested his forehead against hers. "I'm not going to hurt you."

"You won't try, but it'll happen. When we made love, you put your wall down. I saw in your eyes what I always suspected you had. You won me."

His gut twisted. "Then what's the problem?"

"I'm not sure, Justin. I don't know if you're afraid to take a chance or you're just not willing, but you put your wall back up when you went in for your shower. Maybe I'm not the woman for you. I can't force you to love me."

"Was making love a mistake?" A strange heaviness settled into his chest and formed a clamping ache in his throat. "Did we move too fast?"

"Maybe, but I don't regret it." She straightened, and her beautiful eyes glistened with moisture.

"Don't go." His throat began to clog. He swallowed and said, "Tell me you're not involved with another guy."

"I'm not. I promise." She took a step backward. "I've been entirely honest."

The walls of her room began to close in on him. "Please stay."

"It's better if I go. We have to be adults. This has been fun, but I have to return to reality. Staying will only make that harder, and it's already very difficult."

This had been fun? She had to return to reality? Her words crushed him. Time spent with her had been more than real for him. She had grounded him. Given him a tranquil shore when he'd been tossed upon a raging sea of self-doubt and loathing.

He had considered this their beginning, but she stood before him saying goodbye in no uncertain terms. How had he gotten her so wrong?

♪　♪　♪　♪

Three other hotel guests headed to the Norfolk International Airport the next morning, so the concierge arranged a hotel shuttle to take them. It saved Desiree an expensive taxi fare, and she sat at the back of the van with her breaking heart in her throat. It felt wrong to leave him. The pain of it made her nauseous, but her head couldn't deny the logic of her decision.

Making love with him had been the point of no return. It had changed how she viewed him. How she wanted him. Afterward, all or nothing were her only two choices.

She'd wanted all.

Pinpricks of sorrow in her eyes threatened tears. She pressed fingertips to her eyelids and prevented them.

After the way he had touched her, kissed her, there could be no halfway with him. He had acted so easy and relaxed, and it had occurred to her that she'd been alone in her revelations. For her, their joining had meant a physical confirmation and culmination of her love for him. The idea that it had meant nothing more to him than a moment of sexual pleasure, or worse, that he'd used her to help him get through his writer's block, felt like a knife twisting in her belly.

She'd be unfair to expect more from him, though. He hadn't made promises or declared any deep emotion. He had behaved honorably.

The ride to Norfolk was long, so she retrieved her laptop from its case and reviewed the wedding photos. She sorted best shots into a separate folder then began identifying potential keepers and absolute duds. The work calmed her, though it didn't lessen the pain in her heart.

At the airport, she checked her bag and obtained a new boarding pass. Walking away from her suitcase made her keenly aware that now she couldn't change her mind and return to North Carolina. She would board that plane as if her entire world hadn't crumpled under her unreasonable expectations, and she'd go home.

Security passed her through with only a cursory glance in her equipment bag. Then she bought a croissant and bottled water. Sitting at the gate, she managed only a few bites of bread. Her stomach didn't want food. It didn't help that she kept glancing down the walkway as if he would come chasing after her.

"More unreasonable expectations," she mumbled.

When it came to Justin, she had nothing less. She had always dreamed of his love. Even when she thought she'd gotten over him. She guessed she always would.

For the first time in years, Justin had an urge to throw a piece of furniture out a window. He'd grown up, however, and left that cliché rock musician behavior to C.J. Their drummer was better at it than the rest of them, anyway.

Justin paced his cottage, back and forth, replaying yesterday with Desiree. What had he said? Or was it something he had done? He clutched his chest as another deep stab sapped his strength.

"I'm going to die." He sank to the couch and closed his eyes. "I'm having a heart attack and I'm going to die."

His phone rang. Without opening his eyes, he slapped around on the coffee table until he found it.

"Justin?" Jet's voice called through the earpiece.

He groaned inwardly. He seriously couldn't handle Jet telling him C.J. had gotten into trouble again.

"Justin. Say something, would ya?"

"What? What is it now?"

"Geez. You could've said hello."

"Why are you calling me? I'm on vacation."

"Brenda left me, Justin. She broke my heart."

He clenched his jaw against real pain. "Don't talk to me about heartbreak. I swear to God..."

Jet sniffed loudly.

"Are you crying?" Justin smacked a palm to his forehead.

"No way, man. Hey, the studio called to schedule our next recording dates. They want to know how many songs are going to be on our next album. Marge called, too. She said the label wants to get started on our next contract. She needs the name of the new album."

What dim light remaining inside Justin blinked out, extinguished by the weight of his failure. Fighting tears of despair, he fisted a hand then threw it in the air above his head. "You know what, Jet? You write the songs for the next album. I'm done."

Silence hung on the phone line.

"Did you hear me, Jet?"

"Yeah. You said you're done."

"I mean it."

"You're done composing or you're done altogether?"

Justin squeezed his screaming temples between thumb and middle finger. "I quit. I haven't written a song in months. I lost the music. It's been killing me, and I don't want to do this anymore."

"Maybe you're too bottled up. You've been tense. More distant than usual. Maybe you just need to relax and let people get close. We're your friends, but you never hang out with us anymore. You never joke...or even smile."

"I feel responsible for you guys. I'm feeling the pressure."

Jet cleared his throat. "We're grown-ups, man. Let us be responsible for us. You be responsible for you. We'll all share responsibility for the band's success. That's how it should be. Maybe if you let us—"

"No." Justin scraped his fingernails over his scalp. "I can't. I'm done."

"Music's your life," Jet said quietly.

"Not anymore, apparently. I gotta go. I'll tell C.J. and Chaz when I get back to Chicago next week. You're welcome to take over Smashing Glass and keep it alive. You're a great songwriter and you have a strong voice."

"I write rock ballads, man. They're nice for two or three songs on an album or in a concert, but you're our sound. You're the life blood of this band."

"Not anymore. You'll figure something out." Justin ended the call before he said something stupid like he was sorry or how he'd miss them.

Better to break it solidly. He'd make his retirement official when he returned home. Simple as that.

Chapter Eight

A loud pounding woke Justin from an afternoon, depression-induced nap. His heart skipped, and he lay listening to the beat. Was it the beginning of a song?

"Justin! Open up, man," called Jet from the cottage door.

He crammed his pillow over his head and groaned. The pounding continued. His phone began to ring, adding to the noise.

"Damn it!" He launched off of the bed and marched to the living room. Opening the door, he demanded, "Can't a man suffer in peace?"

C.J. shouldered past, ending the call that was making his phone ring. "Not when he's got friends who care, dude."

"Yeah." Jet entered on a single one-legged stride, his blue eyes bright and accusing. "What's this bullshit about your quitting the band?"

Chaz came last but stopped inside the doorframe. In a subdued tone, he said, "It's like Merlin saying he quits magic. You are the music. It's categorical. When people talk about Smashing Glass, they're talking about you. We're just backup."

"Geez." Justin waved him in and closed the door. "You must really want me back, Chaz. That's the most I've ever heard you say at one time. And where's your guitar? You never go anywhere without it."

The bass player hitched a thumb over his

shoulder toward the door then slumped into a chair. "It's in the car we rented in Norfolk."

C.J. transferred food and beer from the refrigerator to the kitchen table. Jet stood glaring at him from behind the sofa, his hands on his waist, which made his meaty shoulders and biceps bulge.

Justin glared in return. "You guys didn't waste any time coming down here, but you did waste the trip. Don't get too comfortable. You're not staying."

"You know us better than that, dude," said the drummer from the kitchen. He withdrew drumsticks from his back jeans pocket and tattooed a sweet rhythm on the table. "We got rooms, but if you keep talkin' crazy, we'll camp out right here in this tiny house."

"Don't think we won't," warned Jet.

Chaz shrugged, the closest he ever came to showing agreement.

Justin flopped into the chair opposite their bass player. "Suit yourselves. It won't do you any good."

"Why not?" Jet vaulted over the sofa's back and sprawled. He kicked off his sneakers and folded his hands behind his head of short, black spiked hair.

"There's no point. I'm all out of songs."

"Like hell." Jet sat straight. "You just started a song right there. He sang, "I'm all out of songs, There's nothing but silence, And I don't know why, Writing words is so hard—"

"Knock it off." Justin slapped his forehead then regretted it when his headache returned.

"What? That was good." Their keyboard player fell backward and resumed reclining against the sofa's arm.

"First, it's a ballad. That's your department, not mine. Second, you stole the tune from *I'm All Out of Love.*"

"Yeah, well, I'm a man of habit. Besides, the music part is your thing. I'm too busy trying to get over Brenda. I really thought she was the one, man."

"Music's not my thing anymore." Justin sighed.

C.J. came from the kitchen bearing two long neck beers in one hand and two sandwiches in the other. He kicked Jet in the calf then sat. He handed a beer and a sandwich to the keyboard player and asked, "How come? What happened, dude?"

"I don't know. Maybe I'm just done."

C.J. eyed his sandwich then Justin's clasped hands. "I'm sorry. Did you want a sandwich?"

"No, thanks."

"Never mind me," said Chaz, his eyebrows low over grayish eyes.

"What? You're never hungry," said the drummer.

"I might be." Chaz widened his eyes and thrust his chin forward.

"Well? Are you hungry?"

The bass player huffed a loud breath then found a spot on the chair and scraped his fingernail across it. "No."

"What the hell, dude?" C.J. gestured wildly, sloshing beer on the carpet. "I'm supposed to offer you food when you're not hungry?"

"I may be quiet, but I'm not invisible."

"No. You may be *crazy,* but you're not hungry." The drummer rolled his eyes and took a bite of sandwich.

Justin relaxed a bit. He'd missed his friends. "I'm sorry you came all this way. I don't know why I stopped writing, but we won't be much of a band if we don't have anything new for our fans. Better to quit while we're ahead, I guess."

C.J.'s chewing slowed, and his brown eyes narrowed. "Oh, shit. You met a girl!"

"Huh?" Jet looked from C.J. to Justin and back as he lost his casual pose. "Did you get serious about someone? Are you in love?"

"No!" Justin shot to his feet. "I've been here four days. You fall in love in four days all the time, but I don't. Ever."

The keyboardist stood. "You're awfully defensive, and C.J.'s love radar is rarely wrong. He pegs me all the time."

"That's because you always think you're in love."

"What's her name?" asked Chaz.

"Yeah," said C.J. "What's her name?"

Justin turned his back on his band as a knife twisted in his chest. Desiree's face appeared in his memory. So the heart attack wasn't a heart attack. It was his heart breaking. How had he fallen for her in such a short time? He hadn't thought he was capable. Not of *real* love, anyway. Shit!

Jet came to his side and clapped a hand on his shoulder. "Is that what happened? Is she the reason you stopped writing?"

"You know I've been struggling with writer's block for months. I met Desiree on the plane in Norfolk. She photographed Cassidy's wedding."

"Sexy Desiree," drawled C.J. with a smirk.

Justin's blood boiled, and he took a lunging step toward the drummer. "Watch your mouth."

C.J. let loose a knowing whistle. "There it is, dude. You're in love. Where is she?"

The proof in his reaction made Justin contrite. He'd missed the signs, but thinking back, it occurred to him that she'd fallen for him, too. Had she thought he didn't share her feelings? Had she thought he couldn't? Was that why she'd left so fast?

He raked both hands through his hair. "I messed up."

"No shit," said the drummer. "But it's not too late. We won't tell anyone you quit the band."

"That's not his reference," said Chaz.

Justin went weak and sank to his chair. "I messed up with Desiree, C.J. I was stupid, and she left me."

His friends said nothing, and their silence unnerved him.

"I've never been such a screw-up. Believe me. She's better off without me. You guys are better off without me. Even I'm better off without me. Unfortunately, I'm stuck with myself."

Jet went to the door. "We're more than a band, Justin. We're friends, and that means you're stuck with us, too. I call dibs on the couch."

♪ ♪ ♪ ♪

"I'm sorry." Desiree gave her fuzzy mind a shake and retreated from her camera stand. "Let's take fifteen."

Her model relaxed and headed for the studio door.

Close to tears most of the day, she'd struggled for focus and couldn't get a halfway decent picture. She blew past stiff lips and clapped her hands. She could do this.

Her subject had stepped outside, so Desiree went to her office and took a long drink of water. She had never fallen so far off her game. What had Justin done to her?

The studio door closed, so she headed back. Her subject hadn't returned, however. A middle-aged man in an expensive suit and intelligent eyes offered her a cursory smile.

"Desiree Renault?" he asked.

"Yes. Are you here to make an appointment?"

"No." His expression turned grave. "My name is Calvin Spence. I'm the agent for Smashing Glass. It seems we have a bit of a crisis, and I'm told you may be able to help."

Her heart plummeted. Had Justin been in an accident?

"I don't believe I'm anyone Mr. Keither would want to see," she said, embarrassed by her trembling.

"Jet says Justin needs you. Please understand my position, Ms. Renault. Justin's the reasonable one. He's the one I rely on to keep this band motivated and moving in the right direction. Jet's a good guy with a steady character, but Justin's a thinker. A planner."

"What has this to do with me?" Desiree went to the stand and checked the settings on her camera to hide her interest and nervous energy.

Calvin came and stood at the edge of a blue drape that covered the floor. "These are superstars we're talking about. They're different from the rest of us. They seem to feel more. They can be volatile."

"I'm very familiar with superstars, Mr. Spence. I've worked with and around them my entire career."

"So it makes sense when I tell you that out of all the talent I represent, I've valued Justin Keither mainly for the fact that he's the one person who doesn't need me to hold his hand and tell him how wonderful he is."

"Please get to the point, Mr. Spence. I have work to do." She swallowed and tried to ignore the fact that her voice had warbled on the last two words.

"Do you care about Justin?"

God help me, yes. "No."

His eyes narrowed, and a slow smile lifted his features.

"What?" she asked, forcing an irritated tone. Averting her gaze, she prayed he hadn't witnessed her concern.

"I think you care more than you admit. I really need to know."

"Why? Is he laying in a hospital somewhere?" Her knees threatened to collapse at the idea.

"That would make it easier for me," he said with a slight grimace. "At least then I could hold out hope."

Alarm knifed through her. She gave him her undivided attention. "What happened?"

"Tell me first that you care what happens to him."

She wilted. "Maybe there's something you need to understand about *my* position. I'm the one who left. I know he's going through a hard time, and I walked away. Under the circumstances, I can't imagine he's interested in seeing me."

Her heart ached, and Calvin's silence didn't help. She wanted to tell him to leave, but she didn't make it a habit of acting rude to anyone, and she refused to start now.

She hated how she missed Justin. In a matter of days, he had resurrected every desire and dream she'd had of him. Only now, it was worse. Now they had no lovers keeping them apart. Now they were adults and could decide to be together...or not.

When the agent didn't say anything, she asked, "Is he asking for me, or is this request coming from you?"

He offered a smile that more resembled a closed-mouthed grimace. "Neither, really. His band is asking for you. They want you to go back to North Carolina and, well, talk some sense into him."

"What do you mean by 'talk some sense into him'?" She ventured a slight step toward the man.

"He's quit, Ms. Renault. Justin Time has quit Smashing Glass."

Chapter Nine

Swiping his finger down the screen of his smart phone, Justin scanned for jobs in the recording industry while trying to block out C.J.'s incessant drumming on a kitchen counter. He didn't need money. Growing up poor had taught him the importance of saving. The band's accountants did nag him about needing to invest, though. He had enough now to live a life of luxury without working another day, so he was in no hurry.

Unfortunately, he'd never idled well. He preferred to stay busy and spend his days around people who appreciated music. He understood music and the kind of people who dedicated their lives to it.

A recording studio in California looked to hire a mixer board technician. Not really his field of expertise. Besides, California was far from Illinois...where Desiree lived.

RAT-TAT-A-TAT!

Justin cut an irritated glance sideways at C.J. He scanned further down. Agents wanted. Contracts, publicity, and babysitting? No thanks.

TAT-A-TATA-TATA-TATA!

Music teachers wanted. Not in a million years. He didn't have the patience. California began to look good. Maybe living far from Desiree wasn't so bad, considering she probably never wanted to see him again, anyway.

RAT-TA-TA-TA-TA-RRRAT!

Through the wall that shared the shower, Jet's voice sang loud and strong on a refrain of their latest top-ten hit. It competed with C.J.'s drumming for domination over the peace. Their combined effort cut into Justin's already precarious focus and made thinking impossible.

He covered his ears, hit a raspy C-note and climbed the octave into a rock-scream as he came to his feet in time to his singing slide. He held the note at the top of his range then bit it off short, like he did when singing *Dogs in the City*, their all-time best-selling single.

Silence reigned, and he breathed a sigh of relief. "You guys, I love you, but you're making this worse. I'm going crazy."

"Hold that thought." C.J. pointed a drumstick toward the ceiling then sent it to the kitchen counter and beat a rhythm. "I've been working on something that might inspire a song. Listen to this."

"Get out." Justin threw one of the small square pillows from the couch and hit the drummer in the chest.

Jet came to the bedroom door. He wore only a towel and the gold pinkie ring his grandfather had left to him. "What's going on out here?"

"All of you." Justin swung his arm to indicate he addressed all three of his friends. "Get out."

"But—"

"No, Jet. No 'but' and no 'we're here to help' and no more noise. This is bullshit. I quit. End of discussion. Now get out." He strode from the cottage, slamming the door, and stopped short in the driveway. He had no car. Why hadn't he rented a car for this vacation?

"Because I figured I'd be writing the whole time," he muttered.

He poked his phone to life and began walking. He let his feet take him where they may. It didn't matter as long as he could have some time alone.

Those guys were his best friends, and despite his

frustration, he couldn't hate them for attempting this intervention. His decision changed their lives, too. But he refused to live a lie. Staying in the band and going on tour without a single new song and no hope of another album would eventually earn them disdain and disappointment from their fans. Better to quit while the world still loved them than a year from now after they'd tanked their reputation.

Acid rose from his stomach into his throat. He swallowed against its burn. This sucked. Everything he'd worked toward would end in a matter of weeks. His crew and all the band's roadies would lose their jobs. Their label would drop Smashing Glass. Without him in the lead, the band would have to start over and find a new sound.

"Justin!"

He brought his mindless trek to a halt and glanced at a car pulling alongside him. Desiree stared up at him from the driver's window, her concern palpable in the crackling air between them. He blinked. Did he imagine her next to him because he desperately wanted her near?

"I thought you left," he said, afraid to move in case she evaporated in the next breeze.

"I did," she said. Her gaze went to his phone then to his face. "Can I give you a ride somewhere?"

"Sure." He couldn't pass a chance to be close to her.

After he'd settled into the passenger seat, she asked, "Where are you headed?"

He shrugged. "Nowhere. Anywhere. I don't care. My friends are at my place. Between C.J.'s drumming and Jet's singing, I had to get out of the noise trap."

A gentle smile touched her full lips. "I know where we can go."

She drove to the Kitty Hawk Monument to a Century of Flight and parked at a secluded section of parking lot. After rolling down their windows, she turned off the engine. A salty breeze blew through the car, stirring her curls and rustling the cuff of her ivory shirt's sleeve.

"Why'd you come back?" he asked, enjoying how her perfume sweetened the refreshing breeze caressing his face.

"I got some alarming news." She unfastened her seatbelt and swiveled to face him.

"About the wedding pictures?"

"About you."

Justin stared out the windshield, hating how she'd said exactly what he expected.

She put cool fingers on the back of his hand. "Is it true? Are you quitting Smashing Glass?"

"Yes." He braced against her disapproval.

He ought to chafe over the fact that he cared so much what she thought. Women had always been more an afterthought than anything. Desiree was different. He had realized it minutes after meeting her on the plane, but it grew more apparent by the day. It bothered him how he hadn't noticed her that night at The Hole.

"Do you think I'm a loser?" he asked. "A quitter?"

"No. I think you're capable of anything you set your mind to."

Goose bumps stood on his arms, and he shivered. "Anything, huh? Are you saying I could get to writing songs if I'd just make up my mind to do it?"

She released a loud sigh. "Justin, I'm not your judge. I like to think I'm your friend, though."

A stab of regret cut him deeply. "So you came back to rescue me from myself. Did Jet call you? Or was it C.J.? I wouldn't put it past either of them to find you in my phone contacts."

"Maybe your band wants me to try and talk you out of quitting, but I'm not here to do that." A tiny smile tugged at her mouth. "I came to tell you...well, that I trust you to know yourself and what you need. Maybe you should quit. Maybe you've taken Smashing Glass as far as it will go."

His entire being shuddered. Hearing her words brought home how wrong he was in this decision. She had been right when she said music was part of him.

When Chaz had said Justin was Smashing Glass.

He hadn't wanted to hear it. He didn't want to know it.

"Shit!" He got out of the car, leaving the door open, and strode ten paces.

He glanced at her over his shoulder. Desiree's beauty distracted him. He couldn't think straight when he looked at her. Why did she have to read him so well? Why did she have to be so gentle and generous? Why did she have to be so smart? The total package.

He took five steps toward the car and stopped. "Why'd you leave?"

Desiree had dreaded this question, but she couldn't ignore or sidestep it. He deserved to know. Even if he didn't return her feelings, he needed to hear from her what stole her sleep and destroyed her peace of mind.

His dark eyebrows angled sharply toward his nose, and he fisted his hands at his sides. She didn't mistake him for angry, however. He was lost. She didn't know how she knew. She simply did.

She left her seat and went to him. Holding his gaze, she gauged his willingness to be touched. When his eyelids dipped a fraction in an almost blink, she closed the distance and wrapped her arms around him.

"Why'd you leave so suddenly?" he whispered, not hugging her in return.

She squeezed closed her eyes. Dread of rejection stiffened her spine. She sank her teeth into her cheek then took a deep breath. "Because I love you."

He didn't move.

"I'm sorry," she said softly, pressing her forehead to his shoulder. "I didn't—"

"You're apologizing for loving me?"

She felt him relax, and his arms came around her. "I didn't want to burden you with it, and I certainly didn't want to become one of those women who clings to a man who can't love her back."

As his arms tightened, she felt a pressure atop her head and realized he kissed her there. She hadn't been kissed on the head since childhood. Not since she'd grown too tall for most to reach it.

"Desiree, you don't love a man who can't love you."

It took a second for his words to sink in. She pulled away only enough to look into his handsome face. "You can love me? Someday?"

He smiled sadly. "I love you now. I loved you before I took you to bed. I just don't know where my head is right now. I don't know where my life is going. And I don't know if I can love you *enough*."

Her mind reeled and her heart pounded. Justin loved her. She wanted to help him.

Settling her palm over his heart, she asked, "What about all those notebooks filled with songs? More than sixty, you said. You must have songs in them worth singing."

"Most of them are crap. I spend five songs dumping garbage onto the page to make room in my head for a good one. Believe me. There's nothing worth singing that we haven't already recorded."

Taking a step back, she asked, "What if you wrote a new song? Would that put you on track?"

He frowned slightly and raked his hand through his hair. "Well, yeah. I can't make that happen, though. I tried."

She couldn't fight a smile as it slowly took control of her lips. "I have an idea. Would you be willing to try it?"

"Hell, Desiree, I'll try anything."

Her stomach fluttered. Tossing him the keys, she turned for the car and said, "Where can we find your band? We need them for this."

He gave her a quirky look. "I can guarantee they're still at my cottage. Especially since I told them to get out. They tend to do the opposite of what I tell them unless it relates to our music."

"Okay then. Let's go to your cottage." She grinned.

Justin loved her. Not the image of the rock star. Not the subject of her girlhood imaginings. Justin. The man whom she'd come to know and love, with flaws and demons and real life intruding. This was so much better. Maybe he doubted he could love her enough, but she didn't. He had it in him. He simply didn't realize it. Yet.

At the cottage, he led the way in.

"Hey, man," someone inside greeted. "We're sorry."

Desiree went in and greeted the band with a smile. She recognized each of them. Jet. C.J. Chaz.

Jet came forward and offered his hand, and she warmly shook it. "How are you, Jethro?"

He frowned a bit. "I know you, don't I?"

"I'm Mandy's friend. She went to your high school."

He grinned and twisted the ring on his pinkie. "That's right. You came for our first gig. Man, that was awful."

"Everyone," said Justin. "This is Desiree."

C.J. waved a greeting with his drumsticks. "Thanks for coming."

Justin closed the door, and Desiree moved to the sofa. She picked his green notebook off the floor and sat. "I think we can help Justin get his songs back."

Chaz set a hardcover copy of *A Tale of Two Cities* onto the arm of his chair. "I don't compose. I continuo."

She chuckled. "Okay, so you don't write, but you live with him. You're around him every day. When you're on tour, there's no getting away from one another, right?"

"What's your point?" Justin came and sat by her side. He took the notebook but didn't open it.

"When I think of my work, I consider the world my studio. If I have a camera in my hand, literally everything I see is a potential picture. It's the same for you."

C.J. sat on Chaz's book and tugged on a braided leather bracelet around his wrist. "I don't follow.

Justin's not a photographer."

The bass player punched him off the book. "Imbecile."

Desiree looked at her handsome songwriter and cupped his cheek. Gazing into his brown eyes, she said, "The scope is the same. Your work is your words. Everything you say is a potential lyric."

"I get it," said Jet. "We all listen to Justin. We can feed him back his own words."

"Brilliant," said Chaz. "You can write a song from things you've said to us."

"I don't know..." Justin lifted one cynical eyebrow.

"You expect us to remember things he said?" C.J. tucked his drumsticks into his back pocket and crossed his arms. "I can't remember what I ate for breakfast. How am I supposed to remember Justin's quotes?"

"We can try," Jet shot at him with a scowl. "Geez. You're supposed to be the party animal. Why do you have to be such a downer?"

The drummer shrugged, on the defensive. "I'm just sayin'."

"Well, don't. I'll start." The keyboard player scratched a spot in his black hair above his ear. "I have one. 'I love you, but you're making this worse.'"

Justin rolled his eyes. "You're throwing my words back at me? Are you trying to make me feel bad?"

Desiree grasped his wrist. "No. Think about it. Those are great lyrics. Write it in your notebook."

His features went from skeptical to curious. Then he brightened. "Okay, yeah. 'I love you, but you're making this worse.'" He opened his notebook, reached for a pen, and wrote it word for word.

"You said you were going crazy, too," said C.J.

"See? You haven't destroyed all your brain cells yet," said Jet with a smirk.

"Okay. 'I'm going crazy.' What else?" Justin asked.

Desiree interjected, "How about when you said 'I like how you don't have to talk all the time'?"

"Good one, but different song." He flipped the page and wrote the line.

They tossed words at him for three hours. When they nearly had four delivered pizzas devoured, he stood. An intense, thoughtful expression hardened his already angular face, but he said nothing. He simply stood there, notebook and pen in hand, and stared at the wall.

Desiree opened her mouth to ask what was wrong, but Jet thrust an open palm her way. He put a finger to his lips then whispered, "He's composing."

Chapter Ten

Jet had told him that when the words came, they would flood him. Justin had been caught in a torrential rush of lyrics and music, lost to the world and terrified it would come to a screeching halt. Scared it would leave him barren like before. It didn't stop this time, though.

Music played over and over, giving his fingers time to get the notes onto paper. Lyrics occurred to him as fast as he could write. With them came harmonies and lyric layers so good they made him tremble with delight.

With each word and each note, he grew happier. The idea that his best friends, so like brothers, and the woman he loved had come to help softened a place buried deep. A place he thought hard and impenetrable. He could love. They showed him that. Not only could he love, but he could love all the way.

Taking a deep breath, he fought a grin and returned his pen to a half-filled page. He wrote feverishly, as though possessed. Every song blossomed from a quote his friends had provided, but the ones Desiree had given him sprouted songs he knew would win spots on the top ten hits, and possibly more awards for his band.

"I'm back." He rolled off of the bed with a groan, stiff from hours of inactivity.

In the living room, C.J. had a blond half undressed and under him on the sofa. How he found these girls everywhere he went, Justin couldn't fathom.

Nobody else was around.

"Where's Desiree?" he asked.

Without breaking his kiss, the drummer pointed at the front door.

She'd gone? Without saying goodbye? He didn't bother his friend with questions. C.J. wouldn't answer, anyway.

He went out, hoping she'd gotten a room at the Radisson. He would check there first. He owed her...well, everything. Never again would he let her simply walk away. She had his heart, and he'd be lost without her.

At the end of the driveway, laughter from the beach stopped him. Jet's voice shouted something about sand, and Desiree's unmistakable laugher rang out. Justin instantly shed ten pounds of worry.

She had stayed.

On the beach, Chaz stood in a hole and played his acoustical guitar while Jet sang silly lyrics and Desiree giggled. When she saw him, her eyes widened on a bright smile.

Justin stilled. He loved these people. More than he thought humanly possible. It scared him how much affection he had for them. How much love he had for Desiree. But he wouldn't run from it. Everything looked different. He'd missed so much by hardening himself against hurt and abandonment. No more.

"There you are!" Desiree cried and got to her feet. She ran to him and wrapped him in a tight hug.

He closed his eyes and basked in her adoration. Her love seemed to come naturally, as if it required no effort on her part, and he marveled at her simplicity. She didn't ask if she could hug him. She didn't ogle him as if he were more than a mere man. She came to him as an equal and showered him with genuine love. Her gesture took his breath away.

He buried his face in her soft hair and breathed her lovely scent. "I've been waiting for you my whole life. Where have you been?"

"Dreaming of you."

"I'm not a dream, though. I'm real."

She gazed at him, her eyes sparkling. "You are now. Did you finish a song?"

He smiled as even more weight lifted from him. "I finished twelve."

"Twelve!" She gasped.

Nodding, he said, "And there are more. I feel them. It's like before. I'm back to myself, and it's thanks to you."

She tilted her head. "I can't take credit. They're your words. All of them."

He released a quiet chuckle. When had he ever been this happy? "Stay with me. I've got four more days here. I'm going to send these guys home in the morning. We'll have the place to ourselves. I'll write. You'll take pictures. We'll make love. It'll be like heaven."

"I can't." Her smile faltered. "I've been called to Israel. There's an important summit forming, and I can't pass up the chance for potentially award-winning photos. At the least, I'll get high-priced journal material for our American papers."

The idea of her going made him weak, but she didn't say goodbye. That was something.

"I'm ready for this," he said. "I *can* love you enough. I'd never ask you to quit your job so you could be with me. I just ask that you make a little room for me. Promise you'll come see me when you get back."

Was this happening? Desiree floated in the clouds. "Don't you know, Justin? I love you. You're not only in my time. You're in my thoughts. You're in my dreams. You're in every second of my life. No matter where I am, I'm with you. You're in my heart."

He studied her, and she held her breath, unable to read him. Then he said, "I love you, Desiree. I want you to know I've never said that to any woman. I never plan to say it to another."

"I was so wrong about you. I knew you were

capable of great love, but I didn't think you wanted it. I'm really sorry."

He sweetly kissed her. "The music may be part of me, but I'm not this job. I'm not the stereotype."

Now she recognized a real future with him. A home. Children. A life full of passion and purpose. "I see that. You're not Justin Time. You're Justin. You're *my* Justin."

His smile turned her insides to pudding. "That's right. I'm your Justin."

He kissed her deeply, and the world fell away. His love surpassed her dreams and brought her a reality where his kiss was his promise of forever.

THE END

C.J.

Chapter One

"Mmm."

"Aaah."

"Ugh." C.J. put a palm to his clammy forehead and opened one eye. A redhead to his right. A blonde to his left. What, no brunette? He was losing his edge. Then again, at the moment, his edge had evaporated. He'd do well not to hurl.

Closing his eye, he groaned. Coffee. He needed coffee...through an I.V.

"Hey, baby," cooed the redhead in his right ear. "I'm up for round three if you are." She grasped his flaccid jimmy and made a disappointed mewl.

"I'm all out of rubbers, doll." A soft strain of keyboard music seeped through the door, giving him the excuse he needed to punt these babes. "Sounds like the band is getting ready for a session."

"Can we stay and watch?" asked the blonde, rolling with a squeak and a stretch.

"Sorry. We don't work that way. You girls have to go." He slid a pillow over his face as the bed jostled. "Had a great time."

A toilet flushed. Water ran. "Will we see you tonight?"

Would they leave already? "Don't know. We have a concert."

"We know."

Fingering his braided leather bracelet, he peeked

from under the pillow. They stood by the door, dressed and wearing expectant expressions.

Damn. "Sorry girls. I don't have any backstage passes. Try to catch me after the show."

"But—"

He sank under the pillow. "See ya later."

The door opened then quietly closed.

He was an ass. They'd never get past security at the amphitheater. After snoozing another thirty minutes, he stumbled from bed and used a hot shower to find the will to join the living.

In the suite's main room, the entire band sprawled across soft-looking upholstered furniture and worked at a new song. Jet and Justin shot him dirty glances, but he ignored them.

"Why do you have to do this here? What's wrong with your suite? You guys know I had a late night." He shuffled to a miniature kitchen and claimed the last coffee in a nearly empty pot, drinking straight from the spout.

"Every night is a late night for you, C.J.," said Justin, jotting lyrics into a notebook.

"Besides," said Jet, fingering keys on his keyboard. "This is my suite, too."

C.J. huffed with disgust and carried the pot to the sitting area. "You guys are a bunch of old men." Never mind they were the same age. Flopping into an armchair, he threw a leg over the side and took a swig of coffee.

Jet leaned forearms across his control panel. "Why? Because we go to bed at a reasonable hour, don't wake up from a tequila-induced coma every morning, and know the names of the girls we hang out with?"

"I'm enjoying the rock-n-roll life, dude. I'm young, single, and famous. Why shouldn't I party hard?"

"I don't know," said Justin. "Maybe because you value your liver, want a brain with at least half its memory cells intact, and hope to live to see forty?"

"Whatever." C.J. wished his head would stop pounding.

Why couldn't Justin and Jet be more like their quiet, moody bass player? Chaz never gave him hell for having a good time. At least he hoped he had a good time. Beyond a midnight limo ride, he couldn't remember much.

Glancing around the suite, he asked, "Jet, has your mom sent a box? I'm out of cum-catchers."

Chaz groaned.

"Gross," shot Justin, tossing his notebook on an end table and picking up his guitar. "Get your mind out of your pants, would you? We've got work to do."

C.J. drained the pot and set it on the carpet beside the chair. "What's the hurry? There's another whole week left in the tour."

"Yeah," said Jet, striking a discordant chord that would sound perfect in a horror movie. "Only a week to compose four more new songs. We start recording the next album when we return to Chicago. Did you forget or did last night's drinking kill those particular brain cells?"

He made a face at him. "No, I didn't forget. How hard is it to write a song?"

Justin plucked warm-up chords on his guitar. "If you'd paid any attention over the years, you'd know. That wasn't exactly a party we had in Kill Devil Hills when I got buried under writer's block. Give us a break. Better yet, why don't you help?"

C.J. stood and put a hand on his chest. "I'll do better. Here's a song for you." At the top of his lungs, he howled, "I'm a rock star and life's good. Women aplenty, booze and food. I play my drums the best in the biz. If you don't like it, I don't give a shiz."

Chaz got to his feet and went to the window.

Launching a wad of paper at C.J.'s head, Jet said, "You suck. Now I remember why you don't help write songs and why you're not allowed to sing. On another note, however, I have an announcement to make. I'm getting married."

Justin and Chaz rolled their eyes as if on a practiced queue.

"I've met the love of my life. Her name is Jennifer, and tomorrow I'm going to ask her to marry me."

"What happened to Cynthia? Isn't Cynthia the babe living in your apartment in Chicago?" C.J. laughed and headed for his room. "All this excitement has my head ready to explode. Knock on my door when you guys head out for lunch."

"A rock concert? Which band?" Sindra eyed her friend's backstage tickets. She didn't consider ear-splitting volumes, a crush of people, and a smoke-filled arena an ideal way to spend a Friday night, but backstage could prove interesting.

"I'm interviewing Smashing Glass tonight." Amy waved a card. "And I've got an after-party invitation good for me plus one."

Now that peaked her interest. It would be like the old days. Not when she'd played percussion in her high school orchestra, but when she'd accompanied her dad on tour. "Okay. I'm there. How are you dressing?"

Amy grinned. "I'm wearing slutty chic."

That meant she couldn't do jeans and a T-shirt. She'd look dumpy next to her friend. "I'll figure something out. Meet you there?"

"Yes. Back entrance. Seven o'clock." Amy waved and headed to her desk. "You'll be glad you broke free from your boring life."

Her life wasn't boring. Sindra shut down her computer and dropped her latest restaurant review in the senior editor's inbox as she left. A rock concert. It beat pizza and a movie rental. Okay, maybe her life was a little boring.

Despite traffic jams that doubled her time getting home and forty-five minutes agonizing over what to wear and do with her hair, she arrived at the amphitheater ten minutes early. She parked her Jeep next to a dark tour bus and strolled toward the rear entrance.

A large man with a clipboard and a silver headset

stood scowling. He intimidated her, and she stopped short. Would he yell when she couldn't produce a pass? Where was her friend?

Amy came around the corner from the side and offered a friendly wave. She looked stunning in a bright red dress that hugged every slender curve. High heels made her legs appear long like a model's, though she only stood five feet four. She had curled her hair, and it swayed in dark brown waves as she sauntered toward the man.

Sindra touched a self-conscious hand to her head. Her blonde twisty-braid surely appeared washed out and plain in comparison. No fair.

She wiped a sweaty palm along the hip of her medium-blue jeans. She should've worn that black miniskirt she'd bought last year on a whim but never wore. Her only saving grace came in a form-fitting white camisole with tiny silver studs that caught any light and sparkled along the cleavage-revealing neckline.

Amy batted impossibly long lashes. She showed the man her press pass and backstage ticket. Handing Sindra a hangtag with the other ticket, she led the way inside.

Equipment and hundreds of hard-sided cases filled the area in no apparent organization. Beyond it, people bustled, carrying clothing, coiled cable, and every manner of electronics.

Sindra followed her friend. As the entertainment reporter for their newspaper, Amy knew her way around the concert epicenter.

"This way," said her friend, beaming over her light brown Puerto Rican shoulder.

Sindra found her excitement contagious. With butterflies in her stomach, she realized Amy enjoyed success in her articles because she truly thrilled in what she did. Sindra loved writing, but she hadn't yet found the one topic that fed her spirit and provided unending inspiration.

Her friend turned into a long hallway where people talked in pairs or clusters, carried drinks and food, or moved racks of clothes. She passed a room arranged like a hair salon.

She realized they had entered the band's show support. She paid more attention to faces but didn't recognize anyone.

At a blue door marked with a gold star, Amy knocked. Sindra bent her head, slipped the nylon strap of her hangtag around her neck, and flipped her long twisted hair over one shoulder. Her hands shook.

Why was she nervous? They were musicians. Rich, famous musicians who made the kind of music millions of people enjoyed. So what? Never mind she hadn't spent time around such a scene in nearly ten years.

The door opened. A thin man wearing a crew T-shirt and headset checked Amy's credentials then waved them in. It wasn't the intimate interview Sindra had imagined.

Fifteen other reporters sat in a line of chairs, vying for answers from four handsome men. All four turned and raked Amy's figure as she swayed her hips on her way to a chair. The beautiful brunette knew how to work a room and could have any at her choosing, Sindra didn't doubt. She, on the other hand...

Shrugging, she turned from the large room and wandered into a smaller, cozier room. Lining the walls hung pictures of the band in concert, meeting fans, or shaking hands with well-known people. One photo grabbed her attention, and she went to it. The man at the center of the other pictures, with a flame tattoo climbing his neck from the collar of his shirt, kissed a beautiful redhead. The woman's shoulder seemed odd in its angle, and she realized she'd been taking the picture. It made Sindra smile.

Black leather furniture made the space inviting. When she spotted a set of drumsticks, a guitar, and a saxophone on a far table, she realized she had discovered the band's sanctuary. Oops. She took a backward step but stopped.

Something about the drumsticks beckoned her.

They offered a dull return of light from a string of bare bulbs draped like a valance above a wide wall mirror. She went to the table and ran two fingers along the smooth, pale wood. These weren't show sticks. No, these reminded her of her own drumsticks. She hadn't been good in high school, but not because she lacked skill. She had lacked motivation.

The sticks had nicks and dents and dull spots where fingers had rubbed through finish. The owner of these sticks had a passion she understood. Taking them in one hand, she swallowed past a lump in her throat. Her fingers slipped into position from memory, and her heart beat a bit faster.

They weren't hers. She shook her head. But her hands and wrists paid no mind. A tip dropped to the table and bounced with a satisfying double beat. She smiled. That felt really good.

Letting the sticks have their way, she began a soft, slow roll. She strolled, following the length of the table, liking the tone. Releasing a ghost of a laugh, she traveled without missing a beat before jumping to the arm of a leather chair. The low thump as wood struck taut hide thrummed a chord in her, and she increased the tempo.

Closing her eyes, she absorbed the rhythm, moving into a combination of beats that flowed from a place she hadn't realized still existed.

"You're not supposed to be in here."

"Aa!" Sindra dropped the sticks onto the seat cushion and stumbled sideways into a coffee table. Ow! She rubbed her knee. "I'm so sorry."

The man in the doorway was a band member from the other room. He was in half the pictures on the walls. Clamping her lips closed, she didn't trust she could speak without uttering something embarrassing. She had heard some of their songs on the radio, but she didn't know their faces, much less names or who played what.

The man considered her with milk chocolate brown eyes. He had the longest hair in the group, his dirty blond waves resting beyond his shoulders and framing strong features. Her gaze found its way to broad shoulders, full chest, and nicely rounded biceps stretching the sleeves of his black T-shirt.

"Well?" he said, putting a hand to the doorframe, which made his chest muscles bunch.

"Nice pecs," she said. Oh, God. Did she say pecs?

"Oh, yeah? Nice tits." In two steps, he reached the chair and collected the sticks. "These are mine."

Chapter Two

Focus

C.J. weaved a drumstick through the fingers of his left hand and adjusted his stool. The packed amphitheater roared, but he had grown used to it. The vision threatening to ruin his rhythm was the stunning blonde pounding her heart into a sweet lick on a leather chair with his sticks. *His* sticks.

Justin stood at the front of the stage and fingered the first five notes of the starting number. Jet joined him with the keyboard on the next five. C.J. would break in on a mean beat with Chaz on bass, and they'd blow the audience's hair back.

Except he missed his place in the queue. Shit! Justin shot him a nasty glance, but the band had mad skills and circled to the beginning as if they'd meant to begin that way.

Focus.

He hit the skins on time, and the jam earned them delighted screams. Slamming his drums with extra energy, he tried to purge the babe from his thoughts but failed.

Hell, she was just a girl. Sending his sticks high overhead, he brought them down with a ferocious growl. She was just a girl like the hundreds he'd had before.

When the song ended, he didn't give the guys a chance to reset. He inhaled a single breath then pounded straight into the next song. Jet had to scramble, switching from his keyboard to an electric guitar, but the band met the challenge. The crowd erupted in dance and screams.

Justin bit the last of the initial refrain into the microphone then marched across stage while his fingers screamed along his guitar's fret in a wicked instrumental. "What the hell? Chill. This isn't a race."

With a nod, C.J. lifted off his seat and drummed a dramatic transition for the second set of lyrics. Jet took the lead vocal, and Justin joined in on harmony. It actually sounded better.

Rocking hard, C.J. closed his eyes and settled into his routine. He pumped back and forth, the sway of his hair against his cheeks providing something tangible to sink his musical pulse into.

His foot working the pedal of the bass drum, he gritted his teeth through a complex beat that incorporated every drum in the set and ended on a wild strike of cymbal. Opening his eyes, he smiled as camera flashes created a sparkling effect in the darkness of audience beyond the bright, multicolored stage lights.

To the immediate right of the stage, another sparkle caught his attention. He recognized it right away. The blonde's halter-top. She moved along the VIP balcony. Was she leaving? Had he disappointed her?

What was he thinking? Giving his head a violent shake, he finished the song with an angry shout. Why should he care if she left? She was just a girl.

Yet his gaze sought that certain sparkle on the balcony time and again.

"So what do you think?" asked Amy, joining Sindra at a line of sinks in an enormous ladies room.

"They're great. That drummer is something else. What's his name?"

"C.J. Brody. Hey, what did he say to you in the green room?"

Reluctant to admit it, she confessed, "He caught

me drumming on a chair with his sticks."

"No." Her friend's eyes went wide with horror. "I can't believe he didn't get you thrown out. You should never touch a musician's instrument."

"I know. Really, I know that." Stepping from the sink, she grabbed a length of paper towel and tore it from the dispenser.

"What did he say?"

"He asked me what I was doing."

"That's it? And?"

Sindra grimaced. "And I was going to compliment him on the pictures they had on the walls, but I looked at his chest and..."

"Oh, good Lord. What did you say?" Amy tossed her paper towel in the trash and moved toward the door.

"I said 'nice pecs' instead of nice pictures."

Her friend barked a laugh. "Great going. I swear I can't leave you alone for two seconds. Did he laugh?" She led the way to the balcony.

"No. Well, sort of. I mean, he said, 'Yeah? Nice tits.'"

Amy's features twisted in disgust. "He's such a pig."

"It wasn't like that. He was joking." At least, she thought he joked. Yes, he had definitely poked fun.

"If you say so."

As they made their way to their seats, the lead singer spoke to the audience about the band's pleasure at playing for their city. Then C.J. exploded into a drum solo that had Sindra halting in her tracks. Amazed by his skill and energy, she moved to the railing.

She couldn't get close enough. Gripping the rail, she leaned over and added her shout of encouragement and appreciation to the crowd's.

Then he looked right at her. He rolled to a stop, rent his T-shirt from neck to hem, and threw it into the front row. Staring without shame, she thoroughly enjoyed the ripple of muscle as he tore through another pounding rhythm. Tattooed drumsticks encircled his arm right below the indentation of muscle that separated bicep, triceps, and shoulder. Digressing into a simple but toe-tapping lick, he dropped his gaze to the keyboardist with spiky black hair. The guy swung an alto saxophone to his mouth and hit a long note.

Disappointed that the drum solo had ended, she left the rail and found her seat. "That was incredible!"

"Except the part when I thought you were going to tumble off the balcony."

Sindra laughed. "I'm having the most fun. He tore off his shirt."

"He always does. It's his thing. He keeps looking at you."

She turned to the stage. Sure enough, he glanced her way. He'd watched to see where she sat? Her heart caught a wave and missed a beat. Wondering if he found her as attractive as she found him, she smiled and waved. He lifted a hand overhead and twirled a stick. Sindra gasped.

"Oh, please." Amy rolled her eyes. "He wants you for one of his one-night stands, and don't expect to be the only girl there."

Her friend's words hurt, and she turned new eyes on the drummer.

"If you watched television, you'd know. Besides, he's not even the cutest. If I had my pick, I'd go with Chaz." Her friend licked red lips.

"Chaz? Which one is he?"

"The serious bass player. I think he's dreamy."

Sindra sighed. "Looking like you do tonight, you could probably have your pick."

"Think so?" Amy sent the unsuspecting bass player a predatory stare while he fingered strings on his guitar. "I might have to see about that at the party."

The party. Sindra had forgotten about it in the excitement. Would C.J. go? Would she get a chance to talk with him?

Bam! Bam! Bam! C.J.'s sweat flew off the ends of

his hair and splattered the stage for the final time that night. Neatly tucking his drumsticks in a back pocket, he sat back on his stool and stretched with a smile. This concert had been a wild ride, nearly as exciting as his first ten thousand-plus audience.

Because of a pair of blue eyes, which had stayed on him the entire show. What was it about her that gave him such a thrill?

"Come on," yelled Jet over the roar of the crowd.

Time for public relations. Amped on adrenaline, C.J. ran for the shower. He shampooed and wondered if he'd get to meet her for real. She had a backstage pass and sat in the VIP balcony, so he figured she'd attend the after-party. He hoped so, anyway. For once in over a year, he planned to spend more than ten minutes at the event.

After toweling dry, he donned clean jeans, his biker boots, and a light green long-sleeved button down. He didn't bother blow-drying his hair. Slicking it with a comb, he studied his reflection. At five feet ten inches, he was the shortest member of the band. It had never bothered him before, but now, he really wanted this girl to notice him.

"You coming?" he asked Chaz who sprawled on the leather couch and plucked an angry sounding chord. C.J. pulled a long-necked bottle from a mini-fridge then headed for the door.

"In a minute."

"See ya in there." He grinned when his friend sent him a puzzled frown.

C.J. shrugged and ducked to the hallway, which buzzed, crammed with people he'd never seen before. Some tried to get his attention, but he ignored them. Twisting off the cap from his beer, he smiled. His stomach fluttered in excitement and anticipation of meeting the blonde. Actual flutters. No woman had ever given him stomach flutters.

He gave the beer cap to a passing crew worker then took a sip and climbed steps two at a time to the VIP lounge. At the top, the door stood open. The hum of conversation slowed him.

What if she didn't like him? What if she found his drumming lame? What if she had a boyfriend? Damn. That would really suck. Only one way to find out. He chugged three swallows of liquid courage.

Taking a deep breath, he went inside. In seconds, he realized he had arrived ahead of the other guys. How had that happened? He was always last.

And she hadn't shown. He'd gotten worked up for nothing. He needed a drink. The hard kind. He set his half-finished beer on a table.

On his way to the bar, he spotted the sexy brunette from the press conference. "Hey," he said. "Where's your friend?"

She gave him a disdainful sniff that caught him off guard. "Sin isn't your type."

C.J. arched his eyebrows, used to women pursuing him, not shunning him. "Sin? With a name like that, I'd say she's perfect for me."

"Ha-ha," she scoffed. "I know all about you. Sin won't get drunk with you or fall into your bed just to be sent on her way the next morning without so much as a thank you. You'll have to look somewhere else for your brand of fun."

"You're mean." He checked if anyone listened.

"No, I'm not. She's my best friend and I'm protecting her. She doesn't hang out with rockers like I do."

He leaned closer and said low, "Seems to me she's grown up and can make decisions for herself. Why don't you tell me where I can find her and let's see what she has to say."

"What who has to say?"

C.J. found her standing behind him. She appeared as beautiful and fresh-faced at eleven-thirty as she had four hours earlier. He said, "You."

"Hey you." She shoved her hands into her front pockets. "You were really great tonight." To her friend, she said, "You should go check out the ladies' bathroom. It's marble."

"They know how to treat the VIPs around here." He hiked a thumb toward the bar. "You wanna get a drink with me, Sin?"

"You know my name." She glanced at her friend with a question in her blue eyes.

"You're on your own. Don't do anything *you* wouldn't do," said the brunette. She stood taller as Chaz joined the party. "I've got trouble of my own to get into."

When Sin's friend sauntered away, C.J. ushered his lovely fan to the bar. "The girls go for Chaz. Especially the teenagers. He hates that."

She laughed. "I bet." Sliding onto a high stool, she asked, "Who goes for you?"

He shrugged. "Trashy ones, I guess. Which is what has me baffled about you. Your friend's right. You're not my type, but there's something about you."

Had he said too much? He told her trashy women were his type. This girl had gone to his head.

"Is that what you talked about with Amy?" Her lids narrowed, accentuating her long lashes. "You asked about me?"

"Actually, I asked where I could find you. She tried to warn me away." He braced. Her answer would determine if he flew or crashed.

"That explains a lot."

"What'll it be?" asked the bartender.

C.J. sighed, frustrated at the interruption. He'd gotten so involved in talking with her he'd forgotten about drinks. Indicating she should order first, he expected such a classy chick to ask for a cosmopolitan or martini. When she told the bartender to bring her a lager, he relaxed. Maybe he needed to stop reading this book by its cover.

He ordered the same. Hard liquor could ruin a night with this beauty. If he was lucky enough to persuade her into his bed, he wanted to remember every minute.

Bringing the conversation around, he said, "So, about your friend telling me I'm not your type..."

She laughed, showing pretty white teeth. "She

tries to protect me. Honestly, I don't get out much. I spend a lot of time in local restaurants as a food critic for the newspaper, but that's about it. I'm trying to get a job with a cuisine magazine. I'd like to travel. See the country."

A food critic and writer. Impressive. "You know gourmet and fancy restaurant stuff?"

"Pretty much. I actually trained at a culinary institute my last two years in college. I was good at it, but when I worked in a real kitchen, I didn't like it. I had to start as a sous-chef, and the stress was ridiculous. No, I like writing about it better. I wrote a cookbook I might try to sell called *Gourmet for Everyday.*"

"You're really serious about food." She had to have an amazing metabolism with her slim lines. Shaking his head, he chuckled. He couldn't remember ever spending so much time talking to a girl, and about her instead of his life as a rocker. He liked it. He liked her.

Chapter Three

"I am serious about food, but I wouldn't say it's my passion. Not like your music is for you." Sindra wished she had his kind of fever for something. For anything.

The bartender placed brown bottles before them, and C.J. took a drink from his. "What makes you say I'm passionate about music?"

Was he kidding? "I could see it in your playing. You have so much energy and enthusiasm. The audience feeds off your beats. Don't you know that?"

He shook his head, quirking his lips into a charming half-smile. "What was with you and my drumsticks? From what I saw, you're pretty good, too."

Groaning inwardly, she hid embarrassment behind a sip of her dry beer. "Sorry about that. I don't know what I was thinking. I couldn't resist."

"Where'd you learn to play?"

She studied him a long moment. Would he treat her differently if she told him about her father? For a second, she considered lying or avoiding the question. What would be the point? He'd leave and she'd probably never see him again.

Taking a steadying breath, she said in a rush, "My dad's George Karriker."

His brown eyes widened, and his mouth went slightly slack while his beer stopped between the counter and his lips. "George Karriker? The George

Karriker of the Karriker Jones Band?" He narrowed his gaze and leaned a bit closer. "Holy shit. Sin. You're Sindra Karriker. You've changed a lot since you were a kid."

Taken aback, she sat straighter. "How would you know?"

He smiled and took a drink. "I can't believe it. Your dad's the best drummer. Ever. He's the reason I took up the sticks. You're in a couple of the band's videos."

"When I was really little," she admitted with a nod.

One corner of his mouth curled upward. "I remember. You're only a few years behind me. I was ten when I saw his 'How You Do It' video."

Sindra grinned. That had been a fun few days of filming. "I was six when we made that. So that makes you what, twenty-eight? Twenty-nine?"

"This is crazy. And cool. Hey, you wanna do something?"

"Isn't talking doing something?"

"Not usually. For me, anyway." He tilted his head with a curious expression. "With you, I'm liking it, though. But I have something better in mind."

Sindra enjoyed their talk, but she couldn't get physical with him. She wouldn't. She glanced at Amy. Her friend stood talking to two of the band members, her notebook out. No help there.

"Look, C.J.," she said. "I know about your reputation—"

"It's not about that. Come on, Sin. Have a little faith. This could be the best time."

She hesitated, but the sparkle of excitement in his eyes won her. "Where are we going?"

"To the stage." He took her hand.

On the way to the door, she waved at Amy. She patted the cell phone clipped to her front pocket. "Don't leave without me. You've got my number."

Her friend frowned, but Sindra could take care of herself. Amy would have to deal with it.

"I don't believe I'm doing this," C.J. said, leading the way downstairs.

"Doing what?" Curiosity sped her feet along behind him.

"Not telling. It's a surprise." He grinned over his shoulder, holding firmly to her hand. He acted more like an eager schoolboy who'd found a treasure than a sex-crazed rock star.

"I'm serious about not—"

"So am I. I promise. You've got to trust me." He led her along a gray hall away from the dressing rooms.

"Trust you? I don't know you." She should've been nervous, but she couldn't wait to see where he took her.

"I'd say you know more than you think."

In the bustling area next to the concert stage, he waved over a stocky, bearded man wearing a T-shirt labeled *Crew Manager*. C.J. whispered in the manager's ear. Smiling, the man gave a nod and blew a whistle hanging around his neck. A drove of workers filed off the stage.

"Our turn," said C.J. with a mischievous smile.

This was going to be good. Sindra hadn't stood on a stage like this since she attended her dad's retirement concert in her sophomore year of high school.

Letting go of his hand, she went straight for his drum set. She ran fingertips along the upper curve of metal framing the large bass drum. "My dad had one exactly like this."

"I know. If you don't mind me asking, why did he quit?"

Not taking her eyes off the shiny set, she traced the edge of a cymbal and said, "He didn't."

"Sure he did. I went to his final concert."

"Me, too. But he didn't quit. He loves music almost as much as he loves my mom and me."

"Then why? The band was more popular than ever."

"It really was." She faced C.J. and hoped with all her heart that he would enjoy a longer career than her father. "He was going deaf."

C.J. took a step back. "No way. That really sucks."

"Tell me about it. He told the band to keep going, but they refused."

"They were right. It wouldn't have been the Karriker Jones Band without the genius drumming of George Karriker."

Sindra smiled. "That's what Patrick Jones said. My dad wears a hearing implant, but now he hears the world differently. He teaches music at the state university down the street."

He shook his head. "Can you imagine learning music from The George Karriker?"

"Actually, yes. I can."

He laughed. "I bet you can." He reached past her then handed her his drumsticks. "You smell good. Have a seat."

"Are you serious?" Her stomach did a little jump.

"Completely."

She moved behind the drums, and as she settled onto a black stool, visions of C.J. in concert played through her mind. A particular beat from one of the songs nagged at her, begging her to give it a try. Glancing at him, she took a stick in each hand and positioned her foot on the base drum's pedal.

He gave a single nod. It was all she needed.

She stole his breath. As if she had played with Smashing Glass for years, Sindra banged a perfect beat to Jet's song, *She's All Mine*. A technician flipped on the sound system, sending the rhythm into a rich fullness that filled the stadium.

Without missing a beat, she smiled and mouthed, "Wow."

She was definitely her father's daughter. The woman could play.

She finished the final rhythm phrase and added a personal signature ending that made him smile. Eyeing the sticks, she said, "That sounded nothing like playing my set in the garage of my parent's house."

"Wait." He glanced backstage. Then he grinned. Here it came.

Two roadies carried an assembled drum set and two cymbal stands onstage. A third brought a stool and a set of sticks.

"What's this?" Sindra asked, a slow smile transforming her beautiful features into something stunning he didn't want to take his eyes off. "You do this with all the ladies?"

"This is the first. You up to the challenge?" He directed the workers to set the drums facing her.

She shrugged. "I don't know. Tonight's the first I've set sticks to skins since I moved out on my own. Usually I bang around my apartment on whatever surface is available."

He nodded. He did the same. Taking a seat, he spun his sticks while a sound technician plugged him in. When the soundman gave him a thumbs-up, C.J. waggled his eyebrows at Sin. "You're doing fine. Ready to jam?"

With a worried stare, she asked, "What are we playing?"

"We're going to jam. Make something up and I'll join you."

Shaking her head, she said, "How about you start?"

"Works for me." Offering her a wink, he said, "Here we go."

He started a simple three-two beat. She met the rhythm with her bass, pedding in time to her bobbing head. Adding a third to the rhythm, C.J. upped the challenge. Sin met it. She came in with a series of half and quarter beats that ripped the sound and took the rhythm to a level no drummer could achieve alone. Blown away, he switched it up, keeping to the original three-two but increasing the complexity and adding his own bass.

She followed, as if they'd practiced this as a routine a hundred times. Their eyes met and held. She laughed, pounding the drums with everything she had.

An electric guitar screamed a wavering high note. C.J. reluctantly dragged his gaze from Sin and glanced over his shoulder. The entire band strolled onto stage. When had they arrived?

Jet and Chaz joined the jam session, filling the amphitheater with wild, wonderful music. After-party guests and roadies spilled onto the stage and danced.

Turning his attention to Sin, he met her joyful gaze. He wanted to knock it up a notch. As if reading his mind, she gave a nod and provided a run of eighth notes that progressed into sixteenths. In her intense concentration, her smile melted.

His heart began to pound. He'd never been so turned on in his life. Letting her take the complex beat, he banged his sticks on the skins in a tempo that matched his foot at the bass drum.

A delicate sheen of perspiration glistened across her chest and brow. Her shoulders and biceps flexed and strained as her slender wrists and fingers worked the sticks across his drums. She had her dad in her, making Karriker magic right before his eyes.

He sent his sticks into an arm-burning rhythm George Karriker used to do and that had taken C.J. a year of practicing to learn. Sin's eyes widened a fraction as her lips formed an O. In an echo effect, she mirrored the rhythm but behind by two beats. She did it like it was nothing.

The dancers hooted their approval.

He didn't know whether to be offended that she drummed better than him or angry that she tossed her obvious skill and talent aside for a two-bit newspaper job writing about food. He needed a shot of tequila.

Winding down the session, he lifted a hand for her to stop. He thumped the base drum twice to signal the band that they had ten beats to wrap the session. Pointing at her to start drumming, he used one drumstick to run a three-two while counting down the ten with his other hand.

At zero, he and Sin signed off with his signature

multi-drum roll and cymbal finish.

C.J. barked a surprised laugh. "How'd you know I was going to do that?"

She stood and placed the sticks on a drum. "You did it during the concert. It seemed fitting."

"Awesome, man," yelled Jet over laughter and hoots from the guests. The crew applauded.

C.J. raised a hand high and gave Justin a wave. "Let's get out of here," he said in Sindra's ear, putting a hand to the small of her back to usher her off stage.

She sidestepped from his touch and gave him a wary look. "This has been a blast, and I really enjoyed meeting you, but I can't. I'm not like that."

Damn it. "I want to spend more time with you."

She retreated a step. "Maybe we could get together for lunch tomorrow. I'm reviewing—"

"We leave in the morning."

Pausing, she peered at the floor. "In that case..." She offered a hand and gazed at him with earnest blue eyes and a wavering smile.

He took her hand but held tight. "Sin. Stay."

She gave her hand a tug, but he refused to let go. She said, "It's late."

"Not for me. We don't pull out for another eight hours. We could go to my hotel's bar, or to an all-night pancake house, or someplace. I swear I won't try anything." Although, if she showed signs of wanting him as much as he wanted her, a quick trip to a drugstore for a refill of condoms would pose no problem.

"I see what you're thinking."

Shit. Was he that transparent?

With an insistent pull, she won her hand from his grip. "Thank you for a great concert and an after-party I'll never forget. I wish you the best."

Her friend hurried over and put an arm around Sindra's shoulder. "Ready to go?'

"Goodbye," she said to him, a sad look elongating her features.

As she left, C.J. fought the urge to chase her. She'd wished him the best. Nobody ever had. Ever.

Chapter Four

"You wanted to stay, didn't you?" Amy pushed open the rear exit.

Cool air hit Sindra full in the face. It went far to clear her head. "Maybe."

"That drummer's no good, Sin. He'd use you and discard you without a second thought."

"Maybe." Somehow she hadn't gotten that vibe from him. Then again, Amy was a far better judge of character.

"You going straight home?"

"Maybe." Definitely.

"Would you please stop saying that? And look at me."

Sindra met her friend's dark gaze.

"I mean it when I say he'll hurt you. That's what he does. He's a rock idol, and he enjoys that life. He's known for it."

Nodding, Sindra dug her Jeep keys from her front pocket. "I hear you. Don't worry. I'm going straight home and hope my dreams can come close to this dream I lived tonight."

Amy smiled. "It was fun, wasn't it?"

"Yes. Thanks for bringing me."

Her friend offered a small wave and headed for her car. "You're welcome. If I don't see you this weekend, I'll see you Monday."

Sindra went to her Jeep and got in but didn't start

the engine. After Amy's red taillights disappeared into the night, she turned her attention to the amphitheater's rear entrance. It appeared peaceful despite the party and work going on inside.

What was she doing? She glanced at her keys then at the door. Nothing happened. She should go home. Why didn't he come after her?

Thirty minutes later, she realized Amy had him right. He wasn't interested in her. He only wanted a good time. She was no man's good time girl.

She inserted the key into the ignition, and when the engine came to life, she inhaled a shaky breath. A wad of disappointment settled into her chest. She had liked him. Really liked him. It had been too long since a man had made her heart pound like this. Why did he have to be a playboy?

She left the parking lot and headed along the deserted street. Her father had warned her against musicians, but it made no sense. Her dad was such a good man. A loving, devoted husband and the best father, he was a musician. Patrick Jones, too.

At home, she took a shower and smiled at the memory of C.J.'s expression when he'd found her beating his drumsticks on a leather chair. He must have thought some lunatic had snuck into the band's dressing room.

She dried then stood at the mirror, wrapping the towel around her. In the reflection, her mother's eyes stared back. Her mother would know what to say to ease Sindra's confusion and hurt. It probably wouldn't be based in truth but in a parent's bias.

Her mother had once said Sindra got the best attributes of both parents, but she'd really gotten only half-measures. Half of her mother's beauty and determination. Half of her father's creativity and talent.

With a sigh, she brushed her teeth then tossed her towel over the shower curtain rod and went to bed naked. She wanted to shine in her own right, her own ability. Maybe she had tonight, creating original beat combinations and using various musical influences to make something new. Something never heard before.

It hadn't been good enough. C.J. would've come after her if it had. He would've seen her as more than a one-night stand.

She huffed. Why did she have to measure her success by the approval of a pleasure-seeker? She had reasons to have pride. She liked reviewing restaurants and writing articles. Well, maybe like was too strong of a word. She appreciated...respected...aw heck. Who was she trying to convince? It stunk. She was good at it, but it didn't make her like it. She knew food and loved writing. Simple as that.

What she liked was the thrill and energy that raced through her as she pounded those drums while staring into C.J.'s eyes. She'd never experienced anything comparable. During the drum set tonight, she came awake. She hadn't realized she'd been moving through life asleep.

"Amy's right. My life is boring."

"Man, you're looking like Chaz." Jet punched C.J.'s arm.

"Ow!" He grabbed the sore spot and glared at his friend.

"That's a compliment," muttered Chaz from a swivel chair near the front of the bus. He gave a newspaper a noisy rustle and pivoted.

"What do you think of this?" asked Justin from the dinette. He lifted his notebook and sang, "Adrift in the ocean of misery, I'm drowning without you. Drowning without you. Fish me out."

"Fish me out?" Jet arched a single ebony eyebrow and twisted his pinkie ring. He erupted in guffaws.

Chaz glanced over his shoulder with an amused grin.

"That's really bad." C.J. gave Jet a shove to move him to the other end of the couch. "You need some loving, Justin. Fish me out? How long has it been since you got some?"

The lead singer scowled and dropped his songbook on the table. "Desiree's been on the European tour thing for three weeks. Besides, love and sex are two different things, C.J. Getting some from a strange girl who throws herself at me after a concert means less than nothing. She's not loving me. Hell, she doesn't know me. Not that I'd do that now, but I learned that our first year on tour. When are you going to?"

Jet nodded and Chaz turned his back.

Crossing arms over his chest, C.J. stared out the window at passing scenery. He knew it. He'd learned it, too, but he refused to let their band get a reputation as a bunch of fuddy-duddies. Besides, it was sex. Sex! Who said no to sex with gorgeous, willing babes?

Though, after last night, he wondered if he could do it anymore. Sin had pitched him off his beat when she refused to stay. Not one hottie at the party could compare. He'd gone to bed alone. When had that ever happened while they toured?

If she were any other girl, he'd knock his head against a wall and call himself a pathetic idiot. But he had met Sindra Karriker. She had been important to him before he ever met her. Damn, but she was worth it.

"I had fun last night," said Jet, resting his head against the couch and staring at the ceiling. "It's been a long time since we jammed for the hell of it." He cut a glance C.J.'s way. "Who was that babe on the drums?"

"Sindra Karriker."

Chaz spun around so fast his newspaper went flying. "You remember a chick's name?"

C.J. got to his feet. "She's no chick."

Jet laughed. "No shit. That babe could play. Hey, did she bang you as well as she banged your drums?"

His face growing hot, he fisted his hands and said, "Watch your mouth, Cavanaugh, before I put my fist in it."

"Defending a girl?" asked Chaz, retrieving his obituaries from the floor. "Who is she?"

Justin went to the refrigerator and got a soda. "Karriker. Isn't there a band by that name?"

C.J. took the can without asking and downed a swallow. "Was. There was a band called the Karriker Jones Band."

Justin got another drink and returned to his seat. "That's right. I remember you were a big fan of theirs back in high school."

C.J. shrugged and slid onto the opposite booth seat.

"This girl, she's a kid of one of those band members?"

"Something like that."

Justin studied him. Jet began to chuckle. Chaz folded and set aside his paper, his gaze on C.J.

"What?" C.J. took another swallow of cola and slid open the curtain covering the window at his shoulder.

"You're always willing to spill the details of your late night adventures." Justin's lips quirked. "And you never know their names."

"Yeah," said Jet. "What's up with this one?"

"Nothing's up." He wished he had a late night adventure to keep secret. Did she wish she'd said yes? She probably hadn't given him a thought after she left. Compared to the rock legends she'd know all her life, he was nobody.

"Why won't you tell us about her?" asked Justin. "Don't tell me she wanted Chaz, instead."

Jet groaned and Chaz rolled his eyes.

C.J. shook his head. "She didn't want anybody."

"She turned you down?" Jet grazed fingers over his black spiked hair. "Damn, man. Has that ever happened?"

"Plenty." C.J. huffed. Girls had rejected him a lot in high school and during those early years when Smashing Glass worked to make a name. Okay, so maybe he was tripping with this success. Maybe he shouldn't take her rejection so hard.

Reasoning didn't help. It still stung.

"You going to see her again?" asked Chaz.

"Damn it, can't we talk about something else?" C.J. squirmed in his seat and finished his soda.

"No," said Justin with a grin. "This is a big deal, drummer boy. You've been this band's wild man and a huge source of free publicity. If you're going straight, you have to say so. We'll be glad and relieved, but our publicist needs to know."

Jet sat forward and planted elbows on his knees. "Yeah, we need to know. Mom's gotta change what she sends you in her care packages if you insist on giving up your prowling ways."

"Don't go telling your mom anything. I swear, that woman already knows too much."

Justin coughed a laugh. "Your personal business makes entertainment news at least once a week. It's not like she has to dig for it."

"Whatever." Was that why Sindra turned him down? Was he too wild for her?

"Are you going to answer my question?" asked Chaz, leaning against his seatback and crossing his arms.

"Fine." C.J. tossed his empty can in the trash. "No, I'm not going to see her again. She didn't give me her number, I don't know where she lives, and she didn't seem interested. Satisfied?"

Chaz sighed and unfolded his paper. "Too bad."

"What a waste." Jet shook his head. "You two were kick-ass on the drums together."

C.J. had to agree. Thinking about it still blew him away. Sure, she hadn't offered him a way to get in touch with her, and he gave his butt a mental kick for not going after her when she'd walked, but he had options. Her friend had interviewed the band for an article in the paper where she worked, which meant their agent had the newspaper's contact information. He smiled.

"Uh-oh," said Justin with a wary narrowing of his eyes. "I don't like the looks of that."

Jet pulled a wallet from his back jeans pocket and opened it. "Sorry man. You're gonna have to put that thought on hold. I don't have enough to bail you out."

Chaz cleared his throat. "I was the one who bailed him out last time."

"You guys crack me up," C.J. said dryly.

Drumming fingers on the table, he stared out the window. He never had patience to wait, though. At the refrigerator, he took another drink then went to his small sleeping compartment. He found his cell phone in his backpack.

Their agent's office closed on the weekends, so he auto-dialed his private number. It only rang twice.

"C.J., I'm going to kill you. I can't get away right now. What kind of trouble are you in?"

"Geez, Spence. Why does everyone think I'm in trouble or looking to get into it?"

Silence answered.

"Cal?"

"Sorry. For a second there, I thought you'd lost your mind. You are trouble, C.J. It's what you do."

The talent agent had a point. "Well, I'm not in trouble right now. We're on the bus on our way to Los Angeles."

"That's good news. So what do you need?"

"A name and number."

"No."

"Come on, dude. This is legit. I swear."

"Could you be more specific?"

How much would Calvin Spence need to know before he gave him what he wanted? He didn't want to admit he had grown desperate to contact a woman. He searched through his pack for a piece of paper. "There was a reporter from a local newspaper at the show last night. She was the only woman in the bunch. I need the number to her paper and the name of our contact."

"I'm in the backyard. I've got to go inside." A dog barked then a closing patio door thumped. "So, what's going on? Did the reporter get some bad info? Or do you want to add something you forgot?"

He thought fast. "Do you know the name George Karriker?"

"Yes. Famous drummer from the nineties. A

legend."

"His daughter was at the concert last night. I was hoping the newspaper might know something."

"Oh, right. He's your idol. Hold on a second. I think I can get you a number from my computer. Do you know the name of the reporter or paper?"

"No."

"Of course you wouldn't. That would be too easy. Hold on. I have a list of the interviewers. Here she is. Amy Diaz."

Yes! C.J. located a broken purple crayon he had no idea about and an album. Opening the CD case, he jotted the name and number on the inside label. "Thanks, dude. You coming to California?"

"No. I've got family in town. I'll meet you guys in Phoenix in a few days."

"See ya then." C.J. ended the call and immediately dialed Sindra's newspaper.

"Daily Post. Local and Entertainment department. John speaking."

"Hey, John. This is C.J. Brody."

"C.J. Brody from Smashing Glass?"

"Yep. That's me. I met one of your writers last night. Sindra Karriker?"

"She works here, but you didn't meet her. We sent Ms. Diaz to interview Smashing Glass. Who are you really?"

"Look, they both came. Is Sindra there today?" What would she say about him calling her at work? Hell, calling at all?

"Ms. Karriker isn't working today. Is there something I can do for you?"

Strike one.

C.J. grimaced.

"Are you really C.J. Brody?"

"I really am, dude."

"Okay, this is cool." The guy sounded happy to have a rock star on the phone.

How far could he play the fame card? "John. You couldn't give me her number, could you?"

"No, I can't do that."

Strike two.

"Not even for a set of free tickets with backstage passes and an invitation to the after-party?" *Come on, dude.*

"For what band?"

Offended, he said too harshly, "Smashing Glass."

"Sorry. I don't listen to that kind of music."

Strike three. Damn.

"That's cool." Not! "I'll just leave a voicemail message for her." C.J. sighed.

"Her voicemail is full."

Full? The man lied. "Would you take a message?"

"Sure. Go ahead."

"Tell her..." What? That he regretted not begging her harder to stay? That he wished he'd followed her like a lovesick puppy? That he couldn't get it up for any other babe after she left? "Tell her I called and that I'd like it if she called me."

Chapter Five

Nearly tripping over the threshold of the newspaper building, Sindra read through a letter she'd received by special delivery that morning. Her heart beat faster, and she smiled.

Hired.

Fine Cuisine Magazine wanted her on their payroll as a traveling restaurant reviewer. Hitting the elevator call button, she extracted an expense card Visa from the envelope and gazed at her first assignment in the letter.

Phoenix. Tomorrow. Plane tickets made the mailing envelope stiff as a board. She'd never visited Arizona. It wouldn't be as exciting as a trip to the east coast, but it still offered a new experience, and that made her catch her breath.

One phrase in the next paragraph grabbed and held her attention. Trial basis. To begin working for the magazine, she'd have to quit her job at the newspaper. Yet the position offered no security.

She could play it safe and decline the job she'd wanted so much, or she could take a risk and try something new. Something outside her comfort zone. Hating to admit it, an hour on stage beating skins with the drummer from Smashing Glass had given her a taste for adventure.

C.J. Brody lived for risks, didn't he? The drummer wouldn't hesitate to quit a newspaper job if it meant he got to do something different and interesting. That said a lot about what he thought of her. If he'd considered her different and interesting, he would've tried to keep her from leaving the party. She would always wonder what could've happened if she'd stayed.

"Hey, girl," said Amy, her voice hitching with surprise.

Sindra stepped off the elevator. "What are you doing at my desk?"

Her friend smiled and held up a wad of sticky notes. "Just phone messages. Don't worry. I took care of them."

"From who?"

Amy waved a dismissive hand. "It's about the interview Friday night."

"Weird." Why would anyone call her when her friend had done the interview and written the article?

"Exactly. So are you done moping? You've been down ever since we left the amphitheater."

"I'm done. Promise."

"Okay." Amy moved to her own desk and threw the notes in a wastepaper basket. "I never knew you could play the drums like that."

She hadn't, either. She'd taken lessons and played from sheet music in school, but freestyle had been her dad's specialty. She couldn't remember a night she'd enjoyed so much.

She sent her friend an apologetic smile and booted her computer. "You know how I applied for a job with Fine Cuisine Magazine?"

"Yeah?" Amy hiked a hip onto the edge of her desk.

"I got it, sort of."

Her friend clapped with delight. "Sin, that's awesome. Wait. What do you mean by sort of?"

"They're sending me to Phoenix to review a couple restaurants. They're paying for everything, but it's a trial. If they like my reviews, they'll hire me as one of their traveling reviewers." She couldn't shake the notion that it wouldn't fulfill her like she hoped. Great food? She was there. Travel? She was all over it. But writing about meals, service and ambiance? Not so much.

"What's wrong?" Amy asked.

Sindra opened her writing program and began typing a resignation. "This might sound strange, but since Friday night when I'd played the drums like someone possessed, I'm having a hard time. Writing about food here in town isn't satisfying. I'm thrilled to get this chance. I have to give it a try. I've wanted it too long."

"So you're taking some time off to go to Phoenix?"

C.J. popped into her mind. Whoa. What did he have to do with anything? She shook her head. "I leave in the morning. I won't be back until Wednesday."

"John's not going to go for that. You know he won't approve vacation if you don't request it at least a month ahead."

Sindra kept her eyes on her monitor. "I'm not going to ask for vacation. I'm quitting."

"What?" Her friend came off her desk with a start. "You can't quit. Who's going to watch out for you?"

"Watch out for me?" She frowned. "What are you talking about?"

"You're so naïve. People will use you if you don't..."

Sindra sighed and returned to typing. "I appreciate your worry, but I'm not stupid. My dad was a rock god. I've seen things that would turn your hair white." She fingered some of her hair and laughed. "See what happened to me? I'm not naïve. I don't need anyone to take care of me."

"I didn't mean it that way."

"Yes, you did." She smiled and sent her resignation to the printer and stood. "You're my friend, not my mother. You worry about Amy. I've got Sin covered."

"Look, I'm sorry—"

"It's fine. I'll call you when I get back." Shoving the magazine's letter in her purse, she took the resignation and headed for John's office. Her heart thumped in time with her footsteps. A wonderful new beginning waited for her in Phoenix. She sensed it deep in her bones.

"We're ordering in. You want something?" Jet reached for a phone and tossed him a box of ribbed condoms from the care package Mrs. Cavanaugh had waiting for them when they arrived in Phoenix.

"I'm going stir-crazy. Hell, no." C.J. headed for the door to their suite. "See ya later."

"Stay out of trouble," called Cal from a corner where he held a cell phone to his ear. "I mean it."

C.J. wanted to shoot him the bird, but they needed Calvin Spence. He really treated them right, and as far as talent agents went, Cal was actually a decent human being. The guys would never forgive him if he offended him.

"Don't do anything you'd do," said Justin with a smirk, waving goodbye with a hotel menu.

Grabbing his drumsticks off a table near the door, he offered a halfhearted kiss-my-ass salute on his way out. He tapped his sticks along the wall to the elevator, used the tip of one to press the call button then put on sunglasses and rapped against the car wall on the ride to the lobby.

Sindra's face haunted him, and he planned to drink it into oblivion. But dinner first. Someplace nice.

He marched to the concierge's counter. A thin woman in a pale blue suit and uptight hairdo already spoke with the concierge, so C.J. stepped behind her and waited his turn. Though she had a pert rear end, he expected pinched features when she turned.

When she pivoted to leave, she wore Sindra Karriker's face. Great, now he saw her where she wasn't. After leaving seven unreturned messages at the newspaper, he'd gotten a clue. She wasn't interested. So why couldn't he let her go? He closed his eyes.

"You."

If the woman asked for his autograph, he'd say something not good for the band's public image. He opened his eyes, surprised she still looked like Sindra. Blinking, he moved closer. She stayed the same.

"I'm here reviewing restaurants. Are you playing Phoenix? You're staying at this hotel?"

"You never called." Shit. How pathetic did he sound? He resisted an overwhelming urge to knock a fist on his forehead.

"Nice to see you, too," she said, her tone laced with sarcasm.

"Sorry, but you never called me back." Okay, he needed to turn around and leave. He removed his sunglasses. Would she notice if he slunk to the hotel's bar? Dinner be damned.

"As I recall," she said, planting a slender hand on her hip, "you let me leave the party without your number."

What kind of game did she play? Leaning close, he scowled. "I didn't let you do anything. I asked you to stay. Besides, I left you my number all seven times I called the newspaper. Haven't you people ever heard of voicemail?"

Her attitude evaporated. "You left messages for me at work?"

"Yeah." Shouldering past, he approached the counter. What was it about this woman that drove him to distraction? He could have any hot babe he wanted, so why did he waste energy wanting the one he couldn't?

"I didn't get them." She touched his arm murmuring, "I'm going to kill Amy."

Halting, he closed his eyes. Her hand burned an aching awareness into him. Opening his lids, he stared straight ahead.

The concierge gave him an impatient but curious glance.

"I would've called you," Sindra said.

Giving his back to the man behind the counter, C.J. offered the beautiful drummer his full attention. "Yeah?"

A small smile curved her pink lips. "Yeah."

"What ya got planned for tonight?" An image of her slowly stripping from her too prim suit and letting down her hair came unbidden to his mind.

"Well, I'm headed for a restaurant called the Phoenix Flame. This very nice gentleman has made the arrangements."

The concierge gave a polite nod.

"Are you asking me out?" C.J. took a step closer.

"A date? Um, sure. Want to come?"

Like she couldn't believe. "Let me think about it."

"Of course. I don't want to interfere with your plans. I've got to go if I'm going to make my reservation. Maybe we'll see each other around." She retreated three paces toward the exit.

"Wait a second." He was a nughead. "I'm not about to watch you walk away a second time. I'm with you."

She smiled.

Slipping on his sunglasses, he flashed her what he hoped passed for a debonair grin and took her elbow. "Will they let me in wearing leather?"

She stopped and eyed his black leather boots, pants, and jacket. "You're going to need a tie."

The concierge cleared his throat and held out a slim black leather tie.

"Cool." C.J. accepted it. "You're good."

"Merely doing my job. I'll call ahead and let the restaurant know the reservation is now for two. Mr. Brody, Ms. Karriker, have a good evening."

C.J. escorted Sindra toward the exit. "Whatever they're paying that guy, it's not enough."

She nodded and laughed. "You didn't even tell him your name."

He shrugged. "I'm used to it."

Outside, a cab waited. The driver asked, "Going to the Phoenix Flame?"

The lessons in good manners Jet's mother had tried to teach him over the years came flooding in. Holding open the cab door for her, he took her hand and assisted her in then slid beside her.

She gave him a bemused smile. "You're quite the gentleman."

He chuckled. He'd never been called a gentleman before. Setting his drumsticks on the seat between them, he got to work on the tie. "Not what you expected from a drummer?"

"Actually, my dad is a complete gentleman." She took the sticks and held them reverently, as if they were made of precious metal.

"He's from a different generation. Most drummers I've met are animals like me." Oops.

"Amy warned me about your reputation." She cut her gaze his way then drummed on his thigh.

A thrill shivered through him. His fingers fumbling with the tie, he stared at her fingers working the sticks in a gentle rhythm. What were they talking about? Reputation. Right. "I've got a rock-n-roll reputation."

She released a sharp breath. "You've got a bad boy rep."

"Same thing."

"Is it?" Her eyes narrowed.

"Maybe. Well, mostly. I tend to get in trouble a lot." Not tonight, though. Not with her.

"I see." Her voice dipped to a soft, sultry quality. "You can't get me kicked out of this restaurant. After dinner, though, you can go wild."

"Promise?" He wanted to go wild on her naked body. He studied her suit. How hard would he have to work to remove it? "You really didn't get any of my messages?"

Sindra shook her head. "Do you remember Amy? She busted your balls Friday night."

Too well. "Yeah."

"I think she threw them out before I got to work yesterday."

"She really hates me."

Sindra stopped drumming and gazed beyond their driver and out the windshield. "It's not that. She doesn't want you to hurt me."

"She thinks I'll hurt you?" Satisfied the tie hung straight, he reclaimed his drumsticks.

"Amy thinks you'll use me."

What could he say? He had done that with a lot of other women. Hell, with every other woman. Every city of every tour for the past three years. How could he convince Sindra he wouldn't treat her the same?

"She doesn't have any reason to worry," she said before he could speak.

"Why?" The taxi pulled to the curb of the restaurant glowing from fire troughs and spotlights, and C.J. paid the driver before sliding out after her. "Why shouldn't she worry?"

"Because I'm not going to be used. By anyone." Inside, she gave the maître d' her name, and the man personally led them immediately to a prime table a few seats from a grand piano where a player massaged elegant music from the keys.

"You're not so impressed by my fame that you'll fall into my bed?" A self-confident woman with a mind of her own who didn't want a piece of him because of what he did for a living? Now there was a refreshing idea.

She laughed while perusing the wine menu. "First, what's so impressive about a guy who does what my dad did? Second, it's not your bed. It's the hotel's."

Setting his drumsticks on the table, he removed and set his sunglasses atop them. So she wouldn't go easily. He liked a challenge. "Both very good points."

Chapter Six

Enjoying the way C.J. stared at her as if she were the gourmet meal, Sindra found it difficult to concentrate. She had a fair idea of the restaurant's wine choices, so she switched to the main menu.

"This is the job you told me about at the party? You got it? I can't imagine the newspaper would send you out of town, much less to another state, to eat at a fancy restaurant." He glanced around.

"Definitely not the newspaper."

"Congratulations."

"Thank you. Aren't you going to look at the menu?" Studying his profile, she enjoyed the strong lines of his face.

"You know food. You pick."

"I know food but I don't know what you like." She hoped he liked her.

"I'm not picky, but don't order me brains or internal organs."

She laughed and nodded.

He turned consuming brown eyes on her. "What's the name of this magazine? You're a restaurant critic, or a food critic?"

She cringed. "I really don't like that term. Critic. I prefer reviewer. I'm reviewing restaurants for Fine Cuisine Magazine."

"You don't like to be called a critic?" He gave her a hard look. "Isn't that what you are?"

"Sure, but critic implies I'm here to be critical and find fault. I'm not." At least, she hoped she had a positive review to give. Nobody had come to offer service yet, and she began to doubt she would write a glowing article.

"So, if the food stinks, the silverware is dirty, and service sucks, you're not going to say so?"

Was he trying to vex her? "I'm not going to lie, but I'm always searching for the wonderful elements."

C.J. shook his head. "Are you sure this is the job for you?"

"No." She supposed the best reviewers were cynical. She lacked that characteristic, but she could develop it. Couldn't she? Did she want to?

"Why don't you play? Drums, I mean. You're really good."

Play? Professionally? "I never thought about it. It was my dad's job."

He leaned forward, his expression intent. "So think about it. Start a band."

Good Lord. Start a band? No way. "As much as I enjoy music and being around the people who make it happen, I'm not one of them. It's fun, and drumming makes me happy, but I don't want to do it for a living."

Leaning back in his seat, he fingered his cloth napkin. "That's too bad. I'd play with you anytime."

"Me, too. So, tell me why you try so hard."

"With you?" He smirked.

A lump formed in her throat, and she swallowed past it. "No. With your antics. The girls. The drinking. The arrests."

"Antics?" Crossing his arms over his chest, he gave her a quizzical stare.

"Yes, you're not really like that." She suspected he acted that way for a reason, but she couldn't discern why.

"You sound confident. What makes you think I'm not a party animal?"

She laughed. Despite near constant news clips showing pictures of him in compromising situations, she couldn't think of him as a party animal. He'd behaved as a gentleman ever since the concert.

Before she could respond, a waitress arrived. She placed water on the table then took Sindra's wine and appetizer order.

"Are you going to be satisfied with wine?" she asked when the waitress left.

"Probably not. Before I found you in the lobby, I'd planned to get wasted tonight." He squared his shoulders as if challenging her to judge him.

"Sounds like fun," she said, refusing to take the bait.

"Well, it's not."

She closed the menu and set it aside. "Then why do it?"

"You know, Sin, maybe you're right." He leaned forward and braced forearms against the edge of the cloth-covered table. "Maybe I'm not a party animal by nature, but I've become one. It's not easy, either. I put a lot of time and effort into it."

How could he make such a ridiculous statement with a straight face? Fighting an amused smile, she said, "Which brings me back to my question. Why do it?"

"Because our band needs the publicity. The other guys – it's all about the music for them. Our first big year, after we landed a top talent agent and went on tour as the opening act for Back Alley, it was great. We went out every night, partied hard, rocked hard, lived the rock-n-roll." Excitement and frustration sparked from his gaze. "Then we got famous. On our world tour, we had a band opening for us. My friends stopped partying."

"So?" Sindra liked how the look in his eyes reminded her of his expression when he played drums.

"What do you mean 'so'? A new rock band that doesn't party? We're twenty-eight. All four of us. Not eighty. None of us are married. Jet's *in love* with a new girl every month, and Chaz never takes women to his room. Never. If he hadn't been as wild as me that first year, I might think he's gay. Only Justin has a woman he's serious about. I couldn't take the chance of having our band get a reputation for being a bunch of boring guys."

"I guess it never occurred to you that your fans might love you for your music and performance, not your lifestyle. I went to one of your concerts. I've heard some of your songs on the radio. Smashing Glass rocks harder than other bands, and you guys put on an exciting show. That's what made you famous."

"Not me. The band. Justin and Jet write the songs. They play the music with Chaz. They're the face of Smashing Glass."

Her heart went out to him. "You really love them. I can tell, but why do you think you're less than they are?"

He frowned. "Less than them? What do you mean?"

Didn't he see his own inferiority complex? She stared him down.

Fidgeting a bit, he ran a finger along the frame of his sunglasses. Did he want to put them on and hide from her? That was it. He spent his life hiding.

She asked, "Do you think they're smarter? More important? More valuable than you?"

A muscle jumped at his jaw, and his eyes went steely. "I hold my own, thank you. I didn't come here to get psychoanalyzed. Where the hell's that wine?"

Sindra reached across the table and took his hand. He froze, and she smiled. "You're important."

"To you?"

She asked, "Do you really want to go there? Because my mama raised a confident daughter. I'll tell you exactly what's on my mind."

His eyes widened a fraction then he grasped her fingers and caressed his thumb across the back of her hand. "Okay, maybe we shouldn't go there yet."

"I know a thing or two about drumming." She stifled a shiver of thrill at his touch.

"No kidding. You slaughtered the skins Friday

night. Impressed the hell out of me."

"Thanks. I was trying hard." Did she admit that aloud? "You say hell a lot."

"Why not? It's where I'm headed." C.J. winked.

"You really believe that?"

"I don't know what I believe."

The waitress arrived with a plate of crab dip and steaming pita chips, which she placed at the center of the table. She poured a sampling of wine into C.J. glass and waited.

He sent Sindra a questioning glance. Fighting a giggle, she gave him a faint nod. He took a sip, made a thoughtful face then approved the bottle. The waitress filled both of their glasses and set the bottle on the table. After taking their meal orders, she headed for the kitchen.

"Sorry about that," he said. "I'm really clueless, aren't I?"

She glanced at their still joined hands. "You should give yourself more credit."

What was it about this girl? She made him want to shed his party attitude and treat her like a lady. Though classy, she slew a set of drums and looked like she stepped from a music video when she wore blue jeans and a halter-top. Plus she drank beer. It blew his mind how she appeared comfortable in a five-star restaurant, dressed in a suit, ordering a meal that would result in a bill higher than a night's stay in his five-hundred-a-night suite.

She made him wish he knew more about cultured living. She made him wish he was a better man.

"You got serious. Did I say something wrong?" she asked.

"No way."

She took a round bread-thing and used it to scoop a white cream sauce with stringy chunks in it. "Careful. It's hot." With delicate precision, she sank straight white teeth into it, biting off half and closing her eyes.

He imagined far more interesting uses for those gorgeous teeth, all involving one part of his body or another. He needed to get a grip.

Releasing her hand, he gave the dish a skeptical glare.

"Try it," she urged. She popped the other half in her mouth, chewed, and swallowed. "You're wild by your own admission. You're supposed to take risks, try new things when other people won't."

He couldn't let her outdo him. Then again, how cool would he look if he vomited at her fancy dinner review? He gulped. Choosing a hot bread chip, he dipped it into the sauce.

"Come on, C.J. Dig some onto your pita."

Pita? This did not look promising. He sent the round chip into the small bowl and piled on the chunky concoction. "What is this, exactly?"

"Try it then I'll tell you."

Uh-oh. Attempting not to grimace, he took the entire chip into his mouth and chewed. An explosion of flavor weakened his spine and made him moan with delight. Sweet seafood combined with soft cheese and the wholesome baked goodness of the pita was delicious.

"My God, that's good," he said after swallowing. He reached for another chip.

"It's blue crab prepared in cream cheese and Parmesan. I can tell they hand-make the pita. These are fabulous."

Her fingers brushed his at the plate. Lingering over the dip to prolong the contact, he dropped his gaze to her lips. He looked forward to the sight of those teeth biting into a chip.

Damn, she was sexy. He sent another smothered chip to his tongue and chewed, imagining the fun if she let him coat her breasts in the dip then feast on her.

"I'd like to talk about why you think you're less important than your band mates."

She was tenacious. He had to give her that. "I

never said I thought I'm less important."

"You don't have to. It shows in the way you behave."

If she weren't so beautiful, he'd tell her to mind her own business. He couldn't take his eyes off her and, in a way, he sort of wanted her in his business. He really was losing it.

"I'd rather not talk about it," he said.

"May I make one comment then?"

She appeared so earnest, how could he deny her? "Fine."

"You're the heartbeat of Smashing Glass." Sindra cemented her statement with a firm nod.

She'd hooked him. "Okay. I'm game. Why am I the heartbeat?"

"It's not a game. It's the truth. Think about your concerts. The opening song begins with an instrumental layering. Other than a few screams and whistles, the audience waits. What are they waiting for?"

"The beat."

"Exactly. The beat heats the blood, makes people move, and gives the band a foundation for the melody. Without you, it's just nice music. With your beat, it's magic. It's rock. There's power in those songs because you put it there."

He'd never thought of it that way. When she said it, though, he heard the truth. "Makes total sense. But any drummer could do it."

"Really?" Taking a sip of wine, she narrowed her eyes and studied him over the rim of her glass. "You're more than the band's drummer. You're their friend. Amy told me you guys have been playing together since high school. They'd never be able to replace you."

"If you asked them, I bet they'd tell you they'd be glad to get rid of me. I irritate the crap out of them." He chuckled.

"You mean you irritate the shit out of them?" Her lips quirked into a half smile.

"Well, yeah. I didn't want to offend you."

"I grew up around a rock band, remember?"

How could he forget?

"Here's something else to consider. You're very good. I'd bet money you could hold your own against my dad."

"What?" Now she blew smoke up his ass. "Nobody's as good as George Karriker. Definitely not me. You're better than I am."

She shook her head. "Don't bring me into it. I'm an amateur. I'm serious, though. You did some combinations in your concert Friday that I doubt my dad could've done without trying really hard and messing up a lot."

"Like I believe that." Who did she try to fool?

"My dad didn't drum like he did without working for it. He practiced constantly. I remember overhearing him talking to my mom once, and he told her he didn't deserve his reputation as the best. He said the best wouldn't have to work as hard as he did to get the rhythms right."

C.J. hesitated. Was it true? "I know how he feels. I beat my drums until my shoulders and back burn. I want perfection, you know? Then again, nobody's out there calling me the best."

She cast him an impish grin. "Maybe after dinner I'll show you a few things."

Chapter Seven

Sindra couldn't remember the last time she'd had so much fun at a five-star restaurant. Halfway through the meal, C.J. made an excuse and headed toward the restaurant bar. He left his sticks and glasses at the table, so she didn't worry that he'd gone. Still, she wondered if he didn't like his beef tips in port reduction sauce with asparagus and risotto.

When he returned, he cleaned his plate. "That was incredible."

"I'm so glad you liked it. You had me scared when you left. I thought maybe I ordered the wrong meal for you." She crossed her knife atop her overturned fork, and the waitress came immediately to clear the plates. "My lamb and artichoke hearts were first-rate."

"What are you going to show me after we leave?"

"You'll have to wait, Mr. Impatient." She gave the waitress a nod, and the woman came and filled their cups with coffee.

"I'm not so great with waiting," he said. After taking a sip of coffee, he glanced toward the service station. "What do you say we pay our check and head out of here?"

Sindra laughed. She suspected she wouldn't get much writing done that night, so she pulled a pen and small notebook from her purse. "You weren't kidding. You really are impatient. First, the check is paid. This particular restaurant is billing the magazine. Second,

I'm working. I can't simply leave. I have to at least taste dessert, check out the ladies room, and visit the bar. How was it, by the way?"

"I wouldn't know. I haven't been. You sure we can't cut out of here?"

"Positive." If he hadn't gone to the bar during the meal, where had he gone? The men's room was in the opposite direction.

Dessert arrived, a single slice of caramel drizzled Bavarian cream confection. C.J. eyed it but didn't move to try it.

"Come on. One bite," she prompted, sinking her fork into the decadent pie.

"I'm not big on sweets. Do you want me to go to the men's room? For your article, I mean?"

She laughed around the smooth textures in her mouth, enjoying the contradiction of firm caramel and soft cream. Swallowing, she decided a single bite would suffice. Any more and she'd go into sugar shock. "Only if you actually need to use it."

He barked a laugh. His approval put her on top of the world. As she rose to head for the ladies' room, he brushed her hand with his fingers. It sent a tingle up her arm that lasted through her viewing of the restroom, a walk around the large bar area, and her stroll to the table. What would a touch like that on a more sensitive part of her body do to her?

"We're on our way," he said into his cell phone, standing as she approached. Flipping it closed, he put on his shades while collecting his drumsticks.

Anxious to go, she took her purse and dropped her business card next to the nearly untouched dessert. She hooked fingers into the crook of his elbow and liked the way he offered her a bemused smile then walked a bit taller toward the exit.

"I think this is the first meal I've had in a restaurant where I wasn't asked for my autograph." He grinned.

"Nice, huh?"

Outside, a black stretch limousine monopolized

the curb.

"That's ours," he said.

"You got us a limo?" Sindra couldn't help being impressed. He made an effort when he really didn't have to, and it meant a lot.

The half bottle of wine she'd consumed with dinner kicked in as she slid onto the backseat. It relaxed her and chipped away at her inhibitions. When he joined her, she didn't scoot to put space between them. She let him get hip-to-hip, thigh-to-thigh.

He bent a bit, his face close. "You want to go dancing?"

"In a business suit? I don't think so."

The driver got in, and C.J. instructed him to drive them to the hotel. Sindra removed the clip holding her hair in a twist and tossed it in her purse. She fluffed her hair so it fell loose to her waist then unfastened her jacket.

He tugged the knot on his tie until it sat low. "This is a much better look on you."

"Thank you. I think."

Settling against the seatback, he put an arm around her shoulders and tucked his sticks into the crease between seat and back.

"Do you take those everywhere you go?" she asked, peering at the jutting wood.

"No. I've been curious about something."

Leaning a shoulder against the backrest, she ran a leisurely fingertip along his leather tie, appreciating his firm body beneath. "Go on."

"At dinner, you said you'd tell me exactly what was on your mind if you wanted me to go there."

"I remember."

"So what was on your mind?"

She laughed and gave his tie a playful tug. Could he handle it? "Now you're ready to go there? Okay. I like you, C.J. Really like you. I get butterflies looking at you. But I think you expect more than I'm willing to give."

He arched his eyebrows. "A kiss?"

"Sex."

"Yeah. I kinda figured after Friday night."

"Then you're not expecting me to...you know? Tonight?"

He grinned, his eyes sparkling. "Why don't we play it by ear and see what happens?"

Finding his smile contagious, she didn't try to fight one of her own. "Don't raise your hopes. There is something I want to do, though."

"What's that?"

"Kiss."

"Now you're talking." He rose from his slouch and leaned close.

She placed a staying hand on his chest. "Not this second. Later."

He frowned. "When later?"

She chuckled. "Gee, what do you say we play it by ear and see what happens?"

"You're so funny," he said dryly.

"Not really." She wanted to kiss him right there, and maybe not stop until they said goodbye. She suspected he would kiss her senseless, and she'd do something she'd regret tomorrow. No, better to wait.

"You're going to make me crazy," he said.

"That could be fun." Especially since he robbed her of any good sense and made her a bit crazy, too. If not for her mother's voice in her head reminding her to make reasonable choices, she'd happily fall into bed with him and let the half-notes fall where they may the next morning.

As the driver pulled to the hotel's main entrance, C.J. wrapped some of her hair around his finger. "I like your hair."

"Don't you think it's boring?"

"No way. I don't think I've seen anything like it since I was a boy."

The driver opened her door.

Without letting go of her hair, C.J. snatched his sticks from the seat's crease and scooted out after her. "There used to be a candy shop on the corner of the block where I lived with my mom."

"In Chicago? You live in Chicago, right?"

"I do." He led the way to the elevators, his thumb stroking the strands around his finger, and pressed the call button. "The lady who owned the shop used to make amazing lemon taffy. It was really pale with streaks of white and yellow. I haven't thought if it in fifteen years until I saw your hair."

By far, that was the coolest compliment she'd ever received. It completely changed her opinion. For the first time since seeing Billy Jo Graham's beautiful curls in first grade, she liked her straight hair.

He released it as the elevator doors slid open, and she swallowed past a thick disappointment. Who knew she'd like him playing with her hair?

"Your place or mine?" he asked, finger poised over the keypad.

"Mine. I have something to show you, remember?"

He waggled his eyebrows.

"Not that," she gently chastised. "Sixth floor."

During the silence of their ride, the anticipation of her promised kiss hung heavily between them. The delicious tension edged her into a slight tremble. Did expectation turn him on as much as it did her? She cut a sideways glance at his lips. Yes. Definitely exciting.

At her room, she unlocked her door and led him in. She threw her jacket on the queen-sized bed. "I'm in town for two nights. How long are you guys here?"

"The concert's tomorrow night then we leave the next morning." He glanced around while she booted her laptop. "What did you want to show me?"

"This." She pointed at the computer screen. "Give it a second and I'll get on the internet. You want anything from the bar?"

"I could use a shot."

She could, too. From the shelf above a miniature refrigerator, she took two tiny bottles of tequila and two shot glasses. She poured, tossed the bottles in a garbage can, and handed him a glass. "Here's to new friends and new adventures."

"Friends and adventures." He swallowed the shot

in a single gulp then bared his teeth. "Oh, yeah. That's the good stuff."

She inhaled a deep breath and downed her drink on a big gulp. Fire burned from her throat to her stomach, making her eyes water. Releasing her breath, she shuddered then sighed as the fire went out and left her warm inside.

Accepting his glass, she stacked it in hers and set it next to the laptop. She typed the National Music Appreciation Association's website address. "Come see. Remember how you said nobody out there calls you the best?"

"Yeah." He came next to her as she maneuvered through a couple pages.

"You're wrong. Look what I found Saturday." She clicked a final link with a flourish. "Ta-da!"

He bent close, as if not believing his eyes. Amidst categories, lists of musicians were proclaimed best in their specialties. C.J. Brody appeared at the top of the page in the largest letters with a picture of him in concert.

"Best Musician of the Year. This is a big deal, right?" he asked.

"It really is. See?" She scrolled down. "You beat out world famous concert pianists, jazz musicians, symphony members. And look. You won Best Performer and Best in Percussion. People are calling you the best." She nudged his arm with her elbow.

"Why don't they tell us about this?"

"I don't know. My dad won Best Musician of the Year and Best Performer in nineteen ninety. He didn't find out until two months later when a reporter asked him about it in an interview. He's never won best in percussion. You're one up on him."

"Way cool." He turned and stared into her eyes. "You're very good for my ego."

"That's not why I'm showing you this. You earned these awards by yourself. Nobody else in the band made the list. You work hard and it shows. People whose opinions matter have noticed. Next time you want to compare yourself with someone, don't look to my dad. Look in the mirror."

"Damn."

"Why'd you say that?" Okay, she didn't want to wait any longer to kiss him.

"You ought to give pep talks for a living."

She smiled. "I'm telling the truth."

His gaze dropped to her mouth. "I like your truth."

"Kiss me." She placed a hand on his shoulder, and not giving him a chance to respond, leaned in and pressed her lips to his.

Chapter Eight

With the top of his head ready to blast off, C.J. pulled Sin close and took over the kiss. The woman was too much. Kind, beautiful, smart. Yet unlike every woman he'd known, she seemed oblivious to the fact that she was special. He marveled at her genuine and giving nature.

She hummed a sweet moan and fitted her curves to him. He adored how she closed her eyes and wrapped her arms around his neck. Even if she hadn't told him she wouldn't sleep with him tonight, he couldn't. He groaned in painful denial, willing his hardening jimmy to wilt. As much as he wanted to bury himself in her, she deserved more than mindless sex with a man who hardly knew her.

She deserved a guy who would value her, spoil her, and love her. Someone who could commit, who could make her a permanent part of his life. She deserved the kind of man he couldn't be. Damn it.

He'd have to walk away, a difficult prospect to say the least. For now, he could spend some time with her. Enjoy her company and kisses. When they had to part, he'd man up and do the right thing. He'd say goodbye.

She touched the tip of her tongue to his top lip, and his resolve faltered. His senses spinning, he urged her to open. She did. Their tongues met in a maddening rush, hers sliding along his and tasting of tequila and the sweet cream of her dessert.

Her perfume, faint and inviting, laced his nostrils and made him want to undress her. Want to press his nose to her stomach and inhale. Want to taste her and touch her and... He groaned.

He hadn't done this outside a drunken stupor in three years. He'd forgotten how intoxicating anticipation could be. Or maybe Sin intoxicated him. His mind whirled, and his senses reeled.

Combing his fingers through her silken hair, he imagined her sliding the gorgeous pale strands along his naked body. He imagined her kisses across his chest, down his stomach, and lower.

He kissed the coolest, most sophisticated, most talented, smartest woman he'd ever met. He couldn't believe she let him. A shiver ran through him, raising goose bumps on his arms, as she stroked fingertips up the sides of his neck then along the outer curves of his ears.

A hunger like nothing he'd ever experienced shook him. The nearby bed beckoned, and he growled with the effort to resist toppling her onto it. Did she have the same response to his kiss? Her soft moan and tightening arms told him she did.

His temperature rose, and his leather became too hot and too tight. Keeping his mouth working against hers, he shrugged his jacket off and flung it aside. He hugged her close and inhaled a sharp breath through his nostrils. His black T-shirt and her thin white blouse did nothing to reduce the feel of her hard nipples against his chest.

Her warmth, her curves, her scent and taste conspired to seduce him. He didn't want to scare her. He had to take it slowly. Could he change her mind about spending the night with him? *No. Don't even think about it.* But the straining crotch on his pants made it impossible to contemplate anything else.

He needed to get out before he peeled off her top. He took her gently by the shoulders and reluctantly pulled away. "I should go."

"You should?" She blinked.

He adored her breathlessness. "Maybe I shouldn't. Maybe I should stay."

She sobered, her eyelids abandoning their sleepy, sexy droop. "No. You were right. Can I see you tomorrow?"

She was so sweet. "I have a concert tomorrow night. We spend most of the day in setup and sound checks."

She headed for the door and gave him a shy smile. "You've got to eat, don't you?"

He found his jacket on the floor at the far side of the bed. Scrunching it in his fist, he followed her to the door. "Sure. What ya got in mind?"

"I have another restaurant to review. Want to come along?"

"Hmm." He stroked his chin, pretending to consider. "The food tonight was pretty good."

"Pretty good?" She gave him a playful swat.

Grasping her arm, he gently pulled her against him. He lowered his face until his lips hovered near hers. "It was good, but not as good as the company. I'll go." Pressing his mouth to hers, he put a hand to her lower back and brought her closer. The woman smelled amazing. Her scent eased inside his head and seduced him as surely as her kiss.

She placed both hands on his chest and urged him away. Though the kiss ended, she stood on swaying legs with her eyes closed. She sent her tongue over her lips as if savoring the taste of him.

His jimmy bucked. He'd never been more turned on. He'd participated in orgies, played at Penthouse sex parties, and been stripped naked and screwed by a bevy of supermodels until his eyes crossed. But nothing turned him on like Sin. He couldn't think. He couldn't move. He could only stare at her fantastic mouth.

Clearing his throat, he shifted to ease the strain in his pants. "If I don't go now, I won't be able to."

She opened her eyes and reached for the door latch.

He didn't miss the tremble in her fingers. She

wanted him. He smiled and gave her a chaste kiss before stepping to the corridor. "What time's your dinner reservation?"

"Seven." She smoothed her hair with a shaking hand.

"That'll work. We don't go on until ten. I'll pick you up here at six-thirty."

She offered a nod and faint smile, but desire shone from her eyes as clearly as a lighthouse beacon. When she didn't close the door, it occurred to him she issued an invitation. If he asked to stay, she'd say yes. The temptation overwhelmed him, and he planted a hand against the wall to keep from wavering.

No. Not tonight. Not like this. Sin wasn't some groupie who only wanted a night with him so she could brag about sleeping with the drummer from Smashing Glass. She was everything he'd wanted when he didn't even known what he wanted. Hell, she was everything and more.

"Goodnight," he managed, dragging the word past reluctant lips – lips that begged to kiss her. Lips that tingled to explore every curve of her.

"Goodnight," she whispered, her features relaxing into a set of resolute disappointment. Without a sound, she closed the door.

God. How was he going to make it through this night? His gait made awkward by the discomfort of his swollen jimmy, he blinked through a haze of need and headed for the suite he shared with Jet.

Sindra slumped against the door. Her legs failed, and she sank to the carpet. That man could kiss. More than that, he really got to her. Maybe because he drummed, like her dad. Maybe because his talent impressed her. She couldn't put her finger on it, but he tipped her past the edge of reason.

Pushing to her feet, she chuckled and made her way to her suitcase. "I'm acting like a star-struck fan.

He's just a guy."

Yet as the words left her lips, she recognized the lie. He wasn't just a guy. He had a special spark in him. An intensity that sucked her in and made her want to dig deeper. He wanted everyone to see him as wild, fun loving, and devil-may-care, but she'd glimpsed another aspect. She suspected he'd given her a peek at the real C.J.

She was in trouble.

She undressed and slipped into a fresh pair of underwear and white tank top. Moving to a vanity with her bag of bathroom essentials, she twisted her hair around her hand. She tied it into a knot-bun and stared at her reflection. "He's a rock star. He sleeps with a different woman every night. He probably does drugs."

Putting toothpaste onto her toothbrush, she leaned closer to the mirror while adding water to the bristles. "He's on a self-destruct course toward an early death. What does he care about me?"

Right. It sounded reasonable. Yet somehow she didn't believe it. He had more to him than rock-n-roll and living in the moment. He hid depth and character.

Brushing her teeth, she narrowed her eyes and wondered how he saw her. Would he open and let her in? Would he consider her worthy of forthright honesty? Or did he simply think of her as another on-the-road conquest?

No. If he meant only to sleep with her, he'd have stopped trying when she walked away Friday night. He certainly wouldn't have come to her room with the understanding that she had no intention of letting him in her bed. Though, heaven help her, she'd have gone there with him both Friday and tonight if he'd made one final attempt after their goodbyes.

She rinsed then smiled. To her reflection, she said. "He's interested. In *you*."

After washing her face, she eyed her laptop. She could go online and dig up his dirt. It's what she meant to do Saturday when she'd discovered his awards and stopped searching. She needed to learn who he really was, not how the public viewed him. Falling on the bed, she hugged a pillow under her and stared at the headboard.

She had never chased bad boys, so why did C.J. hold such fascination for her? Would her parents approve? She rolled onto her back and laughed. For the first time in her life, she didn't care what they thought. Not tonight, anyway. This man was her puzzle. Her secret joy. She couldn't wait to see him again.

Taking a break from writing his first song ever, C.J. spun a drumstick through his fingers then patted a beat on a fabric-covered arm of the sofa next to his chair. He liked the quiet. It hadn't occurred to him how peaceful a hotel room could get in the early morning. Nodding his head to the beat, he sent the sticks back and forth along the sofa's arm until more words came to mind. Then he couldn't get them on the page fast enough.

"Hey, man. Couldn't sleep?" Jet shuffled bare feet across the carpet toward the coffeemaker. He wore red plaid drawstring pajama bottoms and no top. When he rubbed a hand over his face, the thick muscles of his arms and chest bunched.

C.J. turned his attention to Justin's notebook and wrote frantically before the words fled. "Hold on a sec. Let me get this down."

He'd never written a song. Never wanted to. But he awoke with words forming in his mind, and before he finished his shower, the words had gathered into sentences and the sentences into the beginnings of a song. What had Sindra done to him?

Finishing, he closed the notebook with a satisfying thud and tossed it on a coffee table where it landed with a loud slap. He stretched then drummed on the sofa arm. "I slept fine. I can't remember the last night I slept the whole way through."

Jet finished fiddling with the coffeemaker and

flipped the brew switch. Eyeing the notebook, he asked, "What the hell are you talking about? I got back to the room at midnight, and everything was neat and quiet. Justin'll tear your head off if you were messing with his songs."

C.J. shrugged, trying to imitate the beat sequence Sin had done a week ago. "I went to bed early last night. I was unconscious at midnight."

"Yeah, right." Jet guffawed. "You haven't been to sleep before two in the morning since our last year in high school."

"I was last night. Geez, Jet. You always in such a shitty mood first thing in the morning? Battabattabatta Battabatt." He struck an invisible cymbal. "Ching! And if Justin doesn't want us touching his notebook, maybe he shouldn't leave it in our room. Besides, I wasn't messing with his songs. I was writing one."

"He left it so I could finish my second ballad for the next album."

"Whatever." C.J. needed a drum set. This couch wasn't cutting it.

"You expect me to believe you wrote a song? You?" Jet planted a hand on his waist, his pinkie ring glinting in pale sunlight streaming through a window.

C.J. kicked the notebook across the table without missing a beat. "Check it out for yourself, asshole."

Jet blew a breath out his nostrils and picked up the notebook. As he read, his eyebrows slowly climbed his forehead. "Holy shit, Chris."

"C.J."

"Whatever. This is good."

He smiled. "I know."

His friend stared at him. "Okay. Who are you and what have you done with my friend?"

"Funny," he said dully. "Hey, where can I get a suit?"

"What?"

The coffeemaker gurgled, and the smell of fresh coffee filled the room. "I want a cup of that when it's ready. I need to buy a suit. Where can I get one?"

"What for?"

"Dinner tonight. I've got a hot date."

Jet threw his hands high. "What is going on? You promised you'd never get into drugs. So help me—"

"I don't do drugs!" The heat of anger pumped into his face and knotted his stomach. He took a calming breath then quietly said, "You know how I feel about drugs."

Standing statue-still, Jet said, "I know. And I thought I knew you. You're like a brother. What's going on, man?"

"I don't know. I just...well, it's different." He pointed at a laptop with a blackened screen on a table behind the sofa. "Check that out. Someone showed me that last night."

Squinting, his friend went around and slid the mouse. The screen blinked to life and revealed the awards page for the National Music Appreciation Association's website. "No way."

"Cool, huh?"

Jet glanced his way then actually read it. "Damn. I knew you were a genius at percussion, but this blows my mind."

C.J. stopped drumming. "You knew I was a genius?"

"You can't live with someone for more than ten years and not know what makes him special. Man, you're the best. Here's the proof."

He had spent his life trying to shake the smothering shadows of his parents and prove he could do better. Be better. Now, he could believe he'd succeeded.

He relaxed into the chair and grinned. "What's for breakfast?"

Chapter Nine

Biting her lip, Sindra clicked the Send button and released a held breath. Her article about the restaurant would either meet with huge success or miserable failure. No in between on this one. By far, however, it was the easiest, most fun article she'd ever written. She looked forward to writing the next one about her dinner with C.J. tonight. It seemed strange to enjoy her work for a change. She hoped the drummer wouldn't get mad. At least she made deadline...barely.

She stood and smoothed wrinkles from the soft pink skirt of her sleeveless dress then checked her makeup at the vanity. Butterflies upset her stomach. Why was she so nervous? It was only dinner.

But it wasn't. She had to fly home to California tomorrow, and he would leave as the band continued their concert tour. She had no idea what city he played next. No idea when she'd see him again. *If* she'd see him again. A heaviness settled in her chest, and she gave her sternum a thump. She didn't want regret. Especially before she learned what possibilities lay before them.

She hardly knew the man. She wanted to, though. C.J. had layers she wanted to peel.

A knock at the door startled her. Glancing at her watch, she realized the time had gotten away from her. "One sec."

She added gloss to her lips then gathered her purse and jacket from the bed. When she opened the door, her breath caught in her throat. C.J. grinned, his hair tamed and his eyes shining. He looked like a Fortune Five Hundred businessman in a three-piece brown suit shot through with threads of sky blue. He wore a pale blue silk tie with drumsticks embroidered in brown floss, and a blue shirt with brown crisscrossed drumsticks at the points of the collar. His braided leather bracelet peeked from his left cuff. He never appeared to take it off, and she wondered if it had significance.

"You look amazing," she said, stepping into the hallway and letting the door close.

"Thanks. When I took that tie back to the concierge, he told me about a men's shop that could set me up. Didn't think you'd want me wearing leather again, and I figured jeans were out of the question."

"You bought this for today?" She fingered the high-quality material of his lapel.

He pointed to his tie. "Look. Drumsticks. They have an old lady there who did this by hand."

"She did a great job."

Nodding, he asked, "Are you ready?"

She slipped her hand into his. "As ready as I'll be. I tried to research the restaurant but couldn't find much. They don't even have a website."

He led the way to a bank of elevators and pressed the call button. "Do you know what kind of food they serve?"

"I understand they prepare haute cuisine." At his blank stare, she explained, "Food art. Like fancy designer food. A great deal of care is put into presentation to enhance the dining experience. So where are your sticks?"

Ushering her onto an elevator, his hand at the small of her back, he said, "I've been playing all day. I put in two hours this morning and three this afternoon. I'm working on a new lick. Believe me. I had no problem leaving them onstage."

"I guess not," she said. After so much arm work, how could he move? "Five hours already and still a concert to give. Aren't you going to be ready to drop by the end?"

"Nah. I do this for a living, remember?"

In the lobby, she shrugged into her jacket.

"Our ride is here," he said as a limousine arrived at the main entrance.

"You take a limo everywhere?" She tried not to sigh. Why did he try so hard? Didn't he realize she already liked him?

"Pretty much. Except when I'm home. Then I take my motorcycle or drive my car."

She accompanied him outside where the limo's driver held open a door for her. "Why a limo? Why not a taxi or rental car?"

Sliding in beside her, he gathered her in his arms and said low, close to her ear, "Because I'm usually planning to get drunk. Taxis lack discretion, and I shouldn't be driving. Ya can't beat tinted windows for privacy, too. Besides, what's the point of being a rock star if I can't enjoy the perks?"

His warm breath against her ear and cheek caused a shiver of delight to run down her spine and sent the hairs of her arms on end. She whispered, "I want to know more about you."

"What do you want to know?" He pressed a kiss to the curve of her ear then another to the tender spot right behind.

Sindra trembled, wishing he'd do that again. "Well, what are your parents like?"

"Dead."

Oh, God. "I'm so sorry."

"I'm not."

She stiffened. "How can you say that?"

Sighing, he released her and rested against the seatback as the limo inched past bellhops, taxis, and baggage carts. "My dad was a deadbeat. I never knew him. He got my mom pregnant then took off. I heard he died in prison. The only memories I have of my mom are when she was stoned."

Her heart broke for him, and she fought tears.

She could only begin to imagine the loneliness he must have suffered as a child.

He rolled his braided bracelet between thumb and forefinger. "Social Services took me from her when I was eight. She gave me this before I left. She never tried to reclaim me from the foster care system, and she overdosed when I was fifteen."

"I'm so sorry," she whispered past a constricting throat.

Gently touching fingertips to her cheek, he offered a weak smile. "Don't be sad, Sin. I stopped feeling sorry a long time ago. See, I met Jet my first week in high school, and his family was like a dream. I was a real troublemaker my whole life, so none of the foster families kept me longer than a year. When they told me my mom died and they planned to send me to an orphanage in Michigan, I freaked. I ran to Jet's house, and his mom and dad made some phone calls."

She took his hand and leaned a knee against his. "What happened?"

"I don't know how they did it, but they convinced a judge to give them custody of me. They went through a lot to make it happen, and I'll never be able to thank them enough. I got my life straight and lived with them until I was twenty." He smiled. "Jet's like a brother. His mom and dad treated me no differently than they treated him. They really love me, you know? Especially his mom."

"What an incredible gift they gave you."

"It really was. Mrs. Cavanaugh sat me at the kitchen table the day they got the judge's signed Order, and she told me that she knew I'd had a rough life. She said she'd never ask me to be anyone I wasn't or to do anything I didn't want. She simply offered me a home and her love." His lip quivered a bit, and he blinked rapidly before gazing out the window. "That's exactly what she gave me. If I asked for help, she gave it, but she never butted into my personal business. She respected me. I'd never met anyone like her. It's like she completely accepted me for who I was, and she always supported whatever I wanted to do."

"Including the drinking and the women and the arrests?"

He turned and released a breathy laugh. "In a way, I guess. It's like she knew I needed to do it. I could tell she didn't like it and that she worried, but she always sends me condoms in her care packages. Jet's dad tries to talk sense into me, but it's only because he cares about me, too. Every month, she asks me to get a blood test and make sure I haven't caught anything. They're always firm on reminding me that no matter what happens or what I do, they'll never stop loving me. They're real parents. They're what my parents should have been."

Sindra smiled. "Are you serious? She asks you to get tested for STDs?"

"Totally. And I do it because I know it's important to her."

She laughed. "She sounds like an amazing person."

"She is. I love her. Jet, too. And his dad. They're my family, even though I don't live there anymore."

She leaned against him and sighed. What a wonderful support he had. She hoped, one day, she could be part of it.

His heart thudding in heavy two-four time, C.J. stared into Sin's gorgeous eyes and waited for her rejection. He never talked about his past. Other than the band and Jet's parents, few knew about it. He had no clue what made him spill to this beautiful lady, especially since he admired her.

She didn't shy away or lower her lashes. She didn't get a disgusted expression or look at him like he'd grown a second head. What did she think?

He cleared his throat. "I told you my dad was a criminal and my mom was an addict."

"Yes. You did." She straightened and cupped his

face then leaned close and kissed him.

It stunned him into stillness. Then it hit him like a hammer that she wanted him despite the dark ugliness of his childhood. She accepted him with his baggage. Grasping her slender arms, he kissed her as if his life depended on it. Slanting across her mouth, he worked his lips on hers and urged her to open.

She did with a sweet submission. He adored her surrender. It told him she didn't consider him beneath her. Sliding a hand behind his neck, she drew him nearer and sent her tongue into a sensuous dance with his.

She felt soft and delicate and feminine. Her spirit contained strength and fearlessness, though. Next to her, he was more a man than he'd ever been. Kissing her, he absorbed some of her strength. He tasted her determination, and for once, his past didn't matter. What anyone thought didn't matter. Nothing mattered but her.

Winding down the kiss, he stroked fingers through her soft, straight hair. His mouth close to hers, he whispered, "You're amazing."

She opened her eyes, the blue of her irises sparkling like aquamarine. "I was thinking the same about you."

He jerked upright. "You were?"

"Yes." She snuggled against him and settled her head on his shoulder. "Look how far you've come. Look what you've accomplished. You could've let your childhood consume you and turn you into a victim. You could've ended up like your parents."

"Like hell," he murmured.

"Exactly. Like hell. You turned it around and used it as an example of what not to do...though you have been arrested. More than once, according to my friend, Amy."

"I'm not a criminal. Lewd behavior and disturbing the peace stuff. You know. Rock star nonsense."

She laughed. "You behaved that way because you thought you were supposed to? Because you're a rock musician?"

"Well yeah, I mean..."

"Your band doesn't have its huge fan base because of how you behave. It's because you create great music. You guys put on a spectacular show. You shouldn't care what people think. Be yourself and be true to it. People will respect that."

Be himself? He lived in fear of it. Would he be like his criminal dad or his addict mom? Would he be a loser with no personality? "You sound like Justin."

She turned in his arms and gave him a serious stare. "You're with me. Not once have you gotten drunk, behaved rudely, or chased after pretty girls."

He laughed. He couldn't help it. "I chased after you. How do you know I'm not faking it? Maybe I'm pretending to be a decent human being when I really want to get drunk, be rude, and chase you around the restaurant."

Slapping him lightly on the chest, she said, "Knock it off. I mean it. You're not getting by with the minimum effort or abusing your money and fame. You worked really hard to become as great a drummer as you are, and you've got awards to prove it. Doesn't it feel good to receive acknowledgment for a job well done?"

It really did. "I became a drummer because of your father."

"He's so talented. You picked a good role model."

"How far is this restaurant?" He glanced out the window at passing office buildings and storefronts.

She knocked on a glass partition separating them from the driver.

C.J. reached up and pressed a switch that lowered the glass.

"How much further?" she asked.

"Two minutes, ma'am. Right around the corner."

Settling against the backrest, she whispered, "He called me ma'am."

"That's because you're a classy woman." He licked lip-gloss from his lips, liking the sweet flavor.

She took a powder compress from her purse and

checked her face. "Classy, huh? Classy women play the drums, hang out with rock stars, and live in tiny one-bedroom apartments?"

"You do, so yeah."

"You think I'm classy?" She cut a curious, half-smiling glance his way.

"The classiest I've ever met." He envied the wand of her lip-gloss applicator as it glided over her shapely lips. When they pulled in front of the restaurant, he gazed out the window and winced. Heads turned. He had hoped there wouldn't be a scene when he stepped out. Last night had been a dream of anonymity.

"Well, that's sad. Though my mom will be proud to hear it. She'll think she did something right."

"Did she ever," he said under his breath.

The driver opened his door at curbside, and C.J. exited. Avoiding making eye contact with the onlookers, he offered Sin a hand and helped her out. Murmurs began along the sidewalk, and when he turned, someone shouted his name.

"We need to get inside. Hurry," he said low in her ear.

She giggled as they rushed inside, barely missing a press of fans. "That was exciting."

He used to think so, too. Now he worried for her privacy. He didn't want her face printed on the covers of tabloids. Bimbos tended to enjoy it, but Sindra had a life. Had a career. She was the opposite of bimbo.

She flipped her hair over one shoulder and straightened her jacket. "It's like the old days with my dad. I don't think he ever got accosted outside a fancy restaurant, though. His fans tended to be a lot younger and not interested in fine living."

He shook his head. "It's weird. Normally I love the attention. It means people still like what Smashing Glass is doing."

"I sense a 'but'."

He kissed her cheek then led the way to the maître d'. "But this evening, I'm with you. I don't want the craziness."

"If it's any consolation, I don't mind. I'm used to it. Really. It comes with being part of a popular rock band, and being an incredibly talented musician."

"I swear you're the coolest woman I've ever met."

"Good to hear." She laughed. Turning to the maître d', she said, "Reservation for two under Karriker."

More than ever, he realized he didn't deserve her.

Chapter Ten

"Are they kidding?"

Sindra grinned as C.J. shot the waiter's back a glare. She loved how he didn't try to fake refined manners. "Haute cuisine isn't intended for satiation of hunger as much as satiation of the senses."

"Can I have that in English?"

"It's not meant to fill you. It's food in art – attractive to the eye and flavorful in the extreme. Try it."

He chose one of two pâté hors d'oeuvres and popped the entire morsel in his mouth. As an explosion of flavor nearly overwhelmed him, he closed his eyes and chewed slowly. "Wow. That was probably the best thing I've ever tasted. I need about ten more."

"The next course will be bigger. I promise." She ate her hors d'oeuvre in two bites, savoring the tangy combination of goose liver, bacon, and rich cream inserted with crispy sesame sticks and topped by shards of buttery pastry. "If I tell you something, do you promise not to get angry?"

"No." With a twinkle of mischief in his brown eyes, he took a sip of red wine.

Her stomach lurched. She should've broached the subject before she began eating. "I turned in my article about last night's dinner."

"Why would I get mad about that?"

"It's about you, sort of." Hiding a grimace, she waited for him to frown.

He didn't. "What do you mean by sort of?"

She released a held breath. He seemed more open to the idea than she expected. Letting her enthusiasm and hope for the project show, she said, "I'm proposing a series of articles to the magazine called Educating Henry."

"Who's Henry?"

"You. I really enjoyed watching you experience dinner last night. It was fun teaching you about the food. So I wrote my article around you. Of course, I called you Henry and never hinted at who you really are."

He gave a thoughtful nod. "Can I read it?"

"Sure. You absolutely may. I'd love it if you did." Her heart beat faster at the idea of him reading and liking what she wrote. Then again, he might hate it and crush her.

"You didn't make me sound stupid, did you?"

Horrified, she grasped his hand. "No. Never. I wrote you as you are. Curious, adventurous, and intelligent."

He gave her a wary look before giving her hand a squeeze. "Intelligent, huh? Yeah, I definitely want to read it. So, how many of these articles do you plan?"

Tracing a fingertip around the base of her wineglass, she said, "I haven't really planned anything. The magazine may not like my article and refuse to hire me. Or maybe they'll hire me but not like the series idea."

"What if they do?"

"I have tonight's dinner as article number two." She hoped the magazine accepted her proposal. She had worried while writing that story, but when she finished, she honestly believed it her best work yet. For once, she'd found some passion in writing.

"What about after that? Aren't you going back to California tomorrow?"

A sharp pain stabbed her chest at the thought of leaving him right when she began truly getting to know him. And his kisses. She plucked her thin purse from the table's corner and fanned her face. "I am going home tomorrow. I guess if they like the idea...I don't know. I haven't really thought ahead. I think a lot of people are like you, though. They'd like to know more about fine dining but don't know how to go about learning. They don't dine in high-end restaurants because they're afraid of looking foolish in their ignorance. These articles could be the tool that teaches them and gets people into fine dining more often than the occasional birthday or anniversary dinner."

"I have two more stops on this tour. We begin work on a new album in Chicago afterward. I probably won't be free to travel for another four months."

She set her purse on the table and took a sip of wine. "I guess I'll have to find another Henry."

"Like hell," he mumbled.

She hid a smile behind her wine glass, liking his show of possessiveness.

The waiter arrived with the second course, placing a bowl of soup before each of them.

"It's green," said C.J. with a look of distaste pursing his handsome features.

"It's a cool cucumber soup with dill and onion. Try it." She dipped her soupspoon in and tried a sip. The icy liquid washed over her tongue with a mild but tasty flavor and finished with a brief bite from the onion. An utter delight. "How is it?"

He'd already finished half. "It's really good. Who knew?"

She chuckled. She hadn't expected to have so much fun reviewing restaurants, but with him, it became her favorite job.

Drumming his hands on the edge of the table in a rapid beat that blew her mind, he said, "Can I ask for more, or is that forbidden?"

She swallowed another sampling of soup. "It's not forbidden, exactly, but we've got a few more courses coming. You don't realize, but they've planned this meal for us, knowing I'm reviewing for Fine Cuisine. Everything has been prepped and timed. If you get another bowl of soup, it's going to throw off the schedule and push the dishes behind it to a later delivery time."

"That doesn't sound like a good thing."

"Not unless you like your pork dry and the chef in tears."

"Okay. While you finish your soup, I'm going to the men's room."

She smiled. "Good. Then you can tell me about it so I can put it in my article."

He rolled his eyes, making her laugh.

"So how was it?" she asked when he returned.

"Clean." C.J. eyed the anemic stack of fru-fru on his plate. A thin slice of pork, something red, and four spears of white asparagus. Was asparagus supposed to be white? He could devour this course in three bites. Great. His stomach rumbled.

"You've got to give me more than that." She sliced into her food with a butter knife, the pork posing no problem for the dull blade.

"There were sinks and toilets and urinals. Oh, and mirrors, too. And stuff on the counters."

She laughed, a sound more like singing than any laugh he'd heard. "Marble? Tiles? Colors?"

Cutting into his stack of fru-fru, he shrugged. "No clue, but there was a guy sitting in there who made me wash my hands."

"What?" she asked on a chortle. "You mean he like grabbed you and forced your hands under the water?"

"Ha-ha. No. He gave me a look, and when I rinsed, he handed me a towel. A real towel. Not paper."

"Good to know."

He forked a bite and studied her a moment before eating it. As a knee-weakening deliciousness threatened to make him incapable of thought, he struggled past the pleasure to wonder if Sin would be open to an idea he had in the bathroom. They hardly knew each other, yet she put him at ease like nobody else.

"Do you like it?" she asked then took another bite.

"It's mind-melting. Almost as good as sex. I can't believe I just said that, but it's true. It's criminal how stingy they are with the portions." He took another bite and gathered his courage. "I was thinking."

She tilted her head to the side and gave him a curious glance that made him want to grab her and run out of the restaurant so they could get naked.

He cleared his throat. "If they like your article and want you to do the series, maybe you could come on the road with me. We're in Lexington tomorrow and Thursday. We'll be in St. Louis Friday and Saturday. I'd bet there are some great places to eat in those cities. Then Sunday, we're home in Chicago. Everyone knows Chicago's all about food." Had he sounded desperate? Did he scare her?

She finished her last bite with a thoughtful pout. Then her eyes widened and a slow smile stretched her lips. "You know what? That's a great idea."

He couldn't believe his ears. Relaxing, he ate the rest of his pork in a single bite.

"They'd have to approve it, of course. I imagine they have a list of restaurants they want reviewed. I don't know how keen they'd be on a writer setting the agenda. It sure would be fun though, don't you think?"

Fun didn't begin to describe what he thought.

"They'd have to want the project, but I love that idea. I'll pitch it as soon as I hear from them."

His stomach dropped. "I hoped you'd be able to come with us to Lexington tomorrow."

Her features smoothing into seriousness, she shook her head. "I'm not prepared to do that. I've got a plane ticket the magazine already provided. I'm not packed for an extended trip, and I've got family and friends who would worry. I can't simply take off."

"Sure you can."

"You're probably surrounded by people who regularly act on impulse, but I've got a responsibility to the people in my life. They care about me."

He thought about Mrs. Cavanaugh and

understood. He'd never want her frightened for him. "I get it. That's cool. I wish you could come, though."

"Me, too."

The waiter arrived with two tall goblets of sherbet.

"Dessert?" C.J. wouldn't make it another hour if this ended the meal. He'd had what, four bites and some bit-of-nothing soup?

"Not yet. We have four more courses then dessert if we want. The sherbet is to cleanse our palates and ready us for what's next."

"Geez. People eat this way all the time?"

"I can't imagine so. Not anyone below royalty, anyway. Maybe Trump and Gates who can afford a master chef and full kitchen staff, but even then..."

"Yeah. They'd starve."

Sin guffawed. "Well, breakfast and lunch would have to be hearty."

When the bill arrived, Sindra regretted asking C.J. to dine on so little when he had a concert to give. He was right. She had provided him a less than fortifying meal.

He glanced at the receipt. "We've been robbed."

"You didn't like it?" Plunking the magazine's credit card on the bill placard, she stood to go to the restroom.

He took her hand before she could pass. "You look upset. What's wrong?"

She couldn't help but appreciate his concern. "The meal was delicious and beautifully done, but there's no way you took in enough calories to get you through a concert."

"Don't worry about it, Sin. It was really good. I liked it."

She did worry. How could she stand it if his performance suffered because of her? She made a cursory pass through the ladies room, bar, and lobby area then returned. "I have an idea. How long until you have to be at the concert?"

"I don't know. What time is it?" He stood and pushed in his chair.

She signed the receipt and retrieved her card. Glancing at her watch, she said, "It's coming up on eight-thirty."

With a wolfish grin, he said, "That's plenty of time. We don't go on until ten. I hope your idea's the same as mine."

"Doubtful." She chuckled and gave his suit jacket a tug.

Out front, the limo waited where it had delivered them. They raced for the door their driver held open as the crowd erupted at the sight of C.J. Cameras flashed and people shouted his name. She suspected paparazzi peppered the sidewalk. Safely inside, she gave the driver an address.

"Where are we going, beautiful? Tell me you're kidnapping me." C.J. wrapped her in his arms and rained warm kisses along the side of her neck.

She giggled as the thrill of his kisses sent goose bumps across her nape and up her arms. "Someplace that's guaranteed to leave you satisfied."

"Now you're talkin'." He captured her mouth in a hungry domination that left her in no question about how much he wanted her.

She wanted him, too, and poured her yearning into her response. He had opened to her this evening, told her personal and troubling aspects about his childhood. It meant everything to her, and made her admire his strength of character and his determination. The more she got to know him, the more she came to realize how deeply she could love this man. Heaven help her.

When the driver cleared his throat, and she discovered he held open the door, she pulled from C.J. with a jerk. She had gotten lost in his kiss, gotten lost in him. With no time to recover, she straightened her neckline as she exited the limo on shaky legs. Nobody milled about like in the busier section they had left.

C.J. appeared disoriented, too, blinking briefly as

if waking from a nap. He gazed at a neon sign above a quaint white shack. "Is this right? BB's Q?"

"I read about this place. I finally get to try their food and include it in my article." Taking his hand, she led him inside. The place was packed, which said a lot considering they dined out on a Tuesday night. "Do you like barbeque?"

"Depends. Is it the pulled kind with vinegar, or is it the Kansas City style with a tomato-based sweet sauce?"

She laughed. "I'm impressed."

"Beautiful, you're in my element now. What do you prefer?"

"Kansas City style. Let's get the ribs. I understand nothing compares within a five hundred mile radius."

"Damn. I can't wait." He gave a nod toward a sign asking customers to seat themselves then led her to a corner booth at the rear.

Moments after they sat, a young waitress with a cute ponytail and a red and white checked apron arrived with glasses of water and menus. C.J. held up a hand, refusing the menus. With a wink and a smirk at Sindra, he sat taller and proceeded to order for them both, requiring a minimum of guidance from the waitress on the side dishes.

Nobody paid them any notice. Waitresses bustled about the dining room, and though the place was much larger than it appeared from the curb, it handled sound well. Hundreds of people dined and talked, yet in their corner, she couldn't make out a single conversation and appreciated how quiet the place seemed – quieter than the five-star restaurant they'd left minutes ago.

"Now it's my turn. I want to know about you," said C.J., rubbing his ankle up her leg under the table while removing his tie.

Chapter Eleven

Being with Sin came so easily, yet she gave off neither a sister nor a friend vibe. No, this woman practically hummed with sexual energy. It amazed him how she didn't have to wear skin-tight clothes, low-cut tops, or four-inch heels to make him take notice.

Her appeal came in the way she looked at him as if he could reveal the mysteries of life, how she listened when he spoke, and the open respect she showed him. Then there were her kisses and the way she touched him. If he thought about that, however, both the barbequed ribs and the concert would have to do without him because he'd give them both up for an all-night romp in her hotel room.

Romp didn't fit what he wanted to do with her. Neither did getting together, doing the jimmy jump, or even having sex. He studied her a long moment. With no uncertainty, he wanted to make love to her and with her. Slow, sensuous, worshipful, heartfelt lovemaking. It struck him that he'd never met a woman he'd wanted for more than a casual quickie. Not Sin. He wanted to get inside her and stay for hours.

She cleared her throat, yanking him from his erotic daydream. "My father has played drums since before I was born. He met my mom on the road with the band, so rock-n-roll has been part of my life since the beginning. I used to go on every tour with him, but when I started elementary school, Mom and I had to stay behind. I hated that."

"I saw you at a concert of his."

"Right. We talked about that. It was the summer before my sophomore year in high school. I went that summer. It was wonderful to live on tour again, and awful knowing it was his last."

"It's weird you say that because I sorta felt the same. I mean, he was my idol, you know? That was the only concert of his I made it to. I was happy to be there after years of trying to find a way to go to one. After I learned the band had retired, it was horrible to realize I'd never get another chance. I was so glad I got to see him play live."

Sin offered a solemn nod.

The waitress brought beers with two mugs and bread, reminding him of how little he'd had to eat that evening. Trying not to appear piggish, he downed a chunk of buttered bread in seconds.

"You'd think life with a famous rock star would be chaotic and crazy, but my parents worked hard to give me a normal childhood," she said. She ignored her mug and took a sip of beer straight from the bottle. "I went to public school and played halfheartedly in the concert and marching bands. My friends called my dad Mr. Karriker. My mom used to bake brownies for PTA fundraisers and sewed my Halloween costumes every year. Dad was gone three months out of the year to tour, but I got to go when his tour fell in summer months."

He shook his head. "Your father let you tour with the band? The sex and drugs and booze and craziness?"

"It wasn't like that. They didn't live that way. Not around me, anyway. Women offered, but they didn't cheat on their wives. They had families, and we were important to them."

"So what did they do when they weren't performing?" He took a swallow of beer and wondered what his own friends did while he went out partying like a wild ass.

"I remember watching football games on big

screen televisions in fancy hotel rooms. Going to amusement parks and the beach. Fun songwriting sessions. Practical jokes. The list goes on."

It did sound like good times, and he couldn't recall ever thinking the band wasn't cool. In fact, the Karriker Jones Band had remained his favorite for years, even after they retired, yet he'd never paid attention to whether or not they lived the rock-n-roll lifestyle. He hadn't thought about it. He'd only cared about their music.

Geez, Justin was right. Damn him. C.J. hadn't reached his twenty-ninth birthday, but he ached and dragged like an old man. He wouldn't admit it to his friends, but he would gladly leave the models, drinking, and late nights behind. He'd been over it for a while now. With a woman like Sin at his side, he'd never regret it. He'd never look back.

Sitting in the limo and cleaning barbeque sauce from under her fingernails with a wet wipe, Sindra tried not to eavesdrop on C.J. He paced the sidewalk while talking on the driver's cell phone. Why he refused to use hers or didn't carry one of his own, she couldn't understand.

"Just make the reservations. I'll pay for them," he practically shouted before shoving the phone in the driver's hand and sliding in beside her.

"Everything okay?" she asked.

"Sure." He gave her a smile that didn't reach his eyes. "Reconsider. Stay with me. We can buy you whatever you need. We've got runners on staff. All they do is figure out how to get us what we need and want."

Sounded like a devil's deal. Too good to be true. "You don't know what you're asking. It's not about you and me. It's about my family."

"I bet they'd understand." He stared pensively out the window as they headed to the hotel.

"I bet they wouldn't." She balled the moist wipe

and tossed it in her purse. "There's never a good reason for behaving irresponsibly."

"Are you lecturing me?"

"No. I'd never tell you how to live. I'm telling you how I do. I have standards and values, and I don't compromise them."

"I get that. I really do. That's why I'm making arrangements for you to have your own room at the hotels. You can have my room on the bus. It's the size of a closet, but the bed's comfortable. I'll sleep on the sofa." He rubbed a hand over weary eyes.

Did he step out of his comfort zone on this one? Why would he want her tagging along? He'd admitted he sought a good time and liked living the life of a star. She wouldn't contribute to his party nights, and she absolutely refused to become nothing more than his sex toy.

"I'm not a groupie. I won't—"

"I'm asking a lot. I know." Taking her hand, he gazed into her eyes. "I haven't figured this out or I'd explain why. All I know is I want you with me."

Flattered despite her concerns, she sighed as warmth suffused her chest. "You think if I return to California tomorrow, you may never see me again."

"I don't want that to happen. I like you. A lot. More than any girl – woman – I've ever met."

"You tempt me, but I can't." She sighed. She wanted to stay so much she could taste it. On the reality side, however, her job with the magazine still lingered in the maybe category, she had bills to pay, and her father would have a fit. "C.J., if this is right, we have to do it right. We have to be adults."

He flinched. "You make me want things to be different. You make me think about the future and about how my life should be. The drinking and all the rest, I'm done with it."

"You can't say that. People don't change overnight." Now he scared her. Did he believe he could convince her to stay if he promised to change? That would be a formula for certain failure.

"Sin—"

"We're here." She reached for the door, anxious to escape into the hotel before he said something that would guarantee a ruined relationship before one fully formed.

He took her by the wrists. "Sin, please."

Closing her eyes, she whispered, "Don't. Don't say something you'll regret."

"How did this date go so wrong?" Placing a finger under her chin, he turned her to face him.

She refused to open her eyes. She didn't want her final memory of him to be one with a remorseful expression.

"Sin," he said low.

Then his lips touched hers and she melted. She liked him despite his lifestyle and troublemaking. In him, she recognized strength and honor. She could imagine a future with him, a love like her parents shared. She wanted it so much it lit a fire in her belly.

Wrapping her arms around his neck, she drowned in him for a moment. She kissed him with all the passion in her, all the hope and longing and need. Because he was right. When she returned to California, she'd likely never see him again.

C.J. poured his disappointment, frustration, and anger into his performance. He pounded the skins like they were the cause of his pain. He shouted his voice hoarse. He snapped at Justin and growled at Chaz. It didn't make a difference. Try as he might, he couldn't shake the image of Sin running into the hotel.

She hadn't looked back. Had she wanted to forget him?

Rage seared the backs of his eyeballs, making tears pool at his lids. Damn it! He deserved her.

"Damn you!" he cursed his parents. He deserved love and happiness and a healthy life.

Justin glanced over his shoulder and scowled,

mouthing, "What the fuck?"

C.J. shook his head and transitioned from the refrain. Sindra saw him. The real him. He liked that she did. Liked how she accepted him, approved of him. She wanted him. So why did she plan to leave? Why wouldn't she consider staying?

He'd left her at the hotel, yet he spent the entire concert searching the audience for her face, desperate to see her. Wished she'd surprise him by attending. Find him afterward and say she'd made a mistake and would finish the tour with him.

What he really wanted from her were three words he hadn't expected to ever hear from a woman other than Mrs. Cavanaugh. Had never cared to hear. Not said by a fan who loved his fame or money or fantasy ideal. Not murmured in the dark during a meaningless jimmy jump. No. He wanted heartfelt. Forever. Said from the lips of a woman who searched the deepest part of his soul and found the good in him. Said from the lips of Sindra Karriker.

When the concert ended, he scooted from behind his drum set and headed backstage.

"C.J.," shouted Jet.

"Not now, dude." He broke into a jog. He had to discover a way to show her his sincerity. Show her that his feelings for her were real.

Entering the dressing room, he let the door bang the wall. Roadies and caterers scattered.

"Sorry," he mumbled, not slowing as he strode for the shower.

Washing away sweat from the show, he decided words wouldn't do. Nothing he could say would change her mind. He had to show her. Toweling dry, he shook water from his hair. He moved to a mirror above a sink and swiped through a steam film. His brown eyes lacked their usual blood-shot hue and dark smudged eyelids. He actually had color to his skin, and his face didn't sag. Amazing what a good night's rest and some decent food could do.

He couldn't show her what she meant to him with

a mindless gesture like flowers or chocolate or jewelry. She went too deep. She required action.

Dressing quickly, he ignored Chaz's scowl as the bass player headed for a shower stall. He somehow avoided Jet and Justin altogether, though he would get an ear full in the morning. Especially since he bypassed the after-party and went straight to the hotel.

When he stood at her room's door, he had no clue what he could do to change her mind. With his hand poised to knock, he hoped an idea would come to him on the spur.

Chapter Twelve

At a soft knock, Sindra rolled in bed and glanced at the clock. Good Lord, she'd spent the last two hours staring at the ceiling and thinking. The knock sounded again, and she wished her neighbor would open their door. Turning, she stared at a bank of tall windows where a street lamp offered a faint gray glow through unmoving draperies.

"Sindra," came a hiss.

She bolted upright. Someone was at *her* door. She threw aside the covers and swung her legs over the side. Padding to the door, she asked, "Who is it?"

"C.J."

A surge of joy made her stomach leap. Why wasn't he at the concert? She opened the door a crack. "Has something happened?"

"Yes." He ran a hand through damp hair, looking way too awake for twelve-thirty. "Can I come in?"

A thousand thought fragments ran through her mind as she stepped away and widened the gap so he could enter.

"I had to see you," he said, closing the door.

"Why?" She tried to sound irritated but suspected she failed.

He went to the bathroom and flipped the light switch. A sliver of white light sliced across the carpet and cut into the dark room. With narrowed eyes, he said, "You don't look like you've been sleeping."

"Okay. I haven't. I've been thinking."

"About me?"

She hesitated.

He said, "I hope..."

"What happened? You said something happened."

Taking a step closer, he rubbed a palm across the chest of his brown T-shirt. "I realized I can't let you go. I need you to know... Tell me you were thinking about me."

"I was thinking about you." Would he kiss her? She dropped her eyes to his lips. "What do you need me to know?"

In two long strides, he reached her and took her by the waist. "Sin. My God."

Her heart skipped a beat as her legs began to tremble.

Lowering his face to hers, he captured her mouth in a gentle but passionate kiss. His lips worked against hers then he urged her to open and met her tongue in a sensual exploration that had her legs giving out altogether. His arms closed around her, securing her as he continued to kiss her and walked her to the bed.

He smelled clean and sweet, but under the scent, a rich, masculine element appealed to her on a primal level. Inhaling deeply, she filled her lungs with his fragrance. She skimmed her tongue along his, enjoying the low groan her boldness elicited.

She didn't want to think about leaving in the morning, but it niggled at the back of her mind. It refused to let her ignore it. She gave up. Using the knowledge to fuel her hunger, she savored every moment because it could be their one and only night together. She pulled him to the rumpled bedding and let him sink into her. His weight pressed her into the covers, both exciting and comforting.

This man intrigued her, held her attention, and made it hard to concentrate on anything else. She'd never met a man who so completely monopolized her thoughts.

Shifting her hair from her throat, he broke the

kiss and moved his attentions to the side of her neck. A thrill ran through her, making her quiver. This was going to happen. She needed him, and she wouldn't deny it. Not tonight.

"Please tell me you haven't been drinking," she said. She didn't taste alcohol on him, though. She could only detect sweet mint.

"I've never been more sober." He slowly lowered the neckline of her tank top and rained tiny kisses along the upper swell of each breast.

Her nipples hardened.

He gazed into her eyes. "When you look at me, you see me. You see Chris, the man. Not C.J. the rock star. I need that. I've needed you for a really long time."

Her heart warmed.

He kissed her, long and demanding. Lowering to her cleavage, he whispered, "Stay."

When he stretched the neckline further and pressed kisses toward her still-concealed nipples, she shivered with delight. A tingling began between her thighs.

"C.J." It became more difficult to get enough air into her lungs as he inched fingers along the elastic waistband of her panties. "Chris. I want to stay, but I can't."

He rolled off of her. Would he leave without her promise? Fighting disappointment, she reached for him. He yanked his shirt over his head and brought her atop him.

He wore vulnerability and wariness in his gaze. "Kiss me, Sin. Show me you care even a little."

"I care," she said, tracing the drumsticks tattoo around his upper arm. "A lot."

She pressed her lips to his and skimmed her fingertips from his jeans to his ribcage then back. She loved his hard body, his firm muscles attesting to how he put his all into drumming every time.

"You have so many qualities I admire and respect." She dotted pecks along his freshly shaven jaw. She ventured a taste with the tip of her tongue. The

sharp bitterness of his aftershave served as
punishment.

"You drive me crazy." He lifted her top.

Raising her arms, she let him remove it. The feel
of his hot skin against hers sent her nerves humming.
Grinding her pelvis against the delicious bulge in his
jeans, she groaned. The soft flesh between her legs
prickled and swelled, growing slick as her excitement
grew. She squirmed, seeking relief.

"You're so beautiful. I've wanted this since I first
saw you in the green room last Friday." He flipped her to
her back. Taking a nipple between his lips, he grazed
his front teeth over the tip then sucked.

She gasped. Electric pleasure shot from her
breast to her crease, and moisture rushed, coating her
and soaking her panties. Moving slowly, he thoroughly
explored one breast before paying equal attention to the
other. She combed fingers into his nearly dry hair,
amazed by its softness. Her body heated, his mouth
stoking a furnace deep inside her.

Her wet underwear clung to her and had to come
off. She lifted her hips and worked them to her knees.
She hiked a foot and caught the crotch with a toe then
flung it free. Sighing, she wrapped her arms around him
and softly raked nails along his back.

"Take them off," she whispered, slipping a thumb
into the waist of his jeans.

Sending a hand down her abdomen then around
her hip to cup her rear, he exhaled a heavy breath. "I
want you so much."

"Please," she pleaded, her folds throbbing.

Sliding from the bed, he stripped from his boots,
jeans and underwear. He removed a condom from its
package and rolled it onto his jutting erection. Sindra's
throat constricted. The man took her breath away. No
wonder women fell over each other to get naked with
him.

He opened the bathroom door wider, bringing the
light to the bed. "I want to see you."

He came to her and urged her knees apart. She

grasped handfuls of sheet. Would he? He stared at her most private place while inching closer. When he bent and pressed lips to her aching slit, she threw back her head. Yes!

With his fingers, he spread her flesh and stroked. She bent her knees to give him better access. He settled between her thighs and licked her until she panted. Tremors shook her with each pass of his tongue. Pleasure built. Tension stretched. When she wanted to weep with frustration of release dangling out of reach, he found her clit.

He sent his lips over it. The promise of rapture sent a shudder through her. Gently drawing upon the nub, he flicked it with the tip of his tongue. A shock of pleasure-pain jolted her. She cried out. So close. Almost there.

He repeated, and her entire body jerked. Closing her eyes, she groaned and surrendered to a wave of ecstasy. Her inner walls clenched then pulsated, carrying a tide of pleasure to her depths. The tide crashed, and she arched, riding bliss until it released its hold.

She slumped with a sigh. "Wow."

"Sin, I've got to be inside you."

"Yes." She rose to her elbows as he gave her folds a final kiss. So sexy.

His hair fell across his forehead, came across his tan shoulders and brushed her thighs. He was so handsome. Licking his shapely lips, he fitted his tip to her opening. She needed him filling her. Now.

She wrapped her legs around his hips and locked her ankles over his firm backside. She helped him ease in. His size stretched her. Opening her mouth, she fought for air as her passage accommodated him.

"You're so tight," he said, his voice deep and strained.

"Oh, God. Yes. C.J." Her voice hitched on a sob of intense pleasure as he seated fully inside her. Their pelvises met, and he pressed against her resisting womb. Her walls quaked around his length.

Cupping her breasts, he gave each nipple a brief bite then a kiss. Her passage gripped him as reward, sending blasts of heat through her veins. Then he kissed her, and she opened. She tasted herself on his tongue and lips.

Caressing her body downward, he strummed her nerves as if playing her like an instrument. He stopped at her hips. Sliding his hands under, he tilted her.

He withdrew to his tip and broke the kiss. She locked eyes with him as he thrust hard. She gasped. Grabbing his thick shoulders, she squeezed her legs around his hips.

"Again," she said. "Again."

She lit him on fire like a roman candle ready to explode. C.J. had never been so hard. Her sheath milked him. Her body writhed erotically, and yet her gaze, filled with honest affection, didn't leave his. He couldn't get enough. Her soft scent. Her velvety skin. Her tight body.

Pumping in and out, he set a rhythm perfect for a ballad. She arched beneath him. Crying out his name, she dug her fingers into his shoulders as her walls massaged his length. Her orgasm sent a gorgeous pink flush blossoming across her breasts. It crept up her throat and tinged her beautiful face. Heat rose from her, surrounding him like an additional embrace.

He struggled against the need to come. Against his need to claim her. Against the pressure that built deep inside and made his heart pound. She felt tight and hot and slick, but he wanted to rock her world. Maintaining a steady stroke, he cradled her in his arms as she went limp.

Her eyes opened. They appeared bluer than ever. Increasing the pace, he thrust into her heavenly body and took her lips in a savage kiss. She returned it with the same passion, tilting her hips.

The need to come grew painful. Grimacing with

the effort to delay it, he squeezed his eyes closed and held the beat.

"Yes. Yes!" She hugged her legs tighter around his hips. Her sheath quaked then clamped around him. She drew him deeper. "C.J., come with me."

As she arched in release, he let the pressure go. It exploded. He thrust twice more, pouring the last of his need into her.

Not wanting to leave her, he hugged her close and rolled. He lay with her on top, fully seated inside her and realizing he'd never been happier or more satisfied.

She rested her head next to his on the pillow. He blinked at the ceiling before closing his eyes and savoring the feel of her soft skin. He promised, "We're going to do that again."

"Definitely," she murmured, not stirring. "But let me sleep for a minute."

He chuckled and kissed her sweet lips. Then it hit him.

He loved her.

In disbelief, he slowly hugged her tighter and touched his forehead to hers. She smelled like flowers, and her hair felt like Indian silk. Her breathing became steady as she slipped into slumber.

He loved her.

When had it happened? He couldn't pinpoint the moment, but she had haunted him since the second he met her. Everything about her fit him, appealed to him. Her beauty. Her drumming. Her common sense. He'd never known anyone so well adjusted. He adored her lack of vanity, her open passion, and the way she kissed him honestly. To top it, she had values and intelligence.

He'd been wrong at the concert. He didn't deserve her. Not even close. Yet, in a way, he did. She had chosen him, and that made him worthy. He wanted her in his life. At his side. Forever.

Forever.

C.J. shuddered. The idea had always terrified him. He hadn't thought he could pull it off. With Sindra, he would commit to forever in an instant. Life with her would be an adventure. He trusted her, and no matter what happened, he could count on her.

Should he tell her? Sighing, he gazed toward the window. What if she didn't love him in return? She would devastate him. She'd made love with him, though, after she said she wouldn't. Her mind had changed. Had her heart?

If he told her, would she stay? He didn't think so. She clearly cared a lot about the people in her life. He wanted to be one of them. No, he wanted to be the most important one.

With her at his side and her love and loyalty behind him, he could do anything. Be anyone – even a committed, mature man with people relying on him. Sober. Monogamous. Focused on what mattered.

His stomach tensed, but he ignored it. He'd have to let her go, as much pain as it caused him. If they stood a chance, she'd have to come into his life by her choice.

Inside her, he lengthened and grew hard. He grinned. He'd have fun waking her.

Chapter Thirteen

"Mmm." Sindra stretched and smiled. She'd expected to regret sleeping with C.J. last night, but she didn't. He'd made her come five times and kept her up most of the night. She smiled bigger. The man was spectacular.

It hadn't been dirty or raw or meaningless, either. They'd made beautiful, moving love. Touching fingertips to her lashes, she felt a bit of moisture left from tears she'd spilled with her final orgasm.

She rubbed stiff lids and sat. He slept, his head on the other pillow. Unsure why, it surprised her that he'd stayed. She liked that he had. It proved last night meant as much to him as to her.

She went to the bathroom and began her morning routine. After washing her face, she patted dry with a hand towel while returning to the bedroom. She stumbled over one of his boots. Suppressing a laugh, she glanced at the clock.

Eight o'clock.

"No." Her flight left in an hour and a half. She had to get to the airport, pronto.

Retrieving her tank top from the floor, she found her panties hanging from the corner of a mirror above the room's television set. She hurried to her suitcase on a stand in a corner, flipped open the lid, and crammed them inside.

On the bed, C.J. stirred. He gazed through slit lids

and gave her a tired smile. "Hey, gorgeous. Come back to bed."

"I can't. I'll miss my flight. You know what a nightmare it is trying to fly these days." She chose a comfortable pair of shoes she could easily slip off and on at the security check, and dropped them to the carpet.

"So you're just going to run out of here?"

Stepping into a pair of clean underwear, she sent him a pleading look. "You knew I had to leave this morning."

"I knew," he said low and slow as he sat and combed his long, dirty blond hair over the top of his head.

"I have to. I'm having dinner at my parents' tonight. Mom's cooking. It's important."

"I wouldn't know."

Hooking her bra, she said, "Sure you do. If Jet's mother had planned a get-together and asked you to attend, you'd do everything to be there, wouldn't you?"

"You're right." He cut a guarded glance her way then slid from the bed and went to the bathroom.

She pulled on a pair of knee-high stockings, slacks, and a sweater. Working a brush through her tangles, she balanced while slipping her feet into her shoes. She tried to ignore the ache in her heart, but C.J. made it impossible. She wanted to stay. He'd gotten under her skin, and now he had won her deepest affections. Could he give up the party girls and drinking binges? She'd never seen him acting like an out-of-control rock star, but she couldn't disregard his reputation.

A movement near the bathroom caught her eye. He said, "Hey. You were deep in thought."

"Sorry." She tossed the brush in her suitcase and passed him to gather her bathroom items. "I'd bring you to meet my parents if you could get away."

Leaning against the doorframe, he crossed arms over his chest. "I could, technically."

Would he? She feared a burst of hope at the idea he might say yes.

"We don't have a concert until tomorrow night, but I don't think the guys would go for it. If my flight coming back got delayed or canceled..."

"Of course." She nodded. Deflated expectation settled into her stomach like a stone. "Maybe you can come for a visit when the tour is ended."

"We start recording a new album when we return to Chicago next week." He took a step backward.

She collected her bottles and tubes from the sink and shower and moved to the bedroom. He'd given her two excuses why he couldn't come to California. Swallowing past a lump, she began to get the picture.

"No sweat. Really," she managed, her throat gone thick with disillusionment. Refusing to glance his way, she zipped her suitcase. "We had some fun and it was interesting."

The sound of fabric riding skin told her he dressed as she packed her laptop and its chords in a black leather carrier.

"Look, Sin—"

She held up a hand, keeping her face averted. She didn't want him to blow her off, or worse, give her another excuse about why they couldn't see each other. Fighting tears, she pressed a palm to her aching heart. How could they share a night like last night and it not mean anything to him? She should've known better than to get involved with a rock musician, especially after warnings from both her father and Amy.

She willed away her tears. She couldn't let him see how much this hurt.

"Sin."

She shook her head. Placing the straps of her purse and laptop bag over one shoulder, she yanked her suitcase off its stand and headed for the door. She couldn't get out fast enough.

"Let me carry those for you."

"I'm sure the band is looking for you. You're leaving this morning, too, aren't you?"

Yes, but—"

She stopped at the door and turned, the world

crumbling around her. "I really did have a great time. I'm so glad I got to see you again. I hold you in the highest regard."

She hadn't given C.J. a chance. She cut the heart out of him, and it burned. Why had she acted that way? It didn't seem like her. Especially since he'd tried to tell her he wanted to see her again. He should've tried harder. He punched the door then sucked a breath through his teeth as his knuckles smarted.

He had to go after her. Make her listen. He scrambled into his boots, nearly falling when he moved toward the door before his heel landed its insole. By the time he stepped from her room, she had gone.

He jogged to the elevators and hit the down button. Could he say anything that would make her reconsider? So much for manning up and letting her know when the time came. She wanted to be with him. He'd recognized pain and disappointment in the way she'd moved stiffly and wouldn't look at him. He hated that he'd caused her to hurt.

Behind him, an elevator bell binged and doors opened.

"Hey, trouble." Chaz held a battered copy of Ernest Hemmingway's *A Moveable Feast* in one hand. In the other, he lifted a box of seltzer tablets in a see-through bag labeled *Gift Shop*. "Hope you're packed. The bus awaits."

Shit. With a sigh, he joined his friend. "Have you ever been in love?"

Chaz gave him a fierce scowl as the doors closed.

"Geez. I just asked." C.J. held up both hands in surrender. In record time, he had his bag packed, bought a coffee-on-the-go from the hotel restaurant, and sat sipping it on the bus.

Justin walked past and smacked him on the shoulder. "It's about time you joined us. I was about to call the police to see if you'd been arrested. Where were you last night? Drunk in a gutter?"

"Fuck you."

The leader chuckled. "Jet said you were with some blond chick. I figured it had to be a babe since you completely *lost your mind* during the concert then bailed on the after-party."

"She's no chick."

"Didn't look like your type," said Jet.

"What's my type?" C.J. took another sip of coffee and regretted not dumping these guys for a trip to California with an angel.

"Indecent. Promiscuous," said Chaz with a half smirk. "He said the word *love*."

Justin collapsed on the couch in hysterics. Guffawing, he braced an arm across his middle. "Love? Chris? I don't think so."

The bus engine revved, and the hotel slid past the windows.

"To each his own." Chaz opened his book and swiveled his chair from them.

"Is that true?" asked Jet, coming to the dinette and scooting onto the opposite bench. His serious expression and tone soothed C.J.'s stinging pride.

"Me? Love? Couldn't be, right?" He set his coffee on the table and pushed the window curtain closed. He couldn't get her off his mind. Hell, he could still smell her on him and it drove him insane.

"Sure it could." Jet offered him a curious smile and a wink. In a conspiratorial whisper, he said, "I once heard Dad tell Mom that I'd have my heart broken before I found the right girl, but that you'd only love once and it would be one of those all or nothing, forever loves. I was kinda jealous."

He hoped Jet's dad had him pegged wrong. If not, he'd fallen for a woman who'd stolen his heart then run.

"Did it happen? Did you find someone?"

C.J. shook his head. "Nah, dude. I thought maybe, but she..." He couldn't say it. "What happened with Jennifer? Did she say yes?"

His friend crossed his arms. "No, man. She broke

my heart. She was a stunner, too."

"You know what? I feel for you. I actually do." He rubbed gritty eyes. "I was out partying all night. I'm going to sleep. Wake me when we get there."

"Sure, Chris."

"C.J." He took a final sip of coffee, stood, and dropped the cup in the trash. Staring out the window behind Justin's head, he thought of his mother. Chris had loved her, no matter what. Chris needed love and acceptance, could get hurt, and liked it that way. He turned to his friend, so much like a brother, and said, "Chris doesn't exist anymore. Call me C.J."

Chapter Fourteen

"What's bugging you?" Sindra's father took her by the shoulders and maneuvered her from the kitchen sink.

She tossed a washrag into hot, soapy water and let him conduct her to the living room. "Why does something have to be bugging me?"

"Because you hardly spoke at dinner. I expected you to be excited and ready to tell us everything that happened on your trip."

"Didn't I?" She sat on the couch and put a throw pillow on her lap.

"We had to drag it out of you. What're you excluding?" He joined her and propped an elbow onto a back cushion.

Sighing, she traced decorative piping around the pillow's edge. "I met someone. He's someone you wouldn't approve."

"Try me." His eyebrows arched, but his mouth remained relaxed in a slight smile.

She took a bracing breath. "He's a drummer with a rock band."

"A local band in Phoenix?"

"Huh-uh. Mega-famous. I actually met him here last Friday when I went to the Smashing Glass concert with Amy."

His eyes narrowed a fraction. "C.J. Brody? Are you talking about C.J. Brody?"

"You know him?" She swayed slightly in shock.

"I know who he is. That young man is a remarkable drummer. Didn't he recently win the NMAA award for best in percussion?"

She nodded. "And best performer. He happened to be staying in the same hotel in Phoenix, and I spent a lot of time with him."

"And?"

"I foolishly fell in love with a man who can't love me back."

"Why do you say that?" He leaned his head against his hand at the back of the sofa and gazed at her with curiosity.

"He's a rock star, Dad. He does everything but the drugs. You say you know who he is, so you know about his reputation."

"That doesn't mean anything. How was he with you? Was he letting groupies hang on him, getting drunk, being loud and obnoxious?" He chuckled, as if remembering good times.

"Dad?"

"Was he?"

"No. He was a perfect gentleman. We had fun. We talked a lot."

"Sounds like a nice guy."

Was he toying with her? "Dad? Come on."

"Fine. I've gone to a lot of trouble to keep my early band years from you. You're a woman now. How old are you? Twenty-two?"

"Tsk-tsk. Twenty-five."

"Even better. You can make these decisions for yourself. It shouldn't matter if I approve or not. But know this." He straightened and took her hand in both of his. "It was my love for your mother and you that made me want to be a responsible man. I didn't want any woman but her. I didn't want to get drunk or high because I wanted to remember every wonderful moment with you two. I didn't want to do anything that would compromise this incredible life she built with me."

"You think C.J.'s like that? He let me go." She

didn't want to face the pain, which still cut sharply.

"Did you give him any choice?"

Sitting taller, she said, "I did. I invited him to come with me and have dinner here tonight."

"He's on tour?"

She nodded, wilting.

"Not exactly fair of you, sweetheart. You went on tour with me often enough. You know it's a job. He can't take off for a couple days."

"Why are you defending him?" What she wouldn't give to relive this morning. Tears smarted, and she blinked them into submission.

"Because you deserve happiness, and I've never seen you moony over a man like you are for this one. I don't care if he's a drummer. We're not all bad, you know. If he's right for you, it'll work out. Give him a chance."

"I don't know, Dad. I'm out of my head for the man, and that frightens me. What if he doesn't feel the same?"

"Go find out. If you don't, you'll always wonder." He tucked a lock of hair behind her ear then kissed her cheek. "Now how about I take us out for dessert?"

"I swear, man, if you don't snap out of it, I'm gonna knock you upside the head." Jet tossed a stack of music, and the pages landed on his keyboard with a slap. "All this over a stupid chick?"

Rage sent C.J. off their hotel room's sofa. Taking a throw pillow, he crushed it then threw it at his friend. "This is why you can't get a girl to fall for you. No respect, dude. If you call her stupid or a chick again, I'm going to tear off your fuckin' head."

"I'd like to see you try." Waggling his finger, he said, "Come on, Chris."

He'd never been so tempted to hammer Jet into the ground. The keyboard player had serious height, but the guy couldn't fight to save himself. "If I bust my knuckles on your face, I won't be able to play."

His friend huffed in disgust. He collected the pillow from the floor at his feet and threw it back. "What is it with you and this girl?"

C.J. caught it. "I don't know. It's like when she left me in Phoenix three days ago, she took a piece of me."

A loud knock sounded then Justin's voice came through the closed doors. "Let's go, guys. It's time to head to the arena. We've got a show to do."

C.J. closed his eyes and sighed. One more concert and he could go home to his apartment and hide for a couple days while he licked his wounds.

Bam! Boom! Pitta-pitta-datta-datta-botta-botta Shing! C.J. fought for breath as he ripped off his T-shirt.

Jet started the opening melody to the next song. With the tattered cloth, C.J. wiped sweat from his eyes and forehead then chucked the shirt over his shoulder. He blinked, and a silver glitter in the VIP section to his left caught his attention.

He needed to stop searching for her. She was gone. When would he accept that?

Past bright blue and white stage lights trying to blind him, a length of pale blond hair swung past the second level railing. The audience went wild as Justin rock-screamed, picked up the melody on his guitar, and dropped to his knees as he strained for a wicked run of high-pitched notes.

Squinting, C.J. stared, hoping to make out the person at the railing and hating himself for hoping. The stage lights went red when Chaz joined in on bass.

There she stood.

Grinning like mad, Sin swayed from side to side with the song. His heart skipped a beat, but his sticks didn't. On his mark, he took the song to the next level, his skins breathing soul into it and moving the audience around her into a simultaneous rock. He loved that.

Her eyes met his, and her smile wavered. She

stopped moving. She mouthed, "I'm sorry."

It was good enough. At the same time, it wasn't. He needed to hear her voice. He needed to know if she shared the sense of bonding that had tortured him the past few days. Glancing toward the side-stage, he caught the eye of their roadie manager. He gave his head a jerk, and the man bent low to scurry to center stage.

"What's the problem?" he shouted, squatting next to the stool.

"See that woman standing at the railing? The blonde one with the sparkly halter top."

The manager searched for a second. "I see her."

"I need to talk to her. Right now. Her name is Sindra Karriker. Can you handle that?"

The man gave him a mischievous grin. "You got it, Mr. Brody. Give me five minutes. I'll bring her backstage."

C.J. played on, his heart rate outpacing the pounding of his sticks. Any minute. Any minute. He'd thought he would never see her again, but she came.

What would he say? More importantly, what would she say?

Justin and Jet both sent him questioning looks. C.J. could only shrug and smile. Once the smile took over, he couldn't stop. Any minute.

Chaz shot him an irritated glance. C.J. laughed. She had said sorry. It was a start.

They concluded the song, and he stood. "Hold up, guys."

He gazed toward the place offstage where the manager promised to bring her. It remained empty.

"What's going on?" asked Justin, leaving his microphone and swinging his guitar to his back. "We're trying to put on a concert here."

At the front, Jet addressed the crowd. "Bear with us a minute, folks. Is everyone having a good time?"

The audience roared an affirmative.

"Jet's buying you a couple minutes, man, so you better tell me what the hell your problem is." Justin's features tightened, and he narrowed his eyes.

"It's love, Justin. I thought I lost her, but she's here."

"Love? Are you fuckin' with me?" His friend looked ready to strangle him.

Offstage, Sindra appeared. C.J. set down his drumsticks and took a step toward her. The manager whispered in her ear, and she nodded then marched onstage. Her large eyes stared worriedly as she sank teeth into her bottom lip.

While Jet entertained the crowd with a road story, C.J.'s stomach knotted. "I can't believe you're here."

She took his hand. She sent a concerned glance toward the audience. "I had to. Can we talk after the concert?"

Backing away with an indulgent smile, Justin said, "Make it quick."

"We need to talk now." C.J. took her other hand, wanting to hug her. "I've been out of my mind without you."

"Really?" Her eyes widened as her face lifted. "Me, too. I've made mistakes."

"You have?"

"Yes. That first night you asked me to stay, and I wanted to so badly. I didn't want to be used and forgotten."

"I could never forget you." His throat grew thick, and he swallowed.

"Then you asked me to stay on tour with you, and I wanted to so badly."

He grinned at her use of the same phrasing. When she became serious, he held his breath.

"Ask me to stay," she said, inching closer and holding his gaze.

"You'll destroy me if you say you can't." He hated admitting it, but she had to know.

"Ask me to stay."

His throat constricted, but he forced his words past. "Stay, Sin. Stay with me and be my love. Stay."

Beaming a brilliant smile, she said, "Yes. I'll stay.

I love you."

Oh, God. Yes.

She pressed against him and wrapped her arms around his neck.

"I'm sweaty," he said, his gaze on her lips.

"I don't care."

Lowering his mouth to hers, he poured his hopes and fears into the contact. She fed him strength and love in return.

She loved him.

Sindra leaned into him. In that moment, he realized she would depend on him, love him, and bring out the very best in him. She brought out the true man in him, and he adored her for it.

She loved him.

Breaking the kiss, she said, "The magazine hired me. They want me to do reviews for the next six months on Chicago restaurants for a series I pitched. They liked my articles and want me to do a whole set of *Educating Henry* reviews. All I have to do is give them your next tour schedule so they can promote."

"That's incredible." His head spun with her news.

"Hey," called Justin. "Let's get back to work."

Sindra let him go and began moving backward.

He couldn't stand her retreat and grasped at something to say that would make her hesitate. "Wait. Isn't that going to be a lot of traveling back and forth between California and Illinois?"

"Nope." Her eyes lit from within. "I sold my apartment. I'm moving to Chicago."

His stomach did a flip. "When?"

"Right now. I drove my moving van here. It's parked outside."

No way. She really meant it when she said she'd stay. "Live with me, Sin. Stay the night and drive up with us tomorrow."

She halted. "You really mean that? Are you sure?"

Going to her, he said, "I've never been more sure of anything in my life."

"I love you, C.J."

Taking her in a tight hug, he gave her a fierce kiss. "I love you, Sin."

Staring into her beautiful, glistening eyes, he said, "Call me Chris."

THE END

JET

Chapter One

A b-flat hung in the air above Jet. It wavered and wept, a perfect expression of the emotion behind it. His heart squashed and heavy, he clutched his saxophone like a lifeline. As his lungs ached, releasing the last of their air, the note weakened and warbled. It became the sound in his soul.

A tear escaped the corner of his eye, but he didn't care. Let a river rage down his face. Let it drown him.

Out of breath, he let the note go into dreaded silence. He hated the quiet. It allowed him to think. To remember. If he did that, he'd stagger to the kitchen and stab his hurting, limping heart.

In the moment when the only sound in the room consisted of his rushed intake of air, he detected a deep murmur of voices outside his apartment door.

An intervention. Damn them.

Another tear followed the path of the first, and he lit into a run of bluesy half and quarter notes. Inching toward the door, he poured his torment into a lamenting melody. Subdued light from the dining room window turned the white walls of his apartment gray and shared his sadness.

How could his lover reject him so cruelly? How could she end their relationship? Cynthia had been his everything. His life. His future. His one and only.

At the door, he finished his breath on a moaning note then yanked open the door. In the hall outside his apartment door, C.J. sat on the floor, resting against the wall to the left of the doorframe. Justin leaned a shoulder against the opposite wall.

The bandleader took a step toward Jet with an irritated scowl and drew a keycard from his jeans pocket. Shaking it, he said, "You're costing us money. We haven't used this in two days, but we're still paying for the studio time. You going to reimburse the band?"

Whatever. Why did Justin talk like they were still starving up-and-comers? Jet moved to close the door, but a movement at the end of the hall caught his attention. A whiff of coffee made him perk.

When Sindra came carrying a bag from the corner bakery and a tray of covered cups, Jet retreated a step and widened the opening. "Come on in."

She shot his two friends a told-you-so look.

He headed across the living room, running a hand down the cold, smooth side of his saxophone. Propping the instrument against the cushions of his couch, he clutched the front of his robe, wiped his face dry then dropped into an armchair.

"Where's Cynthia?" asked Justin.

"Shut the hell up," snapped C.J., knocking into the lead singer's shoulder as he passed. "We're here for you, dude. When did you eat last?"

Jet shrugged.

The drummer tapped drumsticks in a blindingly fast tattoo along the length of the sofa back.

"Cynthia moved out yesterday. She's gone," said Jet. That was harder to say than he'd expected. Swallowing against a sharp pang in his chest, Jet rubbed stiff eyelids. "Where's the coffee? Is it too early for tequila?"

Sindra kicked closed the door, and Justin took the bag from her as she passed the couch.

Jet accepted a cup from her. Popping off an opening in the lid, he took a sniff of the rich brew. "I think I ate yesterday. I can't remember."

Sindra ruffled his hair and whispered, "I'm available if you need to talk. Desiree's in town, too.

We're both here for you."

When her eyes met his, he understood she meant it. He didn't know why, but her offer helped ease his pain, not that he wouldn't take her up on it. He took a sip of coffee. It didn't matter that it scalded his tongue. The warmth in his stomach and the caffeine jolt brought him to life and induced him to take another sip.

Justin sank to a sofa cushion and shot the saxophone a dirty look. "How long are you gonna stay here feeling sorry for yourself?"

"Why do you have to be such an ass?" C.J. asked the lead singer. "Jet's hurting, dude. Give him a break."

"No, you give me a break." Justin narrowed his eyes on Jet. "How long did Cynthia last? Three months?"

"Four. But she was different."

"You always say that," said C.J., sending a hand into the bag with a noisy rustle and bringing out a muffin. "Want one?"

"No, thanks. Cynthia really was different. I finished our tour with the intention of asking her to marry me. I have an appointment Friday to pick out a ring." He slapped his forehead. "Shit. I need to cancel it."

Justin opened his notebook to a fresh page and retrieved a pencil from above his ear. "She couldn't be all that special. You two went on a couple dates, then she moves in here right before you go on tour for three months. Convenient, if you ask me. And wasn't there some chick named Jennifer in Phoenix you were moony over for a day or two?"

"The idea of picking up a phone and canceling that meeting with the jeweler is twisting my heart."

Sindra made a pitying sound, came to the chair, and patted his shoulder.

Justin huffed. "You buy diamond rings like other guys buy flowers. Honestly, Jet, why do you think every girl who looks twice at you is the one?"

"I'm about to kick you out of here," she warned, flicking a tendril of blond hair over one shoulder while fire sparked in her blue eyes. Sindra threw a banana at the bandleader's head, but he caught it before it could strike. "Do you want me to call Desiree? She remembers when you were hurting and Jet was there for you. The least you can do is be a friend."

"Am I wrong?" He peeled the fruit.

"It's not about right or wrong. It's about having compassion."

"You guys aren't helping," said Jet, touching his cup to his aching head.

Justin sighed. "Look, I'm saying you shouldn't let these chicks mess you over. There aren't a lot of women out there made of forever material. If you keep pushing these girlfriends of yours, you're gonna find yourself married and divorced. If you ask me, you've been lucky to pick women smart enough to leave before it comes to that."

"Nobody's asking you." Jet eyed his sax, sensing its silent call. It wanted his attention. It wanted to give voice to his pain. Swallowing a strangled groan of denial, he tore his gaze to his grandfather's ring. "You guys found your soul mates. You've got your forever love. Am I wrong to want the same?"

The glance of pure adoration C.J. shared with Sindra cut through Jet like a knife. He'd loved those women. He'd seen his future with each and every one of them. Well, the wedding, anyway.

Sindra came and put a hand on his arm. "Of course it's okay to want that. Maybe you want it so much you try to make it happen instead of letting it happen naturally."

He'd had enough. He stood and headed for the door. "Thanks for the advice, but get out. I appreciate the coffee, but you all need to go."

"We have an album to record, and I'm not going anywhere until I know you'll be in the studio. Tomorrow morning. Nine sharp." Justin relaxed further into the couch and took a bite of banana.

"Aaargh!" Sometimes Jet despised him. "I'd like to tell you to eat shit."

"But you won't. You wouldn't let me quit last year,

and I'm not going to let you pull this bullshit that puts our next album on the line."

"You make me regret that trip to Kitty Hawk."

C.J. stood and took Sindra's hand. "He makes me regret it sometimes, too. But we've been a band since high school, and despite our nughead leader's attempt to quit last year, we're still together. So what do you say? We've got an album to record."

"Fine." Jet shot a resentful scowl Justin's way. "Nine tomorrow. I'll be there."

With a satisfied smile, Justin got to his feet and tucked his pencil above his ear. "Good enough for me. See you then."

Sindra followed him to the door while C.J. asked, "Are you sure you don't want us to stay, dude?"

"I want to be alone."

"We understand," said Sindra, waving the drummer to the door.

Justin opened it but blocked the exit. "Hey, Jet. Do me a favor, would you? Leave that damned saxophone here for the next couple weeks. We'll put the sax songs at the end of the schedule."

Jet eyed his instrument with longing. When he turned to say goodbye, the doorway stood empty. He went and slammed the door. He'd said he would show in the morning with every intention of bailing, but he wouldn't. He wasn't that person. No matter how much he didn't want to go, he would.

Today, however, he would give in to his broken heart. He went to the couch and took his saxophone. He drew the strap about his neck and licked the reed. He summoned the agony that had pulled soulful sounds from the sexy woodwind. Somehow, however, the thought of Cynthia's abandonment didn't cut as deeply.

Chapter Two

Fingering his pale blue tie, Jet chirped his tires as he whipped his classic nineteen sixty-nine fire engine red Camaro into the studio parking lot. Justin and C.J. already waited near the side entrance with Chaz thundering onto the lot on a cherry chocolate Harley-Davidson. Cringing, Jet parked in a far corner and braced for a razzing.

"Dude," greeted C.J. as Jet stepped out and began toward the door. "What the f—"

"Chill, man. They're just clothes."

Justin chuckled. "Clothes make the man. Haven't you heard?"

"Then I'm sorry for the lot of you, because your clothes say unwashed, slept in, and low class." Jet shoved his keys into the front pocket of his wool slacks.

Inside, Justin and C.J. led the way along a narrow hall lined with pictures of famous musicians who used this studio. He caught a whiff of flowers and glanced around for a woman. Then he realized it came from C.J.'s long hair.

"Chris, geez, you smell like a girl."

"Can't help it, dude. I ran out of shampoo and had to use Sin's."

Chaz nudged Jet with an elbow and gave him a questioning look.

"I figured if I had to go out in public today, I'm going to look good doing it."

"Damn." The bass player gave the tie a flick. "Warn me next time."

"Why, so you can wear a tie, too?"

Chaz chuckled. "Kiss my ass."

At the end of the hall and around a corner, Justin swiped his card in a reader and pushed open the door to the studio where their instruments waited. They didn't have to say a word. As seasoned musicians who had played together as a band for more than ten years, they went to work setting up for the first song.

Justin thrummed the strings of his electric guitar then stepped to the center microphone of three that protruded from the ceiling. "It feels good to be in here. Finally. Let's do *Fish Out of Water* first."

Jet plugged power into his guitar and leaned it against a padded wall for later.

"Where's Frank?" The lead singer glanced at the window separating them from the sound tech and producer.

Jet snapped a power coupling into the back of his keyboard then followed Justin's gaze and froze. Dark, slanted eyes in a heart-shaped porcelain face stared at him. Definitely not Frank. The lovely woman averted her gaze to the mixing board. Long, graceful fingers adjusted earphones on one side then descended to light upon a flashing red button. He'd never been jealous of a button before.

She pressed it, and a soft pop sounded a moment before the producer's voice came through a speaker on the wall. "He's on maternity leave."

Justin nearly dropped his guitar.

"It's a medical miracle," mumbled Chaz.

C.J. drummed a comical ba-dump bump. "Frank had a baby!"

"Sorry," said the producer. "Paternity leave. His wife had the baby. He's taking three months off."

"Cool, Corey," said Justin.

"Let me introduce you guys to Akiko. She'll be your sound and equipment tech for this album."

"Hey, Akiko," said their lead, sounding less than

enthusiastic. He rolled eyes toward C.J., and Chaz chucked the singer on the shoulder in chastisement.

"Don't be rude." Jet glanced at her, but she appeared not to pay them any mind. Were her headphones on? "Nice to meet you, Akiko. We're glad to have you."

She didn't take her eyes from the mixing board, but a hint of a smile softly lifted the corners of her pretty lips.

She heard him. He fought a smile of his own as he struck a series of chords to stretch his fingers.

"She'd better be good. That's all I'm sayin'," said C.J.

"Nothing but the best will do for Smashing Glass, Mr. Brody. Gentlemen, whenever you're ready." The speaker popped, letting them know Corey had turned off the two-way.

As Chaz and Justin checked their guitars, and C.J. swung his arms in circles, Jet couldn't take his eyes from Akiko. She had a serene quality to her countenance that soothed his upset. Cynthia had walked out and brought all his hopes for their future tumbling about his ears. But something about watching the tech's sweet face gave him a sense that everything would be fine.

Justin gave a thumb up, and Corey's lips moved a moment before the tech gave the okay sign with her fingers. Jet stared at the pretty woman during the silent pause. No, the term pretty didn't do her justice. Lovely. Black hair pulled into a ponytail shined in fluorescent overhead lighting and complimented flawless features set around dark eyes.

Above the large window, a red bulb lit. She had begun recording.

"Let's do this," said Justin. "One and two and one-two-three—"

As if they'd played the song a hundred times instead of three, everyone hit the first note on cue. Jet didn't care for the tune, but Justin had given him a strong vocal. He always appreciated a chance to use his voice. Closing his eyes, he pictured Cynthia walking out the door with suitcases in hand. He used the raw emotion to roughen his voice as he leaned to the microphone and released a howl that softened into a descending scale.

The last note of his scale started the lead's vocals. He concentrated on his fingering at the keyboard while letting Justin solo the first verse. When he joined in on harmony, he glanced at the tech.

She tapped on her left earphone then shook her head.

Corey's voice came over the speaker. "Guys. Hey, guys. Hold up a second. There's a technical difficulty."

"This sounds good to me," said C.J. on a frown.

Jet shared a shrug with Justin, and Chaz sighed when the recording bulb blinked off.

"Where's she going?" asked C.J.

The technician set her earphones on the board and left.

"Great," said Justin, thrumming a discordant note on his guitar. "We finally get Jet in here, and our tech quits."

Chaz went to a loveseat and opened a hardbound copy of *The Count of Monte Cristo.*

"Who says she's quitting?" Jet squeezed a sad melody from his keys.

"Knock it off," said C.J., slipping off his stool and scratching his ass. "You're depressing me."

"Why?" asked Justin. "Got the wedding blues?"

"No way." The drummer began working his hands in a series of finger and palm stretches. "Marrying Sindra was the best thing I've ever done. We're trying to get pregnant. It's not going very well. So I don't need to hear sad songs."

"Deal with it," said Jet. "You've been married a month. You haven't been trying long enough to stress. It'll happen."

"Look, dude—"

A door opened, disturbing gray foam lining the wall opposite the booth entrance. In a soft voice, the technician said, "Please excuse the interruption."

Taller than Jet expected, she carried a microphone in one hand, a stepladder in the other, and looped cable over one shoulder. She wore a pretty white blouse with a flowing skirt in a beige print, and dressy flats. Not the jeans and T-shirt usually worn in the studio.

"You want some privacy?" asked C.J. with a grin.

Jet shot him a warning glare. "Be nice."

"Or what?"

"Or I'll adjust your attitude with a swift kick."

"Promises, promises."

Akiko set the stepstool under Jet's mike and climbed. In a near whisper, she said, "Please excuse me."

"You're fine. What's the problem?" He came from behind his keyboard to stand beside her.

"Your voice was muffled on the track. This is old equipment, and you need new."

He needed new like she couldn't believe. A new heart. New hope. Heck, a new beginning would be ideal.

She removed the old mike from the ceiling connection and handed it to him. As she worked to install the new one, she said, "I like your tie."

"You do?" He put self-conscious fingers to the blue silk. "You don't think I'm overdressed?"

"No. You're working. It's nice to see a musician in professional clothing."

He offered his band mates a grin. "Take a lesson, men."

"Shove it," said C.J., but he rubbed a hand down the design on his black T-shirt and shifted his weight.

Jet chuckled. He'd made them look shabby, and she noticed. When she secured the new microphone, she reached for the old one in his hand. Their fingers brushed, and he straightened as a jolt of awareness sent his arm hairs on end under his sleeve.

Uh-oh. He'd learned his lesson with Cynthia. No more rebound loves. No more rushing into a relationship and expecting the world.

She passed him a shy glance from the corner of her eye. "I'm Akiko."

"That's what Corey said. It's nice to meet you. I'm Jet."

"Jet? Like an airplane?" Unwinding cord from her shoulder, she moved away and began laying it along the back wall behind the amps and spare instruments.

Didn't she know him? "No, not like an airplane. It's short for...well, it's a nickname. Do you want a hand?"

"Clap if you want. I kind of like it."

It took him a second to catch her joke. He was slow, and she was a whole lot of wonderful. She wasn't a fan with expectations of dating a famous rock star. In fact, she hadn't even known his name. She seemed sweet and shy. For heaven's sake, she wore a skirt to work at a recording studio as a technician.

Whoa. He needed to reverse direction. She wasn't for him.

"You're a glutton for punishment," said C.J. with a shake of his head.

"I'm just offering Akiko some help. It's more than you guys are doing."

"Right," drawled Chaz. "*Help.*"

"It's good to be a gentleman." Akiko straightened at the far corner and attached the end of the thick gray cable to a plate jack waist-high on the wall. "I think men have forgotten how. It's nice to meet one who hasn't."

She considered him a gentleman. At least he dressed like one today.

Crossing the studio, she offered him a shy smile, her gaze averted. She made a slight bow at the door, and without a word, disappeared.

Chapter Three

"Good session, *gentlemen*," said Justin with a playful wink in Jet's direction.

"Watch who you're calling a gentleman," mumbled Chaz, checking his watch. "Sure isn't one playing this bass."

"Got a hot date, Chaz?" C.J. tattooed his sticks on his thigh then imitated the bass player's time check.

"You think that's so hard to believe?" Chaz unplugged his guitar and leaned it against the back wall.

Without taking his eyes off the departing tech, Jet said, "It wouldn't be so hard to believe if you actually dated."

Chaz grunted and strode from the studio. Jet followed on his heels, anxious to catch Akiko before she left. He had no idea what he'd say. He found her standing at the edge of the sidewalk where it ended at the parking lot entrance.

He came to a quick halt. She simply stood. Did she wait for him? No, couldn't be, could it? What should he say? Everything in his head sounded idiotic. Then she glanced at him.

"I followed you," he said, blurting the first words that came to mind, and winced. Great. He sounded like a stalker.

Facing him fully, she asked, "Do you need something?"

"No. I mean, yes. I mean... Do you need a ride?"
Geez. Now he had become a stuttering abductor. "I'm
sorry."

"Don't be. You're kind. I have a ride, thank you."

"You're so polite." He ventured a step closer,
encouraged by her lack of censure.

"Thank you. You are gentlemanly."

"Thanks, I think." Was that her way of calling him
a nice guy?

"This is my ride." A silver Toyota sedan pulled
alongside the curb.

Ignoring the hostile expression on the slanted-
eyed driver's face, Jet asked, "Is he your boyfriend?"

Akiko made her way around the front of the car
but stopped before getting in. Gazing at him over the
roof, she said, "I'll see you tomorrow, I hope."

He'd pried. Why should she tell him who drove
her? He'd be lucky if she spoke to him after this.
Dejected, he raised a hand in a half-hearted wave.
"Sure. See you tomorrow."

As the car pulled from the curb, C.J. came to his
side. "Crash and burn?"

"Pretty much. Am I still smoking?"

His friend chuckled. "It's too soon, dude. Cynthia
left, what, three days ago?"

"Thanks for the reminder."

"I'm not trying to bust your chops, dude."

"I'm sure. But you're in love with a great girl. That
makes your perspective a little different. What are you
and Sindra doing tonight?"

"Five-star gourmet. She's doing a review."

Jet shoved a hand in his pocket and retrieved his
keys. "Enjoy. I'm heading home."

"Why don't you come with us? I don't know jack.
You know less. It'll be embarrassing and fun."

"Right. Because embarrassing myself at a stiff,
formal gourmet restaurant is a blast." He headed into
the parking lot.

"Come on, dude."

"Go have *fun*. I'm going home. I'll see you back

here in the morning."

"*Konbanwa.*"

Akiko offered her brother a tired smile. "Good evening to you, too."

"Tough first day?"

"Nothing went right at first. When we finally got the equipment working, there was only time for them to get one song on track."

"Isn't that good?"

"Not for them. I was told they usually do two or three. Corey said we won't charge them today's studio time. It's fair."

He glanced at her then stared out the windshield. "So who was that guy?"

She smiled. "I'm proud of you, Makoto. You made it a whole three minutes before asking."

"Ha-ha. Spill it or I'll tell father you're dating a *gaijin.*"

"This is America. We're the foreigners. Not him."

Her brother laughed. "You better tell me."

Crossing her arms, she stared out the side window. "Fine. He's the keyboard player for Smashing Glass. I'd think, of all people, you'd recognize him."

"I love that band. No way he was a member. I'd know those guys anywhere. Justin. Chaz. Jet and C.J. Those guys don't wear ties."

"Well, today this one did." She hid a secret smile. He'd looked so handsome.

"Introduce me then," he said, his tone insistent and stubborn.

"I can't."

"Why?" He stopped at a red light and shot her an irritated glance.

She didn't dare show her interest. In as nonchalant a voice as she could manage, she said, "I don't know his name. If you love them so much, how come you didn't know who he was?"

"The guy wore business clothes. I didn't even look at him. I thought he was a nobody. If he's Smashing Glass' keyboardist, his name is Jet. Did you know he sings, plays guitar, and writes songs, too? He plays a couple other instruments, and there's a rumor that he's going to play saxophone on some of the songs in their new album."

"That's nice." Akiko kept her face averted.

"Don't pretend you're not into him."

"Why should I be?" Affecting what she hoped passed for a bored expression, she faced him and shrugged. "It's a job."

He narrowed his eyes, but the light changed to green and he had to devote his attention to the road. When they arrived home, Makoto headed for his room. She was safe. For now.

The next morning, Akiko pulled a sheet of meat and vegetable pastries from the oven and glanced at the clock. She removed her apron and thrust it at her mother. "I'm going to be late."

"You haven't packed a lunch," said her mother in Japanese.

"I don't have time." Pulling a ponytail holder out of her hair, she raced from the kitchen.

"We need to talk tonight," her mother called.

Before she could reach her purse near the front door, Makoto stepped from the family room with his keys in hand. "I want an introduction."

"Not today, little brother."

"When?"

"Cool it or I'll get Dad to agree I should have your car. I'm the one with a job."

Makoto's face paled a shade. "You wouldn't. I'd have to take the bus to college like a loser."

"I would. Don't doubt it for a second." She skirted him, grabbed her purse and hurried out the door. "Having you drive me is inconvenient."

"If you'd gotten married like Mom and Dad wanted, your husband would buy you a car." He made a sour expression, jutting his chin in her direction.

"I won't marry for money or things." In the car, she buckled her seatbelt.

Her brother slid behind the wheel. "School."

"Don't start." She didn't want to start her day this way.

"School, school, school. You weren't even supposed to go. Mom made plans for you to marry that Fujiwara guy. What was his name?"

Akiko grimaced. "Michizane."

"Right. That guy." He started the car and backed from the driveway. "Dad may not be willing to pay your school debt, but he's still ready to pay for your wedding to Michizane."

"Michizane is not going to happen. Besides, I'm going to buy my own car. I've got a job now."

"The whole family wants you to marry Fujiwara. Why won't you?"

"Everyone but me. Not that it's any of your business, but Michizane is an uptight accountant living in Nagoya. My dream life doesn't include making a home and raising children for an emotionally unavailable husband who leaves for work at five in the morning, comes home at nine at night, and works half a day on Saturday so he can be considered for the manager's position in eight years."

"Ouch."

"Exactly. Besides, he's secretly in love with our cousin, Miyuki."

"Do Dad and Mom know about all this?"

"I'm not sure about Dad, but Mom does. It doesn't matter, though. It's about family connection, securing a suitable husband for me, and honor."

"Always about honor." Makoto pulled her side of the car to the curb in front of the studio. "Come on, Sis. Introduce me. I'll let you drive my car for an entire week."

"Not today." She wiped a nervous hand across lavender irises on her white skirt and unfastened her seatbelt. "I've got to go. Maybe tomorrow. See you at four-thirty."

"*Hai. Yo-jī han.*"

Opening the door, she shook her head. "You need to speak Japanese more. If Dad heard your accent, he'd cuff you."

Makoto squinted his face into a scrunch that made her laugh. She closed the car door and headed for the studio. Would Jet be waiting with the band? Would he look as nice, or would he wear T-shirt and jeans like his friends?

Her stomach quivered in anticipation. Unable to imagine a man who more greatly epitomized forbidden fruit, she pictured her parents' faces if she brought him home. Disappointing them was her least desire. No, her least desire was marrying Michizane.

Chapter Four

"Two days in a row? What the f—"

"Watch your mouth, C.J." Jet shot an anxious glance toward the sound tech's seat through the window. It remained empty.

"Why? Who's listening? She's late. Is that for her?" The drummer eyed Jet's black leather tie and turquoise button down.

Yes. "No. Maybe it's my new thing."

"She's a strange one," said Chaz, strumming a rhythm on his acoustical guitar. "I like it."

"Not strange. Nice. Not that any of you deviants would know nice if it smacked you."

"Watch it," warned Justin.

"Sorry." Jet pushed his keyboard's switch to the ON position. Its hum was like home. "Sindra's as nice as they come, and Desiree's pretty hard to beat, too."

"Why do you try?" asked C.J.

"Because."

"You're a rock star. It's not for you to try. It's for the girl to try."

Akiko was different. But then he always said that. He needed to get away from his rut. "It's cool chasing after someone instead of being chased. Not that I'm chasing Akiko. She's got a boyfriend."

"Let's drop the subject," said Justin. "Looks like we're ready to get started. How about a once through of *Dreaming* before we begin recording?"

As Chaz and C.J. made sounds of assent, Jet snuck a peak at the technician. She eased into her seat and slid earphones over her shiny dark hair. He took a deep breath. He'd never liked the smell of foam rubber and disinfectant pervading the studio, but if seeing her meant he had to smell it, he could come to like it.

Justin strummed the opening chord, and Jet joined in on the keyboard. When the lead signer hit the first note, C.J. brought the song to life with a strong beat while Chaz filled the tune with bass. Jet added harmony to the vocals on the second verse, his fingers playing from rote memory.

At the board, Akiko's placid features made him believe she didn't have her earphones active. Then she cast him a curious glance, bobbed her head for three beats, and smiled before returning her attention to switches and knobs in front of her.

Did she like his song? He couldn't help a sense of pride, and poured more feeling into his harmony. Of all the songs he'd written, he considered *Dreaming* in the top three best.

Corey arrived, talking on a cell phone. He settled on a sofa against the back wall behind Akiko. Only the top of his head appeared over the edge of the picture window's pane dividing the two rooms. He shared a couple exchanges with her.

When the song ended on a final refrain, Corey stood. At some point, he'd donned headphones, which he now tapped. His voice came through the wall speaker. "Sounds good, guys. Ready to lay one just like it on a track?"

Justin nodded, and the red record sign lit. "And one, and two, and one-two-three-four..."

Corey took a seat at the board, and Akiko's eyes met Jet's. He almost missed his vocal entrance. Why did she have to be so pretty and sweet and polite? Why did she have a boyfriend? Her hands made adjustments on the board, but her eyes stayed on his.

Against his will, he felt a stirring in his pants. He needed to look away. Look at Justin or the wall or his keyboard. Anything but her. But she mesmerized him. The longer she stared, the faster his heart beat until his stomach fluttered and he realized he couldn't step from behind his keyboard for the bulge in his slacks.

When they finished the final refrain, he let his fingers skip along the keys in a jazz-rock fadeout. He licked his lips, trying to remember if he'd ever wanted to kiss a woman as much as he did Akiko.

She lowered her gaze to the soundboard and replayed the recording for Corey. The guys talked about trouble spots on the next song, but Jet couldn't focus.

Why was he fixated on her? The way her lips moved as she discussed the recording with the producer. The way she blinked slowly before nodding agreement. The way her hair moved when she turned. He hoped her boyfriend treated her well, because she sure didn't deserve to be pursued by Jet on the rebound. Not that he'd let either stop him.

He blinked and gave her his back. What was he thinking? What business was it of his how her boyfriend treated her? She offered nothing more than professional courtesy. Friendship at the most. Rebound? How pathetic was he?

He *was* a serial monogamist. Maybe C.J. had it right. Maybe he was trying.

When he thought he had his arousal under control, he faced his keyboard. She glanced at him and smiled. His peter responded, and he sighed. At this rate, his voice would get too tight to perform.

The speaker on the wall popped then Corey said, "Justin, can we get you to sing the third verse again? We'll feed the instrumental to you through a set of headphones. The rest of you go ahead and take a fifteen-minute break."

Escape. Thank goodness. Using his clarinet case as cover for his private embarrassment, Jet followed C.J. out and hurried for the men's bathroom. He set the case on a sink and went into a stall.

Staring at the closed stall door, he sank to the toilet seat. He had to be the biggest loser ever. First he got dumped by a girl he hadn't realized was hardly more than a glorified groupie. Now he had the hots for an unavailable woman.

"You can't have her," he told himself aloud.

"Huh?"

"Chaz?"

"Two points for the moron behind door number two." The sound of a fly unzipping reverberated from the corners of the bathroom.

"Can I ask you—"

"Don't talk to me while you're having a bowel movement. It's unseemly."

His control regained, Jet sighed and left the stall. "I'm not. I was thinking."

Standing at a urinal, Chaz glanced over his shoulder. "Why do you struggle with being unattached?"

"It's not about having a girlfriend." Folding his arms over his chest, Jet leaned against the wall next to the sink where Chaz had set his copy of *The Count of Monte Cristo*. "It's about finding the person who completes me. Don't you ever feel like something's missing? Like someone's missing from your life?"

"Every second of every day." Chaz did a heavy bounce, fastened his jeans then flushed.

"Really? Then why don't you date?"

The bass player moved to the sink while shooting him a don't-go-there look.

Jet took his clarinet case from a metal shelf beneath a huge mirror. "I feel like someone's missing from my life. I want to love someone."

"You force it. I don't believe it's supposed to happen that way."

"What should I do? Go through life alone? Wait for God to drop the love of my life into my lap?"

Chaz turned off the water and took a paper towel. "I'm hardly a love maven."

"Am I a fool?"

"No."

"Then what?" Jet led the way out.

"C.J. and Justin found happiness. Why not you

too?"

"That's all I'm saying."

"Then do it right."

He gave up. At the other end of the hall, Akiko emerged from the equipment room. Okay, so he didn't give up.

She met his gaze and colored pink. As she hesitated, Chaz offered a dismissing wave and disappeared behind a door to the kitchen.

"Hi." Jet took a tentative step toward her.

"I am so sorry," she said. Her eyes glistened as she shared her gaze between the wall and a point of the carpet at his feet. Was she going to cry?

"For what?" He reached her in three long strides and set his clarinet on the floor. He clasped his hands behind his back to keep from reaching for her.

Moving her gaze to his left arm, she said, "For staring at you the way I did. I didn't mean—"

"I liked it." He checked his sleeve for a stain or water spot. It appeared fine.

She wiped palms on her skirt from hips to mid-thigh. "I didn't mean any disrespect."

She was talking about respect? Was that a backward way of saying she respected him? His chest expanded. "Is that a Japanese thing?"

A shy smile softened her features, and the blush vanished but for a tinge of pink shading her high cheekbones. "Most people call me Chinese. How do you know I'm Japanese?"

"Your name's Akiko. Not exactly a Chinese name." He caught a whiff of her perfume, a light fruity fragrance that suited her and made him want to lean closer to breathe more.

"It's nice you recognize my heritage."

Smoothing his tie, he grinned. "So what are you doing for lunch?"

She hesitated, the smile fading.

"Hey, it's cool if you can't eat with me. I'm not trying to step between you and your boyfriend." Well, maybe a little.

"I ran late this morning."

"I noticed." He noticed everything about her. Even the fact that she didn't wear a ring of any kind.

"I didn't get a chance to pack a lunch. I'll probably order something."

"Let me take you out." He shoved fingers up to the knuckles into a front pocket and attempted a casual stance.

"Why?"

Because he couldn't stop staring at her and didn't want to stop. Because she turned him on simply by looking at him, and nobody had ever done that. Because he wanted to know about her, her boyfriend be damned. "You've got to eat. I've got to eat. Let's eat together."

"Alone?" She took a half step backward.

Lifting one corner of his mouth in an unsure smile, he said, "No. In a crowded restaurant. Lots of people around. I promise I'll behave. I'm a gentleman, remember?" Had he sounded like a schmuck?

Shyly, she glanced through her lashes at him and relaxed. "You could invite a friend from the band to come along."

"Believe me, you don't want any of those guys along. Am I so bad? I don't stink, do I?" He lowered his nose to his shoulder and sniffed.

She released a quiet laugh. "No. You smell good."

So do you, gorgeous. "Then you'll have lunch with me? I know a great place. Very crowded, I promise."

Chapter Five

If Father found out about this... Akiko shifted in the passenger seat of Jet's fancy classic sports car. Going alone with a strange man would earn her serious trouble at home, not that he was a stranger. He was unknown by her parents, however. She couldn't recall riding in a car that smelled so clean. Leather, lemon, and was that foaming carpet cleaner?

He seemed so at ease behind the wheel. At ease and handsome. When she had first met him, his eyes captivated her. He had a lot of Japanese features – black hair, olive skin, high cheekbones with a somewhat small nose and shapely, thin lips.

Those amazing blue eyes amidst such familiar features struck her as startling and wonderful. And his height. Her heart thumped with delight. If he went to Japan, he'd spend half his standing time stooping to keep from hitting his head. His build also proclaimed him athletic. The opposite of thin, soft-bellied Michizane.

She had never put much stock in a man's looks. As her mother had taught, she'd cared more about his character, interests, and treatment of people. She would gladly marry an unattractive man if he shared her interests and values, treated her with respect and consideration, and loved her and their children. A man who helped others, spent time with people in his life, and cared to make a difference.

Jet had demonstrated some of these qualities, and she intensely wanted to learn more. It was like torture, though. If he proved to be what she suspected within a body and countenance that made her want to do things she shouldn't, she'd want to scream over longing for a man she couldn't have. A man her parents would never approve.

"You're staring," he said without taking his eyes from the windshield.

"I am so sorry. I was raised better than this." She resisted the urge to smack her forehead. A Japanese man would turn right around, take her back to work and avoid her from then on for such rude, confrontational behavior. She wasn't confrontational, however. She just couldn't seem to stop looking at his attractive face.

"No, really. I know it's a cultural thing, but I love how you look at me." He glanced at her with amusement twinkling in his brilliant eyes. "We're here."

He pulled into the parking lot of a building that looked like a three-story white mansion. *La Maison,* said the sign at the entrance. He found the last space available and parked.

"This place looks expensive." Akiko tucked hair behind her ear and eyed her conservative one-inch pumps.

"It's lunch. You're perfect. And it's on me. Now, wait here." He pulled the keys from the ignition and got out. Before she could reach for the door handle, he opened her door.

Such a gentleman. Makoto could take lessons. She stepped out, and then it hit her. He'd said he would pay for lunch. Did he consider this a kind of date? Stumbling at the thought, she reached for the door and found his steadying arm instead.

She had underestimated his firm athleticism. Her hand landed on soft cotton covering hard, unmoving muscle. Letting her hand linger a bit too long on his forearm, she fought the urge to explore higher to his bicep and shoulder. An image of him without his shirt flashed in her mind and left her breathless. She swayed.

"Are you okay?" he asked, concern lowering his eyebrows.

"Fine," she said with a suddenly dry mouth. Clearing her throat and standing straight, she reluctantly removed her hand from him. "Thank you. I'm fine. But I can't let you pay for my lunch. It's not right."

"Because of your boyfriend?" He closed the car door.

For a moment, she considered telling him Makoto was her brother, but she had trouble keeping her distance from him as it was. If he knew she didn't date, he might really turn on the charm. Then she'd be in a major hurting.

"My parents wouldn't approve," she said. A couple made their way from the restaurant to a nearby car, and Akiko breathed a sigh of relief to see them dressed like Jet and her.

Escorting her to the door, he said, "Yeah, my parents' opinions mean a lot to me, too. That's why I'm paying. I'd never hear the end of it if my dad found out I invited a lady to lunch and let her pay."

"Sounds like we have a dilemma. Though if it helps, I'm not a lady."

He opened the door then followed her through. "You are more a lady than any woman I've ever met other than my mother."

Flattered by his compliment, she tried to staunch heat flooding her cheeks. It didn't work. Two blushes in the same day? He had her head spinning. Ignoring his knowing smile, she said, "Maybe it would be better if we went back to the studio."

"Mr. Cavanaugh. Such a delight to see you. Two for lunch?" A balding older man with a distinguished mustache and smart suit joined them and slid two menus from a stack next to a maître d' podium.

"Too late," Jet whispered. To the man, he said, "Yes. Two. You look packed, if the parking lot's anything to judge."

"We are. But we always have a table for you, Mr.

Cavanaugh. If you'll please follow me..." He led the way through a brimming dining room to a staircase at the rear.

Akiko liked the way Jet walked at her side with his warm hand on the small of her back. Upstairs, a lovely table waited next to a window in a dining room with fewer tables and even fewer diners. She appreciated the quiet, looking forward to talking with him. Perhaps she could let him pay and her father wouldn't learn of it. Still, she hated keeping secrets from him, and it was bad enough she hid her interest in the rock musician.

Consistent with his gentlemanly ways, Jet slid her chair out as she sat. He took the opposite one and sent her a conspiratorial wink she enjoyed entirely too much. The man's bright eyes fascinated her.

After accepting her menu, she said, "You're different from the others in the band."

"Not really." He opened his menu and began reading. "They're my friends. They're like brothers to me. We're more alike than you'd think."

Though his features and tone were relaxed, she didn't miss the fierce loyalty and dedication toward his band mates that came across in the set of his shoulders and a telltale tick of muscle at his jaw. It stirred a deep respect in her.

Opening her menu, she stared at the words without seeing. "You dress differently. Speak differently. You even move differently. When I watch them, I think *rock band*. When I watch you, I think *classical concert performer*."

"You think so? They're definitely rock band. So am I." He glanced at her from his menu. "I don't know if that's a good thing or not. But I am classically trained."

"You play many instruments?"

"Sure. Piano and keyboard, obviously. Guitar. Saxophone and clarinet. Flute, oboe, and recorder." His eyes narrowed.

Did he expect her to criticize? "I play flute and a couple traditional Japanese instruments."

"You hide your talents?" He folded his menu and set it aside.

"Not at all. In the Tadaka family, our music is meant to entertain in the home. It is not for public display."

"Is that your way of saying you disapprove of what I do?"

"No! No, of course not. Tadakas value performance. It is a profession of great honor." Had she offended him?

"But not in the Tadaka family?"

"We don't aspire to perform, but we greatly appreciate others who do. My father prefers that we put our efforts into academics."

A waiter arrived with a pitcher of ice water and filled their goblets. It made Akiko realize she hadn't studied the menu. Letting Jet place his order first, she made a hasty selection then gave the waiter her choices. She swallowed. The prices would pain her already meager bank account.

When the man took the menus and left, she traced a wavy line through condensation beading the glass of her water goblet. "I gather you don't approve of my family's position on music."

He leaned forward and placed his hand so close to hers on the table she felt heat from his fingers. "I didn't mean to sound critical."

She fought a smile. "More like defensive."

Shifting his gaze to the window, he sat back and took his warm hand with him. Any hint of amusement that had played about his features melted away. Instantly sorry for causing tension, she glanced at his averted eyes. The sadness she found there surprised her.

Relaxing, she took a sip of ice water then sighed. "I can't imagine you would understand my parents. They're first-generation Japanese in America, and they're very traditional. It was the way they were raised, and it's the way they raised me."

"So that's why you dress up to work at the

studio?" His blue eyes softened around the edges.

"That has less to do with Japanese tradition and more to do with how my mother instilled in me the importance of first impressions and public perception. Judging by the way you dress, you understand."

"I don't dress this way all the time." His gaze slid from the window and met hers. "Do you even own a pair of jeans?"

Akiko laughed, put at ease by his teasing. "I do. And sneakers. And flip-flops, too." Growing more serious, she sent him a hard look. "I can't figure you out."

"I've been getting that a lot lately."

"You're so nice, and you really made an effort to get me here at lunch with you, but now you seem so distant. Are you one of those men who enjoy the chase but lose interest once you've caught the girl?"

"Are you saying I caught you?" A corner of his mouth quirked as if he fought a smile. Still, that sadness clung to his eyes.

"Far from it, Jet. I'm not easily won."

"Did you give your boyfriend a hard time before you agreed to date him?"

She weighed the benefit of letting him believe her unavailable against the discomfort of leading him in a lie. In opposition to her better judgment, she lowered her gaze and said, "I wouldn't be here with you if I had a boyfriend. And you haven't answered my question."

He opened his mouth to speak, but lunch arrived. When the waiter set a dish of baked fish and broccoli before her, she couldn't, hard as she might, remember ordering such a light meal. With her fast metabolism, she'd be starving by dinnertime.

Across the table, Jet sent her a predatory grin. Uh-oh.

Chapter Six

No boyfriend. Had the sun gotten brighter? Jet stirred noodles on his plate to coat them evenly in white cheese sauce. "I apologize if I seem distant. I'm going through something tough right now."

"I'm sorry. I won't ask you to tell me about it." Akiko rolled broccoli this way and that with her fork before choosing a piece to spear.

"Thanks. To answer your question, no. I don't chase after women then dump them. Would you be here if you thought I was a creep?" He wiped a chunk of chicken through the sauce then put it in his mouth. The rich combination of ricotta and white cheddar mixed with a smoky grilled tang of the chicken to create a goodness that dominated his world for a second.

"You are a rock star."

He groaned inwardly. "I guess rock stars don't have good reputations."

"In general. I suspect you're the exception to the rule." Her dark eyes searched his face a second before dropping to her plate.

"Actually, we all are. Smashing Glass, I mean. C.J. was wild until he met Sindra. Now he's as normal as the rest of us. We're guys." He shrugged, not sure if he could put it any other way. "We're about the music and our friendship. The money and fame come with it but don't drive us. Does that make sense?"

"Completely."

"You said your father emphasizes academics, but you're a sound technician. Hardly what I'd consider scholarly."

She quietly laughed. "I know, but I really love it. It's so strange how I came into the work."

Intrigued, he said, "Tell me what happened."

"I graduated from the University of California with a degree in ancient world literature last year. Talk about a degree that doesn't result in a job."

"Man, Akiko." Ancient world literature? He couldn't comprehend studying such a subject.

She nodded and downed a bite of fish. "I know. Anyway, there was a young man my mother had introduced me to in hopes we would date. Ever since my betrothed and I announced our lack of interest in one another, my mother's been trying to set me up with nice Japanese men." Using quotation fingers around *nice Japanese men,* she rolled her eyes.

Betrothed? What? "Whoa. Back up a second. You were engaged?"

"Not really. Not officially, anyway. It was a match our parents had arranged. More hopeful than anything. It's nothing."

She hadn't kidded when she said her family was traditional. "I didn't think people did that anymore."

Finishing her broccoli, she offered a sweet, closed-mouthed smile. "Anyway, the last guy my mother tried to get me to date came by the house to let us know he'd been asked to go to Japan to care for his sick grandmother, and he mentioned that he had recently begun studying at the technical college. The school refused to refund his tuition, and he was going to offer his place to my brother."

"So you went." Jet wiped cheese from his lip with a napkin and waived away the waiter headed their way.

"Absolutely. I couldn't find a decent job, and I didn't want to teach literature. Besides, I love music and I have a gift with electronics. I've always been a gadget freak like my dad. Only one problem."

"What?" He adored how she seemed to open. This

was the most she'd said since they met.

"Chicago has a lot of music, but it's nothing like Los Angeles or New York. There's not a huge demand for technicians. The jobs are already held by people who've been doing it for years."

"That's true. You lucked out when Frank took leave, huh?"

"I really did." Her eyes danced with happiness.

As she finished her meal, he leaned back and admired her delicate beauty. She was a feast for the eyes with her smooth skin and hair, shining dark eyes, pretty pink lips, and slight body. In appearance, she would make a stunning ballerina. She had a mind, too. A degree in ancient world literature. That must have taken serious studying.

"What does a person do with a degree in ancient literature?" he asked.

"Teach. Research. Write books nobody wants to buy." She chuckled.

"You didn't want to do any of those?"

"Exactly. If I had been smarter, I'd have chosen a profession first then a major to support it. I picked my major based on my personal interests. I'm fascinated by ancient languages and the writings that have come out of those civilizations."

"It's not useful in a practical way, though."

"That was my problem." With a sigh, she dabbed her napkin on her shapely lips then draped it on her plate.

"No dessert?" he asked. Unbidden, the picture of her with chocolate pudding smeared across small, firm breasts and flat stomach had him shifting in his chair.

Her face lit for a brief moment then she wilted a bit. "We'd better not. I need to get back to work. You have music to make."

Waving to the waiter for the check, he tossed his own napkin on his plate. "You're right. So this brother you mentioned – he's the one who picks you up after work? I don't think he likes me."

"Ha. He's a big fan. In fact, he's been begging me

for an introduction."

"Could've fooled me."

She laughed. "He didn't recognize you dressed like that."

He doubted many would. He liked dressing for Akiko. It made him more adult somehow. More responsible.

The check arrived, and he slid his credit card into the bill booklet after confirming the total.

"Wait," said Akiko, reaching for her small purse.

"No way." Jet handed the booklet to the waiter. "I told you. We Cavanaughs live by a certain code. I asked you to lunch. I pay."

"I can't offer you anything more than friendship." Her eyes lost a bit of their light, and the tightness of her lips told him she had made an effort to say so.

He studied her a moment. She had such an exotic, fragile loveliness, and he could stare at her all afternoon. In fact, the longer he gazed at her, the closer he grew. "Friendship? I can accept that." For now.

The waiter returned, and Jet settled the bill before escorting Akiko to his car. Her quiet both comforted and worried him. He didn't try to understand the contradiction.

Pulling onto the main avenue, he said, "My parents didn't care for my choice of majors."

"Music?"

"You bet. My father complained that he wasted money on my tuition, and my mother worried I'd turn out to be a miserable music teacher in some middle school somewhere." He grinned.

"You're rich, aren't you? From your music?"

"I am. Smashing Glass was on the rise in those days. We've been playing together since high school, and by the time I attended the university, we were playing clubs on the weekends and opening for some big names at local concerts. My parents didn't think anything would come of it, though."

"They thought you would outgrow it?"

"I guess."

"Music is your passion?"

Cutting his gaze her way, he found her watching him intently. Nervous, he licked dry lips. "Definitely. They know it now, but I don't think they understood it then."

"My parents are the same. They think I can only be happy if I'm married or working behind a desk. They don't realize that I love troubleshooting. I'm happiest when I'm enhancing a track to make a song sound better or trying to figure out why a piece of equipment isn't working."

"You're good at it."

"Thank you. You're an excellent musician."

"It feels good to do something well. There's satisfaction, you know?"

"I do."

He pulled into the studio parking lot and chose a space at the far end. Turning off the engine, he hesitated to get out. He enjoyed the peace and curiosity she inspired in him. He didn't want to leave.

"We should go in before they come searching for us," she said with a shy smile.

That overwhelming urge to kiss her returned. He would *not* practice bad habits by telling her he liked her. He'd go slowly. "Thanks for joining me for lunch."

"You're welcome. Thank you for asking me, and paying."

"Let's do it again tomorrow."

Averting her gaze, she said, "I don't think that's a good idea."

So much for going slowly. He was a dufus.

Chapter Seven

When they called it a wrap on the album's fourth song, Jet couldn't wait to leave. Every glance at Akiko increased his desire to tell her how much he liked her until the tension made the top of his head ready to explode. He flicked his keyboard off-switch and forced his feet not to run to his car. He couldn't linger, however. He'd find her outside, like he had the day before, and say something he'd regret.

He growled as he merged into highway traffic. This obsessive attraction wasn't healthy. Hating to admit it, he slapped the steering wheel at the acknowledgement that his friends had him pegged. He didn't like bachelorhood. Simple friendship with an attractive woman opposed his very nature.

"What's wrong with me?" Nudging the volume knob of his radio, he tried to drown the words whirling through his head. It didn't work.

Why did Akiko monopolize his thoughts? With past girlfriends, he had looked forward to going on dates, anticipated first kisses, and experienced excitement at the prospect of getting them into bed. Making the ultimate commitment plagued him during his downtime. Yet he couldn't isolate Akiko into the personal part of his life. She seeped into every part – his music, his conversations with the guys, and even his sleep. Was it because he'd met her at the studio, as a professional part of his work? Was it because he imagined she embodied his dream girl? His ideal? She'd only disappoint him like the others, wouldn't she?

"I'm insane." He had no other explanation. Why else would he go to sleep thinking about a woman he'd just met and wake the next morning still thinking about her? It wasn't normal.

He parked in front of his apartment building and turned off his engine. Nothing awaited him here. Not peace. Not rest. Solitude brought sorrow, and he reeked of sadness. When would he find happiness?

He made his way inside then to his bedroom where he shed his business wear for a pair of ragged jeans and an old gray T-shirt with a hole at the neckline. Would Akiko find him appealing now?

Aaa! Akiko-Akiko-Akiko! He had to get her out of his head.

In the kitchen, the answering machine's light blinked in triple succession. Three messages. The first was his mother asking him to a cookout at the house Saturday. The second delivered the voice of the band's agent, Calvin Spence, who needed him to confirm his plan to play at Boston's benefit concert next month. The third had C.J. on a warbling and crackling cell phone, inviting him to a party that started in two hours.

A party. Now there was an idea. Maybe Akiko held so much allure because she was essentially the only single woman in his world at the moment. At a party, he would meet lots of women anxious to meet him.

Grimacing, he went to the refrigerator and stared at the meager offerings on practically bare shelves. Fans. Ugh. Cynthia had been a fan, and the two women before her. Look where they had gotten him. Heartbroken and nowhere. Akiko appealed because she didn't idolize him. She hadn't entered their friendship with preconceived and incorrect notions. She actually made an effort to get to know him.

Disgusted, he shut the fridge and scratched his right shoulder even though he had no itch. Fans or not, he'd go to the party and try to meet women who didn't know him. Not everybody liked rock music. There had to be people tonight who wouldn't recognize him.

Through a sheer force of will, he thrust Akiko
from his mind and changed into black. Black jeans,
black T-shirt, black leather jacket, and black pointed-
toe boots. He glanced in the mirror and approved his
bad-boy appearance. He looked sharp. As he headed out
the door, he called C.J. on his cell.

"Hey, dude," greeting his friend. "Did you get my
message?"

"Yeah. A party sounds great. I'll be at your place
in thirty."

"Are you bringing a date?"

"Nope. I'm going alone for once. Is Sindra going?"

"Like I'd go to a party without her." C.J. barked a
laugh. "Besides, this shindig is her thing."

"Right. What was I thinking? I hope you don't
mind a third wheel."

"You're never a third wheel, Jet. You're my
brother. See you in a bit."

Jet stepped outside as evening began to hint at
night. Rush hour had passed, so traffic moved
smoothly. He reached C.J.'s house in twenty minutes
instead of thirty. When his stomach grumbled, he
regretted not grabbing dinner on the way.

"What kind of party is this?" he asked when
Sindra opened the front door.

"Hello to you, too, Jet." She laughed and headed
for their dining room. "Come on in."

She had her pale hair twisted into a fancy knot on
the back of her head, and her fine figure showed at its
best in a pink version of the dress Audrey Hepburn wore
in *Breakfast at Tiffany's*. She was an amazing woman,
and perfect for his friend.

He stepped inside and closed the door.

With a wave and a welcoming glint in her blue
eyes, she said, "It's a meet and greet. Fine Cuisine
Magazine's owners are throwing it for their writers and
the Chicago's top chefs and restaurateurs. It's going to
be fun."

Chefs? Good, the food would be fantastic.

Writers? Restaurant owners? Probably not a lot of Smashing Glass fans. The night looked better every minute.

"You're beautiful, as usual," he said.

"Thanks. Are you going to your parents' cookout? C.J. already told them we would."

"I'm thinking about it."

"Good. How've you been? I've been worried about you."

"I'm okay. You're so nice. C.J. doesn't deserve you."

She grinned.

"It's true," said his friend, coming from the back of the house. He wore brown leather pants and boots and a red silk button-down. "Damn, dude, it doesn't matter how hard I try, you always look better than me."

"You clean up well," said Jet. "I swear I haven't seen you look this good since Phoenix."

"Yeah, I gotta do it up right for my sweetheart." C.J. jerked his head to the side to get his long hair out of his eyes. He laughed and stuck a pair of drumsticks in a back pocket.

"I appreciate it." Sindra pressed her curves against her husband and kissed his cheek.

Jet hadn't seen C.J. so content. Jealousy twisted in his gut, but he stifled it. His friend had earned this.

Sindra collected a shiny gold purse from a table in the living room and said, "I've got to stay for the whole party, so why don't you follow us? That way, if you want to leave, you can."

He fought a grin. She was hoping he'd find a babe to take his mind off of Cynthia. He adored her transparency. What he needed, though, was somebody to take his mind off of Akiko. He could only shake his head. He was an ass for wanting Akiko mere days after Cynthia had gone. Then again, that made C.J. right. He'd prepared to ask a woman he didn't love to marry him. If he'd loved her, Akiko wouldn't impact him so hard.

He tailed them to a large art museum where

floodlights lit welcome banners and valets parked expensive cars. Limousines glimmered in a line of streetlights at the far end of a parking lot across the street, and more delivered partygoers at curbside. This wasn't a party. This was an event.

"No joyriding, man." Jet reluctantly handed his keys to an eager valet who practically drooled over his classic Camaro. He joined C.J. and Sindra at the front door and went inside.

Immediately, squeals echoed off the walls of the museum's wide entry showroom. Sindra chuckled and strode away as a mob of people blocked C.J. and him at the door. Jet's stomach dropped. So much for any measure of anonymity. With his hunger growing, he signed napkins and scraps of paper until he could edge his way around the crowd and to a side room. He offered a half-hearted smile and wave then turned on his heel.

An older, distinguished group of elegantly attired guests milled about a gallery of subdued oil paintings. Where was the food? In a far corner, Sindra spoke to a tall gentleman with a head full of white hair, his black tuxedo gently gleaming in a spot of recessed lighting from overhead. Another man, dressed more on a level with C.J., stood with them, nodding and sipping champagne.

Jet headed toward the corner where a server passed with a tray of hors d'oeuvres. He snatched one without stopping and popped it in his mouth. Sinking his teeth into it, he was instantly sorry. An overwhelming flavor of fish caused his step to falter. Anchovy? When a sticky, bitter substance wrapped around his front teeth and refused to dislodge, he nearly spit the foul mess from his mouth.

He took a napkin from a stack next to a small statue of a mid-nineteenth century lady, and deposited the partially chewed hors d'oeuvre into it. He wadded the disaster and searched for a trashcan. Unable to find one, he shoved the napkin in his pocket.

Sindra waved him over and introduced the older man as her publisher and host of the party. The younger man was a master chef at one of the top restaurants in town. Jet didn't care. He wanted food.

A server approached and presented them a tray of tidbits. Leery after his last experience, he eyed the delicious-looking morsels.

"Try one," said the chef. "These are my own recipe."

Each chose one. Hoping for the best, Jet took a cracker set with a square of white meat pressed into some kind of brown paste. Sindra and the publisher ate theirs in a single bite. Their raised eyebrows and nods indicated they considered the appetizer delicious.

He slid the cracker onto his tongue. So far so good. Biting into it, he almost gagged. The paste had so much garlic it stung, and the meat gritted against his teeth, fishy and rubbery.

"I do love a good squid," said the chef.

Squid? Somebody help him. Moving away, Jet said around his food, "Excuse me."

Searching his pocket for the napkin, he blinked watering eyes from the garlic. He successfully expelled the nastiness and left the room in hopes of finding something to wash the unsavory taste from his mouth.

In the main showroom, C.J. beat drumsticks on the base of an enormous elephant sculpture. Two men stood with him, singing lyrics to a song from their previous album. Jet envied his friend's ability to have a good time anywhere.

Giggles caught his attention as a group of young women headed his way, waving napkins and pens. This was not what he'd had in mind when he agreed to come. On the other side of the room, a cluster of unmistakable high-maintenance models raked their greedy eyes over him.

When his stomach growled loudly, a fan raised her eyebrows, and he began inching his way to the exit. He signed napkins on the way while ignoring suggestive overtures and outright propositions. He wanted something real. Something deep and lasting. Not a one-night-stand with a girl whose name he wouldn't remember in the morning. He hadn't enjoyed meaningless sexual encounters since their early years of success.

Worse yet, he could end the night with another Cynthia. Forget that. At the front door, he answered C.J.'s questioning glance with a wave goodbye.

Chapter Eight

Akiko made her way along the back wall of her neighborhood video store, one of the few brick and mortar ones remaining in the city. It grew harder and harder to find movies her parents would enjoy.

"If you rent two movies, you can get popcorn, candy, and a drink for just three dollars." A smiling store employee with free-flying blond curls and mirroring a lightness in happy blue eyes tried to hand her a coupon.

"No, thank you." Akiko moved toward the foreign films section. Maybe they had a Japanese thriller. Her mom loved those.

"We have Easter nerds." The pretty clerk's full lips quirked. "How can you pass on those?"

"Easter nerds?" Akiko assumed she talked of candy.

The woman laughed as if she had held it in. "I know. I can't even say that with a straight face." Not missing a beat, she handed a coupon to an unsuspecting patron who took it without thought. "I'm good," she said low with a wink. "What can I help you find this evening?"

"Probably a better idea not to get involved," warned Akiko, appreciating that the woman didn't try again to press her into accepting a coupon. "I'm trying to please two people who can't be pleased."

"Ah." She gave a knowing nod, the playful glimmer changing to one of wisdom. The clerk hurried to the front where a customer waited at a register, and called, "I'm Teak if you need anything."

Wondering if Teak had any new Japanese releases, Akiko looked out a huge plate glass window as a pristine red Camaro rolled past. The driver glanced her way.

Jet.

Her heart found a pounding rhythm as recognition lit his features. Trying to pretend he wouldn't care about spotting her, she perused movie titles. It didn't matter. He was probably on his way somewhere important or fun. He wouldn't stop.

When the door issued a loud ding with someone's entry, however, she knew he had come. She refused to turn as she ran a finger along a shelf of French movies.

"Hello, Akiko." His deep voice washed over her, and she closed her eyes, savoring it a moment.

Sighing, she faced him. Her knees went weak. Why did he have to be so handsome? And interested? She couldn't have him.

"Hi, Jet. Are you getting a movie for tonight?"

"No. I stream movies on my home theater. I'm here to see you."

Was that relief she detected in his voice? He appeared pleased, anyway. "How did you know I was here?"

"I didn't. I happened to pass by and see you. I'm glad you are." He glanced past her shoulder and shoved his hands into the back pockets of his black jeans. His tight black jeans. His sexy black jeans.

She squeezed her eyes closed. This was torture.

"You're renting a French film?" he asked, no censure in his tone.

"No. I've got to get something my parents will want to watch."

"Together? Yikes," he said casually.

"Exactly." She caught a movement near the exit and found Teak at the counter waggling eyebrows at her. Stifling a laugh, Akiko shrugged. "I don't know what to get."

"Here." Jet stepped around the case and chose a movie off the back wall.

She took it and stared at a leaping ninja on the cover. "For my parents?"

"Trust me. They'll love it because the story's based on an ancient Japanese legend. Don't ask me. I forget. If they're anything like my folks, your dad will like the action and intrigue. Your mom will like the love story."

She couldn't argue with that. "Thanks. I'll try it, and if they don't like it, I'll blame you."

"Now wait a minute."

She chuckled. "I'm kidding."

A low growl rumbled from him, and she took a step back.

"Sorry." Putting a hand on his middle, he said, "I haven't eaten."

"Me, neither." She moved to the counter. Despite a knowing smile, Teak didn't say a word while checking out the movie. Akiko was grateful. "I ate too light a lunch, and now I'm famished. Luckily, dinner should be about ready now."

"Is that an invitation?"

Ignoring the clerk's encouraging and enthusiastic nod, she stammered, "T-t-to dinner? With my family?"

"It's a little early between us, but sure. I'd love to." He grinned and put a hand to the small of her back. She adored the protective gesture.

He was coming to dinner. How had that happened? Stunned, she accepted the movie from the clerk.

"Are you sure you don't want to get some Easter nerds for dessert?" asked Teak before barking a charming laugh.

"Easter what?" Jet shot the clerk a curious smirk.

"Hey, aren't you Jet Cavanaugh from Smashing Glass?"

"No. I get that a lot, though."

Trying to figure out how to tell her father she'd invited a rock star to dinner, Akiko let Jet take her hand and practically drag her from the store.

Handsome Jet in her house. Sexy Jet sitting next to her while they ate. The idea thrilled her, sending fluttering sensations into her belly. What would her parents say?

Makoto was going to flip.

She opened her mouth to tell him not to come, but before she could speak, he said, "I'll follow you."

"Jet—"

"Don't worry. I won't get lost."

This was going to be a train wreck, and somebody would come out the other end never wanting to talk to her again.

True to his word, he followed her home without incident. Her throat went dry when she pulled into the driveway while Jet parked at the curb.

Meeting her at the front door, he said, "That's a really high fence."

"My parents value their privacy. It goes all the way around." If her father had his way, it would completely encompass the property, blocking people from knocking on the front door.

"Our dads would get along great."

"Come inside and meet my family." Swallowing past a lump, she opened the door and called, "*Tadaima.*"

"Akiko-san, *okaerinasai*," called her mother from the kitchen.

Closing the door, she whispered, "I announced I'm back, and my mother welcomed me."

"She sounds nice."

She put the movie and her purse on a table by the door then slid bare feet out of her slip-ons and curled toes into lush carpet. Teriyaki, ginger, and grilled meat scents wafted from the kitchen, making her lightheaded with hunger. She paused, taking in his stiff shoulders and set mouth. "They're not expecting you, but they don't bite...hard."

He released a heavy breath on a smile, his shoulders relaxing. Balancing with impressive skill, he removed his boots. "Something smells delicious."

"Akiko? Who is this?" Her father stood in the

doorway to the dining room, a frown adding an edge to his already dour demeanor.

"Father, please meet Jet Cavanaugh. He hasn't eaten, so I invited him to dinner." Expecting a sharp reprimand in rapid Japanese, she blinked and glanced at the floor.

"Mr. Tadaka, it's a real honor." Jet took a step toward her father and offered a hand. "Thank you so much for having me this evening."

He accepted Jet's hand with a slight bow, and Akiko covered her bemused smile. Her father's features softened. "Meestah Cavanaugh. You a fu-riend of Akiko? Come in. We ah about to eat. Join us."

"Thank you, sir."

He pumped Jet's hand as though meeting an important business partner then indicated the way to the dining table.

"Please call me Jet." He shot her a smile over his shoulder and moved further into the house.

"Help your mother," her father said in Japanese, shaking his head like he used to when she stepped out of line as a little girl. A curl to his lip let her know he faked his anger.

Maybe it would turn out well. She hurried to the kitchen and gathered an extra set of dishes from the cabinet. "We have a guest, Mother."

Her mom's face brightened. "A man?"

Akiko coughed. "Yes. A man."

"A nice man? The one Makoto mentioned? From the studio?"

She froze. Her brother told them about Jet? "I guess so."

"He isn't Japanese."

"No, Mother. He's American."

"He's just a friend."

No. "Yes." Not in a million years.

"Good. Good. Because I called my sister in Kyoto this morning. You will go."

Aghast, Akiko nearly dropped a bowl. "Why did you do that? I started a new job. I can't go abroad."

"You told us this job was only temporary. Besides, finding a husband is more important."

Shaking with anger, she snatched a set of chopsticks from a drawer and headed for the door. "Now isn't the time to discuss this."

"Of course." Her mother removed her apron and made to follow with a tureen of soba.

Chapter Nine

As a low table filled with steaming dish after dish, Jet tried not to get excited. Home cooking. It all looked and smelled incredible. Now his stomach hurt in hunger.

Akiko arrived with a plate of skewered meat. "This is the last."

Her father settled cross-legged onto a large mustard-colored cushion on the floor at the head of the table. He motioned Jet to sit on a red one along the side. Too hungry to question anything, he eagerly took his seat, glad when Akiko sank to a pale blue cushion to his right. Her brother took a seat across the table with an *I've got you right where I want you* grin.

"Tell us of your work," said her father, placing food into a bowl before him.

"I'm a musician." Leaning toward Akiko, he whispered, "Where's your mother?"

"In the kitchen. She won't sit with us until we're halfway through. Help yourself." She poured a clear liquid from a small gray vase-like container into a tiny cup next to his bowl. "Sake. Drink it slowly."

He spooned rice then bright vegetables in a sauce and skewered chicken into his bowl. His fingers hovered over a set of chopsticks. Casting a sideways glance, he tried to figure out how to hold them by watching her father manipulate a pair.

Her brother leaned forward with wide eyes.

"You're a famous musician. You're really great. I can't believe you're in my house. This is unbel—"

"Makoto," said Akiko in a soothing voice. "Let's not harass our guest."

While her father chuckled, Jet whispered, "Thanks."

Her arm brushed his knee as she leaned near. She reached across him and took his chopsticks, her pretty fragrance filling his nostrils and stirring a new kind of hunger. Taking his left hand, her long, soft fingers positioned the tools in his hold. He adored how she knew he was left-handed. She had paid attention.

Her ebony lashes fluttered a second then her dark eyes gazed at him in smiling seduction. For a moment, he forgot to breathe. Her open, easy manner contrasted so drastically with the behavior of every other woman at the party earlier that he couldn't help enjoying her company. Enjoying her. Wanting her.

His temperature rose, and he needed out of his jacket, but he didn't dare let go of the chopsticks. Plus, she'd have to release his hand, and he didn't want to lose the cherished contact.

As she guided his hand to the bowl and put his fingers through the motions necessary to grasp food with the chopsticks, he said to her father, "I play music in a band. We do pretty well."

"Pretty well?" Makoto snorted. "Smashing Glass is world-famous. You guys tour the planet. I've got friends in Japan who've seen you in concert and have all your CDs."

"Like I said, we do pretty well." Jet attempted a carrot slice on his own and managed to get it to his lips. Tangy sauce complimented the carrot's sweet flavor. "Mmm. Delicious."

"Thank you," said her mother who carried in a plate of small round cookies.

Mrs. Tadaka. Here was the person he needed to impress most. Eying the feast, he asked, "Do you eat like this every night?"

She didn't answer. As she left, Mr. Tadaka said,

"Only when we ah all he-ah to eat togeth-ah."

Akiko patted his hand and returned to her own
meal. Though she sat next to him, he missed her
nearness. Her fragrance. Her touch.

Setting his chopsticks on the lip of the bowl like
he'd seen Makoto do, he shrugged out of his jacket then
folded it and set it on the floor next to his cushion.
Instantly more comfortable, he tackled the task of
positioning the sticks in his hand. Akiko offered an
encouraging smile and nod. His mom would love her.

Succeeding in getting the chopsticks into working
position, he chose a piece of chicken and inclined his
head toward her father. "Akiko tells me you're skilled
with electronics. Is that what you do for a living?"

"I do. I am Vice PU-resident of Research and
Development for Tendime Systems."

The chicken, moist and tender, graced his tongue
with a rich barbeque flavor that hinted at a delicate
smokiness. Hibachi-cooked maybe? "Tendime. They do
the high-tech alarm clocks, kitchen gadgets, and stereo
systems."

"Yes. It's hard work but rewarding. You know
Akiko from the studio." He wrapped noodles around the
tips of his chopsticks with no effort and rid his bowl of
half its remaining contents in a single, noisy slurp.

"My band is recording an album, and Akiko's
working the mixing board." He gave her a smile of
thanks. "You're the one who's going to make this album
worth listening to."

"But the songs are very good."

"I can't wait," said Makoto, fairly bouncing on his
cushion. "Dad, did you know half the songs are written
by Jet?"

Nearly to the rice at the bottom of his bowl, he
said, "Not as many as half. I write three songs for each
album. Justin's our composer. All the tunes are his.
Mine are ballads, though. Embarrassing as it is, I have
to admit I'm a poet at heart."

"You feel deeply, I think," said Akiko in a reverent
tone. Her face in profile, she gazed at her dinner, yet an

invisible part of her reached out to him.

He didn't know if he imagined it, but he felt the connection as surely as if she had put a hand on his arm.

Her father took a sip of drink then said, "You should not be embarrassed. Poets ah highly venerated in Japan. It is a way of expressing what we hide inside. An appreciation for nature, emotion, a human's pu-lace in the world. A glimpse into the poet's soul."

Akiko cleared her throat. "Poetry is personal, first to the one who writes it, and then to the one who reads or hears it. Your songs touch me."

Jet frowned, not liking the idea that Justin's song might move her as easily. "Most of the songs are Justin's. How do you know if we've recorded any of mine?"

"I can tell yours apart. Two of the four you've recorded are yours. I know because they are the songs that make me melt."

Melt? His songs made her melt? Her admission made *him* melt. "Yeah? Then tell me. Which ones do you think I wrote?"

"Easy." She smiled. "*Dreaming* and *Catch Me in a Lie.*"

She did know. "That's amazing."

"Not really." She showed him how to put the sticks together to form a scraper-like scoop and encouraged him to pick up his bowl. "Justin's a genius with lyrics, I think. But your songs come from a deep place. They're simpler in word composition but more complex in emotion. Always there's this message of pain and searching, but with an underlying hope."

She totally got him. He stared at her in awe, his chopsticks suspended over his raised bowl.

Her mother came in and settled between Makoto and her husband. "I missed something impo-ru-tant?"

Jet blinked and reluctantly tore his gaze from Akiko. "You have a remarkable daughter."

"You ah remarkable to recognize that." The woman's happy eyes slowly closed as she made a shallow bow. "We ah honored you share our meal."

He eyed his almost empty bowl and asked, "Is it polite to have seconds?"

"Oh, yes!" Akiko's mother passed him a dish of tempura. "And thirds and fourths."

Her father chuckled with a nod and moved for a second helping of noodles. "We su-poke of poetry, Hanako-san."

"My favorite subject. Ah you familiar with Haiku, Meestah Cavanaugh?"

"I am, though I don't write it. Please call me Jet."

"Jet-san, I write Haiku. Perhaps you would like to read my poetry sometime?"

He didn't miss Akiko's arching eyebrows and gentle smile. Did it mean her family liked him? He hoped so. They made him welcome in their home. "I would love to. And maybe you would be willing to take a look at some of my poetry that never got turned into songs?"

"I would be most honored, Jet-san." Akiko's mother took an empty bowl from a stack at the center of the table and served herself modest portions. "You ah welcome to visit us anytime."

"Anytime," agreed Makoto. "But don't make me read poetry. Set it to music and I'm there, but don't make me read or write the stuff. I'm not a poetry kind of guy."

"I would be honored, too," said Akiko, placing a hand on his knee.

A rush of awareness raced along his thigh to his loins. As they stirred, it continued upward to twist a knot into his stomach. His imagination took over, sending her hand to the crotch of his jeans, making her family evaporate, and converting the table into a bed.

When she removed her hand, her cheeks went pink. Had she shared his vision? Could she want more than the friendship she claimed to offer?

Chapter Ten

"I should probably go. I've imposed long enough," said Jet an hour later as he shrugged into his leather jacket. "Thank you for having me to dinner."

Akiko and her mother wiped tears of mirth left from his telling of his party experience earlier that evening.

"Aw, man. I still have so many questions." Makoto came down from the second floor, trying to hide a CD behind his back and failing.

Akiko sighed. Her brother seemed determined to embarrass her.

"Is that one of our albums?" Jet stepped to the bottom of the stairs.

Makoto had the decency to color. "The first one."

"No way." He held out a strong hand. "Did you know we only sold about five hundred of these? I bet at least half wound up in the garbage. Do you want me to sign it?"

"Would you?"

"How about I do one better? Let me take it to the studio and I'll get all the guys to sign it. Then it might be worth something someday."

"Cool." Makoto handed it over but didn't let go right away. "You won't forget? Or lose it?"

"Trust me, man. I'll set you up right. Akiko will bring it to you tomorrow, okay?"

"Okay." He released the case and took a step

back, his eyes never leaving the album.

Akiko went to Jet's side, adoring his height and strength. She couldn't remember ever being so proud to have a friend meet her family. Not because he had money or success, but because he was such a goodhearted person.

"Thank you for the delicious meal," he said to her mother. Offering her father a handshake, he said, "Thank you for welcoming me into your charming home. It's been a long time since I've enjoyed myself so much."

Her father shook his hand and said to Akiko, "Why don't you take him through the garden? It is a beautiful night."

The garden? She held in a gasp. It was his way of saying he considered Jet a friend of the family, and he meant for her to visit longer with him.

When Jet sent her a questioning glance, she said, "Bring your boots and come this way."

She led him through the living room and out a set of French doors to a concrete walkway under an awning that ran the length of the house. There, she slipped on a pair of *tatami* straw sandals with red velvet thongs while he donned his boots.

In a near whisper, he said, "I never would've guessed this was back here."

She took his hand and closed the door. Moonlight glistened off a snaking stream that quietly rippled into a pond at the far end. White stone pathways gleamed between artfully arranged groupings of flowers, trees, and bushes. Her father found peace when working this garden, and it showed.

Jet glanced at her. Unwilling to speak earnestly so close to the house, she gave him a gentle tug and moved onto a pebbled pathway. The rocks made a cheerful sound as they shifted under their feet.

"Do you have to leave right away?" she asked.

"No, it's only nine." His low voice had an intimate quality in the night.

She led him toward a pagoda-style gazebo. Three-quarters of the way there, lantern lights flickered on, casting a gentle glow across the garden. Akiko glanced over her shoulder to the house as her father passed the French doors on his way to the staircase inside.

"You impressed my parents," she said, taking three steps into the gazebo. "They like you."

"I'm glad. I wasn't sure. You've got a really nice family."

"Thank you." Not letting go of his hand, she sat on a bench and patted the place next to her. In the garden behind them, a frog chirped a three-note melody.

As he took a seat, the light of a tan lantern reflected from his features in a warm radiance, the angles and planes of his face made less sharp in the faint gleam.

"It's so quiet. I can almost believe we're in some small town in Japan instead of at the heart of Chicago."

"It's restful." She boldly skimmed her thumb across the back of his hand, enjoying the coarse resistance of a few hairs near his wrist. Anticipation coursed through her. She wanted to taste this forbidden fruit, and the idea thrilled her.

"Private," he whispered. Leaning forward, he planted his elbows on his knees and took her hand in both of his. "It makes me want to say things I shouldn't."

"Like what?" She held her breath. A cool breeze brushed her arm and cheek, and she closed her eyes, soaking in the magic.

"Like that you're so different from anyone I've known, and I don't want to blow it with you."

Her belly quivered with delight. "You are unlike any man I've met. I like you very much."

"Very much?" He pulled her hand, forcing her to lean against his shoulder.

"Yes, very much."

"We've known each other two days. I don't want to rush and take the chance of pushing you away. We're friends, right?"

A heavy stone sank to the bottom of her stomach. She wanted to be more, but she had so many reasons why they couldn't. "Friends. Yes."

Squeezing her hand, he pressed warm lips to her knuckles. "I told you at lunch that I'm going through a tough time."

"I remember." She rested her cheek on his thick shoulder. Layers of shirt and jacket couldn't hide the firmness of his muscles.

"My girlfriend left me a few days ago."

Why would anyone in possession of his heart walk away from him? He was wonderful. The rock in her stomach grew heavier. "I'm sorry."

"I don't want you to be a rebound."

The rock became a boulder. "I'm not a rebound if we're not romantic, Jet."

"Right. Just friends." He closed his eyes, and though his profile appeared peaceful, she felt his tension against her cheek. "Is it that you deserve better?"

"No. How could you think that?"

"Because you do."

Akiko sighed. "It's about perspective, I guess. My father thinks better is honor, character and the ability to support a family. My mother thinks better is about nationality and social connections. But I think the man best for me is the one who can love me for who I am, who can allow me the freedom to pursue my happiness, and who shares my values. A man who wants to share in the life I create and who wants me to share in the life he creates."

He nodded. "When the two lives combine, they are one and the same yet separate."

"You understand." She had taken a chance, and he comprehended.

"I do. So is it that I'm not good looking enough for you?"

Okay, maybe he didn't get it. Disgusted, she pulled her hand free and stood. She crossed the gazebo to stare over the koi pond. "I don't care what you look like. It doesn't matter that I've had romantic feelings about you from the moment I met you. What matters is that I can't have you."

His warm breath brushed her ear, alerting her that he had come near. She gripped the gazebo's railing, afraid to move. Afraid she would lean against his strength and never want to leave it.

"You have romantic feelings for me?" he asked, his hands finding the curve of her waist.

"Yes," she whispered, wishing the word didn't hurt so much to say. A lump of emotion clogged her throat, and she closed her eyes.

"But you can have me."

"I can't." She fought tears. She wanted him so much her heart ached.

Putting pressure on the upper flare of her hips, he turned her to face him. The sadness in his eyes drew the corners of his lids downward. "Tell me to leave."

"No."

He touched his lips to her forehead.

Heaven.

"Tell me you never want to see me again." His gentle lips met with the tip of her nose.

"I can't. I want to see you every day, and when we're apart, you haunt my thoughts."

"It's the same for me." His gaze held hers. Steady. Unwavering.

"Is this crazy? Are we wrong to feel so strongly after only two days?"

"Maybe it's just attraction." The intensity of his voice belied the lightness of his words.

"It feels like more. Maybe we are drawn to one another because we know we shouldn't."

He put his forehead to hers. "All I know is I think you're sweet and gentle and good for me. I like being with you, and being away from you only makes me want to be with you more."

Against everything she knew, she slowly lifted her eyes to meet his stare. Her hands found his chest, but she didn't push. For once, she let instinct and desire override logic. She tilted her face until her nose touched his.

He took over, tenderly grazing his lips across hers. As he lazily moved back and forth, Akiko sucked a quick breath through her nostrils, her body immediately coming to life. He sent his hands to her back then urged her closer. His mouth pressed to hers, and she wrapped her arms around his neck.

His cologne, a fragrance of cedar and bergamot she hadn't noticed before, filled her head with a heady fog of hunger. She let him hug her close, and she melted against Jet's hard lines. Her curves fit to him. She'd never wanted to peel a man out of his clothes so badly.

When he added pressure to her lips, she opened in complete submission. His tongue, smooth and hot, swept hers. He tasted of smoky-sweet yakitori and clean remnants of sake. The earth tilted, and she clung to him.

Jet Cavanaugh. American. Rock star. Her parents would never approve. But this man made her heart pound. Made her palms sweat. Made her want, for the first time in her life, to defy her family. He was rebounding. He was wrong for her, but he made her happy. For now, he lit her world on fire.

She couldn't help envisioning a future with him. As their lips worked and their tongues danced, images flashed in her mind. Life with him on the road, in hotels and at concerts. Going to parties, dinners, and scrounging for time alone. Time in his arms. Time in his bed.

Bending her slightly backward, he deepened the kiss and caressed the outer curve of her breast. All thought disappeared in a blink. Sending fingers into his hair, she enjoyed the thick softness of it despite generous gel making the ends spike to the sky. His chin sported a bit of stubble that gently grazed her cheek as his kiss grew more needy. More passionate.

Though his hunger matched her own, he remained respectful. She never doubted he would stop if she asked. She didn't want to. Fully cupping her breast, he lowered his other hand to her rear where he measured her with the press of his fingers. She fitted her body tighter against him, wanting closer yet never satisfied.

She needed to stop.

Sliding a hand down the contours of his muscled torso, she panted with excitement while seeking the hem of his T-shirt. To feel him. To experience him by fingertips. Inching under the soft material, she tentatively touched the hot skin of his well-worked torso.

She needed to stop or she wouldn't be able to.

He broke from the kiss and regarded her with a curious but engaging stare. Placing his thumb to the dip at the base of her throat and splaying his long fingers along her collarbone, he said, "You're inside me. You're here before me, with me. But you're in my head. Please don't let me scare you away."

As she flattened her palms and drove them to the slabs of his chest, her breath caught on a hitch. "You really are a poet. Please don't..."

"Don't what?"

"I can't be your good time, Jet. Don't let me come to mean nothing."

"Nothing?" He rolled his eyes and took her softly by the shoulders. "You'll never be just a good time to me, Akiko. Never."

He kissed her in a way that made her legs threaten to buckle. His mouth slanted over hers, and his hands held her face as if he cherished her more than anything.

But how could he? Could their souls be connected already? The romantic in her wanted to believe it. Her head, however, told her he said what she needed to hear so he could have his way. He didn't seem the type, but what did she know?

Chapter Eleven

As the sound of Jet's car faded in the night, Akiko entered the quiet house with her heart still beating fast and her entire body in acute awareness. She turned off a lamp left lit in the living room then headed for her bedroom. Upstairs, she paused in the hallway at a muted conversation seeping through her parents' closed door.

"...not Japanese." Her mother's voice rose in agitation.

Her father fired off a rapid response. "...musician...works with her...make her quit?"

Make her quit? They wouldn't ask her to quit her job because of Jet, would they? She had known the man two days, and already he unknowingly put her in the position of having to choose between him and her family.

Her mother's voice grew louder, and Akiko could make out a bit more. "...my sister in Kyoto...serious about a man...time for Akiko to marry. I want grandchildren!"

Good gracious. She was twenty-two. What was the rush? With a frustrated huff, she went to her room and flopped on her bed. She should've defied tradition and moved out after graduating. It would've caused them worry and hurt. Who did she kid? As much as she wanted to be angry with them, she wouldn't intentionally pain them. Still, she couldn't get past the residual effects of Jet's kisses and caresses. Her lips tingled. Her body hummed. He was all she could think about for the rest of her sleepless night.

"And in entertainment news this morning, Cynthia Blalock, ex-girlfriend of Jet Cavanaugh of Smashing Glass, was seen last night with another rocker, Back Alley's lead singer, Brian Bryant. Apparently, the couple is now living together."

Jet froze, his hand poised over a red silk tie still on its hanger in his closet. He faced the television in disbelief. Five days? She'd left five days ago and already she'd found someone else? It could only mean she'd been seeing Brian while she'd lived with Jet.

"The slut."

A sly smirk on his face, the new announcer continued. "It seems Ms. Blalock has found serious interest in Brian Bryant, if the diamond ring on her left ring finger is any indication."

"What?" Enraged, Jet threw a shoe at the television. It struck the power button and the screen blinked to black.

With Akiko warming his heart, he didn't care what Cynthia did, or with whom. But he couldn't understand it. Cynthia had lived with him for four months, and the moment he'd hinted at marriage, she went running. They all did. So what did Brian have that he didn't? How long until Akiko discovered he was missing this long-term appeal other guys seemed to have?

In the main room, his phone rang. He slumped. He couldn't handle more bad news. Tightening the towel around his hips, he ran a hand through his still-wet hair and padded down the hall. His cell phone warbled on the kitchen counter.

The display screen showed C.J. No doubt his friend had seen the same news and wanted to make sure he was okay. As much as he appreciated C.J.'s concern, he didn't need his sympathy at the moment.

He let the call go to voicemail.

In the bedroom, he stared at the clothes he'd set out. Brownish-purple slacks with dark brown shoes, one of which now lay in front of the television, and a purple dress shirt draped the front of his bed. For what? To impress Akiko?

She'd introduced him to her parents and said things in the gazebo that made him hope. Then she'd kissed him like she meant it. He wanted to pull out his hair.

Usually, the only activity that helped him obtain his footing when the world tilted like this was working with weights. Increasing his body's strength somehow brought him a measure of inner steadiness. These past few days, however, Akiko had seemed to ground him in a way he'd never experienced. Working out had turned into an exercise he enjoyed, instead.

Now, however, that foundation slipped out from under him. Leaving the towel around his hips, he stalked to the apartment's second bedroom, which he'd converted into a gym. He grasped a couple thirty-pound dumbbells and moved to a mirror for a set of bicep curl warm-ups.

His reflection mocked him. He'd never find love. Not the real kind. Like most celebrities, the best he could hope for was serial monogamy. Marriage would be a waste of time, so what was the point?

Not caring if he went late to the studio, Jet bent over a weight bench and worked his triceps. Normally, he couldn't wait to see Akiko. Instinct told him she differed from the other women, but instinct had failed him in every previous relationship. He couldn't trust it.

For the next forty minutes, he mentally berated his trusting nature and worked his muscles until he headed, weak and sweaty, toward his second shower of the morning.

Afterward, he donned a faded pair of jeans, a plain white T-shirt, and old but comfortable sneakers. Why try to impress a woman who'd only disappoint him in the long run?

♪   ♪   ♪   ♪

The music sounded amazing despite the late start and thick tension. Akiko attributed it to the band's unusual professionalism and the fact that, according to Makoto, this group of friends had seen more than their share of hardship and trials.

Still, it hurt how Jet avoided her eyes and appeared so hard-edged and angry. After their kisses, she'd expected smiles and at least a greeting of some kind.

Something had happened. When Jet arrived at the studio nearly an hour late, his band mates hadn't said a word to him. He wore casual clothes, though he continued to look more stylish than his friends.

In fact, twice Cory had to nudge her because she couldn't stop staring. Jet's thin white T-shirt stretched delightfully across his thick chest and arms, a constant reminder of how good it had felt when he held her. His jeans hugged his shapely thighs and rear like his slacks never had.

Dressed like that, he made her long for leisurely Saturday mornings, throwing a Frisbee in the park, and long walks through the neighborhood – things she hadn't done since a girl.

After they had the first song where they wanted, the band broke for lunch. Akiko stayed at the mixing board and worked the song's dynamics, trying to ignore her unease at how Jet had left without a glance in her direction. She couldn't have done or said something to offend. She'd had no chance.

Well into the break, she took her lunchbox and went outside to eat a sandwich in the sun. She settled at a picnic table in a grassy area edging the parking lot. Halfway through her meal, Jet parked in a space near her table. Though he gazed directly at her while turning off his car, he didn't say anything when he emerged.

"Hi, Jet," she said.

He stopped but didn't look her way.

"I really enjoyed having you visit my home. I'm sorry we didn't get a chance to talk this morning." She got to her feet, silently begging him not to walk away.

He spun on his heel, dark emotion adding edginess to his handsome features. "Cut the crap, Akiko. Admit that you're biding your time with me until somebody better comes along."

She blinked, flinching as his words slapped her. "Why do you say that? Have my parents said something?" When had they talked to him? Was that why he was late this morning?

"I took a real chance letting you get close after..." He took a step closer and jabbed a finger toward her. "Why are women so heartless?"

"Heartless?" Was he being insecure? "What have I done?"

"It's what you're going to do. You act sweet and kind, but when it really counts, you'll stomp on me as you walk out the door. No, thank you."

"It's not fair to say women are the same, and especially that I'm being nice to you so I can hurt you later. I'm taking a huge risk here, too." Her face grew hot and her voice climbed an octave, regardless of her intention to remain calm.

"What risk are you taking? I'm a sure bet."

"Not judging by the way you're acting today. And how do I know you're a sure bet? You're a rock star. You could break my heart easier than I could break yours. You have far more opportunities." At the idea, her voice began to shake and she sliced a hand through the air. "You'll go off on tour and meet some supermodel, and here I'll be, without my family and without you." She sniffed.

"What the hell are you talking about? Without your family?"

Stuffing the remnants of her lunch into her lunchbox with angry shoves, she blinked back tears. "You've obviously missed my many hints this week. My parents won't approve of you, Jet. I'm defying them. Going to lunch with you. Letting you come to dinner at my home. And then in the garden..."

He took a step closer to her.

She shook her head and zipped the lid closed. "They'll make me choose, and I won't choose them."

"You won't?" His voice grew softer and he came to the table. "They disapprove of me because I'm a rock musician?"

"No. Because you're not Japanese." She hugged the box to her chest.

"And you would choose me?" His gaze never wavered from her face. "After three days, you'd give up your family for me? Damn. I thought I moved too fast. Why didn't you tell me?"

"Are you serious? I want a chance with you. Telling you about my struggle would send you running."

"Not me. I'm different."

"I'm beginning to see that." Her anger dissipated. "So what now?"

She sighed and set the lunchbox on the table. She indicated his clothes. "So now how about you explain...all of this?"

"This is how I normally dress." He sat at the end of the picnic bench. "I'm sorry if it disappoints you."

"It doesn't. I want you to be yourself. I can't truly get to know you otherwise."

"You actually want to get to know me? You're not just interested in hanging out with a celebrity?"

Akiko chuckled and joined him on the bench. "I want to know Jet Cavanaugh, the man who happens to be a rock musician. Not the other way around. That you're so handsome is a bonus."

He gave her his charming half-smile that made her melt a bit. "You think I'm handsome?"

"Very." Her cheeks warmed. "So why were you acting like you didn't like me this morning? Did something happen?"

"Nothing that I want to talk about. Not right now, anyway. Do you really want to get to know me?"

"Yes."

He scooted closer. "Well, I think you're beautiful.

So beautiful it's hard to look at you sometimes."

Now that was a compliment. Her cheeks caught fire, and she pressed cool fingers to them.

"This is for your brother." He pulled Makoto's album from the waist of his jeans and handed it to her. "There's only one way to get to know me."

"How's that?"

"Got any plans tomorrow?"

"Saturday? I usually help my mother with chores, but I'm sure I could get out of it for one day."

Narrowing his eyes, he stood. He twisted a golden pinkie ring and glanced at the studio. "I can't believe I'm going to do this. I'll pick you up at ten tomorrow morning."

Chapter Twelve

It was official. Jet had lost his mind. What would his mom say?

He snuck a peek at Akiko in his passenger seat and licked his lips. She looked like one of those serene oriental ladies painted on silk. Her black hair lay straight and unbound down her back. Why hadn't he noticed how long it was?

Wearing a touch of makeup, something she hadn't done until now, she met his ideal for beauty. Not the attractiveness he'd though was his ideal – blond hair, the body of a lingerie model, and tan. No, she formed a new ideal. Something natural and real. A loveliness that made him want to touch her. Constantly. Her pale skin hinted at an olive glow that became unmistakable in sunlight. Makeup enhanced the slant of her dark eyes and arched, delicate brows. A touch of red color under dewy lip-gloss provided a vibrant contrast.

He wished he had skill with a paintbrush so he could capture her on canvas. He said, "You're unusually quiet."

"I'm nervous."

"You don't even know where we're going."

"That's why I'm nervous."

He laughed, merging right in anticipation of his highway exit. "We're going to a cookout."

"A barbeque party? With your band?"

"C.J. will be there, but no. With my parents."

"I'm really nervous now." Her lovely lips pursed slightly, making him want to kiss them. "By the way, thank you for the movie suggestion. You were right. The whole family liked it."

"I'm glad." Pulling off the freeway, he gripped the steering wheel like a boy going to prom with the prettiest girl in school. He drove streets that had hardly changed since his days as a teenager with big dreams. At his childhood home, vehicles clogged the curbs. He had to park two houses down. "This way, my lady."

Taking his hand, she said, "I'm really not a lady. I'm common."

"There's nothing common about you, Akiko." Not bothering with the front door, he led her directly around back where more than forty people milled in the spacious backyard.

"Hey! Jethro!" His dad waved a spatula in greeting a second before a breeze sent smoke in his face from a sizzling grill. He sputtered and ducked out from behind the grill.

"Jethro?" Akiko shot him an amused glance, her eyes smiling but her lips relaxed.

"Go ahead. Make your jokes."

"No joking. I like it."

Scanning the party for his mother, he snorted. "Nobody likes the name Jethro."

"Really? Not Jethro Tull? And somebody liked it enough to name one of television's most interesting characters Jethro."

"Who?"

"Jethro Gibbs."

"I don't watch much T.V. I'll have to look that one up." Locating his mom, he offered a wave. Twisting his pinkie ring, he said, "It's a family name. My grandfather's, to be specific. He left me this ring."

Akiko put her soft hand in his. "It's a beautiful ring. Is that your mother?"

"Yes." He gave her cool fingers a squeeze.

"She's a lovely woman. You look a lot like her."

"I've got her face and her black hair. My blue eyes

come from my dad."

"Jethro, my handsome son," said his mother as she approached. "I'm so glad you could make it. C.J. and Sindra are inside doing...something. I don't know. Probably beating dents in the walls and furniture with drumsticks, knowing those two."

He laughed and nodded.

His mother beamed then turned a friendly smile to Akiko.

"Mom, I'd like you to meet Akiko Tadaka. She works at the studio."

"I'm pleased to meet you, Mrs. Cavanaugh," said Akiko with a slight bow.

"So polite. You're working with Smashing Glass on their new album?"

"Yes, ma'am."

"Has he told you how the band got their name?"

"No, he hasn't."

She released a hearty chortle. "Oh-ho! You'll have to ask him about it later."

"Thanks, Mom," he said dryly. "Thanks a lot."

She put an arm around Akiko's shoulders and headed for the kitchen's sliding glass door. "Call me Pat. I'm so glad you came with Jet."

Sindra came out the door. "Jet! There you are." She jogged over and hooked an arm through Akiko's. "You must be Akiko. C.J. calls you Magic Fingers."

"He does? I thought he didn't like me." She shot Jet an incredulous look.

"Yep. He says you work the sound board like nobody's business and will make this their best-sounding album yet." The blonde grinned and tugged her arm. "Come inside so we can give you all the dirt on Jet."

He groaned. This couldn't be good. "You can stay here with me, if you'd prefer."

"And miss out on the dirt? Not in a million." Akiko laughed and let Sindra guide her into the house.

His mother stayed and took his hand. She fingered his pinkie ring and said, "I thought you would take a break from women after the way Cynthia treated you."

He sighed and followed her to a table set along the fence where cakes, pies, and puddings sat in colorful display. "I intended to. I promise I didn't go looking for love two days after Cynthia walked out."

She cast him an I-know-you glance then rearranged pies at the center of the table.

"I didn't. I swear. You can believe I fought my attraction for Akiko."

"What? For ten minutes?"

"Listen, I've been struggling with this, but she doesn't deserve a man who's warm and interested one minute then cold another. She's not exactly chasing me, either. Her family wants her to date a Japanese guy, not some upstart American rock musician."

"Upstart?" She barked a laugh. "You're the least upstart person I know."

"It's about appearances."

"Have you slept with her?"

"None of your business."

She straightened and placed a hand on her hip. "She seems very nice."

"She's the nicest, most honest and gentle person I've ever met."

"So she's good for you."

"Too good. And we're all wrong. I mean, we shouldn't be together. I'm on the rebound, and that's not fair to her. She can't tell her family we're romantic. They think we're friendly co-workers."

"You met them?"

"I had dinner at their house."

"Interesting."

Interesting like she couldn't believe.

"I'd like to talk to her." His mother waved to a newly arriving couple. "If you don't mind."

"You won't give her the third degree, will you?" Jet eyed the house. What kind of mischief did C.J. embroil Akiko in right now?

"Of course not, Jethro. You know me better than

that. She sounds different than your other girlfriends. I'd like to see for myself."

"Fine. Be gentle."

"I always am, sweetheart."

He somehow managed to get through a halfway decent conversation with the girl who'd grown up across the street and her new husband. C.J. and Sindra emerged from the house and cajoled him to a table near the grill. His mother and Akiko, both giggling, went to another table.

"This isn't right," he said. "I brought her. She should sit with me."

Sindra nudged his arm then handed him a plate with grilled chicken and a generous portion of potato salad. C.J. plunked a plastic cup of beer in front of him while sipping from another.

"This is ridiculous." He eyed Akiko, who had slipped into a serious discussion with his mother. "I haven't had fifteen minutes with her since we got here."

"She's a great girl, Jet." Sindra passed him a bowl of baked beans. "Genuine and sweet. I guess you're in new territory."

He passed the beans along without taking any. "I knew nice girls in high school, but there aren't a lot of sweet-natured knockouts like her in the industry."

"That's for sure. Akiko really is stunning. Inside and out."

Akiko and his mother burst into laughter. Part of him cringed, dreading to learn what about him they found so funny. Part of him rejoiced, however. They enjoyed each other's company, and that meant a lot.

"Leave it up to you to bring a woman to meet your parents after dating only a week." C.J. shook his head and popped a cherry tomato into his mouth.

With a smug grin, Jet said, "She took me home to meet her family a couple days ago. Don't point a finger at me."

His friend rolled his eyes then kissed Sindra's bare shoulder. "Dude, I can't really talk."

She took a biscuit and passed the basket to Jet.

"When it's right, it's right."

"I'm not saying it's right."

"Then what is it?" she asked.

"Impulsive. Crazy. Stupid and ill-advised." Jet chuckled and held out his plate for his dad to dish a grilled bell pepper onto it. "Exciting. Amazing. A whole lot of wonderful trouble."

C.J. snickered. "So you're telling us it's your typical whirlwind romance. It's the only kind you ever have."

"It's nuts. I know. The harder I try to take it slow, the faster we seem to go. On her part, too."

Akiko and his mother came and sat. His father joined them, completing the table. They talked and laughed as if Akiko had been dating Jet and coming to these cookouts for years. Soon, other guests crowded around and added to the fun.

"Tell us how the band got its name," said Akiko, her eyes bright and happy, as if lit from within.

He couldn't deny her when she looked at him like that. "Fine. It was C.J.'s fault."

His friend threw back his head and laughed loud. "It's true."

"Chaz was new to our group, and he and Justin had come over to practice in the garage."

C.J. drummed his hands on the table. "I wanted to impress Chaz, so I was already in the garage practicing the Karriker lick. I wanted to do it perfect."

"He was concentrating so hard that he didn't hear us coming through the house."

"Yeah. I thought they were going to come up the driveway."

Jet chuckled. "When I opened the door, he shouted and threw his sticks."

"Oh, it was a disaster," said his mother.

"And painful," declared C.J. "I fell backward off my stool and rolled."

"He went right through the drywall," said Jet's father, shaking his head. "I still don't know how he managed to land right between two studs like that."

"Yeah," said C.J. "I went right through the wall into the formal living room! My foot caught a cabinet, which crashed. Its glass door and all the glass trinkets smashed."

"But that's not all," Jet told Akiko over the laughter around the table. "There was a crystal bowl on top of the cabinet, and it went flying. It flew into the kitchen and took out the sliding glass door."

His mother guffawed. "There was smashed glass everywhere."

His father thumped the table in his mirth then took a deep breath. "The boys were in shock. The fear and amazement was palpable. Then Chaz put his shoe on some of the glass and crunched it. I'll never forget. He said, 'The legend begins. From the shards of rubble arises Smashing Glass, the band to lead all bands.' Only Chaz could come up with the name with such drama."

Akiko's mouth quirked at one corner, and her eyebrows crinkled. "Is that really how you got your name? This is a true story?"

"Every bit." Jet shared a look with C.J. then burst into laughter. "We were still finding pieces of glass a month later."

Jet tried to remember the last time he'd enjoyed a woman's company as much as he did Akiko's. Now, if only he could shake a sense of impending doom that kept the afternoon from achieving perfection.

Chapter Thirteen

"What's this?" Akiko lifted an airline brochure from the kitchen counter. Inside rested a one-way ticket to Japan with her name on it. "Absolutely not!"

Her mother shrugged and continued to work dough into loose flour for noodles. "It's all arranged. There will be no discussion."

"I'm a week into a new job and already working with famous musicians. This is my chance to make a name for myself." And she was falling in love with Jet. "I graduated a few weeks ago. I wanted some time. I can't leave. It's irresponsible. Are you trying to ruin my reputation in the music industry?"

"It's irresponsible for a woman your age to ignore the importance of beginning a family early. We never thought you should've gone to that technical college, anyway."

Akiko sighed. "This is America. I can choose to be a career woman."

"No, this is your family." Her mother threw the dough on the kitchen counter in a rare show of pique. "I will not be challenged by my own daughter! You will go and honor your family."

"Don't force this." Akiko trembled, hating how her mother pushed so hard and didn't realize she would push her away forever. The ticket showed Tuesday's date.

"Too late."

"What if I don't go?"

"You disgrace your father and me. It's all arranged. No more talk."

Frustrated and confused, Akiko marched to the garden where her father worked to clean the pond. She wouldn't bother him. He had to leave this afternoon for a business trip to New York, and he needed some solitude. He didn't look her way as she strode to the gazebo. The structure used to mean peace, but now it bombarded her with memories of Jet's kisses. His eyes. His hands. The way he'd held her.

She couldn't stand it. She returned to the house, collected Makoto's car keys and went for a Sunday morning drive. It got her out of the house, but it didn't get her any closer to a decision. If she went to Japan, she'd lose Jet. If she didn't, she'd lose her family. How would she survive this?

Belting out the final note on their eighth song for the album, Jet cut his gaze to Akiko's pale face for the hundredth time that day. Was she sick? Her eyes lacked their usual life, and her expression revealed nothing. Not even pleasure at seeing him.

When Corey called it a wrap, Jet turned off his keyboard and raced out the door. He stood outside the technician's booth and ignored the glances his friends sent him as they passed. Screw them. Akiko appeared to need someone to talk to, and he wanted to be there for her.

"Hey," he said when she opened the door. "You looked like you were having a bad day."

"Bad day. Bad week. Bad life."

"Do you want to tell me about it?"

"Yes. That would be wise. Can we go outside?"

"Sure."

Corey came out and put a hand on Akiko's shoulder. "Call me and let me know, okay?"

She nodded. "As soon as I know for sure."

Jet let her take his hand and headed out behind the producer. "Know what for sure? Is something going on?"

She said nothing, leading the way to the picnic table at the far corner of the parking lot. Heat rose from the baking asphalt still sweltering in late afternoon sun. After singing all day, he didn't welcome the warmth. But she needed him, and he didn't like the impression that she prepared to crush him.

In bright rays illuminating the spot of grass where she stopped, she faced him. She avoided his gaze, however. "I have a decision. A difficult decision I'm not prepared to make."

His stomach sank. "What kind of decision?"

"The kind that changes lives."

"Lives. As in yours and mine?"

"Yes." She nodded and her bottom lip trembled.

He expected her to cry, but no tears came. "Since this is going to change my life, maybe I could help you make it?"

She lifted hopeful eyes. "My parents have purchased a ticket for me to go to Japan. To stay with my aunt."

His stomach dropped to his feet. "Because of me?"

"Not because of you." She placed cool fingers on his forearm. Her wary gaze let him know, however, that if they knew the extent of her attachment to him, it would be because of him.

"To find a Japanese man," he said. "A Japanese husband."

"Yes," she whispered.

"And you think you should go."

"No." Her dark eyes went wide. "I think I should not. If I stay, I defy my parents. I dishonor my family. It will not be forgiven."

"Then you should go." Ouch. That had hurt to say. "Family means everything."

Her lips parted, but no sound came. She showed him her profile as she watched Chaz thunder onto the street on his motorcycle. Did she want Jet to make her a promise he couldn't? Maybe she wanted him now, but in a couple months, she wouldn't. Women never did.

He wanted Akiko to love him. Commit to him. He'd give her his heart and never stray. With her, happily ever after was possible. Or at least he thought so. He could no longer trust his feelings, though. They had misled him too many times.

"You want me to go? To leave?" she asked on a shaking voice.

Her poignant disappointment cracked his heart down the center. He ached from the pain his words caused her. He couldn't have her lose her family on a false hope. She'd hate him if she abandoned her family for him and then their relationship didn't work.

"I'm sorry," he said, meaning it to his soul. "Maybe if we had longer, we could've decided how far we're willing to take this. I—"

"Jet—"

"When are you supposed to leave?"

"Tomorrow."

His heart skipped a beat. This was ending before they'd had a chance to take it far enough to know anything.

"Jet, I told you I am not easily won." Her face went taut.

Here it came. The final kiss-off. He tensed for the killing blow. "I know. We've had a few meals and a couple kisses."

A tear spilled free from her liquid eyes. "It wasn't the meals or kisses. It was the dream of a beautiful future. You won my loyalty in your kind treatment of my family. Your dedication to work and friends won my respect. Your kisses in my father's garden won my heart. You won me, Jethro, but it's clear I haven't won you. I thought maybe I had." Her voice cracked. "So I'll go, as you suggest. I will go."

Stunned, he could only stand unmoving. Without looking back, she ran for the street where her brother waited. He ached to chase her. To ask her to ignore his foolishness and reconsider, but his feet wouldn't move.

He couldn't summon the air from his lungs to issue forth and call to her. Everything in him cried out to her, cried out to the joy and completeness he'd found with her. He couldn't, however, get past the knowledge that if he did, she'd have to leave her family.

For the second time that month, his world crumbled around him. Unlike Cynthia's, Akiko's farewell carried a sense of permanence. As if he lost his one and only chance at true love.

Jet blinked and found himself in his car. He blinked again and discovered he had somehow driven home. Shaken, he parked and made his way to his apartment. He tossed his keys on the coffee table and eyed his saxophone.

Where was the music? Where was the jazz and blues his sad breakups inspired? For once, he had no music in him.

He went to his weight room, but the equipment didn't beckon him, either. The idea of Akiko leaving the country, leaving him and marrying another man, sapped the strength from him

"God. It's been a week. How did this happen?"

Swallowing hard past a lump of fear so great it threatened to suffocate him, he unclipped his cell phone from his belt loop and called his father.

"Hi, Jethro."

"Is this a bad time, Dad?" He despised the neediness in his voice.

"I'm playing golf. We're walking the green to the next hole, so you timed it right. What's on your mind?"

"It's about Akiko. I think I blew it."

"I'm sorry, Son. She was different. I really thought she could be the one for you."

"She is. Her parents want to send her to Japan to find a husband, and I told her she should go."

A long pause on the line made Jet nervous. Then his father said, "You two haven't really had a chance to get to know one another, have you?"

"I think I love her, Dad." He took a deep breath as he envisioned her smile. Her words echoed in his ears.

Her intelligence. Her competence. Her gentle strength. "It was so different with her."

"How?"

"I pictured my other girlfriends in wedding gowns and walking down the aisle of a church. I loved the idea of the wedding. Of love. Akiko, though, makes me want to be with her. It's not about the wedding. It's about the after. Living with her. Sharing our lives. Am I being stupid? Is it too soon to think about this?"

"I don't know, Jethro. I don't think you're being stupid. Sometimes when we meet the one, we know. You've tried hard to force it to happen with so many girls. Maybe when it really happened, you couldn't see it. You've had a difficult go with Akiko?"

He switched the phone to his other ear. "Yes and no. Yes because I tried to resist her and convince myself she wasn't for me. No because I couldn't *not* be around her. When we're together, I'm at home. Comfortable. Calm."

"Complete." His father's sigh came through, loud and unmistakable. "That's how your mother made me feel. Still makes me feel."

Jet closed his eyes on a mixture of agony and joy. He'd found it. Finally, he'd found the real thing. "I blew it. I told her to leave."

"Sleep on it, Son. Take tonight to breathe, and if you feel the same in the morning, go talk to her. Listen, they're teeing up, so I've got to go."

"Thanks, Dad."

"Good luck."

Jet hit the end key, went to the living room and flopped on the couch. His dad was right. If he went to her house tonight, he'd beg and plead and make her despise him. He wasn't a teenager asking a girl on a date. He wasn't a dreamer hunting a fantasy. No, he had to be a man. Akiko deserved a real man who would bring as much to their life together as she did. He only hoped his words this afternoon didn't make it too late.

Chapter Fourteen

"Isn't Father coming?" Akiko handed her suitcase to Makoto at the foot of the staircase.

Her brother sniffed with disgust. "You've been so out of it. Dad doesn't get back from New York until later. He's coming back this morning. We're meeting him at the airport after your flight leaves."

"That's right. I knew that. I forgot."

Her mother handed Akiko a jacket and hurried for the front door. "Let's get going."

Fighting tears, Akiko forced her feet to carry her outside into predawn darkness. The weight of the night pressed her hopelessness to the surface. How could she have such strong love for a man who didn't return it? How was she so wrong about Jet?

He'd told her to go. His words hurt with every echoing repeat in her memory, and they hadn't stopped all night.

She inhaled a shaky breath. Japan had a lot of great men, especially since she had fully escaped her match with Michizane. But none would be Jet. None would have his incredible blue eyes, his way of kissing her, his unique energy.

"I'm a fool," she said, sliding into the backseat of her brother's car.

"Maybe so," said her mother from the front passenger seat. "We'll take care of that with this trip."

Tension filled the silence on the drive, and Akiko

couldn't cease wondering if she'd see Jet again. Her heart wept with shame for a future left unlived. For the hope of true happiness unfulfilled.

He hadn't wanted her. Staring out the window, she let her eyes blur so streetlights became streaks and lines of amber, white and red.

At the airport, Makoto dropped their mother and her at the entrance then went to park. How did the rest of the city barely stir when this place bustled at five in the morning? It seemed she'd stepped into another world. Taking her suitcase to the baggage check, she ignored her mother's firm nod of approval. She didn't know Akiko's heart broke. She didn't know Akiko had offered her heart, her life, to a man who told her to leave.

"What do you expect me to find in Kyoto?" she asked, adjusting the strap of her carry-on and heading for a set of escalators.

"A man who will make you content and bring honor to your family."

"Content? Is that what life is about? Finding contentment?"

"It is good enough, Akiko-san."

"I think you are more than content with Father."

"I am, lovely daughter. You will be, too. You will see."

At the top, Akiko stepped off the escalator and paused as her mother's figure continued toward a coffee stand. What had her mother sacrificed to be with her father? And what had Akiko lost in saying goodbye to Jet?

A sharp pain shot through Jet's neck a moment before he realized his eyes hurt because bright morning sunlight pierced his lids. He opened his eyes, immediately blinded by the light.

"Aah!" he cried, putting up a hand to block the beams. He regretted the move as a worse pinch bunched the muscles of his neck. Jerking, he toppled from the couch and landed on the floor with a grunt.

Akiko. He pushed to his feet and staggered to the bathroom. His watch said seven-thirty. How much time did he have before she left for the airport? He undressed and started a shower. If he asked her to stay, could he maintain any sense of dignity?

The night hadn't caused his adoration to wane. In fact, it had cemented his affection. Stepping into the hot water, he didn't want to live another day without her in it. She'd been willing to turn her back on her family for him. She loved him that much.

For once, a woman moved faster than him. She'd made a commitment before he had. "Two weeks. Not even. This is a record."

Akiko. Amazing, gorgeous, peaceful Akiko. Smart. Grounded. Loyal to a fault. Loyal to her parents to the point where she let them send her to Japan to go husband-hunting when she'd already fallen in love. She'd offered Jet her loyalty. He'd been a fool to decline.

A sense of urgency had him turning off the water when he'd barely rinsed. He dressed in items close at hand without a care to whether or not he looked good. He brushed his teeth while running for his car.

"Please be home." He tried not to speed, but his foot had other ideas.

He arrived in front of her house right behind her father, who emerged from his Mercedes with a grocery bag in hand.

"Mr. Tadaka." Jet waved for the man to wait. He yanked his keys from the ignition and practically fell out of the car. He met her father at the front door. "I know it's early, but I was hoping to have a word with Akiko before she leaves. If that's okay."

"She has already gone. You can talk to her at the studio."

Jet shook his head. "What?"

Her father gave him an impatient look. "I am just returned from a business tu-rip. Akiko-san had gone to work before I got home."

"But she said you and Mrs. Tadaka were sending her to Japan today."

The man's eyes widened. With a low growl, he gave Jet a curt wave to follow then marched inside. "*Kanai!*" he bellowed, his voice coarse and grading up a full octave on the three syllables.

"Seigo-san, *okaerinasai*," came a wavering answer from the kitchen.

"This is going to get ugly," said Makoto, speaking softly as he approached from a side room. His father carried the grocery bag to the back of the house.

Closing the door, Jet asked, "How do you know?"

The boy winked. "Two ways. First, he only calls my mom *kanai*, wife, when he's seriously pissed. Second, he didn't remove his shoes."

"I just came here to—"

"Shh." Makoto scowled and tilted an ear toward the kitchen. "Dad says Akiko loves you and they should honor that. Mom says Akiko needs to honor the family and not marry some American man they hardly know."

"That's fair," said Jet. When Makoto punched his shoulder, he released a breathy laugh. "Where is she?"

"Shh!" Her brother have him a hard look. "Ooh, that's interesting."

"What? Where's Akiko?"

"Listen. Dad just told Mom that they'd both be miserable if they had honored their families and married elsewhere. He said he's mad that she sent Akiko away after he already expressed his support of you as Akiko's suitor. He doesn't regret marrying for love, and who are they to deny their daughter the same." The boy slapped the wall. "Huh. You learn something new every day."

The house went silent.

"I think they're kissing." Making a sour face, Makoto returned to the other room where he'd paused a video game on a large screen television.

"Wait a second." Jet's stomach lurched. "Akiko's gone, isn't she?"

"Yeah. Sorry."

Jet twisted his pinkie ring. If he believed in

ancestors who watched over the living, he'd call upon his namesake. This was a disaster.

Mr. Tadaka emerged from the kitchen with a smudge of lipstick at the corner of his mouth. "Come to the garden, Jet-san. I have words to say to you."

Chapter Fifteen

"We did it, guys," said Justin with a grin. "Twelve songs. I think that's the fastest we've ever recorded an album." He set aside his guitar and sent Jet a heavy glance. "Be back in time for the concert in Boston. Don't make me hunt you."

With his insides wringing with anxiety, Jet put his saxophone in its case then turned off his keyboard and unplugged his guitar. "It's do or die, man. Wish me luck."

Justin slapped his back. "Actually, how about I wish you bring her home. Stan quit. Said he was tired of working as a roadie. Idiot. Now we need a new sound tech in the crew. Akiko's perfect, if she wants the job."

"All I can do is ask."

C.J. came from behind his drums. "Do you want a ride to the airport?"

"I've got one, thanks." Jet checked his watch and hitched his bag over one shoulder. "Gotta go."

Outside, Mr. Tadaka waited at the curb in his Mercedes. Jet put the bag in the backseat then slid into the front. "I appreciate your driving me."

Akiko's father offered a nod before pulling from the curb. "She is my only daughter. She loves you, and her happiness is important to me."

"Me, too"

"Good." He handed Jet a folded paper. "This is where you ah going. Hand it to the taxi du-river when you leave the airport and he will du-rive you to the house."

"Thanks." He slid the paper into his wallet. "I hope it's not too late."

"You should have gone Tuesday."

"I know. I know."

"Akiko," called her aunt from the other room. "I'm taking the girls out for ice cream. Do you want us to bring you some?"

Akiko tore her gaze from pretty city lights out the living room window. "No, thank you."

Her aunt came to the doorway. "I don't like seeing you so sad."

"I'm sorry. Thank you for not making me go to the matchmaker yet. I realize I'm a miserable guest." If only she could get her heart to stop hurting.

"I expect a delivery this evening. If it comes while I'm gone, do you mind signing for it?"

"Of course not." She'd spent the last five days imagining what she could've had with Jet and regretting leaving Chicago. "I should've been stronger. I should've defied my parents."

Her aunt shook her head. "I'm sure it will come right in the end."

She didn't know the man Akiko had lost. The love she'd sacrificed. How could this come right in any way?

Her nieces scampered past, pulling on jackets as they hurried to the door. "We'll be back in about an hour. You've got the house to yourself," said her aunt, following the girls outside.

Akiko offered a small wave and returned to the window. She pretended she stared at the lights of Chicago and that Jet would arrive any moment to take her to dinner.

"Jet," she whispered. Was he at the studio right now, starting his day with music and his friends? Did he think of her?

A knock startled her, and she hesitated. Then she recalled the delivery. With a sigh, she went to the door and opened it.

Jet stood in yellow light from the porch lamp and offered her an unsure smile. He stole her breath. With his hair mussed, bags under his eyes and the opening of his black leather jacket showing a wrinkled T-shirt, he looked a mess. He looked like heaven. It took everything in her not to fly into his arms.

"I came straight from the airport."

"I can tell." Her heart raced.

"I look that bad, huh?" He scratched his right shoulder, though she couldn't imagine it did much good through the leather. "Can I come in?"

"Please." She held the door wide and motioned him to set his bag next to an umbrella stand. "You shouldn't have come."

"Because of your parents?"

Because her heart couldn't take losing him twice. She closed the door. She leaned against the wall, trying to hide her trembling and unable to take her eyes from his handsome face. "Partly. And partly because you don't share my feelings. You made that clear."

He took a tentative step toward her but shoved his hands in his jeans pockets. "Yeah, but that... Family is everything to me, Akiko. My mom and dad have always been there for me no matter what, and C.J.'s my soul brother. We'd do anything for each other. I didn't want you to lose that with your own family."

"I understand," she said on a shaky voice. "You didn't have to fly halfway around the world to tell me why you let me go. You could've called. Makoto would've given you the number."

"I have it." He tilted his head and gave her a lopsided smile.

The pieces came together. No wonder her aunt hadn't pushed her to make an appointment with the matchmaker. She knew he was coming. That's why she and the girls had run out so fast. How had she kept such a secret?

"It's been a week. I thought you'd really let me go." Her breath caught.

"We were in the middle of an album. I couldn't leave." He took a step closer. "Believe me, I would have in a second. My breakup with Cynthia had already delayed our recording and cost us a bunch of money on unused studio time. I couldn't do that to the band again." He released a short laugh and sent her a pleading look, his eyes bluer than she'd ever seen them. "If I had known that I'd meet you and learn how real love feels, I wouldn't have waited for Cynthia to leave. I'd have kicked her out and never given her a second thought."

Love. He said love. Her heart went from racing to nearly stopped. "Are you saying you're willing to let me forsake my family to be with you?"

He opened his arms in silent invitation.

Without hesitation, she went to him. She embraced him, elated by his returned love while also devastated by her choice to defy her parents. Welcoming the strength of his arms, she admitted, "I'm scared."

"Don't be. When I make a commitment, it's forever. I'm yours, Akiko, if you'll have me."

Have him? Did he mean what it sounded like? Loosening her hold, she glanced up to gauge his expression. He bore such tender affection it nearly undid her.

"I didn't come this far to give you a hug," he said. "I have something for you."

He sank to one knee and drew the ring off his pinkie. "Akiko, I've never felt whole until I met you. You complete me. I wish I had written you a poem or a song, but maybe this is the best way to tell you how much I love you."

Akiko could not hold in her joy. It poured from her in the form of happy sobbing, and she buried her face in her hands from disbelief. She didn't want to miss a second, so dropping her hands to her elbows, she stared upon the man who had come to fill her heart. To fill her life. To represent her future and the love she would share with him.

He presented the ring on the palm of his hand. "This was my grandfather's. He was a man of honor and integrity. He was the most generous person I ever knew before I met you, and he set the example I live. To me, this ring is forever. It's unending love with no limits and no measure. That's what you are. Wear this ring, Akiko. Be my wife? Marry me and make me the happiest man?"

"Yes," she whispered. "The first moment I saw you at the studio, I knew you were meant for me. I tried to ignore it, but the more I did, the more I wanted to be with you."

He took her hand and slid the ring onto her finger. "It was the same for me. The more I saw you and spoke with you, the more I loved you."

She stared at the ring, dazzled by its significance and amazed he gave her something so personal. No diamond in the world could be more breathtaking in its beauty than this ring. "We still have a lot to learn about each other."

He stood. Cupping her cheeks, he sent long fingers into her hair. He placed a soft kiss upon her lips. "I don't want to be apart from you anymore. I figure it's going to take a lifetime to get to know you, and I don't want to wait another minute to get started."

His lips met hers in a kiss full of promise and gentle passion. She succumbed, swept away on a thrilling current of hope and delight as she returned his kiss. Still she couldn't ignore the sadness of not sharing her happiness with her parents.

"What is this?" he asked, breaking the kiss and touching the tip of his thumb to the outer corner of her eye. "You're thinking of your mom and dad?"

She nodded, needing him to understand why she couldn't completely drown in the jubilation of the moment.

"Your parents argued."

"Yes, but how do you know?" They had done it in their bedroom after he had gone following dinner.

"The morning you left, I came to your house, and

they fought."

"You came to my house." He had come for her! Her soul rejoiced.

"I shouldn't have let you come here in the first place. Your father was irate."

"That you came to the house?"

"No. That your mother went behind his back and sent you here while he was gone on a business trip." He stroked fingers along her cheek.

It made no sense. "I thought both my parents wanted me to come to my aunt's house."

"Your parents have been arguing because your mom wanted you to marry a Japanese guy, but your dad likes me." He pulled a piece of paper from his pocket. "He gave me this."

She took it and unfolded it. Her father's handwriting stated her aunt's address and telephone number. Revelation shocked her speechless for a moment. "My father wanted you for me?"

"Yes." He kissed her forehead. "Stop frowning. When he reminded her that they had defied their own parents when they married, your mom came around pretty fast. She wants you home so you can start planning the wedding."

A burst of laughter escaped her throat. It was too much. "I never knew. My father supports this match. That explains why he sent us to the garden after dinner."

"You might have to put off starting your wedding planning a week or so. If you agree, that is."

"Why? To what?"

"The band is doing a charity concert next week in Boston, and we need a new sound tech. Smashing Glass wants to hire you. I like the idea of having you on the road with me when I have to travel. Will you consider taking the job?"

Charity work. This man was truly a dream come true. "I do need a job."

Jet laughed. He took both of her hands. "I love you, Akiko."

She marveled how the world had seemed a dark and lonely place before he arrived at the door and brought her head-on with a bright life full of love and adventure. She kissed him, her head spinning. Her parents approved her love match. She would marry Jethro Cavanaugh, the most incredible man. Now she had a purpose beyond home and children. She couldn't have imagined a more delightful happily ever after.

THE END

CHAZ

Chapter One

"Billy's dead."

Justin set aside his songwriting notebook. "Did you say somebody died?"

Chaz blinked, gave his head a shake, and read the obituary once more. William Garrison Hall had died three days ago in the Chicago Metropolitan Correctional Center. His hands trembled, and he dropped the newspaper on the floor of their practice room at the back of his house.

"Hey, man," said Jet. He came from around his keyboard where he'd been working through fingering of their new song while they waited for Akiko to bring drinks from the kitchen. "Who's Billy?"

Chaz stood, his gaze still on the obituary. He'd watched for those words every day for eight years. Ever since he'd agreed to Billy's senseless promise. Every day he had dreaded. Every day he had hoped.

There for a few years when Smashing Glass first hit it big and they lived drugs, sex, and rock-n-roll, he thought he might beat Billy to the grave.

The walls began to close in. A buzzing sounded in his ears. He was free. In an instant, everything he wanted had come into reach...if he wasn't too late. At the same time, an overwhelming grief slammed the air out of him.

"Are you going to pass out?" asked C.J.

"I have to go." Chaz dragged his eyes from the

paper and glanced around the large room. They still had six more songs to practice and perfect from their new album. Four more days of rehearsing and then a new tour to plan. This couldn't have happened at a busier time.

Justin came and plucked the paper from his feet. "What's going on?"

Chaz took a step toward the door. "I have to go."

"You're coming right back? We've got to get this song right before we can quit for the day."

"I'm sorry to do this to you, but—" His throat closed, blocking the words that followed. Tears welled, and he gave his head a violent shake.

The lead singer took a step toward him, a scowl of concern darkening his features. "Are you in some kind of trouble? Is this something I can help you handle?"

Chaz's heart dropped into a lethargic thud, and for a second, everything slowed. For once, he didn't have Billy's crime drowning him. He didn't have foolish promises holding him in shackles of his own. But he'd lost a friend he'd once loved like a brother. It felt like a solid kick to his chest.

"This is important." He spared a glance for each of his band mates. His best friends. His family. "I really need to go."

Justin followed him to the garage. "Wait, would ya? Talk to me."

He took a set of keys from a hook next to the door leading from the kitchen to the garage. As he passed through the doorway, he hit a button on a wall panel, and one of three garage doors began to lift with a motorized hum. At his motorcycle, he stopped and faced his friend. "Do you remember when you and the guys bailed me out of jail?"

"Sure. That's when you officially joined Smashing Glass. I'll never forget it."

"Me, neither. I thanked you, but I never told you that you guys saved me. I can't get into it right now, but I do have to go. I have to." His stomach tensed, and he fought an urge to vomit.

"This is about that, huh? I get it, sort of. Will you be here tomorrow?"

"I'll be at a funeral." He began to shake. To hide it, he slid onto the seat of his Harley and took hold of the handles.

"Do you want me to come? It can suck going to those things alone."

Chaz shook his head then donned his helmet. "This is beyond personal. It's intimate."

Justin nodded and retreated a step. You take as long as you need. I'll keep Jet and C.J. off your back. We'll finish practicing when you're ready. Just give me a call."

"I appreciate that. Give me two or three days, okay?"

"You came through for me when I hit bottom. You've been there for Jet and C.J., too. This is the least we can do for you. Let me know if there's anything more I can do. We'll pack up and be out of here shortly. I'll lock everything on our way out."

He didn't trust his voice, so he offered a nod and started his engine. As he pulled from the house, he began to lose control.

He clutched the handles as if they provided a lifeline, and he held tears at bay through sheer will. He had to keep it together until he got to Billy's house. Until he had the comfort of Billy's parents to cry with him. Then he'd go to pieces. Then he'd decide whether he grieved, rejoiced, or both.

Smoothing a hand down the skirt of her black rayon dress, Emily stood a moment and surveyed her brother's hilltop gravesite before stepping on unsteady legs from the funeral home's limousine. Her father came around and took her by the elbow. At her other side, Mark held her hand.

She didn't bother to wipe her tears. They flowed so steadily that new ones would keep her cheeks wet, anyway.

It made no sense. Billy had only been twenty-nine. A life sentence didn't have to mean life in prison. Surely parole would've eventually become an option. Why had he taken his own life?

The thought wrenched a racking sob from her, and Mark gave her hand a squeeze. Her father let go of her elbow and went to her mother.

People already waited. Their heads appeared past the hill's rise and stood in relief against the bright gray of the cloudy sky. So many had taken off from work to attend on this overcast, miserable Wednesday. It meant a lot that they cared.

Pastor Archer stood unsmiling at the head of the casket suspended above the grave's opening. She refused to look at anyone else, not needing their sympathy to make her sorrow complete. As she neared, a mixture of various colognes and perfumes mingled with fresh flowers and the scent of freshly turned soil. Her stomach roiled. She swallowed hard.

At the hilltop, Mark helped her sit in one of three folding chairs. When he moved to stand behind her, he placed cool, heavy hands upon her shoulders. The weight comforted her a small degree, though she couldn't take her eyes off the gaping grave beneath Billy's casket.

It bothered her that she couldn't see him for herself. The prison report said he'd gone headfirst into machining equipment. He'd been mutilated, so a viewing hadn't been possible. She wanted someone to blame. Someone to suffer. Her father had watched the shop's security recording. He confirmed that her brother had been alone in that section of workspace.

Billy had done this to himself.

She could imagine his despair. She'd suffered her own twelve years ago when she'd lost her brother and Charles on the same night – the night Billy had murdered that boy and gone to jail. The night Charles had gone to jail with him then disappeared.

Her grief magnified to include anger. Where had

Charles gone? How could he abandon her brother that way? How could he abandon her?

Pastor Archer began to speak. His voice droned, but his actual words didn't register past her pain. Numbness would be a blessing if it sent this agony of her soul into oblivion. Her family prepared to send her brother into that dark, cold hole, and it tore her apart.

To keep from screaming, she fisted her hands in the fabric of her skirt. The gossamer fabric didn't have strength enough to hold against the pressure of her fingers. The material separated, and then individual fibers snapped. She didn't care. She squeezed until her fingernails bit into her palms.

Damn Billy for giving up.

Damn Charles for running away.

His heart breaking, Chaz stood opposite the grave from Emily. He half wished she would come out of her daze and see him, yet he also hoped she wouldn't. What had Billy told her? What did she think of him?

The minister's somber tone matched the faces around the grave. He suspected these guests had come more out of love and respect for Billy's wonderful family than to say farewell to the felon in the casket.

Chaz had loved him, though. Billy's crime had come from grief and passion. He had loved a shallow girl who couldn't love him in return. It didn't help that she'd been a slut. Chaz had recognized it, but his friend couldn't. Wouldn't.

Billy had lost it when he found her in another boy's backseat. Chaz covered his eyes, unable to look at the coffin as tears came. He'd tried to stop him, but his friend's rage had made him incredibly strong. Youth, stupidity, and passion had proved a lethal combination. He'd beaten that boy to death.

Chaz shook from the memory. It had been horrific. The girl's screams rang in his ears. Plaintiff's attorney had manipulated the evidence to make his friend appear meditative. He'd accused him of stalking and plotting.

Billy's attorney had failed him, and Chaz's testimony hadn't seemed to make a difference with the jury. The crime had been too heinous.

His eyes stung, and he rubbed them. Thank goodness his band didn't see him like this.

The minister's voice changed, and Chaz opened his aching eyes. Emily gave a tiny start as the casket began to lower. Her wan face contorted in grief, her lips parted on a silent cry, and her dark blue, bloodshot eyes went wide. His heart twisted as he shared her pain, and his breaths caught in convulsions when he could no longer stave off sobs.

When the coffin completed its descent, she lifted her gaze. Emily went still. He held his breath as his sorrow released its hold and the world became quiet. A shadow passed over her features. Then it bled into her gaze as her eyebrows lowered and her lips formed a thin line. He felt her slap as surely as if she had delivered it by hand.

He didn't flinch. He'd expected her anger. She had a right to it. Now he had to somehow win a few minutes alone with her. To learn what understanding, if any, Billy had given her. To discern if she had any room left in her heart for him. To explain.

She stood and followed her parents in tossing a handful of dirt into Billy's grave. Her left hand sparkled from a diamond on her ring finger a moment before it slid into the hand of a tall, Nordic-looking man in a well-tailored black suit.

Chaz's heart wilted.

Chapter Two

"I'm furious." Emily shook both fists in front of her face. How could she go from sad to angry in a second? She gasped from the intensity. "I'm so mad I want to hit him."

"Calm down," said Mark. He wrapped one of her fists in both of his hands. "Hitting a dead man won't help anything."

"She means Charles," said her father from the opposite limousine seat. He patted her mother's folded hands.

"Who's Charles?" asked her fiancé.

She took a deep breath. "You know what? It doesn't matter."

"If you're this angry, it matters. Who is he?"

Her mother's tear-strangled voice said, "It matters. It means everything."

"It means nothing!" Emily immediately regretted her shout. "I'm sorry."

Mark sent her a wary look, but he didn't release her hand and he held his tongue.

Why had Charles come now? He was too late to make a difference. Where had he been when Billy sat on trial? When Billy rotted in prison? When her family needed him to explain? He'd seen what happened. Her parents had to learn about it in a courtroom and from newspapers.

Nobody had told her anything, but Charles would

have if only he hadn't run. Twelve years ago, her parents had said she was too young to know the details, and they wouldn't let her cut school to attend the trial. Newspapers hadn't run her brother's story long, and they provided generalized information about his crime.

Charles had held a brotherly place in her heart. She went from having two brothers to none in a single night. The word 'alone' didn't begin to touch on the desolation she'd suffered.

At her parent's home, her aunt and cousins had opened the house and prepared food. Her father invited the funeral procession's police escort to come in and eat, and guests arrived in a steady stream. Many who hadn't attended the burial and service now came to the house to express condolences. Emily sat on the living room sofa next to her mother.

She remained at the edge of tears, but it was better than the stunned shock that had robbed her of the past four days. Seeing her brother's casket buried had given her a measure of closure, even if she didn't get to view him.

Mark went to the kitchen. When he didn't return, she took her mother's hand and searched faces filling the house. She realized on her second scan that she looked for Charles. Miffed, she lowered her gaze to her lap. She fingered the spot on her skirt she'd destroyed at the burial.

"Maybe I should change," she said, showing her mother the damage.

Her mother nodded on a sniffle then dabbed her handkerchief to her damp cheek. "I should have something you can wear."

Keeping her head down so nobody would try to stop her for a chat, Emily made her way to the stairs. As she entered her parent's bedroom, she muttered, "Now I'm the one running."

She took her time finding something black of her mother's that fit. Then she stood at a window overlooking the backyard. Everywhere had memories of Billy and Charles. Hotdogs and ice cream on the deck during lazy summer days. Late night talks of school and dreams for the future on the swing set. Building a snowman, and having snowball fights during holiday break. When they went to jail, it was like part of her childhood got stolen. Especially when Charles went free but never came to the house.

She sighed, wiped a tear, and went to the door. She couldn't hide all afternoon.

"Hi, Emily."

Her lungs seized on an inhale. Charles stood at the top of the stairs, his suit jacket open and his tie loosened. He wore his hair longer than she remembered. In fact, nearly everything except his eyes had changed. He'd grown wider in the shoulders and taller. His face had angles where he'd had rounded lines at seventeen. Even his hands looked different. Honed. Masculine.

"Sorry if I scared you," he said, his voice that of a man. Nothing remained of the boy. "Your father said I could find you up here."

Irritation straightened her spine. "I have to get back."

"Don't be mad." He stepped into the light of a skylight, and the redness and suffering in his eyes robbed her of her ire.

"I can't help it." Her voice caught on a hitch, and she took a deep breath to steady her raw nerves. "I blame you."

Chaz grasped the stair railing's newel post as the dagger of her accusation stabbed him deep. He closed his eyes against the pain. "I think we have to talk."

"I have nothing to say to you."

"Please." He opened his eyes and drank her in.

She'd grown lovelier than he'd expected. Age had darkened the brown of her hair, which made her blue eyes more stunning. Sorrow had made her pale, but now she pinked a bit in anger. He'd adored her pixie-like face, which had evolved into refined features of an elegant, graceful woman.

She had gained height, too. Where she had been a willowy, unsure teenager, now she had shapely curves and confident beauty. If only he knew what to say to soften the wrath flashing in her stare.

"It's too late for 'please'." She brushed past to the staircase.

Honesty. As a girl, she'd valued honesty above all else. Chaz took a deep breath, swallowed any amount of pride he'd mustered amidst this disaster of a past, and said, "They made me promise not to see you."

She stopped in mid-stride. Her gaze didn't leave the top step when she asked, "Who? When?"

"Your parents still have those swings in the backyard. Will you hear me out? Let's go sit there like we used to, and let me explain." He gripped the newel post so hard his knuckles hurt.

"This isn't exactly a party, Charles. My parents need me."

"Nobody understands better than I, Emily. Billy was...I loved him."

"Then why did you abandon him?"

He staggered under the shock of her words. "Abandon him? I didn't. I couldn't. Is that what you believe?"

She faced him. After studying him long seconds, she relaxed. The fire left her eyes. "I don't know what to believe. I wanted you to come see me. To come and tell me what happened. What was going on? Nobody talked to me, but you would have."

A weight lifted off of his chest, allowing him to breathe. "I would have. It's true. Let me tell you now."

She glanced downstairs at a throng of milling guests. "Conversations grew in volume. Soon, funereal tones would escalate as people attempted to be heard.

"Okay," she said. "Let's go to the backyard."

She led the way, and he couldn't help noticing how the shiny length of her wavy hair swayed seductively on each step she took. Signaling him to follow her through the crowd, she made her way to a hall that took them past her father's study then out the back door at the end.

Chaz traced her footsteps across the lawn and sat on the swing to the left of hers. "I really would've told you everything. I thought so much of you."

"I don't understand. What kept you away?"

He sighed. "It's complicated. When Billy and I had our initial hearing a few days after our arrest, and the judge set my bail, your parents asked me not to come see you. Then they saw me every day at the trial. They didn't want you to hate Billy for what he had done, and they knew me well enough to realize I'd spill it all to you."

"You were at the trial? My parents told you not to talk to me?" Her eyebrows came together above her fine nose. "Hold on a second. My head is spinning."

"I can imagine. You know my dad was never around. Your parents became like mine. I respect them. I couldn't say no. I understand what they were trying to do, and I trusted them to know you better than I did." He fingered chain links of his swing while studying her pensive profile.

She clutched her swing's chain, and he got a good look at her engagement ring. A one-carat diamond, clear and brilliant, sat clutched in the mouths of two dragons – one gold and one silver. When she adjusted her hold, he glimpsed the underside where the dragon bodies entwined. It made for a unique and unusual ring.

"What about me?" she whispered. "I was left out. I thought you ran."

The muscles of his neck bunched at the idea that she believed him capable of turning his back on any of them. "I tried so hard. I was there every day. I went on the stand twice. I couldn't comprehend why they tried him as an adult and sentenced him to life in prison. I'd failed him. Failed you and your parents, too."

"God, Charles. I never knew."

"Don't hate your parents. Your dad told me he didn't want you to know what violence your brother had committed because it broke his heart that he'd been so wrong about him. But he wasn't wrong about him. Billy had lost his mind. When the police told him what he'd done, he didn't even believe it at first."

"It was temporary insanity? The newspapers—"

"There you are." The Nordic-looking guy came across the lawn, his tie and jacket now absent. His pale blue button-down did nothing to hide the sheer size of him. He could give Jet competition in the weight room.

She stood and took the man's hand. "Mark, this is Charles Preston. He was Billy's best friend. Charles, this is Mark Van Scoten, my fiancé."

Chaz's stomach bottomed. Here stood confirmation of his fear. He got to his feet and offered a hand. "Nice to meet you."

"Charles Preston? *Chaz* Preston?" Mark's wary brow relaxed as a genuine grin overtook his hard angles. "I thought I recognized you."

"Chaz?" asked Emily. "You let people call you that?"

"Let?" Mark's eyebrows shot high. "This is Chaz Preston, the bass player for Smashing Glass. You grew up with him and you don't know he's in one of the world's best rock bands?"

Chaz shrugged. "It's not important. Not everyone likes rock. Besides, we're here to remember Billy."

The man sized him up and said, "You're smaller in real life."

"Real life has a way of disappointing us like that."

Mark put a possessive arm around Emily's shoulders. "She needs to get back. People are asking for her."

"I'm sorry," she said, her eyes sad.

Chaz took a step toward her. "There's more to say. Can we meet? Maybe tomorrow?"

Her fiancé steered her to the house. He said over his shoulder, "Enough has been said. This'll be over tomorrow."

When they disappeared inside, Chaz said under his breath, "This won't be over tomorrow or the day after. This is far from over."

Chapter Three

"Good morning, Charles," said Emily's father when he answered Chaz's knock the next day. "It's a comfort to have you coming around again."

"Good morning, Mr. Hall. It's good to be allowed back. Is Emily here?"

"She has her own place now. You know, Mark has decided you're a problem."

"Maybe I am."

A glint of humor glimmered in her father's eyes. "Will you come in?"

"For a few minutes. I really need to talk to Emily." He stepped inside and followed Mr. Hall to the kitchen.

"Have a seat," the man said, indicating one of the stools at a marble island. "Want some coffee?"

"No, thanks." He sat and ran fingers across the island's cool, smooth surface. "This is new. It's nice."

"Thank you. So you want to speak to Emily, huh? About Billy?"

"Yes. She deserves to know. Her life was changed, too." He braced for opposition.

Her father nodded slowly. "It's past time. I agree. I should've told her. She asked, you know. On her twenty-first birthday. It'd been six years at that point, and I didn't want to think about it anymore."

Chaz relaxed some.

"She chose Mark. We have to respect it," said Mr. Hall.

He narrowed his eyes. "Why do you say that?"

Her father offered a small smile and wrapped his hands around a coffee cup. "Becky and I knew you were sweet on our girl. We watched, afraid you'd make a move."

Leaning from the island as his mind reeled, he said, "Emily was only fifteen. I was waiting for her to catch up."

"I can't tell you how much we appreciated that."

"How did you know? Billy was my confidant. I never told anyone else."

"Becky caught it. She pointed out the way you looked at Emily when you thought nobody saw."

Heat climbed his face, and he hoped he didn't flush. "How long has she been engaged? He seems protective of her."

"Two weeks, but they've been dating nearly six months."

No wonder her ring appeared fresh from the jewelers. She hadn't worn it long enough to dull the metals. A new engagement meant a strong, renewed connection. He couldn't help a sense of discouragement.

"How's Mrs. Hall holding up?"

"Becky's having a hard time. She expected us to win our appeal to change his count from first-degree murder to temporary insanity. I think that's why he took his life. When we failed in the appeal, he lost hope."

Chaz traced the rounded edge of the island. "I couldn't understand why they bypassed consideration of an insanity charge."

Mr. Hall nodded. "I learned later that the boy he'd killed was a judge's son. Odd how that fact never surfaced during the trial. Billy never stood a chance."

The injustice of it stabbed Chaz in the gut, and he squeezed his eyes closed. "Whatever happened to the girl?"

"I'm not sure. Last I heard, she'd moved to Las Vegas. You've done well for yourself. Becky and I are proud of you."

"Thanks. So where does Emily work?" He studied

her father. Would she get in trouble if he went to see her there?

"She's a financial advisor at Stan Schenk's office, but he's given her the week off. Why don't you try her at home?" Her father jotted an address on a piece of paper that said *grocery list* at the top. He ripped it from the pad and handed it over.

Chaz stood and moved to leave but stopped at the kitchen doorway. "You didn't act surprised when I said I might make trouble for Mark."

Mr. Hall took a sip of coffee, his eyes thoughtful over the rim of the cup. Then he said. "Mark is Emily's choice, and he's alright, I guess."

Chaz could almost smell anticipation in the air. "But...?"

"But Becky and I have loved you like a son. Sure would be nice if we could call you son for real." Her father didn't smile, which added weight to his words.

Chaz glanced at the floor then at the man who had been more a father at times than his own dad. "Sure would be nice."

A knock at the door forced Emily from bed. Mark had said he might swing by on his way to work to check on her, so she didn't bother with a robe. Her feet swished across her apartment's Berber carpet as she shuffled through the living room.

"Hi, Emily," said Charles when she opened the door. His gaze dropped to her chest.

Cripes! That's what she got for not checking the peephole. She crossed her arms over her camisole and felt her hard nipples against the thin skin of her inner arms. Thank goodness she'd worn pajama pants to bed.

"I thought you were Mark," she said.

"Are you expecting him?" He raised his eyebrows slightly, and his lips quirked one way into a sort of incredulous half-smile that made her more uncomfortable.

She stared at him a second. "What time is it?"

"A little after ten. Why?"

"Never mind. How did you get my address?"

He waved a paper she recognized from her parents' kitchen notepad. "Your dad. Are you just getting out of bed? Do you want me to come back?"

His hazel eyes appeared grayer than she remembered, and he'd grown a chiseled edge to his jaw. His hair curled a bit at the ends and formed a wave of bangs across his forehead. What struck her most, however, was the width of his shoulders. Had he been this good-looking when they were kids?

"Emily?"

She startled. "Huh?"

"Do you want me to come back later?"

She wanted to say yes because she had a bizarre urge to get pretty for him, but she forced a laugh at such an absurdity and took a step from the doorway. "Of course not. You're like a brother. I'm not as mad at you as I was yesterday. Come on in."

He stepped inside and closed the door. "Not *as* mad? So you're still mad at me?"

"I have a lot of questions. Wait. Give me a minute to get dressed."

She hurried to her bedroom and exchanged her bedclothes for thin, gray sweat pants and a plain pink knit top. Her padded bra would save her from further embarrassment. In her bathroom, she picked up her toothpaste and toothbrush then glanced in the mirror.

A shriek escaped her before she could stifle it. Her eyelids had swollen to twice their normal size and turned red from yesterday's endless tears. Her sickly pallor made it appear worse, and a night of restless sleep had left one side of her hair so ratted it looked like a maniac had taken a teasing comb to it.

"Are you okay in there?" he called.

"Fine," she squeaked, mortified he'd seen her this way. Averting her gaze from the hideous sight, she cleared her throat and yelled, "I'm fine. I'll be right out."

She brushed her teeth with one hand while

working tangles out with a brush in her other. After rinsing, she splashed cold water on her face then smoothed her wet hands over her hair to get it to lie properly.

Her eyes still swelled, so she went to the kitchen and took an icepack from the freezer. Charles handed her a small glass of orange juice and sent her icepack a questioning glance.

"Too much crying yesterday," she said, settling at her tiny dinette.

"You want some coffee?"

"I'm not a coffee drinker, but thanks." She stared at his jean-clad ass then gasped and jerked her gaze to where his hands took a couple pieces of toast from her toaster. The wholesome smell made her stomach rumble.

He put a jar of apricot preserves on the table, and she couldn't help but smile at how he remembered she didn't take butter on her toast. After placing the toast and a butter knife before her, he brought a glass of water and joined her at the table.

"You're a member of Smashing Glass?" she asked, opening the jar.

"Yesterday, you acted like you'd never heard of us."

"I don't know anything except the drummer, C.J., used to be in the news pretty often. Now I know you're their bass player. Does that make you famous?"

"Not really."

"Mark seemed excited to meet you until he decided to get jealous." She chuckled.

"What's funny?" He took a drink of water, his eyes not leaving hers.

"Mark being jealous of you of all people. It's silly."

"If you say so."

She stopped spreading preserves on a piece of toast. He didn't smile or shrug or anything, but she clearly understood him. He had a quiet intensity she'd witnessed at the burial. This side of him was new to her, and it sent an unwanted thrill through her.

Using a bite of toast to buy a much-needed pause and steady her senses, she stared at a skeleton horse graphic on his gray T-shirt and pressed an icepack to one of her eyes. "I'm sorry I didn't know you were famous."

"How could you? You don't listen to rock-n-roll." His intensity didn't lessen.

"Please stop looking at me like that," she said quietly, unable to tear her gaze from him.

"Like what?"

"Like I'm ice cream on a hundred degree day."

A slow smile softened his eyes and broke the spell.

She inhaled, aware for the first time that she'd held her breath. "I stay busy between work and Mark. But you're right. I'm not into rock. In fact, I only listen to music on the radio in my car. I don't watch gossip or entertainment shows. If C.J. weren't in the news, I might never have heard of your band. It's been a while since they've reported on his troublemaking."

"He got married. She's good for him."

"Mark said you play guitar."

He nodded. "Bass."

"Do you remember that guitar I gave you for your sixteenth birthday?" That day held such wonderful memories. Perfect weather. Steaks on the grill. Chocolate cake. And the way he'd smiled at her when he opened her gift, as if she'd given him his greatest wish.

"I still have it." His intensity returned. "I don't go anywhere without it."

"Really? Even after everything that happened with Billy?" She moved the icepack to her other eye.

"Especially after everything."

Her heart beat harder. "Why especially?"

"First, your parents asked me not to see you. Then on my last visit to Billy in prison, he made me promise to disappear from your life. You can't imagine-" He averted his gaze to the wall. His voice sounded thick when he said, "When I have your guitar with me, I have you with me."

Chapter Four

He'd said it. Now his words floated above the table between them as evident as a flashing neon sign. Chaz waited on a trepidatious breath, not sure what to expect from her. At fifteen, Emily would have laughed and likely punched him in the arm while telling him to stop jesting.

At twenty-seven, however, she had become an enigma. She appeared fragile, so unlike the hearty, energetic girl he had known. How much did Billy's death influence her tenuous demeanor, and how much came from busy living? None of her youthful guilelessness remained.

"I don't know what to do with that," she said, sinking into a slouch.

"It's alright. I tossed it out there, but I wanted you to know how much you mean to me. How much I thought about you. I never forgot you. Not for a second." He leaned forward, planting his elbows on the table and folding his hands together inches from her saucer.

Her gaze went to his hands. "I understand why my parents asked what they did, but why Billy? And why was it your last visit?"

He sighed. "I've pondered that time so much. I didn't expect talking about it to be so hard."

She put the icepack on the table and closed her eyes.

He studied the grim set of her mouth. She didn't

expect to hear him praise anyone, and her resolution somehow eased his recollection. He could deliver the truth and not worry he would broadside her.

"In a lot of ways, those first few months were the easiest. The trial hadn't started. Billy was positive he had a good attorney, so he had a lot of hope. I had cleared my name, and I spent my time finishing my senior year and practicing with the band. I visited Billy every week."

Her blue eyes opened, dark and deep. They held no censure. Yet. "Every week? I wanted to see him so badly, but I wasn't allowed. It makes me feel better that you went. I had worried he thought we had forgotten him."

"He didn't. He knew what was going on because I told him. After high school, the band started working. We began playing original songs, and we had a couple opportunities to open at some big-name concerts. Shortly after Jet graduated from college, we got a recording contract and made our first album. The label lined us up with a good agent, and by the end of the next year, we had a decent fan following."

She nodded encouragement for him to continue.

"The trial had been torture, but the appeal was worse. The final verdict was too much. After fighting for so many years, nothing had changed." Shame weighed on him. "I couldn't deal. Smashing Glass was getting ready to go on our first concert tour as an opening band when the judge's decision came through."

"I remember that day. I was home from school on spring break. My dad came home a wreck."

He hesitated. He wanted her to have the whole truth, so he had to say what came next. "I'm not proud of myself when I admit I became the typical rock musician. Parties. Drugs. Booze. Girls. We lived it. I thought we were having fun, but it was ugly.

"We practically lived in L.A. because we had as many as three promotional opportunities every week that year." He unfolded his hands and spread his fingers across the table's surface. "We were twenty-two and stupid and had more time and money than we could handle. What made it worse was how every time I got stoned, I forgot about what Billy had done and the pain it caused. So I got stoned a lot. I only made it back here to Chicago about once a month, but I always visited him when I came."

Chaz couldn't face the disappointment that dulled Emily's eyes. He lowered his gaze to the table between his elbows. She rose, dumped the remnants of her breakfast in the garbage, and put her dishes in the dishwasher. He stiffened, willing her not to ask him to leave. When she resumed her seat, he relaxed.

"Right before we began work on our second album, Billy told me not to visit him at the penitentiary. He said seeing me strung out and hung over was killing him." His temples began to throb. "He made me promise not to see you. He thought I was like him. That we both had wicked tendencies."

"Why would he say that?" she asked softly, sadness weighing upon her features.

Chaz shook his head. "I can only guess he suffered depression. He'd committed a crime he didn't recall, spent the last three and a half years in prison and on trial, and faced a lifetime in federal corrections. He was twenty-one, and he'd never finished high school."

"Neither of you were bad. Young, unthinking, and way too sensitive maybe, but not evil." She put a hand on his.

He soaked in her touch and met her gaze. "I tried to visit him a few years ago, after I sobered for good. He refused my visit."

Her swollen eyes grew sadder, but her mouth softened. "He refused all of my attempted visits. I tried. I'm glad you tried, too."

"I wrote him, but my letters came back unopened."

A tear formed at her lower lid, hung suspended a moment at the tips of her lashes then coursed a path to the corner of her lips. It disappeared onto the tip of her tongue. "You were a much better friend than I credited you. I'm sorry I misjudged you, and I'm especially sorry for accusing you of abandoning him."

"I loved him." His voice broke. Taking a second to regain his composure, he rested against his chair's back. "I promised him, you know? I couldn't break that promise, so I stayed gone from your life. I waited. I'd have waited until we were old if that's what it took to see you again."

She shot to her feet, and her lovely face contorted in grief. Her lips trembled before she said, "You should go, Charles. I'm exhausted."

He fought his own tears as he stood and nodded. "I understand. When can we talk again?"

Covering her face with both hands, she merely shook her head.

Did she want him to leave and never return? The idea rattled him. "Please," he whispered.

Tears coursed her cheeks as she led him to her apartment door. He opened it but couldn't force his feet to step across her threshold. He'd waited too long. He refused to give up.

"Please," he said.

Her eyes went to his chest. "Tomorrow. Come by tomorrow."

After tossing the icepack into the freezer, Emily collapsed on her bed and wept into her pillow until the pain of loss eased enough to allow her mind to clear. Charles confused her. The longings he stirred and his words contradicted everything she'd held true about their relationship.

He'd been Billy's friend who treated her like a sister, and then he'd gone. She had missed him for a while. By the time she reached college, however, she'd hardly spared him a thought. She had lived her life. Worked. Dated. Gotten engaged.

Not Charles. He not only still had the guitar she'd

given to him, he claimed to take it everywhere because it reminded him of her. What did that mean? She didn't want to be credulous, but he'd had such a modest and forthright manner. He had delivered his confession without any air of expectation that she should reciprocate. In fact, he hadn't acted as if he waited for a reaction from her of any kind.

Emily rolled onto her back and stared at the ceiling. She couldn't deny a magnetism she hadn't experienced with him before. It didn't bode well for her, especially concerning Mark. What had she thought to invite Charles tomorrow?

Nearly all the news reports about his band mate, C.J., had involved some kind of hedonism. Charles admitted to lasciviousness and substance abuse, but he placed it in the past. Did she dare believe him?

"What do I care?" She went to the bathroom and washed stiff, dried tears from her face.

Her eyes had puffed worse than earlier, and she retrieved the icepack from the freezer before flopping on her couch. The chill plastic felt soothing on her hot eyelids.

Charles' cologne lingered. She tried to imagine him audaciously jumping around a concert stage and partying like a rock star. She couldn't. It didn't fit the boy she had known. His pleasure had come from badinage and from taking things apart so he could learn how to reassemble them. He'd read as if prohibition on novels loomed. He had never behaved in any way to suggest a capricious nature.

Then again, neither had Billy. She had to question the fundamental makeup of Charles' motives. Of his thinking. Of his morals. If her brother believed they shared this, she had to afford it consideration.

It didn't make sense, though. Believing Charles capable of such a crime was antithetical to the courageous, kind, and cerebral person she knew. Twelve years could change a person, she supposed, but he hadn't shown her anything different during their two talks. He looked different, but his character seemed intact. Still, it didn't hurt to stay on her guard.

Her phone rang, and she removed the icepack before answering. "Hello?"

"Hello, sexy. It's Mark. Sorry I didn't stop by this morning. I didn't want to get out of bed. I barely made it to work on time." He snickered.

"It's alright. I slept in." She patted an eye, trying to determine if the swelling had reduced.

"I need you to go to the post office for me. I left a package with my doorman, so—"

"Mark, I'm not running your errands." Irritation roused a hoarse edge in her voice.

"Come on, sexy. You've got the day off. What are you doing but sitting around?"

Her jaw dropped, and she snapped it closed with a clink of her teeth. How could he be so sweet the day of the funeral and so callus the day after? "I'm grieving, Mark. I'm in no condition to go out in public."

He said nothing for a long moment. "Is this about Chaz Preston? Is he still at your place?"

She blinked, trying to process his implication. "He's not here. How do you know he stopped by?"

"I have my sources."

"Since when?" Her heart began to pound. She glanced around then realized he'd know Charles had gone if he had a camera hidden in her apartment. "Don't answer that. It's creepy."

"It's not creepy, baby. I'm just protecting my investment."

Investment? She sat stunned.

"I'm kidding, sexy. I'm not having you watched."

"Then how did you know Charles stopped in?"

"Your dad told me. I didn't mean to scare you. I was trying to make you laugh." He cleared his throat.

"I'm hardly in a frame of mind to find humor, particularly when my fiancé says he's spying on me. For cripes' sake, Mark."

"So there's no way I can talk you into running that box to the post office?"

"Seriously?" She reclined and put the icepack on

her eyes. "Who are you, and what have you done with my fiancé?"

He chuckled. "Fine. I'll get my secretary to do it tomorrow."

"I don't understand why you didn't simply have her do it today. Why didn't you take the box to the office with you? Are you trying to test me or something?"

He didn't answer.

"Mark?"

"So what's the deal between you and Chaz Preston, anyway?"

She softened her tone in response to the tension in his. "There's no deal. He was Billy's friend. He's catching me up on history. Nothing more."

"Are you sure, baby?"

"Positive. Shall we have dinner tonight?"

"Can't. I have to take a client out."

"Since when do you go on dinner meetings with clients? I thought only the partners did."

"Maybe I'm in line for partnership." He sniffed.

"Are you?"

"I'm trying. I'll talk to you tomorrow."

"Wait—"

A click told her he had ended the call. What in the world? Ever since Charles arrived, Mark had acted strange. If he was jealous, he had no reason. Hopefully when life returned to normal, Charles would step away, and Mark would stop acting insecure.

Still, it bothered her that her fiancé could behave this way. Maybe six months hadn't been enough to know him as well as an engagement required. Definitely not as well as she'd thought.

Chapter Five

When Emily opened her apartment door the next morning, Chaz caught his breath. Color had returned to her face, and the swelling had gone from her eyes. She wore a white sweater and blue jeans, and had a purse on one shoulder. He couldn't recall seeing her so lovely.

She offered a faint smile. "I'm glad you came. How about we go to the park? It's a few blocks down the street. We can walk, and I could use some fresh air."

"You look better. Did you get some rest?" He presented his elbow, but she didn't take it.

"Not really." She stood next to him as they waited for the elevator. "I did take a nap yesterday, but I haven't been sleeping well since Billy died. There's so much I never got to say to him."

He stared at her profile. In morning light streaming through a window near the elevator, her skin appeared incandescent. Her mood eluded him, however. How did she regard his confession yesterday? Did he stand any chance?

The doors opened, and he followed her in. Tension laced their ride down, but he wanted to find the right words before he spoke. Outside, she went right and headed along a street lined by small businesses.

"You know Billy loved you, don't you?" he asked.

"I do. He wouldn't have tried to protect me from you, otherwise. He wrote me a letter. Only one. It came when he'd been in the MCC a year. Right before my eighteenth birthday."

He shoved his hands in his back pockets to keep from touching her. "Do you mind if I ask what he said?"

She cut him a furtive glance. Then she stopped at a street corner. "He said you were like him, wild and out of control, and that I should avoid you if you ever came around."

So Billy hadn't trusted him to keep his promise. He checked for traffic then escorted her across. "Then what I told you after the funeral wasn't anything you hadn't already heard."

"I read his letter again last night. It helped. I was feeling guilty for not trying harder to see him in prison." She headed into a large garden park with wrought iron benches, cobblestone walkways, and long stretches of flowerbeds lining sprawling lawns. "He told me not to attempt to see him. That he would decline my visit. He didn't want me to see what he'd become."

"How many times did you try?"

"Three."

He had done the same, but many more than three. Billy hadn't budged. "He was stubborn that way. Once he made up his mind, he became resolute."

Emily nodded. "I guess that's what cost him. He decided that girl should be his girlfriend."

"She encouraged him. It's not an excuse for what he did, but he hadn't imagined her interest. She had sex with him and told him she loved him. A week later, she was chasing after somebody else. She played with people." He shuddered at what she had done to his friend. He hardly recognized Billy when she'd done with him.

"That's sick. There's no justification for murder, but I hope she suffers with the understanding of her part in it."

"I doubt it. I've never met anyone so inane, which says a lot. I meet a lot of silly girls in my business." He inhaled deeply and received a whiff of pollen-perfumed breeze as reward.

He indicated an empty bench, and when she sat,

he joined her. The landscape presented an almost bucolic view at odds with the city sounds beyond a far line of trees. A hum of distant traffic didn't detract from the park's peace, and Chaz smiled when he imagined sheep grazing on the expansive green.

"It's fascinating to me that you play guitar for a living." She stared across the lawn. "I don't know why I bought you that guitar for your birthday. You hadn't shown an interest in music."

He chuckled. "An imperfect gift choice became the perfect present. I'm glad you improvised. I was delighted when I opened your package. It became my career."

"I try to imagine you on stage and rocking hard. I can't." She looked at him, her features open and curious.

He met and held her gaze. "It's a different world. Concerts, I mean. It's three hours of adrenaline rush and feeding off the energy of a sold-out crowd. It's amazing."

"You've always been innately understated. How do you go out there and become bigger than life?"

He laughed. "Bigger than life? Give me a break."

"I didn't mean... Well, I guess I have no idea what I mean."

"No, you're right." He boldly took her hand, and when she didn't pull from him, he stroked the backs of her soft fingers with his thumb. "When we first made it big, I was ignorant. We were a menagerie."

"A menagerie?"

"Yes. We were wild animals trained for exhibition."

She laughed, a lilting sound that added to the morning's beauty.

"I thought our fans loved us. Screamed for us. I'm not sure why I realized later that they love our music. They scream for the idea of us, not who we really are. Maybe I sobered. I don't know."

"So you don't need your fans to worship you?"

"Huh-uh. It's too much pressure. I want to make great music, deliver a message if we're lucky, and put on a hell of a show. For twelve years, we've got four albums and countless concerts to prove we work hard. It's a job. It's my career."

"Does the rest of your band take the same stance?" Her eyes went to where he caressed her.

"Justin snapped out of the stupor first. Jet and I came to our senses about the same time during the Loud Voices tour eight years ago. C.J. clung to it, though. He never did drugs, and gave us no end of grief when we did, but he seemed to thrive on that egocentric mind-set."

"It's destructive behavior. He was forever getting in trouble."

"I know, but he didn't want to hear it. Then he met Sindra, and everything changed."

"Why?"

"Because she showed him what it means to live an extraordinary life. How much pleasure comes from putting someone else first? That love changes what we want." He stared at a patch of flowers where delicate petals danced in the breeze.

"Do you ascribe to that, Charles? Do you really believe love changes what we want?"

"Without a doubt."

She shook her head. "Loving Mark hasn't changed anything for me. I still want to be a partner at the financial firm. I still want an exotic vacation every year, and a big house, and..."

"And what?" He gave her hand a squeeze.

"And Mark conforms to my plan. He plugs in like a puzzle piece. He'll help me get these things faster so I can put my efforts into my career."

His gaze dropped to her lips. He wanted to kiss some sense into her. Where was her heart? "You talk about a life money can buy. Those are good goals to set, but what happens when you reach them?"

"I'm not sure what you mean." Her eyebrows lowered.

"Work isn't life. Existing in a big house isn't life. Are you devoted to Mark? Is he your reason?"

She blinked. "My reason for what?"

"Exactly."

♪　♪　♪　♪

"Are you accusing me of being modal?" Emily couldn't decide whether to take offense or question her thinking.

True, she didn't spend much time contemplating substance in her life. She had her parents' love and support. Mark had his droll moments, but overall he was a romantic and attentive lover. At twenty-seven, shouldn't she focus on acquiring material comforts and securing her financial future? After all, it's what she did for her clients.

"I can't judge your modality," said Charles. "I haven't seen you in twelve years."

His warm fingers holding hers created an awareness she couldn't disregard. The fragrance of his cologne, spiced and masculine, wafted to her from time to time. Longing to touch him, she wanted to test the firmness of his muscles. He appeared naturally shaped, sexy without excessive bulk. Mark had muscles built through weightlifting, which gave him a hard, stretched quality.

"What about you?" she asked. "Has love changed you?"

"Yes," he said without hesitation.

"How, Charles?"

"Chaz. Call me Chaz."

She released a breathy, unsure laugh. "I can't. That's what I called you when I was too young to form my R's. I'm not a little girl anymore."

"You gave me this name. It's what I go by." He gazed at her with hazel eyes that appeared more green than gray in the morning sun.

"Chaz," she said, testing it on her tongue. It felt strange, and she chortled. "I don't know. It'll take getting used to."

A hint of a smile softened his eyes. "Then say it often. You'll get used to it faster."

She tugged her hand, and he let go. "Fine. Then how, *Chaz*? How has love changed you?"

"Easy." He stood and offered his hand.

She didn't take it, fearful further contact with him would re-ignite sensations she shouldn't have from anyone but her fiancé. She stood, however, and joined him for a stroll along the stone pathway.

"Love changed me from an impetuous boy to a man who understands that the best is worth waiting for." He smiled at a spot on the path ahead of them. "It taught me that true love isn't emphatic or blatant, but understatedly constant. I'm not perfect, and I don't come close to having the answers. True love will forgive me my past mistakes, accept me as the man I am today, and see the potential in me for the future."

A streak of envy raged through her, faltering her step. Who was this woman who could love him like that?

"Are you okay?" he asked, taking her elbow.

"I'm fine. What's her name?"

"Whose?"

"The woman you love. The source of this true love. It doesn't sound real."

His eyes became hooded as he stopped and faced her. "I'm not ready to tell you."

Her palms started to sweat, and she wiped them on her jeans. "Why? Do I know her?"

"Yes."

His single word hit her like a bolt of lightning, and her knees threatened to give. What was wrong with her? Why did this bother her? He was as entitled to happiness as she.

Her mind spun with questions. What single women did she know who loved rock music and would date a musician? More importantly, who had enough strength of character to keep secret the fact that she dated a celebrity?

"Marabelle? Is it Marabelle?"

He laughed and resumed his stroll.

"It is, isn't it? She's so pretty," she spat then

stopped short. She'd said that aloud.

He halted and half turned. "I'm not dating anyone named Marabelle. Sounds like a Disney princess. Now, come on."

She regained his side as faces of friends and acquaintances floated through her mind. "Is it Diane?"

He shook his head.

"Caitlin?"

"No."

"Karrie? Or Holly? Wait, it's Stacy, right?"

His laughing smile faded. "No, no, and no. Now stop. It hasn't become important yet. As you said, it's not real. I'm waiting to learn if a future is possible. I promise you'll be the first to know the second I do. Okay?"

"I think it's important."

"Why?"

Good question. She wished she had the answer. "How is it not important? You're like family to me. I want to know you're happy."

He stopped and gently grasped her shoulders. "I'm happy now. I get to see you again."

Her heart thumped. "Billy didn't have a reason to keep you away, did he? You're not a bad person."

"He had every reason then, Em. Now I'm a different person. I have been for a long time."

Chapter Six

Chaz buttoned and unbuttoned the second hole on his shirt. He stared at his reflection. Nothing in it hinted at his rock life. No tattoos like Justin or C.J. No drug-induced pallor. No bloodshot eyes.

He had cut his hair to collar-length and had it layered right before their last concert tour. Justin worried Chaz would receive criticism for it, but girls had screamed louder for him. Even entertainment polls had announced positive results.

He liked the cut. It didn't hang lank or whip in his face, and it stayed clean between washings. He liked this look, too. It more closely resembled his self-image.

Emily's father asked for trouble. Why invite him and Mark to dine at the house? Chaz wouldn't bend for her fiancé, and he'd learn it sooner than later.

Emily wanted Chaz. He'd witnessed it. First at her apartment and then at the park. It made her uncomfortable. How long until she accepted it? How long until she signaled him to make a move?

Turning his back to the mirror, he shrugged into a suit jacket then went to his bookcase in the living room. It filled an entire wall. Unfortunately, he'd read every book in his collection, and he wasn't in the mood to reread one. He placed *The Count of Monte Cristo* with his books by authors whose last name began with D and checked the clock on his phone.

At the garage door in his kitchen, he plucked his

keys from a wall peg then surveyed his house. He tried to see it as Emily would. He'd bought this place with her in mind, but if she didn't like it, he'd sell. House shopping with her could be fun.

If she gave him a chance. If her attachment to Mark lacked depth, as he suspected. If she could love him. If, if, if. He left, got in his favorite car, a blue and silver Mustang GT, and headed for the other side of town.

Yes, he'd come back to try and win her, but regardless of what his friend had thought, Chaz wasn't anything like Billy. He paid special consideration before saying or doing anything. Emily's happiness meant more than his own. If her happiness meant she married someone else, he'd deal with it. Right now, however, he had to hope.

His fingers tightened on the steering wheel at the idea of Mark facing her at the altar. He said aloud, "Relax. Relax."

Parking at the curb in front of her parents' house, he took a deep breath. He had to keep his cool. To win her, he'd have to act nonchalant in the face of Mark's protectiveness. Her fiancé had already warned him off in not so many words. He expected a thinly veiled animosity from the man tonight.

At the door, Mr. Hall greeted him with a smile and a hug. "How are you?"

"I'm alright, sir. I'm still trying to come to terms with everything. How's Mrs. Hall?"

"Becky's better today, thanks. She's been cooking all afternoon. It's done her some good." He indicated they should go in.

Chaz led the way and found Emily with Mark in the living room. She looked devastating in a black dress that wrapped snuggly around her curves and gathered at the tight curve of her narrow waist. She had her hair up in a loose, flattering style that left tendrils gently curling along her face from her temples. A modest silver chain sparkled with a single sapphire, drawing his eye to the swells of her décolletage.

"Good evening," Chaz greeted.

She smiled. "You came"

Her father patted his shoulder then headed for the dining room.

Chaz entered and shared an obligatory handshake with her fiancé. "Mark, it's good to see you again."

"Likewise." The man put a thick arm around her shoulders then lifted her hand and placed an obsequious kiss on her knuckles. "Doesn't my bride look gorgeous?"

A pink flush bloomed along her neck to her cheeks.

Chaz stepped closer to her. "Yes. As always."

Mark snorted. "Didn't you see her at the funeral? I'm afraid tears don't become my sexy lady."

"I'm standing right here," she said, her blush dissipating. She shot Mark a disgruntled, sideways glance then met Chaz's gaze. "Sorry about the short notice. We weren't sure Mom would be up for this until this afternoon."

He raised a dismissive hand. "Don't apologize. I've taken time off, so the short notice is fine. I'm grateful to be included."

"I'll bet you are," said Mark. "So where's your family? How come you insinuated yourself into Emily's?"

She cast her fiancé an irritated glance then shrugged from his embrace. "He didn't insinuate himself."

Chaz met Mark's gaze straight on. "My mother had advanced Parkinson's Disease and lived in a nursing home, and my father was active duty military. The marines had him on deployment eight months out of twelve, so I lived with his sister most of the time. She worked, so I studied and snacked here with Billy. He was my best friend."

"Seems to me you did more than study here." Mark crossed his arms over his chest.

"The Halls are kind people. They fed me. Often." He chuckled and went down the hall to her father's study.

Emily followed. "Need a book?"

He ran a finger along book bindings filling shelves more extensive than his. "I recently finished *The Count of Monte Cristo*. I need something else. I ordered Hemingway's complete works online last night, but it won't come until next week."

She hiked a hip onto her father's desk. "I'm glad you're still reading. I am, too. I'm in the middle of Charlotte Bronte's *The Green Dwarf*. It's fascinating."

"I haven't read that one. I read her sister's novel, *The Tenant of Wildfell Hall* last year. It was alright." He chose a leather-bound book with title lettering worn to the point of illegibility. The front cover showed it as Sir Arthur Conan Doyle's *The Sign of Four*. "Do you think your dad would mind?"

She ignored the book in his hand. "Alright? I really enjoyed Ann Bronte's *The Tenant*. But then, you're a man. I guess I can see where it might not keep your interest in some places." She glanced at the book he held. "That's one of my dad's favorites. I've read it twice."

Chaz went closer to her. "It's that good, huh?"

Her eyes met his. "Who doesn't love Sherlock Holmes? Especially an early one. This is Doyle's second Sherlock Holmes mystery."

He moved close enough to smell her perfume. "Your dad used to lend me books. It's his fault I'm hooked on the classics."

She chuckled but didn't drop her gaze. A light of playful humor lifted her features. "That was before you joined a famous band. What if you go on tour and lose it?"

He leaned near until their noses nearly touched. His heart beat faster, though he had no intention of kissing her. He needed to see how close she'd let him get. "I'm not going to lose it."

A throat clearing made Emily startle, and Charles

slowly straightened. Mark leaned a meaty shoulder against the study's doorframe. His face appeared relaxed, but his voice conveyed a tense threat when he asked, "You want to step away from my bride?"

Irritation graduated to outright anger. "What is wrong with you?"

His eyebrows inched upward, giving him a haughty manner. "I'm simply asserting domain over what's mine."

She actually saw red as she got to her feet. "Domain? I'm not your possession, Mark."

"He's envious," whispered Charles.

Her aggravation diminished. She went to her fiancé and put a hand on his chest. "Charles is a close friend of the family. You have no reason for this posturing. It's insensible."

"Maybe. Maybe not." His eyes narrowed at Charles.

She pushed, and he let her take him to the hallway. Over her shoulder, she said, "My dad loves you. Ask him about the book. He's never said no before."

"What?" Mark glanced toward the study then went with her to the hallway's end and out onto the back deck. "No way is your father going to let him borrow that book. He never lets me step foot outside this house with one of his books, much less one of his favorites."

She smoothed her hands over his shoulders and dropped her voice to a seductive tone. "You have no reason for this defensiveness."

"That so-called friend in there is a world-class rock star. I guarantee he's got nothing on his mind beyond getting high, getting paid, and getting between your legs. In that order."

She placed tiny kisses along his neck. "Since when are you an expert on the lives of rock musicians?"

The tension left his voice when he said, "I read magazines sometimes, and watch television."

"Seriously?" She laughed quietly then put her lips to his.

His arms came around her, but she sensed his

reticence. When he ended the kiss, he gave her a slight smile and started the word game he liked. "I still think he's *odious*."

"Your attitude toward him is *onerous*," she tossed in response.

His smile grew. "He was *obtrusive* to get in your face in the study."

She laughed. "You're being *obstinate*."

"Don't you think his sudden appearance after your brother's death is *ominous*?"

"No." She went to the door. "Dinner's probably ready, so this isn't an *opportune* time for this discussion."

"Fine, but I have a lot more to say on the subject." He followed her inside.

At the front door, Charles stood and raised the book. "Thanks, Mr. Hall. I'll go lock it in my car and be right back."

Emily put a staying hand on Mark's arm. She felt him tremble, and she grimaced. Her mother emerged from the kitchen. She bore a china platter displaying a picture-perfect ham, and continued to the dining room.

"Please behave during dinner," she whispered to him. "For my mother's sake. She's still fragile."

In truth, Emily was fragile, too. The information Charles had shared with her helped bring the past into perspective. It removed a lot of her guilt, and she no longer fostered a burning animosity toward either Billy or Charles. It didn't lessen her sorrow, however. She'd lost her brother and any hope of regaining a relationship with him.

She waved Mark into the dining room then went to the kitchen. While her mother removed dinner rolls from the oven, Emily put a serving spoon into a bowl of roasted redskin potatoes and carried it out.

Charles came through the front door as she exited the kitchen, and they both halted. Their eyes met, and her stomach flipped. She opened her mouth to say something, anything, to break the charge electrifying the air between them, but no words came to mind.

When he took a step toward her, his expression intense and his eyes dropping to her mouth, she shivered in anticipation.

Her mother cut between them with a sweet smile and a basket of rolls. "Let's eat."

Emily stumbled a step backward into the kitchen, breathing hard in shock over what had almost happened. Or had it? Did she imagine it, or was Mark right?

Straightening her shoulders, she heaved a long exhale. She marched to the dining room, wearing as cheerful and carefree a smile as she could manage, and avoiding looking Charles' way. When she sat and placed the bowl of potatoes right on her plate, however, she suspected she didn't have a shot of getting through this meal unscathed.

Chapter Seven

It took a Herculean effort not to reach across the table for Emily, but Chaz somehow managed to maintain a conversation and keep his hands at his plate. She approached the culmination point. He hadn't mistaken the asking in her eyes during their quiet moment in her father's study. He suspected Mark's asinine behavior pushed her faster to the realization that she had chemistry with Chaz.

Mrs. Hall brought banana pudding to the table and said, "This was Billy's favorite. He was such a good boy."

Chaz nodded. "He didn't deserve—"

"Nonsense," Mark spat. "Billy was deserving of opprobrium."

Emily gasped.

Horrified, Chaz glanced at Mrs. Hall. Her questioning alarm told him she didn't comprehend. He turned on Emily's fiancé, and his voice shook when he said, "Billy didn't deserve the trial he got. He deserved consideration for his age and character. That you would say such a thing in this company makes *you* opprobrious."

"I'm impressed," said Mark on a smug smile.

"This isn't a contest." Emily stood and hooked a hand around her fiancé's bicep.

"Please, darling," Mark drawled as he got to his feet. "Show some modicum of dignity. It's disgusting how you all treat this lubricious lothario with a kind of twisted nepotism. He's not even related. It's like he's come to you as an emotional mendicant, and you've opened your home out of a misplaced sense of charity."

Chaz shot out of his chair and fisted his hand to keep from slapping the table. "That's enough. Your caustic, misinformed observations only reveal you as a narcissistic, nocuous, ophidian malcontent, and I can't help but wonder where your motive lies. Are your remarks merely invidious, or is there something more sinister under your glossy façade?"

Mark's eyes grew wider and wider until his jaw slackened. His stupefaction was comical.

Chaz gestured toward the front door. "As you can see, using big words doesn't make you smarter. It makes you condescending. With that said, your mendacious presence is offensive."

"Yes," said Mr. Hall. "Maybe it's time for you to go."

Emily released Mark's arm and retreated a step, saying to her fiancé, "I don't know you at all, do I?"

The man recovered his countenance. He shot flames at Chaz in his squint then faced her. "Baby, you know me."

She shook her head, twisted the engagement ring from her finger, and slapped it into his entreating hand. "You're despicable. That you would think those things about my brother and our dear friend, much less say them aloud, shows me I was blind. I don't know you, and I'm not interested in knowing you a moment longer."

"But baby—"

"Get out!" She squeezed her eyes shut and stood stiff, shaking.

Mark glanced at her father's hard, set expression then strode from the house.

"I don't feel well," said Mrs. Hall who silently wept.

Mr. Hall helped his wife up and from the room. Emily hitched a forearm across her face and collapsed into her chair. Her shoulders convulsed.

At a loss for what to say, and fearing anything he said would only make it worse, Chaz stayed put. He'd provided the catalyst for ousting that toolbox, but he refused to apologize. How could he say anything that would possibly soothe her? He couldn't simply stand aside while she cried, however.

He went to her and sank a knee to the floor beside her chair. Putting a comforting hand on her shoulder, he waited for her to calm.

"That was awful," she finally said. Using her napkin, she dried her face and wiped at smeared and running eye makeup.

"I'm sorry," he said quietly.

"Don't be. Mark's been selfish lately. I think that's who he is, but he's hidden it from me until now." She plunked the napkin on the table and stood.

When she headed for the bathroom, her father was coming down the stairs. Chaz climbed the steps and met him halfway. "Is Mrs. Hall going to be okay?"

"My Becky's resilient. She'll be fine. I want to thank you." The man offered him a tired smile.

"Why?"

"For shining a light on the wolf in the room. I never did like that young man, but I couldn't put my finger on why. So, thank you."

"I was actually coming to apologize for ruining dinner."

Mr. Hall gave a dismissive flick of his hand and accompanied Chaz to the bottom of the staircase. "Dinner was fine, son. It was certain company we found objectionable, but you took care of that. And in remarkable form, I have to say. Well done."

Chaz nodded. This man's approval meant so much.

"I haven't had a chance to ask. How's your father? Do you see him much?"

"No, Mr. Hall. My dad passed away two years ago."

"I'm so sorry, Charles."

Chaz accepted the man's comforting pat on his shoulder. "Thanks. It was lung cancer. He could've fought it, but he didn't want to. He joked and said he had dreaded retirement from the marines and the cancer was his solution. I think he spent his life missing Mom, and looked forward to being with her again."

"You know you're welcome here anytime."

"I appreciate that. Besides my band, you're my only real family. Listen, Emily's upset. I'd like to take her home."

"Of course." Her father went to the dining room and began stacking dishes. "Take care of her."

"I will."

"Dad, let me do this." Emily moved the ham platter to the end of the table.

"No, honey. Go home. Charles will take you. Get some rest. It's been a rough evening." Her father pretended to slap her hand as she reached for a dish of leftover green beans. "I mean it. Now, go on."

She kissed his cheek and moved toward the front door. "I'll talk to you tomorrow."

"I love you, sweetie."

Charles came to her side and put a hand to the small of her back. The slight pressure reassured her. She met his gray gaze then let him take her to his car.

He opened her passenger door, tossed her father's book into the backseat, and waited for her to settle before he closed her door. Behind the wheel, he strapped on his seatbelt and started the engine. He didn't pull away from the curb, however.

"I'm not mad at you," she said.

"You have a right to be." He stared out the windshield.

"Maybe, but I'm not stupid. In a way, you rescued me from a marriage doomed to fail."

She studied his profile, astounded by how little he'd changed from this angle. For a moment, it took her back to girlhood when he'd been her favorite person. When her parents had been too busy and her brother couldn't care less, Charles had always shown a genuine interest in what she did and what she had to say. He hadn't treated her like a little girl. He had conversed with her as an equal. She had loved him for it.

He faced her, and the teenage Charles disappeared. His voice sounded deeper than usual when he said, "I'm glad you see it that way."

As he drove her home, tension between them grew. She wanted to say something to ease it, but everything coming to mind seemed inappropriate. She didn't want to talk about Mark, and the subject of Billy would add to her unease.

Nearly at her apartment, he said, "He was wrong. I'm not lubricious. In fact, I've avoided sex for a couple years now. When it's meaningless, I hate the way I feel the next morning."

"You haven't had sex in two years?" But he was only a couple years older than her. Why would he choose abstinence, especially considering his profession?

"There are plenty of opportunities. Especially when we go on tour, women practically beg for it. It's not real, though. They either want bragging rights to sex with a famous rock star, or they think they're in love with some fantasy. Either way, there's not much in it for me other than the obvious." He chuckled. "Believe me, I was fine with that for a long time. Not anymore."

"Why?" She studied his handsome face.

He pulled into her apartment complex and parked in the space next to her car. "I guess it's like reading a comic book. There's no substance there. I'd rather read Tolstoy or Fitzgerald. I need a lasting, meaningful relationship."

"That's hard to find in your line of work?"

"Sure, hard if I'm hoping to find it with a groupie. I'm not. Jet found it in a cute Japanese-American sound tech. Justin's in deep with a world-renowned photographer. C.J. fell in love with a food critic who also happens to be an amazing drummer. It can happen."

"So you might find what you're looking for

anywhere."

He smiled.

When he didn't say anything, she glanced up at the dark window of her apartment. Loneliness settled around her like a chill frost, and she shivered.

"Do you want me to walk you to your door?" he asked.

Why did he have to be so good-looking? "Do you mind?"

He turned off his engine and pulled the key free. "How could I mind? Don't you know you're my favorite person in the world?"

"I can't believe you said that." She got out, and as he came around the car, she confessed, "I was thinking a short while ago how you were my favorite person when I was a girl."

He put his arm around her waist and kissed her cheek. "You've always been mine. Come on. Let's get you inside."

Her face grew warm, and when he didn't let go of her as they headed to the door, her body began to stir at the feel of him, strong and lean, against her. His peck hadn't exceeded the brotherly kisses he used to give her when they were young, but the new adult attraction she struggled to fight altered his gesture into something far more significant.

In the elevator, he pressed the button for her floor then stepped away. Immediately, she missed his closeness. The gap between them formed a chasm. Did he sense her awareness of him? Did he share in the temptation? His neutral expression obscured any emotion or thought he had as he gazed at the elevator's display showing the floors they passed.

The doors opened, and his hand returned to the small of her back. At her apartment, her hands trembled as she tried to unlock her door. His fingers closed around hers, and she met his gaze.

She wanted him to lean near and put his mouth to hers. Butterflies flitted in her stomach, and she licked suddenly dry lips. When his gaze dipped to her mouth, her lungs arrested. Rather than kissing her, however, he slid the key from her grip and unlocked the door.

She deflated. His friendship had been the most important of her life, and he clearly offered it anew. Why did her body betray that? Why did her thoughts wander on a brazen vein? She didn't want to lose him. Especially after losing him once, and for so long.

"What is it?" he asked, closing the door.

"What's what?" She stared at his arms and fervently wished he would wrap her in them.

He placed her key on the sofa's end table. "You're staring. Do you want me to go?"

"No!" She gasped. "I'm sorry. I just...I need..."

He studied her a second. "You need a hug?"

"So much." She sighed.

"Come here." He went to the sofa, his face relaxed and his smoky eyes kind as he removed his jacket. Sitting, he waved her over and extended his arms.

She didn't hesitate. Stepping from her pumps, she said, "I'm going to pieces. Nothing is what I expected."

"Who said, 'Suffering is permanent, obscure and dark, and shares the nature of infinity'?"

"Wordsworth." She sat next to him, and when he leaned backward against the couch's padded armrest, she cuddled atop him. "But I disagree. When your arm is around me, the pieces start coming together and I'm less lost and confused."

He kicked off his shoes then brought his legs onto the cushions. She rearranged, sliding into the space between him and the backrest. She stretched alongside with her head on his chest and her knee bent across his thigh. His heart beat strong and steady, and the rise and fall of his chest lulled her.

"This has to be the hardest week of your life," he said.

"No." She closed her eyes and wrapped an arm over his firm abdomen. "The hardest week of my life was when you and Billy got arrested. I overheard my parents talking about how you'd made bail, and I waited and waited for you to come. To tell me what happened. To show me you were okay and tell me Billy would be home soon. You didn't. That was unbearable."

"I'm sorry."

"I know." She pinched a wrinkle in his shirt and rolled the soft material between her thumb and finger. She couldn't recall feeling this comfortable next to a man. Her body fit well to his. "Thank you for staying."

"It's no problem." He slowly rubbed the curve of her waist.

"I really didn't want to be alone tonight. Not after Mark left the way he did, and especially since he told me a few days ago that he's having me watched."

Charles' hand stilled. "He's having you watched?"

"I'm not sure. When I told him it was creepy, he claimed he was joking."

"Did you believe him?"

"I wanted to, but after his behavior at dinner, what he said about Billy in front of my parents, I'm inclined to trust my instinct. The man's a rat."

Chapter Eight

A chill climbing his spine, Chaz sat up, forcing Emily to do the same. "I'm not going to tell you what to do, but may I induce you to stay at my house? At least through the weekend?"

She pursed her lips. "Do you think he's capable of hurting me?"

"I don't know, and I don't want to find out." When she hesitated further, he said, "Indulge me. Mark's formidable. Let's not underestimate him."

She whispered, "I don't know if I can trust myself."

"Why?" He fought a surge of excitement.

She'd wanted him to kiss her at the door. He'd seen her invitation as clearly as if she'd spoken the words. Then she had practically asked him to hold her, and snuggled against him like a longtime lover.

For now, though, he would keep her physically close but at an emotional arm's length. When she surrendered, it couldn't be from weakness. She had to want him. Need him. Not merely his comfort. He wouldn't give in until he perceived she sought his love, because he wanted nothing less from her.

"Did I say that out loud?" She released a breathy chuckle then grew serious. "Do you think Mark's a threat? I know he decided he didn't like you from the start, but I've been involved with him for six months. This is the first time he's ever behaved in such an ugly manner."

He stood and offered his hand. "Well, I don't know anything beyond what I've seen. He's a jealous controller who viewed you as belonging to him. Now he probably thinks I've stolen you from him. I don't trust him to leave you alone."

She took his hand and came to her feet. "I don't want to inconvenience you. I could stay with my parents."

He followed her to her bedroom. "It's better if you go somewhere he can't find you."

She pulled a duffle-style gym bag from her closet and opened it on the bed. "Maybe we're overreacting. Maybe he was joking about his surveillance."

He folded his arms. "You know him better. Is he the type to accept defeat? Will he go quietly into this good night?"

She stopped, holding a pair of sneakers in one hand and a pair of jeans in the other. "A week ago, I would've said I didn't think him capable of anything nefarious. Now, I have no idea. I'm realizing I never really knew him."

"Alright. I have a call to make. I'll meet you at the front door." He went to the living room and got their agent on the phone. "Hey, Spence. It's Chaz."

"I never get calls from you, Preston. Is everything okay?"

He peered out a window and scanned the street below. "I need a personal favor. Am I permitted to ask Leon to play private investigator for me? I need somebody watched, and since Leon used to be a cop, he's perfect. He could call me if the guy decided to come for me."

"Do we need to get the police involved? This sounds bigger than your tour company's head of security would normally handle."

"I can't answer. It may be nothing. I don't know what this guy's about. If he's going to become a threat, I'll get the police into it. For now, I merely need him watched."

"Okay. Leon will eat this up. He says he misses those old days sometimes. What's the guy's name?"

"Mark Van Scoten. I don't have much else other than I know he lives here in Chicago and he works as a professional of some kind." The street remained peaceful. Streetlights cast golden light onto parked cars and sidewalks, but nothing moved. "He looks like Thor, if Thor cut his hair and wore a suit."

"Gotcha. Van Scoten can't be a common name. I'll give Leon a call right now. He can call you if he needs more."

"Absolutely. Thank you, Cal."

"Anything for you, Preston. You're my favorite."

He smiled. "Because I never bother you?"

"Yep. Pretty much. In the ten years I've represented Smashing Glass, you've called me twice. The other time was because C.J. had gotten in trouble."

"I remember." He gave Emily an acknowledging nod as she went past toward the door. "I've got to go. Have Leon call me tomorrow so I can capture his number on my cell."

"Will do. Take care."

Chaz ended his call and slid his phone into the front pocket of his slacks. He looked long and hard at the beauty awaiting him. She had changed from the curve-hugging dress into a gray V-neck knit top and black skinny jeans. Flip-flops left her toes bare, and she had taken her hair down.

He felt her fire. Her desire. It brought to mind Aerosmith's song *Beautiful*. As he headed for her, he sang, "You and me, my friend, we're out of here. Beautiful."

A slow smile revealed her straight teeth. "You really are a rock star. I didn't know you could sing."

"I can't. Not really. Come on." He placed her keys in her hand and took her bag before opening the door. Here came the real test. She was about to see how he lived.

♪ ♪ ♪ ♪

My friend. Charles had sung, *You and me, my friend*. Emily stared out his car window as they sped along the highway. Was that why he hadn't kissed her?

She squeezed her eyes shut. What was her problem? Until an hour ago, she'd been engaged. She fingered the empty place Mark's ring had rode for weeks. She flicked her fingernail across the faint indentation it left.

She glanced at Charles' profile. Other than her father, no man put her at ease like him. Billy may have had doubts about his character, but she didn't. Charles had always opened to her like a book. She understood how to read him. She trusted him like nobody else.

He activated his blinker and began to exit. She recognized this area of town. Her boss lived nearby. Charles drove along a busy thoroughfare lined by nice restaurants and high-end service shops. Then he turned into a neighborhood with large homes.

He owned a house. All the singles she knew, including her, enjoyed the benefits of leasing an apartment. No yard work. No maintenance. Someone to call when something broke. The fact that Charles had bought a house went to show his level of responsibility. In high school, he had studied hard and helped around the house while his friends partied. He's been on his own for the most part. It didn't surprise her that he made right choices.

The farther they progressed into back streets, the bigger the houses grew. It began to dawn on her that this man lived in a way she hadn't imagined.

He was rich.

He was world-famous.

Mark had said so, but it didn't hit her until now.

Charles pulled to a high-fenced gate and guardhouse that blocked the roadway. He swiped a card over a reader and continued through. Slowly, they climbed a winding road where she glimpsed bits of mansions along the way. He pressed a clicker clipped to his sun visor, and a tall white gate opened on a driveway half hidden by bushes and trees that also obscured his house.

Her heart began beating harder. The driveway curved left then descended around a dark hillside. The pale roof of his house came into view and took her breath away. It sprawled in the moonlight. He followed the drive to an asphalt parking area. A light came on and illuminated a space twenty cars could fit.

One of three doors lifted at the front of a huge garage. He pulled inside the bright interior where a motorcycle and two other classic sports cars parked. The space appeared neat and clean. The exact opposite of her father's cluttered, oil-stained garage.

He took the Sherlock Holmes book and her bag from the backseat as the door lowered on a low hum. He led her inside to a large, immaculate kitchen. She suspected, despite a few countertop appliances and gadgets, that he never used this room. He punched buttons on a security panel on a wall next to the door leading to the garage then hung his keys on a hook underneath.

"Do you live here by yourself?" she asked.

"Mostly. C.J. used to crash here every now and then before he got married. We rehearse here, too, so the guys sleep over when practice goes late. Mainly when we're working on new songs. I also employ helpers, so there are people here during the day. Gardeners twice a week. A housekeeper Monday through Friday, and a maid a few days. You know." He touched a light switch panel.

Right. She knew all about it. She chuckled and followed him to a long living room where inset lighting shone on black leather furniture, shiny hardwood floors, and a wall-length bookcase completely filled with books. She went over and touched the paper cover on his copy of *The Count of Monte Cristo*, which leaned against a stack.

"You read all of these?" She eyed the length of the wall. He had more than a thousand books in his collection.

"More, actually. These are the ones I kept. Let me show you to your room." He put *The Sign of Four* on a coffee table and headed down a short hall that led to a long one running the length of the house's back section.

Double doors formed each end. He went left and opened a door nearest that end's set. A queen-sized bed, full dresser, television stand, and sitting area complete with full sofa and two upholstered chairs barely did justice to the room's expanse. A bathroom door stood open to her right. Beyond it, another door led to a walk-in closet.

"Will you be comfortable here?"

She laughed. "I could fit half my apartment in here. Is this where C.J. slept?"

"No way. Nobody stays here. It's right next to me in the master suite." He gestured to the double doors then put her bag next to the dresser. "Do you need anything?"

"I could use a drink."

He offered a small smile from the doorway. "Sorry. No booze. C.J. had no self-control, and the rest of us stopped drinking hard liquor years ago. I have beer and soda, though. Iced tea. Juice. Bottled water. Whatever you want."

"A beer sounds great." She headed to the kitchen with him. "I feel so awkward. You always came to my house."

He took two beers from the refrigerator and handed her one. "Do you like it? My house, I mean."

She glanced around, taking in oil paintings, an unlit fireplace, and a couple potted ferns growing tall in corners. Despite its showplace appeal, it appeared comfortable and inviting, like her father's library.

"It's exquisite," she said and smiled.

"Would you live here?" He came to her side and took a swallow from his bottle.

"Sure."

"No." His hazel eyes darkened to almost pure gray. "I mean really. Could you live here?"

Her stomach somersaulted. "With you?"

His eyebrows lifted a fraction, but he didn't speak.

She studied the living room and imagined curling on the couch with a book. She pictured a Christmas tree with presents and her parents visiting. What meals she could prepare in a kitchen like this. It would be fun to take cooking classes.

She gazed at Charles. He'd be here, too. Encouraging her like he always had. Inspiring her to work hard and be a better person. Squeezing both hands around her beer, she fought an urge to reach for him.

"Yes. I could happily live here." She lowered her eyes and moved to the living room.

He dimmed the recessed lighting to half then followed her to the couch. He settled on the opposite end and relaxed against its cushions. Weaving his fingers behind his head, he spread his knees wide. "I'm sorry your fiancé turned contrary."

Somehow, she didn't believe him. "Why? He clearly didn't care for you."

He slowly met her gaze. "Because he hurt you. He didn't seem concerned for your feelings or your parents'. You deserve better. That's why I'm sorry." Closing his eyes, he reclined his head onto the leather sofa back.

Tension built in her belly and crept outward along her limbs. He tempted her, as if he invited her to crawl atop him. "I think he hid his true self."

He barely nodded.

"You don't, do you? You don't hide anything from me."

"Never," he said in a low, quiet voice. "Never."

Chapter Nine

In all the years he had given free rein to his baser desires, Chaz had never wanted a woman more. Sober and well rested, he had no excuse but love for his overwhelming need for Emily. He clenched his jaw and continued to feign sleepy indifference.

Without opening his eyes, he put his beer to his lips and took a swallow. He didn't dare look at her. The mere sight of her fueled fantasies that had him hardening in his slacks.

She didn't need to deal with his advances. Besides, it wouldn't mean much tonight – the night she had ended her engagement with Mark. He refused to risk it. Sleeping with her now carried too high a price, and he wouldn't lose her over a single night's pleasure.

"I'm going to bed." Not sparing her a glance, he took his half-full beer to the kitchen and poured it in the sink. As he passed the sofa on his way to the hall, he picked up her father's book and said, "Stay up as late as you like. The television is behind the wall above the fireplace, and the remote is in that wooden box on the coffee table."

"Thanks."

He practically felt her gaze on him until he turned the corner to his room. At the double doors, he stood for a second and massaged bunched muscles at his nape. He had her safe in his home. That's what counted.

In his room, he undressed for bed. He wanted

nothing more than to march to the living room and kiss her senseless. He'd waited twelve years. It killed him that he had to wait longer, but she was worth it.

He donned a pair of flannel pajama bottoms and brushed his teeth. Then he cracked his bedroom door. Talking from the television quietly carried along the hall. Emily didn't make a sound.

He closed the door and flopped into bed. Staring at a pleated shade over the room's largest window, he couldn't get his brain to stall. He pictured her on his couch, finishing her beer. Sitting alone. Did she cry for Mark?

He hoped she found his home comfortable. He hoped she recovered quickly from her fiancé's betrayal. Most of all, he hoped she could love him.

When his mind continued running circles around Emily, he sat and turned on his light. He read the first three chapters of *The Sign of Four*, but it held his interest too well to allow sleep. He pulled a bookmark from a stack in his nightstand and marked his place. He'd go to his converted theater and practice some of Smashing Glass' new songs.

The television no longer played, but the living room was still lit. Had she gone to bed and left the lights on? Instead of going straight to the theater behind the other set of double doors, he turned and headed for the front of the house.

Emily paced, her eyes on the floor and her feet bare. One of his books lay open on the couch. Her empty beer bottle sat next to his remote. She came his way, but her gaze remained downcast. Her mouth bore hard lines, and her hands jerked at her sides.

"Are you okay?" he asked.

She startled then stared dumbfounded at him a long second.

He ventured a step toward her. "I thought you went to bed."

"I'm too angry to sleep," she said, whipping a hand through the air before her.

So much for finding her weak and crying. He took

another step. "You're mad at me?"

"No." She resumed pacing. "Of course not. I'm pissed. At myself for not seeing through Mark's pretense. At him for believing me stupid enough to stay with him after he showed his true character. Do you think I'm an idiot? Because I'm beginning to wonder myself."

He closed the distance and wrapped his arms around her. "I would never consider you an idiot. In fact, I'm glad to see you like this."

"Like what?" She pressed her warm cheek to his bare chest and hugged her arms around his middle. "Like a bitch?"

He chuckled. Resting his chin atop her head, he inhaled the floral fragrance of her hair. "Like the spunky, independent girl I once knew."

"I'm tired of resentment. I raged at Billy for committing that crime and then refusing to let me visit him. I resented you for abandoning us. When he died, I thought I could let it go, but you came to the funeral. I was enraged. It's embarrassing. Now, I'm seething over Mark. This is exhausting."

"I guess so." As he kissed her soft hair, a stirring began in his loins.

"I want everything to make sense again."

"It will."

She leaned on him in silence for endless, blissful minutes. "I didn't wake you, did I?"

"No. I couldn't sleep. You should try, though." When he grew semi-hard, he released her and stepped backward. Another minute would have him full hard and aching.

She crossed her arms and went to the bank of windows. Gazing into dark night, she shook her head. "I can't explain it."

He retreated another step. He wanted to go to her so badly only one outcome could result.

She faced him, her countenance calm. Not a hint of anger marred her gorgeous features. "I haven't seen you in so long, yet you seem to know me as well now as you did then."

He swallowed hard. It took all his strength to fight a need to pull her close and kiss her into surrender.

"Nobody knew me better than you. Not even my parents."

He crossed his arms over his pounding heart.

Her hands went to her sides, and she tilted her head a bit. "I don't know why, but I suspect nobody knows me better than you right now. Why is that?"

He shrugged while taking another step away. "It seems only fair. We could be fifty, and nobody would understand me better than you."

The ceiling offered no answers as Emily studied its painted plaster swirls. The more she saw of Charles' home, the more she loved it. How did he live here alone? The place was huge.

An occasional metallic whine pricked at her hearing, and now it stirred her curiosity. It sounded like machinery, but what work took place at two in the morning?

She swung her legs from bed and shuffled to the hallway. The whine accompanied a rumble, like music blasting in a closed car at an intersection. She knocked softly on one of Charles' bedroom doors, but he didn't answer.

The sound seemed to come from the other end of the hall. She slowly made her way to the double doors and put a hand to one. It vibrated.

Fascinated, she pressed the door latch and pushed it open. Rock music flooded the hallway. She peeked in and realized he had converted a theater. A wide screen, enormous and lifeless, filled the wall to her left. Two rows of movie theater chairs faced it, but the rest of the room behind those seats had been cleared.

Charles stood at the center of the cleared area, guitar in hand. It's chord snaked on the carpet to a boxy amp. He rocked forward and backward in time to his music, and his fingers danced effortlessly along the strings.

His hair swayed, and his bare shoulders reflected yellow light from sconce-like fixtures on the walls. He still wore pajama bottoms and bare feet.

Muscles on his arms and torso bunched and relaxed. He had his eyes closed, and his lips bore a faint, relaxed smile.

The sight of him, sexy and strong as he ripped a melody from his electric guitar, elicited an immediate longing in her. His rhythm struck a primal nerve and didn't let up. She gripped the doorframe as a throbbing began between her thighs.

She comprehended why women vied for attention from him. Her breathing increased. Her nipples hardened. When he ended the song and sent his arm straight and in a big circle, her knees weakened.

His eyes opened and met hers. His bare chest heaved on two breaths. Then he put the guitar on the floor. He strode to her, his gaze dropping to her mouth.

She whimpered her need a second before he cupped her face and pressed his mouth to hers. Grasping his firm shoulders, she opened and invited him in. Her heart raced.

She kissed Charles.

Sexy, smart, caring Charles. Her best friend. Famous rock star. Charles.

His hand went to her waist and squeezed while his other slid to her nape and drew her deeper into the kiss. Thought fled under an onslaught of sheer sensation. She could only want. Need. Desire.

She put a hand to his chest, loving the feel of his skin over muscle. He had a natural-made body, not one sculpted and bulked by weights. The picture of him naked and entering her wrenched a moan from her.

He withdrew his tongue and worked his lips on her a moment longer. Ending the kiss, he held her gaze. "God, Emily."

"Yeah," she whispered. "Why didn't you do that at my apartment?"

He barely shook his head. "We have to be in the same place for this to work. You were struggling with the idea that I'm like a brother."

"Am I so transparent?"

He retreated a step and kept hold of her waist but moved his other hand to her bare shoulder. Running a finger under the strap of her camisole, he said, "You've been an open book to me. The best book I ever read. A classic unparalleled."

Her heart thudded. "You were my brother's—"

"I was yours, Emily. The moment I opened your gift and found that guitar. The moment you looked at me like I was somebody special. Everything changed at that birthday party. I've been waiting for you ever since."

Her heart stopped thudding and skipped a beat. This wasn't new for him. "I didn't think of you this way."

"I know," he said and caressed her cheek. "You do now."

She looked at her fingers on his skin. Nobody had kissed her as thoroughly. "What if I had chosen Mark?"

A small smile graced his sensual mouth. "You've always been smarter than me. You'd have eventually seen through him. I just brought out the worst in him sooner than later."

The throbbing between her legs grew more insistent. She wanted to lure him to his bedroom and have her way with him the rest of this night. "So now what?"

Touching his nose to hers, he said low, "I see what you're thinking. I want that, too. But not yet. We've waited years. We can wait a little longer."

"Wait?" A sharp pang of disappointment cut across her belly. "Wait for what?"

"You'll know it when you feel it. You and me, there's no middle ground. It's all or nothing. No room for regret. No room for foolish pride."

He captured her lips. Bracing an arm across her lower back, he bent her backward. She threw her arms around his neck and rode his amazing loving. Her head swam. Her body cried out to his. What more did he expect her to feel? She had never wanted a man as much as she wanted him that second.

When he broke the kiss, she gasped. Raging desire shook her to her core. How would she make it to morning lying alone in her guest bed? She clung to him.

He held her a while then said, "I'm probably going to practice a few more hours. You're welcome to stay and listen."

Relaxing, she smiled. "You're not self-conscious?"

He laughed and returned to his guitar. "There's no point. I've played in front of audiences of thousands, but there's only one audience I've ever wanted. Come see what I learned to do on that guitar you gave me."

She sat sideways in a back row seat and drew her knees under her chin. As he closed his eyes and strummed a fast thread, she narrowed her eyes. Nothing would be the same. She marveled at how his kiss changed her world. Charles shined a light on the misconceptions she had mistakenly held as truths.

He wasn't whom she'd thought. He was more. Now she had to turn her back on the past and realize that maybe *she* wasn't who she thought, either.

Chapter Ten

A ringing woke Chaz from a sound sleep. Groaning, he rolled and clapped a hand on his alarm clock. The ringing continued. He cracked open one eye. The display on his phone glowed.

He yanked his cell phone off of its charger and draped a forearm across his eyes. "This better be important."

"Justin called a meeting," said Jet. "Says he has an announcement."

"He better not be quitting again."

"Are you still in bed?"

"I was up all night."

"Having a hard time, huh?"

Chaz glanced at his clock. Eleven thirty. "You have no idea."

"Do you want us to leave you out of it? I could call you later and fill you in."

"No, that's okay. I'll attend."

"Good, because we're all on our way to your place."

Chaz sat up and forced his dry eyes open. "What kind of bullshit—"

"Twenty minutes, man. See ya." Jet ended the call.

"Sonofabitch." He set his phone on his nightstand and scrambled out of bed. He went to the hall and knocked on his guestroom door. "Emily? Are you awake?"

She opened the door, her hair dripping wet. Only a towel covered her, and not by much. "What's wrong?"

He swallowed hard as his groin tightened. "The band's coming over. I'm really sorry. They didn't give me any notice."

Her eyes widened a bit. "You mean now?"

"Twenty minutes. Listen, you don't need to make an appearance if you don't want."

"I want to meet them. I'll be ready." Smiling, she shut her door.

He grinned. They would adore her, and it meant a lot that she showed genuine interest in the people who had become family to him. Racing through a shower, he couldn't stop smiling at the memory of her rapt attention as he'd played through the night. Did she like their music?

Skipping shaving, he ran a brush through his hair then hurried into a T-shirt and jeans. His doorbell rang before he reached his bedroom door. His feet bare, he jogged to the front door, unlocked it, and found Jet and Akiko.

"I like this scruffy look on you," she said, indicating his unshaven face with a pale, slender hand.

"You look lovely, as usual." Chaz held the door wide. "Come on in."

"Stop hitting on my girl," Jet said with a smirk and a light punch as he entered, ushering Akiko ahead of him. He held up a large bag with handles. "We brought lunch. I guess in your case, it's breakfast."

Chaz chuckled and closed the door. "There's someone I want you to meet."

Jet came to a halt and faced him. "Are you serious? Is this one of your secrets?"

"I don't have secrets." He passed his friend and took the bag, following the pretty Japanese woman into the living room.

"Ha! You have nothing but secrets."

Emily came from the kitchen carrying two cups of coffee. She had tied her wet hair into a fancy knot at her nape and had managed to apply enough makeup to give her a flawless finish. Small diamond earrings glittered on her earlobes, and she wore a frilly white blouse that hugged her curves and revealed a bit of firm, round cleavage. Skinny jeans left little to his imagination, and her cute toes clung to a pair of white flip-flops. She oozed casual sophistication.

Jet released a soft whistle. "I can't remember the last time I saw you with a woman, and never in your house."

"This is Emily Hall. Emily, please meet Jet and Akiko," said Chaz, accepting a cup from her. He placed the bag on a kitchen counter.

She met the Japanese woman's smile of greeting. *"Konnichiwa. Hajimemashite. Dozo yoroshiku."*

Akiko offered a bow then beamed. "I am so pleased to meet you, too, Emily. Where did you learn to speak Japanese? Your accent is very good."

"At the university. I thought I wanted to move to Hawaii, and most companies there require employees to speak Japanese. I understand they have a large number of tourists from Japan."

Jet came forward and took her hand for a shake. "Beautiful and smart. It's going to be fun having you around." He faced Chaz. "She is going to be around, right?"

He shrugged. "That's up to her."

"Good Lord. More mystery." The doorbell rang, and Jet headed to the near hall. "That's C.J. I'll get it."

He had a sip of coffee and raised his eyebrows at how good it tasted. For being a non-drinker of coffee, she sure could brew it. Making coffee had never been a strength of his, and he enjoyed that Emily had mastered the task. Especially this morning when he needed the caffeine. Who knew what bombshell Justin planned to drop?

Akiko gracefully sank to the sofa, her knees tight together beneath the hem of her pale blue dress. Sin entered with a nod and smile for each of them and carried a case of beer to the kitchen.

"How the hell should I know?" asked C.J., entering and scowling at Jet. "Justin tells you more than anyone. I should be asking you what this meeting's about."

Jet unfastened a button at his throat. "He wouldn't say."

C.J.'s eyes went to Emily, and Chaz made brief introductions, including Sindra when she returned from putting the beer in his refrigerator. The gorgeous blond went and hugged Emily then sat in one of the chairs. For the thousandth time, Chaz thought C.J. didn't deserve such a wonderful woman.

Akiko gestured to the cushion next to her. "What kept you from moving to Hawaii?"

Emily joined her, both hands around her steaming cup. "A few things. At first, I couldn't afford the move. I found a job in my field immediately after graduation, and by the time I paid off my student loans and had a decent savings, I had reached a position in the company I couldn't easily leave. I'd worked so hard to get there. It's been a bit stagnant this past year, but I met Mark six months ago and got engaged, so I haven't considered moving."

Both Akiko and Jet sent Chaz questioning looks. He ignored them and joined C.J. behind the couch. Emily's damp hair radiated the fragrance of her shampoo, and he took a deep breath.

Leaning forward, Sindra asked, "What do you do?"

"I'm a financial advisor and analyst for Schenk, Cooper, and Row. I head the Bonds and Cash division, but I'm up for another promotion next year." She took a sip of coffee and made a face.

"How do you know Chaz?"

He studied her, wondering how much she would reveal to these near strangers. The doorbell saved her, however. The front door opened.

"We're in here," called Jet.

Justin strolled in, grinning.

"Desiree!" Akiko and Sin cried at once, getting to their feet.

The redhead beamed a greeting and came first to hug Chaz. He gave her a one-armed hug. "Welcome home."

Emily remained seated. Her gaze didn't leave him. Was that a hint of jealousy he detected? He hoped so.

"You were right," Desiree said, taking a step toward Justin and accepting hugs from the other women who appeared tiny next to her height. "South Korea was spectacular. Next time you guys tour there, I'm coming along."

Jet came around the sofa and patted her shoulder. "You always say that, but you never have time."

She shared a conspiratorial glance with Justin that had Chaz suspecting his announcement had to do with her work. He took a step to the couch and gently tugged Emily's arm. She stood.

"Justin and Desiree, please let me introduce Emily Hall. She's the one who gave me my nickname. She also gave me my first guitar. If not for her, I wouldn't have met any of you or have you as the best friends a guy could want."

C.J. laughed. "Damn. Nice speech, dude. Where did all those words come from?"

"My heart." He met Emily's eyes and urged her to come to his side.

The room went silent.

Putting his arm around her waist, he said to Justin, "So what's this announcement you need to make?"

Desiree grinned and showed a diamond on her left ring finger.

"We're getting married," said the band's leader.

Chaz warmed with joy as the room erupted in chatter and congratulations. Desiree came near and spoke quietly with Emily. He couldn't discern their words over Jet's and C.J.'s shouts.

"Since we're making announcements, I should probably tell you that Akiko and I have set our date. May twenty-fifth. Mark your calendars because your presence is demanded." Jet laughed then kissed his bride-to-be.

Chaz hoped Emily would be there, too. At his side. In his soul.

C.J. stepped to the center of the gathering and yelled to be heard. "Just remember who spoke his vows first."

Sin smiled sweetly and took her husband's hand. "Justin and Desiree, we couldn't be happier for you. It's been too long coming. Jet and Akiko, congratulations. We'll do everything we can to be at your wedding. Only one event might keep us away."

C.J. put a hand to his wife's belly and kissed her cheek.

Akiko squealed, and Desiree wrapped long arms around the expecting couple. Chaz's stomach somersaulted at the idea of a baby joining their ranks. They'd all found such happiness, and he had gotten close enough to it with Emily that he could almost taste it.

"Congratulations, Chris and Sin," he said.

Emily leaned near and whispered, "What an exciting day."

He nodded. Her blue eyes went soft. "Thank you. Thank you for letting me be part of this."

The more she learned about these amazing people, the more Emily realized why Charles loved them. They accepted and included her without hesitation, as if her presence was natural to the gathering.

After her coffee brought alertness, a beer relaxed her. Soon, she laughed at their funny stories and leaned against Charles like he'd never left her. This was more real than anything she'd lived since Billy's trouble began.

She ate with them, enjoying homemade sushi Akiko had prepared. It made an unexpectedly satisfying breakfast. Charles hardly said a word. She couldn't remember him saying so little, yet the band seemed used to his silence. When he did speak, everyone listened. Their respect for him hung in the air next to their tremendous love for one another.

When the meal ended, the band went to the theater to play. Akiko and Desiree accompanied them, but Sindra stayed back.

"Can we talk?" asked the blonde.

"Sure." Emily removed her flip-flops and settled on the couch. She drew her feet under a hip and patted the next cushion. "Congratulations on your baby. I'm thrilled to meet the woman who tamed C.J."

Sindra chuckled and joined her. "I can't tame a wild man like my drummer-man. He tamed himself."

"You two seem so happy."

"We are. You look really happy with Chaz."

"He's a good friend."

The blonde studied her a long second. "I've never seen him so interactive. I think it's you."

Emily blinked. "Interactive? What do you mean?"

Sin propped an elbow onto the sofa back and rested her head against her hand. "He's been the background member. He usually hangs in the periphery and rarely contributes to conversation or interviews beyond a brief sentence here and there."

"Charles? My Charles?" This didn't describe the boy, and now the man, she knew.

"Is he? Is he *your* Charles?"

Emily opened her mouth to say no then shut it before a sound emerged. She dropped her gaze. "I want him to be. He's sort of keeping me at arm's length. You have to understand that I ended my engagement with Mark only last night."

"I see." The blonde put a cool hand on Emily's. "Chaz doesn't talk about his past or his family, but we gather it was rough. He went through a lot of pain?"

"It wasn't ideal. It's true. Until a couple days go, I thought of him like a brother."

"And now?"

Emily shook her head, unable to assign mere

words to the daunting yet exultant emotions he stirred in her. The hope for a future that exceeded her most daring dreams.

"I realize you hardly know me," said Sindra with a kind smile. "I must seem out of line to ask you for a confession. We love him. This band is tight-knit, and we women who love them become part of the family. You seem right for him, and I want to see you both happy."

"That's so sweet of you. I can't tell you how much I appreciate how you want to protect him. There's a long history between us you can't begin to fathom. Despite what we may want, maybe he's right to force us to go slowly. We've got a lot of baggage to sort through before we can even begin to decide where our relationship is headed."

The blonde tilted her head. "You're just like him. So wise. You said there's a long history. How long have you known him?"

She gazed out at his peaceful, landscaped lawn as memories flashed in a myriad of moments. A childhood filled with his helping hands and encouraging smiles. A sad sort of contentment weighed upon her shoulders. Was she foolish to want more than friendship? Was he?

"Forever," Emily said wistfully. She met the blonde's blue gaze. "He was my brother's best friend since elementary school. Remember how he said I gave him his nickname?"

Sindra nodded.

"I couldn't say my R's when he first started coming to our house. I was three, according to my dad. I couldn't say Charles, so I called him Chaz for the longest time." Emily shook her head. "I think it's funny how he prefers that nickname."

"I'm guessing, but maybe the name makes him think of you." The blonde arched her eyebrows.

"Maybe. One thing I do know concerning Charles is that supposition is never a good idea."

Chapter Eleven

Exhaustion burned Chaz's eyes, but he couldn't sleep. Emily had fit in with his friends, and the women seemed to accept her. He rubbed his eyes then punched his pillow to fluff it. Why had she danced with Akiko and Desiree during their jam session? The woman was too sexy. Too beautiful. He'd tried to shred it with the guys, but he couldn't stop thinking how badly he wanted to get her naked in his bed.

His phone rang, and he grabbed it before it could ring again and wake her. "It's one in the morning, damn it."

"I'm sorry, Mr. Preston," said Leon. "I thought you'd want to know what's happening with Mark Van Scoten. I called twice today, but you never answered. I really don't think he's a threat. He's got his hands full."

Chaz sat up and brushed away a tickle of hair from his forehead. "Why do you say that?"

"I've been tailing him for seventeen hours, and in that time, he's visited three women. Two, he slept with. He literally just went into his condo building with woman number three. When he met her for dinner at nine o'clock, she wore a necklace and earrings. Now, she's wearing a ring on her left ring finger. See what I'm saying?"

"Shit. He spent the day hunting for another fiancée. The guy's a bigger snake than I thought. You didn't, by any chance, get a good look at that ring?"

"Better than that. I've got a close-up digital picture."

"Is it two dragons with the diamond in their mouths?"

"Yes. One silver and one gold. Kind of weird for an engagement ring, don't you think?"

Chaz's stomach burned. His first thought went to Emily. How would she take this?

"Anyway, sir, I don't think he's a problem for you. I'd be happy to follow him another day or two if you want. This has been fun."

"Probably a good idea. Do me a favor? Print those pictures and run them by here later today." He'd make sure Leon saw a sizeable bonus in his next paycheck, fun or not.

"Sure thing, Mr. Preston. Sorry to disturb you." The security manager ended the call.

Chaz flopped onto his pillow, but a quiet knock had him upright again. "Emily?"

"I heard a phone ring," she said through the door. "Is everything okay?"

He switched on his bedside lamp and opened the door.

"A call in the middle of the night is never a good thing," she said. Her hair flipped every which way at the ends, and she wore no makeup. She looked young and vulnerable and more delicious than ever.

"Come in." He gestured toward a sitting area.

While she settled sideways into one of his brown upholstered chairs, he changed the ring tone on his phone then took a T-shirt from a dresser drawer. At the fireplace, he flicked a lever that activated flames then donned the shirt. He joined her in an adjacent chair.

"Could there be a reason why Mark asked you to marry him other than love?" he asked.

Her eyebrows lowered. "Of course not. Why would you ask such a question?"

"Maybe he stands to gain an inheritance?" he guessed.

"That's silly. No. His father worked on a railroad,

and his mother taught school. He's got three other brothers. What's this about?" Her frown deepened.

Heat began to reach him from the fire, and he stretched his feet toward the hearth. "I've been having him followed."

She leaned over the arm of her chair. "For how long?"

"The past day. I made the arrangements before we came here last night."

She didn't relax.

He released a heavy sigh. "Don't be angry. You have to admit he was enraged when he left your parents' house. After you told me he might've been spying on you, I had to deem him potentially dangerous. You know that. It's why you came here to stay."

"So you stooped to his level?"

Irritation prickled along his sternum. "I needed to know if he was going to hunt us. A little warning goes a long way."

She leaned back and swatted hair off her shoulder. "That call was to tell you Mark's on his way here? I can't imagine it would make a difference. How would he get past all the gates and fences?"

"He's not coming." He agonized over how to tell her the truth.

Concern replaced her frown. "What aren't you telling me?"

He stood, fisted a hand, and wrapped his fingers around it. "This is speculation on my part, but based on what my guy told me, I think Mark was seeing other women. A lot of other women. While he dated you. He visited three of them today."

Tucking hair behind her ear, she said, "I don't believe it. They're probably clients. He often works on Saturdays."

"He visits clients in their homes and has sex with them?"

She gasped and shook her head.

"Leon's got pictures. He's going to bring them to the house. I'm sorry." Wanting to hold and comfort her, he stepped to the fireplace and kept her at his back. With a bed in easy access, he'd likely lose his battle to resist his need of her.

"That scoundrel."

Chaz turned on his heel.

Emily's face burned red, and she pounded on the chair arm. "That asshole!"

"The engagement ring you gave back...he put it on another woman's finger a few hours ago."

She stood and planted her hands on her hips. "Of all the intolerable, manipulative, ignoble—" She sliced a hand in front of her. "That bastard. I shed tears over him."

He moved to her and took hold of her slender, cool fingers. "The day after you broke your engagement, he's got the ring on somebody else. He's got something to gain."

Blinking rapidly, she dropped her gaze to the floor. "I can't... I don't— Wait. The party."

"What party?"

"He's brought it up four times since our engagement. He sounded seriously concerned I wouldn't want to go when I told him Billy had died. He's got a party to attend for work, and his bosses are bringing their families."

Chaz urged her to sit then resumed his seat.

Tapping her finger on the chair's fabric, she said, "He used to complain how his bosses accused him of lacking stability. He claimed they passed him over for the last promotion because of it."

"Do you think they knew he dated multiple women?"

"I don't know. I only know he was adamant that I go to that party on his arm and wearing his ring. I guess he was using me to get a promotion." Anger flickered to disappointment in the set of her lips. "Why didn't I see it?"

He admired her quick mind. The fact that she could admit to her failing made her more appealing yet. He'd never wanted to kiss her more.

♪ ♪ ♪ ♪

Mark had played her. Emily hadn't been anything more than a right fit for his ring. Marriageable material to impress his employer. Had he even intended to marry her, or had he planned to end it the moment he climbed a rung at work?

She refused to surrender to melancholia. He wasn't worth it. Was Charles right? Had he cheated on her the entire time they'd dated? It had to be true. It explained his weekend work, late nights supposedly at the office, and why he'd laughed weirdly when he said he'd had a hard time getting out of bed the morning after Billy's funeral. That's why he hadn't come by like he promised. He'd been with another woman. Besides, he had to have a well-established relationship with a woman to get her to accept his proposal.

"I'm so small all of a sudden," she admitted, unable to look Charles in the eye. "He made me a dupe."

Charles didn't say anything. Did he think less of her? Why shouldn't he? She certainly thought less of herself.

Six months wasted. She could've taken her Japanese and her impressive resume and moved to Hawaii. Then again, it would've put her far from her parents. Far from Charles, and he grew more and more important to her by the minute.

His opinion had always meant more to her than anyone's. She hadn't wanted to be with anyone as much as him. So quickly, she had returned to this. Only now, their dynamic had changed.

The mere sight of him or sound of his voice created a yearning. Sitting in the same room with him left her distracted and physically bothered. She liked it yet simultaneously resented it.

"It's probably best if I go to bed," she said.

He cleared his throat.

Venturing a sideways glance his way, she tried to gauge his mood. His thoughts. The moment their eyes met, however, she couldn't tear her gaze from his. Slowly, she faced him. Electricity charged the air.

In his hooded stare and taut neck muscles, she read a need that mirrored her own. It was implicit in the flex of his fingers on his knee and the brief emergence of his tongue as he wet his lips.

Desire superseded fatigue. His seductive gaze scorched her. Her blood roared through her veins, and she trembled under the sheer force of her pounding heart. The thought of his touch made her nipples harden uncomfortably against her tight camisole. Made her folds quicken and swell around a pulsating ache that forced her to fidget.

When a wrong move pressed her awakened clit to the firm seat cushion, she shot to her feet. "Ah! Um...well, I'll go then."

He stood, and he said in a sleepy tone, "I'm sorry about Mark."

"I'm not." She took three steps toward the bedroom doors. "As far as I'm concerned, I escaped in good time. I hate to imagine if you hadn't come and I'd married him. What a nightmare."

He moved in her direction, but she thrust a hand toward him.

"No need to show me out," she said, her voice tight and too high. She released a laugh that sounded forced even to her own ears. "I know the way."

"Would you like a goodnight kiss?"

Her knees gave, but she hid it in a shuffle closer to the doors. "You know what? Not tonight. Let's talk tomorrow."

"Are you sure?"

"Positive." She grabbed one of the door latches and made available her exit. "We'll talk tomorrow. Lots to say. Lots to...well, decide."

"Goodnight, Emily."

"Mm-hmm," she managed on a half squeak and hurried to her room.

She collapsed on her bed in a throbbing puddle of mush. What that man did to her! It scared her to realize that if he hadn't spent the last two days inspiring reason in her, she'd have jumped on him. She'd have sought solace in his kisses and his bed, but regretted it in the morning.

He was worthy of better. So was she.

Chapter Twelve

Her head hurt. These late nights had Emily groggy and hung over from sleep-deprivation. She snuggled lower into her covers and put a hand over her closed eyes. An incessant drone invaded her peace, though. She opened her eyes enough to test them in light. When a spike didn't pierce her brain, she glanced at the clock. It read eleven o'clock.

She hadn't slept so late on a Sunday since college. Why hadn't Charles woken her? And what made that low rumbling? Was he practicing?

Swinging her legs over the edge of her bed, she slumped then went still. She took another thirty seconds to wake then trod to her bedroom window. Pulling aside its drapery, she squinted in dread of a sun that didn't shine. Rain fell so hard it formed a smooth flowing sheet on the outer glass. Another rumble of thunder growled at the miserable morning.

Her body moved stiffly as she headed for her bathroom. This unsatisfied lust took its toll. Between the rain and her through-the-roof blood pressure last night, no wonder she had a headache.

Thirty minutes later, her stomach's protests competed against the storm. She tied a bow in the string of her sweat pants and trekked to the kitchen. She broke the house's eerie silence by locating pans and making breakfast. His well-stocked refrigerator, pantry, and cabinets had her reassessing. The man did use this room.

She found a wooden serving tray standing on end in his pantry. Arranging it with their meal, she wondered if he'd bark if she woke him to eat. He hadn't during sleepovers with Billy, but she couldn't discount that he was no longer a boy. He'd been through hell because of her brother. He'd lived a wild rock star life for years by his own admission. He'd traveled the world. Experience tended to change people, and he had more than a fair share.

She carried the tray to his room and bumped her knee against his door by way of knocking. A groan met her request.

Then he said, "Come in."

Carefully balancing the tray on her left forearm and hand, she pressed down on the latch and went in. Charles stretched in bed, a blanket riding just below his bellybutton and a grimace contorting his handsome face.

"Have a headache?" she asked quietly.

He grunted an affirmative.

"Me, too. I thought it was because my sleep schedule's a mess, but I think it's this storm. I made us breakfast." She set the tray next to his hip and had a seat at the edge of his king-sized bed. "Are you hungry?"

He opened his eyes, gave her a long look, glanced at the tray, and closed his eyelids. He sank further into his pillows. "You're beautiful. Do you know that?"

"I get by."

A small smile overtook his grimace. "You do more than get by, Emily."

His compliment warmed her. "Do you have any pain medication?"

He pointed at his nightstand drawer without looking.

Expecting condoms, porno, and who knew what else a bachelor kept by his bed, she slid open the drawer. Instead, she found a bottle each of ibuprofen and acetaminophen, her father's copy of *The Sign of Four* with a bookmark halfway through. Behind the book, an opened bag of peanut butter cups spilled a few foil-covered candies.

She opened the ibuprofen, took two, and put two in his hand. Returning the bottle to the drawer, she popped the capsules into her mouth then downed them with a swallow of white grape juice.

Charles pushed to a sitting position and did the same using a sip of coffee. Switching on his lamp, he said, "You were strong last night. Thank you. I was losing the battle."

"I didn't realize we were in a battle." She held out a saucer containing a couple pieces of lightly buttered toast done the way she knew he liked.

He accepted one. "I wanted you. You felt it. It was written all over you."

Using her placement of the saucer on the tray to avoid his gaze, she tried to ignore a flutter in her stomach that had nothing to do with hunger. "I don't deny it."

"I think it's best if we don't go there. Not until you're straight in your head about Mark...and about where in your life I fit." He bit into his toast.

It meant so much that he didn't expect her to give up her life to follow him. His world was bigger than hers, yet he slowed for her to make room for him. Not vice versa.

Chewing a piece of apple, she stalled to find the right words. "I can confidently assure you that I'm well straight in my mind about that cad. I've already wasted too much energy on a man who obviously hasn't given me a second thought."

"He's a fool."

She grinned. "I agree, Charles."

"Chaz. I could've sworn I asked you to call me Chaz." He leaned forward and took an apple slice.

"It's weird for me. That was my baby name for you. I want to giggle every time people use it."

"You'll get over it. This is the name I chose. It's what I go by. Respect it." He sounded serious, but a playful glint shimmered in his eyes as he put the entire slice of fruit in his mouth.

"Are you joking?"

He chewed and swallowed. "Not even a little bit. The whole world knows me as Chaz. Calls me Chaz. I like it. Am I out of line to ask the person who gave me my awesome name to do the same?"

"I suppose not." She doubted she'd ever get used to it, but she would try. "Awesome, huh?"

"Yeah. Awesome."

She laughed, but quickly sobered. "I wish you hadn't stayed away so long."

"Me, too." He scratched along his jaw where stubble sparkled in lamplight. "But I'd made a promise. As long as Billy lived, I had to honor it."

"What if he'd lived to be an old man?"

"I would've waited." His nostrils flared. A sign of displeasure?

"You wouldn't have gotten married? Had children?" The idea of him alone and waiting a lifetime saddened her.

"I honestly couldn't say. I will tell you that I never stopped thinking of you. Not for one day. Not for one hour. For twelve years, I carried your guitar to every city I went. You were near me when I played it. You were near me every time someone called me Chaz." His eyes lost their hint of green and went to steely gray. "I never gave up, Emily. Never stopped hoping. Never."

Had he been anyone less than Charles, she'd have shivered at the creepiness of such a confession and gone running. But he wasn't obsessed. Wasn't a stalker. As always, he had honor and integrity. He had loved her brother, and showed it by keeping his promise.

"I was just your best friend's kid sister. Why were you so diligent about me, of all people?" she asked.

"I meant it when I said that birthday party changed how I saw you. How I felt about you. You weren't just my best friend's younger sister anymore. You became my center. My reason. I learned to play that guitar so I could play you songs someday. I finished high school instead of dropping out because I needed to be someone you'd be proud to have by your side."

Her thoughts careened. "That's a lot of pressure to put on me."

"Don't get me wrong. That was then. You were the anchor that got me through Billy's trial and through those early years of Smashing Glass when none of us handled our new fame and wealth with any measure of moderation. I was so close to losing my mind a few times."

She wanted to reach out to him. To touch him. She didn't dare, however. Since his kiss in the theater, she hung suspended over a state of near constant sexual readiness. She couldn't trust she'd be as strong this morning as she'd been last night.

"The guilt was the worst. Especially when I sobered. Then I matured and resolved to make a meaningful life."

"Guilt for what?"

He looked away, and when he spoke, his voice held a strangled, tortured quality. "The only way I could see you, speak to you, stand any kind of chance with you was if Billy freed me from my promise. Since he wouldn't free me when I asked, there was only one way. If Billy died. I checked the obituaries every day. Every day, I dreaded seeing his name. Every day, I hoped to see his name." His voice broke on the last word.

"Oh, God." Tears rushed to her lids as she trembled.

He faced her, and a tear rolled down his cheek. He whispered hoarsely, "I honored my obligation to him."

She struggled to her feet. Her vision blurred.

"I'm sorry to reveal the ugly truth," he said, his voice stronger. "I vowed to be honest with you. I always will."

Holding up a hand, she stumbled to the door. "I need to be alone."

Chaz wanted to regret his disclosure, but he

couldn't. If she decided to love him, it had to include his faults. Granted, this one was a whopper.

He took a quick shower and shaved. How long should he leave her alone? This was their last day together. He had to take her home tonight so she could work tomorrow.

He dressed then headed for the kitchen with the breakfast tray. The doorbell rang before he made it through the living room. He set the tray on the coffee table and answered the door.

"Hey, Leon. Come in."

"I hope I'm not disturbing you, Mr. Preston. I'm taking a lunch break and thought it might be a good time to bring these by." He held up a thin data tablet.

"It's fine. I was expecting you." He took the man's dripping umbrella and propped it in a holder he kept in a corner near the door.

Emily stood at the hallway leading to the bedrooms. He didn't like her pallor nor the bleak sag of her face. Worse was a dull disappointment shading her usually brilliant eyes.

Waving her to the kitchen, he turned on bright overhead lights. Leon followed, his shoes squeaking on the marble floor. He started the tablet and opened the first picture.

Emily came and stood silently staring at a photo of Mark in bed with a black-haired woman. Their positions left no question as to their activity. A camera date and time stamp showed in red that this had happened yesterday at nine in the morning. Two more images memorialized Mark's morning jaunt.

The next three pictures appeared essentially the same except this woman had short blond hair, and the activity took place in early afternoon. Emily wore no expression.

When the seventh picture showed him entering a building with a third woman, Leon zoomed to the engagement ring. As Chaz had suspected, they couldn't mistake it.

"I've seen enough." Emily went to the living room

and sank to the sofa.

Leon quickly forwarded through the remaining pictures then said, "He's not going to be a problem for you, Mr. Preston. He and his fiancée haven't left his condo. I'd have taken photos, but they haven't gotten dressed all day. I kinda figured you wouldn't be interested in seeing two naked people walking around."

"You figured right. Can I get you anything while you're here?"

The security manager powered down his pad. "No, sir. Nothing. If it's okay, I'll call it quits on this job. The rain is miserable, and my wife wants me to take her out to lunch."

Chaz walked him to the door and handed over his umbrella. "Sure. Thanks for everything."

Leon stepped outside, and while he opened his umbrella, he said, "I'm glad that he-man didn't have a mind to come after you. He's huge."

Chaz closed the door and went to Emily. "Looks like Mark didn't skip a beat."

She released a heavy breath. "Since he's not a danger, I want to go home."

"We still have a few hours."

Standing, she tugged at the hem of her baggy blue T-shirt. "We really don't. I lost my brother a week ago. Then the one person I trusted most tells me he welcomed it. You watched for Billy's death. You wanted it. I can't be around you."

Heartbreak tore him in half. The pain of it stole his breath. He whispered, "I tried to see him, to ask him again to release me from that promise. He wouldn't see me. He wouldn't read my letters. I didn't want his death."

"I'm packed. I want to leave. Now."

Chapter Thirteen

The drive home held more silence and tension than Emily's ride to Charles' house two nights earlier. In the quiet, she realized she'd considered him benevolent. Saint-like. At what point during her girlhood had she placed him on a pedestal?

It didn't make a difference. No reason could possibly justify his long wish for Billy's demise. Still, the idea that he considered her unfair ate at her.

"You think I'm indulging in sentiment," she said.

"You couldn't be more wrong."

"Then why aren't you defending yourself?" She gripped the handle of her gym bag, anxious for a handhold in her slipping world.

"I told you how it was for me. What's to defend? You're right to be upset. That I even entertained the notion of benefiting from Billy's death is unconscionable. I know it intimately. It's been my personal torture since I realized he would never release me from that infernal promise."

Fire licked torrid fingers in her gut. "You shouldn't have made it."

"Don't you think I know this? I was young and foolish and suffered a misplaced conception that I had contributed to his conviction because I hadn't prevented him from searching for the slut. I hadn't pulled him off that boy in time. I hadn't said the right words in his trial to convince the judge and jury that he hadn't premeditated the murder." He punched the steering wheel. "Damn it, Emily. He condemned me. I condemned myself. You're in good company if you choose to add yours to the mix, but don't expect me to plead innocent. I'm not."

Her face grew hot as her stomach wrung. She wanted to hate him but couldn't without some kind of denial from him of his wrongdoing. He admitted it. Claimed it. Anger and frustration formed a vortex that threatened to drown her.

Clamping her jaw shut, she stared out her window. Running raindrops obstructed her view, but she didn't care. A tumult of thoughts and memories rendered her eyes unseeing, anyway.

What was it about him that created such a tempest in her? The word 'passion' sprang to mind, but she flung it aside as quickly as it occurred. Mark had stirred her ire, but she'd dismissed the man the second she concluded their connection had been an illusion. Six months couldn't compare to the twelve she'd lost with Charles. Was she forever doomed to choose men who were bad for her?

Not a single word Chaz could say would sway Emily, so he didn't try. He refused to simply drive her home and say goodbye for good, however. The idea stabbed him like a dagger in the chest.

Before the funeral, he'd worried she had changed in the important ways. Of course she had grown from a girl into a woman, and her priorities had evolved into those of an adult's. Yet the qualities he'd valued in her had remained.

Her spunk. Her love of learning and reading. Her quick mind and sense of right from wrong. Most of all, she'd kept that way of looking at him as though she recognized his true self. As though she peered into his very soul and approved of what she found.

This disappointment she now had for him left him

stricken. He'd time travel if he could, and undo his promise. Undo the miserable loneliness and separation they'd both suffered.

Words gnawed at his resistant tongue. They swirled inside his head. Words from thousands of books. From verbose authors who had supplied him a vocabulary worthy of an Ivy League study. Words that failed him.

He wouldn't have her tractable, though. It wasn't in her nature. But neither would he have her unmovable in her determination to put him from her life. She hadn't said she never wanted to see him again, but the flex of her jaw and her hard-set eyes spoke intrinsically.

Indomitable. Magnanimous. A spontaneous maverick staunch in her support of family and friends. Versatile. Whimsical. Wholly and unwaveringly winsome. Words pulled from the pages of his favorite books, and every one an apt reflection of her character.

He'd lived without her long enough. He wouldn't surrender without a fight. Lifting the lever of his turn signal, he glanced over his shoulder then changed lanes.

"This isn't my exit," she said.

"I know."

"Where are you going?" Emily's knuckles ached from their death grip on her bag's handle. "I just want to go home."

"Not yet." Charles turned into a residential neighborhood filled with older, brick homes. "I want to stop by your parents'."

Weariness stole her strength, and her hands eased their hold. "This isn't the way. Besides, I'm on edge right now. I can't deal with my mother's sullenness."

He kept driving.

"Charles."

He turned onto a large boulevard then into a new

neighborhood. She didn't recognize anything.

"Charles." Irritation made her tone impatient. She glanced at his profile then out the windshield. "Charles. Chaz."

"Finally." He pulled to a curb in front of a two-story plantation-style house. "Thank you."

"For what?" She sideways punched his arm with the soft, outer part of her fist.

He caught and held her by the wrist. "For calling me by my name."

Rolling her eyes, she huffed. "Stop being charming. I need to stay angry."

"No, you don't."

"Don't be flippant." She gave her arm a tug against his hold.

"With you? Never."

"I can't forgive you." An acid burn seared her throat, and she swallowed. "I mean, what an atrocity."

His eyebrows slammed toward one another. "An atrocity? I didn't kill Billy. He killed himself. Did you expect me to turn my back on your family? Your father, who was more a father to me than my own? To you, the only woman I've ever loved? Did you expect me to forget about you?"

His words ripped through her like a storm wind that blew through trees and took leaves and limbs in its force. Love. He'd said the one word she'd dance around and avoided for nearly a week.

Love.

Trembling, she yanked her wrist free of his hold. "How dare you?"

He studied her then put the car in gear and pulled from the curb. "Fine. But this isn't over."

Scowling, she crossed her arms atop her bag. Her lower lip quivered, so she sank her teeth into it to make it stop. How could she have hoped? Chaz was a rock star. A celebrity. How could she consider for one second that she wanted a part of his life? That she had room for jealousy and drama?

Love? What did a man who claimed to love

someone he hoped would die know of love?

Chaz parked in her parents' driveway and removed his key from the ignition. His entire future hinged on this visit.

"You can leave your bag in the backseat," he said. "I'll take you home when we're done here."

"We're already done here." Emily's face reddened. "Take me home now."

"I admire your obstinacy, but you're not having your way. Not in this." He stepped out and fought the urge to slam the door. He had to keep control. He had too much to lose, if he hadn't already.

He strode to the house and knocked.

Mrs. Hall answered, wearing a lacy green apron and wiping her hands on a kitchen towel. She offered him a wan smile. "Hello, Charles. It's always such a pleasure to see you. Please come in."

As he crossed the threshold, he asked, "Is Mr. Hall in?"

"He is. There's nowhere to go after church when the weather's so bad. He's in his study." She headed for the kitchen and flicked her wrist toward the hallway. "Go see him. He'll be glad for your company."

Chaz couldn't agree. He was about to bring the hurricane brewing between Emily and him into the house. Any Sunday peace would soon cease. Knocking on the study door, he took a deep, bracing breath. He had to tell her father everything. Would he hate Chaz, too?

"Come in, dear. I was— Oh, Charles. How are you?" Mr. Hall removed a pair of reading glasses and set an open book on the desk before him.

"Not great, sir." He closed the door and settled onto a short couch facing the desk. "I'm here about your daughter."

He told him about what Leon had found, about how Emily had spent the weekend at his house, and about what he'd shared with her concerning the obituaries. The front door slammed, and women's raised voices carried from the kitchen. Chaz didn't stop talking until he'd revealed everything.

"Why did you feel the need to share such a thing, Charles?" asked her father.

"Secrets and promises have stood between us. I won't foster them any longer. It has to be complete honesty and trust or nothing. No matter how ugly or difficult the truth is."

A sharp knock sounded on the door.

"Five minutes, Emily," called Mr. Hall.

A frustrated groan preceded rapid steps on hardwood.

"How does she feel about you?" her father asked.

"I can't say for sure. I do know that I've been asking her for days to call me Chaz, and she finally did this morning while I drove her here. That's got to count for something."

Her father stroked his chin then gave a decisive nod. "Let me talk to her alone."

"But—"

"She needs to lower her guard before she hears reason. She won't if you're in the room, son."

A hot poker twisted in his gut, but he conceded. "I love her, sir. I mean to make her my wife if she'll have me."

Mr. Hall offered a small, sad smile. "You're the only man who's ever deserved her, Charles. I hope, for your sake and hers, that she's capable of loving you back."

Chaz stood, his heart heavy and aching.

"Emily," her father called.

Chapter Fourteen

"He told me. I think you're being too hard on both of you." Her father came from his desk chair and urged her to sit with him on the loveseat.

"He couldn't have told you," said Emily. "You wouldn't be so calm if he had."

"He told me," he said in a quiet but firm tone.

"About how he searched the obituaries every day?"

He nodded.

"Why aren't you upset?" She threw her hand high then landed it upon her knee.

He took it, folding it within the warmth of both of his. "I am, but I understand."

"What do you understand? Because I don't get it." She fought tears.

"I understand why he did it. It wasn't easy for him, you know. He didn't want Billy to die. He needed him to. There's a huge difference."

Shock left her speechless. She shook her head.

"Yes, there is." He patted the back of her hand. "Sweetheart, I've always taken great pride in what an intelligent, logical woman you are. I've never seen you let emotion overrule reason like this. Take a minute. Think about it."

"I can't," she whispered. "What he did was wrong."

"What he did was seek a way to get you back in his life without betraying Billy, no matter how painful it was for him. Look at you." He wiped a tear from her cheek with his thumb. "Why are you so emotional about him? Even at the funeral, nothing worked you into a frenzy quite like the sight of him."

She sniffed her tear-runny nose. "I don't know. He makes me crazy. One minute I hate him. The next I wonder if I might love him. Then I hate him again."

"You know, the opposite of love isn't hate."

That stopped her careening thoughts, and she paused. "It's not?"

"No. The opposite of love is indifference."

She could never be indifferent to him.

"My fear, Emily, is that you'll let him walk away again. This time for good. And you'll regret it for the rest of your days."

"I'm so appalled by what he did. Every day, Dad. He read them every day." Tremors shook her.

Her father gathered her close and hugged her. "I don't believe for an instant he ever thought *I hope Billy dies*. It was probably more like *When can I see Emily again?*"

"It's the same thing."

"Is it?" He gave her a squeeze. "Don't you think everything would've been different if your brother had relented? How do you think Charles reacted when he finally saw the obituary?"

"I can't imagine. Why are you taking Chaz's side?"

"Chaz? When did you stop calling him Charles?"

She hesitated, trying to remember. He'd cajoled her into using the name at the park near her apartment, but when did she start doing it without thought?

She straightened and shrugged. "Does it matter?"

"It's what he wants you to call him. Maybe if you're bending to his wishes, you haven't completely given up on him." He stood and went to the door.

Emily didn't move. "It crushes my spirit to contemplate what he did."

"I'm not asking you to like it. I'm asking you to put yourself in his place for a minute. Put aside these feelings of betrayal. Stop acting so maudlin. It's not you.

If you can clear your head, you might comprehend what he suffered. His motive wasn't vulgar. It was singular."

"Why don't you cry, Dad? For Billy?"

Her father deflated. "I cry alone, sweetheart. I wept for years over my son's fate. Since his death, I haven't gone a day without shedding more tears. Mainly for what could've been. What if? Your mother needs me to be the strong one, so I mourn in solitude. I don't mind. I love her that much. Consider that for a second. How much must Charles love you if he'd be willing to maintain a vigil for the death of a friend he loved like a brother?"

Standing at the backdoor, Chaz vacillated about joining Emily in the rain. Drops hit the deck in a steady drumming he would've found comforting if not for his breaking heart. He hated how his forthrightness had hurt her.

He took a deep breath and stepped outside. Cold rain spattered his face and bare arms. By the time he reached her side at the railing, water ran along his skin, and his T-shirt clung to him.

She stared across the backyard. As raindrops hit near her eyes, she double-blinked. Not wanting to push, he held his tongue.

She made him wait. When she finally granted him a sideways glance, the rain had thoroughly soaked him.

"My dad filled you in on our conversation?" she asked.

He shook his head. "I didn't ask, either. If you want me to know, I'd rather hear it from you."

Putting pale fingers on the rain-darkened rail, she bent her head. Her drenched hair hung heavily and hid her profile.

"I'm not sorry I told you, but I am sorry I caused you pain." He fisted his hands to keep from reaching for her.

"Did you want my brother to die?" she asked

without moving.

His heart skipped a beat. "God, no. I didn't want any of what happened."

"If he hadn't killed that boy, how do you think our lives would've turned out?"

He gripped the railing, close to her hand but not touching. "I've thought about that a lot. I like to imagine he'd have gone into restoring classic cars. He loved working on his old Mustang. I figured you'd become a novelist. I adored it when you read me those stories you wrote."

She faced him. Wiping her eyes, she straightened. "I forgot about those. I wonder what happened to them."

He shrugged, unable to take his eyes off her. Did she have any idea how much he feared losing her?

"My dad says he understands why you did it."

"Do you?"

"I'm trying."

Her two words resuscitated his hope. "Emily."

She held up a hand. "I care."

Chaz held his breath.

"About you." Her gaze dropped to his chest. "I need to know something."

"Ask me anything. To you, I'm an open book." The rain's chill sank to his bones, and he shivered.

She trembled, too. "When you saw Billy's obituary, what did you feel?"

His throat thickened at the raw memory. "I was at the house, rehearsing songs from our new album with the guys. It was like hitting a concrete wall at fifty miles an hour. My heart got torn out. I remember going weak. I couldn't even hold onto the newspaper. Justin had to pick it off the floor when I dropped it."

"You were sad?"

"I was devastated, Emily. I honestly didn't expect it. I may have looked every day, but I never thought I'd actually find it."

Her shoulders dropped a bit, and her features relaxed. "I don't want you to go away again."

He drew her close and pressed her heart to his. "I

love you."

"Will you take me home now?"

Pulling onto her street, Chaz asked, "What about you? What did you do when you learned of Billy's death?"

She didn't answer immediately. Staring at her folded hands in her lap, she released a sad, sibilant chuckle. "I sat stunned. I couldn't wrap my brain around the idea that he had died so young, much less taken his own life. Then I was on the floor, and my dad was saying I had passed out."

She had taken it incredibly hard. He nodded. It made sense. At least Chaz had gotten the chance to visit him during the trial and for a while after his incarceration at the federal penitentiary. She hadn't. Both her parents and Billy had denied her any chance to say goodbye or obtain closure.

He turned into her apartment building's parking lot and stopped in a spot fairly close to the front door. "I guess you were holding out hope he'd let you visit him someday."

"I did. He was my only brother." She faced him and offered a tiny smile. "I need you to walk me up."

Relief washed over him. Nodding, he removed his key and opened his door. He got her bag from the back then followed her inside. She said nothing on the elevator ride, and he couldn't escape his racing thoughts to break the silence.

What did she want from him? Could she forgive him? Did they stand a chance? What had her father said? Had it made any difference?

They reached her door, and he touched her slender shoulder. "Don't let this be goodbye."

"It's not." She unlocked her door. "Come in."

He should've rejoiced, but anxiety gave him a sense that he walked upon a thin sheet of glass suspended ten stories from the ground. Each step into her apartment cracked the glass and threatened to send him plummeting to the death of his dreams.

She took the bag from him and headed for her room. Her expression unreadable, she said, "Come with me."

Confusion made his footsteps tentative. "Do we need to talk?"

Tossing the bag into a chair next to her dresser, she faced him. She flipped a switch that lit a lamp on her bedside table. Then she removed her shirt in a single move and let it drop to the carpet. "No. No talking."

"Whoa. Wait a minute." His heart hammered as his gaze dropped to the swell of her breasts above white satin trim on her bra. He shook his head.

She untied her sweat pants and slowly revealed white lace panties, smooth thighs, and shapely calves. Her mouth went soft and inviting as her blue eyes darkened. Her pants landed atop her shirt.

"Emily," he said, his voice rough and deep as desire constricted his throat. "We can't."

"We must." She took a condom from a small top dresser drawer and put the foil packet between her lips. She reached behind and unfastened her bra. She shrugged from its straps, and it fell to her feet.

He stopped breathing. Her breasts, firm and round, presented hardened nipples to his hungry gaze. Her skin appeared soft, its pale contours following a svelte waistline to a gentle flare of hips then long, shapely legs. She was magnificent.

"I don't want it this way between us." He swallowed against a lump of need. His heart beat so hard he could hear its rhythm in his ears. In his pants, an aching hardness formed.

She took a step toward him. Tentatively, he accepted the condom from her. She gathered her wet hair at her nape and gave it a twist. "How do you want it? Just about us? Sweet? Romantic? Spontaneous?"

He blinked. She really had him figured out. It shouldn't have surprised him. She'd forever had the ability to read him. He adored that quality in her.

"Billy's always going to be between us, Chaz. It's never going to be solely about us. And spontaneity isn't how either of us works. We're too cerebral." She closed the distance and gathered a fistful of T-shirt at the center of his chest. "No more dancing. No more skating. We're going to decide, here and now, if this will work or if we'll go our separate ways. There's only one way to know."

A test. His stomach balled. This was a test he couldn't fail, and he would if he rushed. He slowly exhaled. Holding her gaze, he ran the backs of his fingers along her cold, silken cheek. He concentrated on her beauty. Her strength. Her inner sweetness.

He had to take a chance. For both their sakes, he had to risk ultimate heartbreak and let this happen. He welcomed the vulnerability. This represented a culmination of twelve years of lonely yearning followed by a week's worth of poignant desire.

The wait ended here.

Chapter Fifteen

Emily released his shirt, and Chaz removed it. His hooded gaze spoke of the same passion welling within her. He stepped out of his shoes and wrapped his arms around her. He began a leisurely descent toward her lips. He moved by inches, his eyes never leaving hers, until she could only manage feathery breaths against the band of intense anticipation closing about her chest.

His gray-green eyes closed, and he captured her mouth. Her heart racing, she sent her arms around his neck and pressed her bare torso to his. He felt incredibly hot against her cold skin, and she hugged tighter, soaking in his heat.

Adding pressure to her bottom lip, he urged her to open. Their tongues met then entered into a sensual duel. He tasted of cinnamon and vanilla, and she realized he'd eaten some of her mother's cookies. Emily's favorite.

A pulling need created a heaviness low in her belly. Moisture crept along her gently throbbing folds. Pressing her pelvis to his jeans, she felt the proof of his arousal.

He broke the kiss only to tilt his face the other way and come in for a kiss so filled with raw need it drew a groan from her throat. He backed her to the bed and eased her further until she kneeled at the edge of the mattress.

He retreated a step and unfastened his jeans. His

gaze devoured her, heightening her excitement. He said, "You're stunning."

"You, too," she whispered.

His muscles bunched and flexed as he removed his pants and underwear. His hair nearly dry somehow, swayed forward across his forehead. When he stood, his turgid length jutted. He rolled the condom on.

Her heart beat so hard it physically rocked her. The man was sexy. Proportioned by the activity of his life, naturally lean, Chaz resembled the statue of David more than Hercules. He stole her breath.

He came to the bed and cupped her breasts in his warm hands. Closing her eyes, she inhaled sharply as he grazed his thumbs across her erect nipples. An electric charge surged to her womb.

Leaning into his hands, she arched, surrendering completely to the fire he had stoked in her the past week. He was consummate at playing guitar, and he proved that his skill at strumming her to pleasure well matched it.

She melted to the bed, and he bent over her. He took a nipple in his mouth as his member slid along her inner thigh. Sparks shot from her breast to her belly with each flick of his tongue, her crease aching for relief.

She wanted him like nothing else. "Please."

He pressed kisses between her breasts then down her stomach, speaking words between each. "We're in no hurry. I waited so long for this. I won't rush."

He brushed fingertips through the curls of her mons. Her swelling, pulsing flesh begged for his touch.

He slipped a finger into her folds and slid it from her opening to her awakening clit. "You're so wet. So gorgeous."

He scooted lower and dipped his face to his stroking finger. When his tongue took over, she gasped. His expert mouth circled, flicked, and sweetly sucked upon her emerging nerve bundle while his finger explored through her juices. She trembled under a blossoming ecstasy.

She sent a hand into his soft, barely damp hair.

"Chaz, I need you."

He looked at her but didn't cease his pleasuring. Her body tightened. Her desire pulled from deep within. Silently, she willed him to send one of his slick fingers inside of her.

The coil of excitement wound tighter yet, becoming almost painful. She moaned. It grew nearly unbearable then released. Orgasm quaked within her.

Chaz straightened, grasped her hips, and thrust inside. Her body grabbed him so hard that her abdominal muscles flexed and her shoulders lifted off the bed. Pleasure-pain seared her through. She screamed his name, taking hold of his forearms.

"My God, Emily," he shouted. His eyelids squeezed shut, and his features grew taut.

When her passage let go, she relaxed. He didn't give her a chance to catch her breath, however. Immediately, he stroked into her, creating a primal rhythm her body recognized. As if of their own will, her hips rocked to meet him at each thrust, seating him deeper and deeper.

The coil of excitement began to tighten, but slower. The gradual climb gave her a chance to savor the pleasure. Gave her a chance to explore the contours and textures of his body. Gave her a chance to invite him for a lingering, sensual kiss that took her to the next level.

She raised her knees, changing the tilt of her pelvis, and inhaled in delight as he thrust to her greatest depth. She climbed fast. Each of his thrusts took her a leap closer to the edge.

He broke the kiss and hovered above her, his arms braced on either side of her. Strain colored his face. His hips worked faster.

Unable to bring in enough air for her burning lungs, she parted her lips. The pleasure intensified. Her entire body responded, stiffening in readiness.

Then he sent her over the edge and into orgasm's abyss. Stars flashed behind her closed lids as meteoric bliss shook her. She barely registered his cry mingling with hers.

When her senses returned, she whispered, "Amazing."

"Life changing," he said breathlessly and kissed her cheek. He dropped to the bed beside her.

Joy overwhelmed her. She'd never experienced such rapture. Instinctively, she realized her heart had never truly engaged with any other man. She'd only ever had sex. With Chaz, however, she'd made love. This was the confirmation she'd sought.

He hadn't disappointed. He certainly hadn't cooled her need. If anything, joining with him had further whetted her appetite for his touch. He had kindled a new excitement in her. She wanted this – him – for the rest of her life. But how would their lives coincide?

"What is it?" He urged her to her side and gathered her against him.

Resting her cheek on his shoulder, she hiked a knee across his thigh and said, "I can't say goodbye to you."

"Thank God." He hugged her tighter and kissed her temple. "I can't say goodbye, either."

"But..." She released a heavy sigh.

But. The one word Chaz hadn't wanted Emily to say.

He closed his eyes, trying not to tense. "But what?"

"I live an ordinary life. Monday through Friday, nine to six. Saturday and Sunday off. Three weeks of vacation a year. There's not a lot of room for, well... How exactly is your life?"

He smiled. "It's not what you probably think. I'm here in Chicago nine months of the year and on tour for three. We do a lot of Skype interviews. We record at Jet's house. About the only time I'm away is when we do in-person interviews, photo shots for magazine spreads, or attend award events."

"I didn't realize you were home so much." She snuggled closer and moved her head to his chest.

Running fingers along soft skin where her back curved, he said, "You mentioned Hawaii."

"That's an old dream. I wouldn't want to be so far from my family now. My mom, especially. She seems to need me around more than ever."

"She's had a rough time. I gathered you didn't plan on staying with this company. I love that you work, but with me, you can do anything you want."

She rose onto an elbow. "I love my work. This company's a good one, and they've treated me fairly well. But I love the challenge of investment."

"Fairly well?"

"I've lost promotions to men with lesser qualifications, but that's part of the dynamic of working in a company run by men. Most of the financial firms are, so I understood going in that I could expect it."

He studied her a moment. She had an independent streak, so he couldn't imagine her rolling over for nonsense when it came to her career. "Have you ever considered working for yourself?"

She settled against him. "I'm not the only one who dreams of consulting. It's not realistic, though. It takes five years to build enough clientele to fully support a business like mine. I don't have the money, and banks won't loan since the fail rate is too high. I refuse to steal clients from the company. It's unethical."

"Hmm. I know four rock stars who could use a top notch financial advisor."

She gently slapped him. "Be serious."

He took the hand and kissed her fingertips. "I am serious. We've got so much money on the move that we had to hire a third accountant this year, and all three are telling us we need to invest. Start your business with us. Let me be your bank. I'll give you a loan with great terms."

She chuckled. "I'll just bet you would."

He put her on her back and pinned her with his

body. Her sweet curves under him had him stirring to life. Nuzzling her neck, he pressed kisses to her silken skin. "The best terms."

"Low interest rate?" She laughed and tilted her face, giving him better access.

"Uh-huh."

"Extended payment contract?"

"Life-long." He found her breast, smiling at her gasp when he tweaked her hardening nipple.

She stilled and pushed his shoulder. He lifted and met her gaze.

"Are you in earnest?" she asked.

"I really am. I know how smart you are. I can't think of anyone we can trust more with our investments. If it means you get to take your career in the direction you want, I'm going to support you all the way. I want you to be happy."

A slow smile made her lovelier than ever. "You're completely wonderful."

"Funny. That's what I think of you. Be mine forever, Emily." His stomach somersaulted at the idea that she would agree to be by his side. "Tell me you can forgive me. Tell me you can love me."

She cupped his cheek, and affection shone from her dark blue eyes. "I need a little more time, but I will forgive you. I'll forgive you because love is patient and kind. Love is not easily angered and keeps no record of wrongs. Love always protects, trusts, hopes, and preserves."

"Corinthians." His heart took flight. "Declare it."

"I love you, Chaz."

He beamed. "Again."

"I love you. I always did. I just didn't realize it. I always will."

He kissed her long and hard. Every worry evaporated. "I love you, Emily. You're my past, my present, and my future. You're the music in my soul."

THE END

ABOUT THE AUTHOR

Laura Kitchell lives in Virginia with her husband, daughter, and their spunky, affectionate, black Labrador retriever. She was published for the first time in 2007, and became a member of the Quality Novelists Coalition in 2013. She is a member of Romance Writers of America and Chesapeake Romance Writers. Contact her at laurakitchell@cox.net, visit her website at www.laurakitchell.vpweb.com, and follow her at laura.kitchell.1@facebook.com.

If you like this book, you might like **Man of My Dreams:**

Cole Pennington thinks getting a job as host on the reality dating show The Man of My Dreams is his dream come true. Then he meets Annasil Pakstasia. As a contestant, Annasil's job is to win the heart of The Man. She doesn't expect to find real love on a television show, much less with the host. Cole is charming, genuine, and completely irresistible. What's he doing in show business? Annasil is beautiful, successful, and intelligent. What's she doing on this show? One thing's for certain. Per their contracts, to each other, they're off limits.

Available in Print and Electronic versions!

http://tinyurl.com/kgvn8yp

30586331R00223

Made in the USA
Charleston, SC
19 June 2014